Never in Anger

Never in Anger

ANTHONY 'BUGS' BENDELL

First published in Great Britain
in 1998 by Orion

An imprint of Orion Books Ltd
Orion House, 5 Upper St Martin's Lane,
London WC2H 9EA

A CIP catalogue record for this book
is available from the British Library

ISBN 0 75281 796 5

Typeset by Selwood Systems Ltd
Printed in Great Britain by
Butler & Tanner Ltd, Frome and London

Acknowledgements

For reasons which become clear in the reading, it has taken more than ten years to write this book. Even then I would have been hard pressed to produce the finished manuscript without the generous assistance of friends and family. Right from the outset – before I invested in a word processor – I have owed my thanks to Carol Lineman for transcribing my first, amateurish audio tapes into hard copy. I am indebted also to the library staffs at RAF College, Cranwell, for lending me copies of the Defence White Papers for the 1960s, and I owe a similar debt to the librarians at the Army Staff College, Camberley, who provided background information on the Military Staff Course of 1972. I have to thank the Air Historical branch (MoD) for their help in clearing the use of certain Crown Copyright photographs. In the later stages, my thanks have been due to: Sister Mary Loreto, for reading the draft to correct my deliberate spelling errors; Patrick Walmsley, for transferring many photographs to compact disc; Terry Sadler, for copying the manuscript; and Peter Biddiscombe, for the final scissors and paste collation. Finally I must thank Air Marshal Sir Kenneth Hayr for suggesting to Paul Bowen, chief executive of the Royal Air Force Benevolent Fund Enterprises, that the script was worthy of further consideration – which, in due course, led to its acceptance for publication.

Bugs Bendell
April 1998

To Juliet
and our children
Stuart and Emma

Contents

List of Illustrations

Unless otherwise indicated, these illustrations were supplied either by the author or by the RAF Benevolent Fund Enterprises, for which grateful thanks.

Foreword

by Air Chief Marshal Sir Richard Johns GCB, CBE, LVO, ADC, FRAeS, Chief of the Air Staff

After thirty-four years in the Royal Air Force, and having flown more than 4000 hours on fighter aircraft, Wing Commander 'Bugs' Bendell concludes that his career represents 'a wholly enjoyable challenge in which I experienced more success than failure'. Such professional modesty is characteristic of Bugs, but within the ranks of his service contemporaries he was recognised as one of the finest fighter pilots of his generation. While he was blessed with enviable natural aptitude, Bugs's flying had that extra measure of disciplined aggression and flinty determination that raised his standing to exceptional – and while he may raise a sardonic eyebrow at my words, they need to be said if this foreword is to have any meaning.

As his career spanned more than three decades of the Cold War, Bugs's story presents a much needed personal contribution to supplement more formal histories covering the years of uneasy peace. Enthusiasm for flying is pervasive, but it is his perceptive comments on character, events, tactics, aircraft and service life that add weight to a thoroughly entertaining autobiography which will be enjoyed by past and serving members of the Royal Air Force as well as others with a general interest in military aviation and our armed forces.

In the final paragraph of his book, Bugs claims that his story is 'not one of blood and guts'. This is the one point in the account of his life where I found cause to disagree with his judgement. While I may exclude 'blood' from consideration – because he never fired a gun in anger – guts is another matter. Both before and after the onset of the multiple sclerosis that was eventually to compel his early retirement from the service, courage has illuminated all aspects of Bugs's life. They do not come any gutsier than Bugs Bendell and his book, modest in telling and honest in word, should not disguise this singular truth.

Never in Anger

1
Earliest memories and growing up during World War II

I was born in a bucket on 30 March 1936. Of course I have no personal recollection of the event, although Mother probably remembered it until the day she died. It was a breech birth – I was the wrong way up – and by all accounts I remained difficult throughout childhood. But then, what could one expect from my turbulent brew of English, French and Scots blood? I would go to sleep only after being driven for miles in the car, and I would perform only after sitting on the pot for hours. The latter made a deep impression on me – I could easily have been scarred for life.

My paternal grandfather, Frederick Bendell, was born in Bermuda, the son of a British Army colour sergeant. But for ill health he would probably have followed his father into the Army, as by all accounts he inherited a strong belief in military discipline – although happily this didn't apply to his grandchildren. Grandad was a dapper little man with twinkling eyes, a neatly trimmed moustache and a wry sense of humour that bubbled away just beneath the surface. He worked for the post office in Lymington, and while delivering letters to one of the big houses across the river he fell for the diminutive French maid, who had emigrated from Alsace in the 1890s. She was an attractive young woman, very determined and suspicious of anything not French, but fiercely loyal to family and friends. She found Fred amusing, and he was clearly an expert on the dance floor – what more could a girl ask? She once reminisced wistfully, 'You know, your grandad would pirouette on the same spot all evening to the Viennese Waltz.' It occurred to me that this might have been due to his limp – one leg being almost two inches shorter than t'other – but that was unkind. Grandad's dancing days were over long before my time, and I never knew the cause of his disability. He regularly visited the doctor for treatment for pernicious anaemia and there was some mention of osteoarthritis, but I wasn't sufficiently interested to enquire further. Sad, really – we should have talked much more.

My father, Frederick George (but known as 'Kelly'), was the youngest of three children and the only boy. It was not easy raising a young family on a postman's pay, but Grandma made sure that her children were properly fed and brought up in the Catholic faith. Grandad was not the church-going type, come to think of it; the porch would probably have fallen in on him as he opened the door. But while Grandma looked after her children's spiritual needs, Grandad imposed the discipline. This combination created great stability, but it may also have discouraged freedom of spirit.

Kelly was five years old when the First World War was declared, and to add to the family's problems he contracted poliomyelitis. The prognosis was not good, but Grandma spent hours massaging his limbs in salt water and praying. Dad eventually made a fully recovery.

In those days, boys were expected to hide their feelings – to show them at all was considered to be a sign of weakness – and this might explain why Dad found it so difficult to show his emotions. He left school at fourteen because he had to find work and contribute to the family income, but jobs were scarce and wage packets slim in the early twenties and, as a young man, Dad was unemployed for long periods. As a result, work later became an obsession for him.

His sporting interests centred mainly on rowing, water polo and football, but he also learned to play the drums and he helped form a local dance band.

Mother, who was christened Anne Barbara but was always known to family and friends as 'Bubbles', came from an entirely different stratum of society, definitely up-town compared to Dad's. Her parents, Dot and Harry Darney, came from Glenfinnan in the Highlands of Scotland. Harry was a highly qualified marine architect, but I remember him as he was after he had retired from ship building, and was proprietor of the Forest Heath Hotel in Sway: a tall, generous man – a patriarchal figure to us grandchildren.

My mother's first marriage was to a gentleman called Frank Philpot, and they had one daughter – my sister Paddy. Sadly, Frank was knocked down by a car while out walking with my mother; later that day, when she visited the hospital, she was told that he had died. At that time the male population in England was still recovering from the ravages of the Great War. To put it bluntly, men of the generation that fought during the First World War were in short supply, and Mother was worried that no one would take on the responsibility of a ready-made family. But perhaps it was inevitable that the handsome young man on the drums should fall for the attractive widow whose father owned a pub. They got married in 1935, and Mother was later to impress upon Paddy that they owed a debt of gratitude to Dad for giving them a home.

As children we were taught that hard work is the key to success – and that still holds good today. But the validity of a second lesson – that women were in some way superior to other mortals – was questionable to say the least. Mother had a vested interest, of course, and girls may have been superior in her day; but when I grew up they were just as ordinary as anyone else, and frequently more so.

When I was three and a half, I sat at the bottom of the stairs in our house in Belmore Lane, idly chipping away at the wall plaster with a hammer – the only effective tool in my toy carpentry set. I had cleared a large area of plaster down to the battens underneath before Mother caught me. 'Just wait until your father gets home,' she stormed – and in our house that was just cause for concern. It was 1 September 1939, the same day that Hitler's armies invaded Poland and the opening shots of the Second World War were fired. Not that such momentous events meant a lot to me then; I was far more worried about a probable hiding for the damned hole in the wall, which seemed to grow larger by the hour. As things turned out, I can't even remember being punished for the wall, but the war was to have a pervasive influence on what I chose to do with my life.

There was an urgency in the air in those days, although I was too young to appreciate it. My memories now may not be in strict chronological order. Of course, some incidents were significant enough to be on public record, and these I have accurately dated. But for the most part my recollections are imperfect snapshots of moments in time. The public parks, where we used to play ball, were soon scarred by networks of trenches for protection during air raids. Fortified pillboxes appeared as if from nowhere. Signposts were removed from all the roads (we were told this was to confuse enemy parachutists, and if the effect on the local population was anything to go by it might well have achieved the desired result). The cast-iron railings and ornate gates that adorned many of the houses in the town were cut down to provide raw material for the war effort. Everyone was issued with a gas mask. My own was made of blue rubber, with round eyepieces and a large, red, beak-like nose; Paddy was issued with the adult version made of black rubber; and for baby Therese there was a soft rubber holdall with a transparent panel on top and separate bellows to supply air. We had to carry our gas masks in a cardboard box, slung from the shoulder on a piece of string. Workmen arrived to build an Anderson shelter at the bottom of the garden, which we were to share with our neighbours. The neighbours moved a lot of furniture into their part of the shelter, while we made little effort to improve our side. Mother said it was ridiculous to go to such lengths over an air-raid shelter. The woman next door was quite upset when I let her know where she was going wrong; and thereafter the relationship between my family and theirs was rather strained. We seldom used the shelter anyway. It was cold, damp and uncomfortable – at least, our half of it was.

Mother used to take us for walks along the quiet lanes on the outskirts of town. I well remember the countryside, the farm at the end of the road and the smell of rain on newly laid tarmac. It was the fashion in those days for boys to wear black lace-up boots, short trousers and – most important of all – a grey cap, the sole purpose of which was to give the wearer something to raise whenever he met a lady. It was the polite thing to do. Mother insisted that I walk in front where she could keep an eye on me, and I was forever lifting my cap. On one occasion we met a herd of cows and out of sheer devilment I swept off my cap and bowed low to each passing animal. Mother gave me a sharp clip around the ear for my pains.

In August 1940, German aircraft attacked shipping in the Solent and off Bournemouth, heralding the opening phase of the Battle of Britain. We got used to the undulating wail of the alert siren, the scramble for the shelters and the anxious wait for the steady note of the 'all clear'. It was an exciting time to be growing up, as vapour trails high in the sky bore silent witness to the great battles that were being fought.

By 1941 the family had abandoned the use of the Anderson shelter during night raids, not simply because we had fallen out with the neighbours, but more to do with my parents' determination to die in their own bed. Up to that time Lymington had escaped damage, but during the early months of that year the Luftwaffe's routes to and from the industrial Midlands lay over the south coast. So for us the alert siren became a nightly ritual. We children slept under the stairs, with pencils ready to clench between our teeth when the anti-aircraft guns started firing. (The pencil was supposed to stop you biting your tongue when the bombs exploded, but no one explained how to wear the gas mask – even the blue one with the red beak – with a pencil between your teeth.)

One night in May the alert had sounded, and I was lying under the stairs, watching the gun flashes reflecting through the windows, when the front door burst off its hinges as if propelled by some giant hand. The field opposite was littered with small fires started by incendiary bombs. A high-explosive bomb had gone off in the adjacent field. On our way to church the following Sunday we passed the charred remains of Fords, the furniture shop. A solitary roll of carpet was left standing on end, blackened and still smouldering amidst heaps of shattered masonry. In the days that followed we were more attentive to the air-raid drills at school, but nothing could persuade my parents to return to the shelter at the bottom of the garden.

About that time, Dad moved to Salisbury, where he set up a new piston-ring factory for Wellworthy Ltd as part of the dispersal plan for vital war industries. The family, now enlarged to mother and four children – Paddy, myself, Therese and Ian – moved up to join him in August 1941. Dad was officially commended for his work on the new factory, but within a few months he had a disagreement with the senior management over fire pickets, and we were on the move again. This time it was to Totnes in Devon, where Grandard Darney had been recalled to serve as managing director of Frank Curtis's shipyard on the River Dart. Dad was taken on as a manager in the timber sawmill across the river.

Initially we moved in to share the grandparents' bungalow, which was cosy to say the least – especially when Aunty Kathleen and Uncle Micky also moved in after their home in Southampton had been bombed. We shared everything: four to a bed, head-to-toe. When one of us got the mumps, we all got the mumps. Life would have been easier if Mother had not relied upon old wives' remedies barely one step removed from witchcraft; to call the doctor in was an expensive last resort. I well remember, when I had mumps, lying on the camp bed reserved for the critically ill, steaming hot, but still piled high with blankets to keep out the chill, with an evil-smelling poultice arrangement wrapped tightly around my ears.

We survived, of course, but after Mother's treatment none could accuse us of getting off lightly. We had had the mumps, or the measles, or the chickenpox, and we were not going to forget it. Then there was the time Therese attempted to hang herself; she had tied the light-pull cord around her neck and had gently slid off the bed. The light switched on, and Therese's face turned a congested shade of purple before she was rescued by Paddy. The grandparents must have been mightily relieved when eventually we moved out.

My first school in Totnes was at a convent run by the nuns of St Mary's, Folkestone, who had been evacuated earlier in the war. It was not a cissy establishment; the nuns were annoyed at having been ousted from Folkestone and were determined that their young charges, particularly the boys, should grow up to defend King and Country. On 21 October 1942 the siren sounded during the morning break, and before anyone could move, a grey twin-engined Junkers JU-88, with black crosses on the underside of its wings, swept low over the playground. It seemed close enough to touch. As I watched, a bomb lazily drifted away from the aircraft's belly on the end of a wire which probably withdrew the final arming pin. Then it was gone, and a split second later an RAF fighter flashed over in hot pursuit. A faint cheer went up from the playground as we were hustled away to safety by the nuns.

Fore Street was in chaos when we arrived home for lunch; broken glass littered the pavements, and groups of people stood around discussing the morning's events. The JU-88 was one of five enemy aircraft – the other four were Focke Wolfe 190s – engaged on a hit-and-run raid. Four bombs were dropped, causing minor damage and a few casualties in the town. Some houses were hit by machine-gun fire. It was rumoured that one of the German aircraft had been shot down, which was good for the town's morale, although there was no mention of this in the official records.

It may have been this episode that first aroused my interest in aviation, although my first attempt to fly – some years before, when I had climbed over the top rail of my cot and fallen off, breaking six front teeth in the process – had ended in disaster. I had been admitted to Lymington hospital to have the stumps removed. But I remember asking Mother how long it would take to fly to Germany; in my childish imagination I had visualised Germany as being on the other side of the world. It came as something of a shock to learn that one could get there and back on the same night. England was not as safe as I had thought. But security was not really a problem for us; Dad's work at the sawmill was a reserved occupation – which meant that he was unlikely to be called up for military service – and although money was tight we were no worse off than any other large family.

By now there were five children, as Tim had just arrived. The only cloud on our horizon was the parents' insistence on going out to the pub every evening. It was almost an article of faith with them; failure to turn up was taken as a sign of serious illness. Not that they drank a great deal; it was probably more for the company – or in Mother's case, respite from the family. But they never missed a night out and they seldom came home before closing time. As children we accepted the pub routine as normal, but looking back, the responsibility that fell upon Paddy to take care of us all while the parents were out was grossly unfair. After all, she was only three years older than me, there was always a baby in the house, and she had no means of contacting the parents in an emergency.

The nuns were righteously indignant about the hit-and-run raid. Later that year they produced a school play in which the boys played the part of an RAF aircrew. I was decked out in brown overalls, Wellington boots and an old flying helmet. I can still remember my lines:

> I am the wireless operator,
> It's a job that's made for skill,
> If anyone can guide you there and get you back I will,
> I have been on operations for fifty times or more,
> And I'll do another fifty to help to win the war.

Heady stuff for a six-year-old. I would have preferred to be the pilot, but that role was given to Bruce Anderson, who had provided the helmets and whose father was serving in the RAF.

In March 1943 the convent moved to Ashburton, so Paddy and I had to commute to school by train. The Dart Valley branch line threaded its way from Totnes to Buckfastleigh and Ashburton, through lush Devon countryside – part of the line is still used to this day as a holiday route. Of course, it was imperative that we caught the train every day: at a pinch one could talk one's way out of being two minutes late for school, but it was a great deal harder to excuse half a day. Missing the train meant big trouble, at both ends of the line. Not that we ever left home in good time; my long-suffering sister was constantly dragging me along the road to the station on a string of threats.

My memories of the convent at Ashburton are dominated by the unappetising lunches of boiled fish and potatoes with liberal helpings of parsnips, for which I developed an abiding dislike. Therese eventually joined us on the school run. On one occasion she came home from school with nits. Mother was horrified. Paddy and I were also inspected and declared unclean. Mother's remedy, which consisted of wrapping our heads in brown paper soaked in paraffin oil, soon got rid of the nits – along with much of our scalps.

I left my cap at school on the last day of the summer term, and was sent to retrieve it next day. Paddy, who according to Mother bore some responsibility for my carelessness, and another girl called Anne Plaister accompanied me. At Ashburton the girls planned to run to school, collect the cap and jump back on the train before it started back. It was an ill-conceived plan, doomed to failure. We missed the return train and, rather than wait an hour for the next one, the girls decided to walk the nine miles back to Totnes. The hike took over three hours – the train passed us five times on its way to and from Ashburton – and the girls had to carry me for the last two miles. Paddy was furious, but by the time we got home I had developed a crush on Anne Plaister. Next time she visited our house, I sent a note declaring my love. This was greeted with shrieks of laughter from the female members of the family and I had to hide in a wardrobe until things cooled off.

In January 1944 the United States Army set up a camp on the old racecourse just outside the town. A Bailey bridge was erected across the River Dart, giving the Americans direct access to the main Newton Abbot road. A substantial tract of land south of Totnes was commandeered for military training, prior to the Allied invasion of France. This was to be the big push.

The American soldiers did not intrude overmuch, except perhaps in the pubs, but they injected new life and money into the town. Overpaid, over-sexed and over here – no doubt they were, but they were generous to a fault with us children. On Sundays the tiny Catholic church bulged to overflowing with American GIs, and the corrugated-iron church hall alongside had to be opened up to accept the excess. After Mass the GIs would hand out chewing gum, Superman comics and Lifesavers – fruit-flavoured boiled sweets shaped like Polo mints. Riches indeed, the likes of which we had not seen since 1939. We soon learned to avoid the laxative brands of chewing gum.

The Americans disappeared from the town early in June, and a few days later we heard about the D-Day landings in Normandy. I sometimes wonder how many of those Americans who shared their sweets survived the war – but at the time I had other things on my mind.

The maximum age for boys at the convent was eight, and in September 1944 I moved to the church school in Totnes to prepare for my scholarship. This was an important examination: if I passed, I would get into the King Edward VI Grammar School, one of the best in the local area; failure would mean the secondary modern school, which did not entirely meet with Mother's approval.

I remember very little about the church school, but apparently I worked quite hard and Mum arranged for me to have extra lessons from Mrs McKenna, a retired teacher who could do with the extra money.

I also attended religious instruction, given by the parish priest – Fr Russell – who barely concealed his disapproval of Catholic children attending non-Catholic schools. He declared that I was unlikely to succeed. Later on I was obliged to serve as an altar boy, which involved attending Mass every day – twice on Sundays – because Dad had done so as a boy. I regret to say that neither Fr Russell's coaching nor my reluctant service as an altar boy added much to my religious fervour. But I suppose I should be thankful; Fr Russell's obvious lack of approval made me even more determined to succeed.

In autumn 1944 we moved to a spacious house in Bridgetown called Heckwood. This was gracious living indeed; I even had a bedroom of my own. The garden, surrounded by mature laurel bushes and fir trees, was a great adventure playground.

My first pal was a chap called Brian Taylor. We shared similar interests, including a preoccupation with fire that bordered on pyromania. We would spend hours crouching behind protective cover, peering at miniature bonfires containing a home-made explosive device – usually a sealed .303 cartridge case – filled with our latest concoction of match heads and gunpowder. The great attraction of this game was the uncertainty. If all went according to plan the bonfire would be blown apart in a satisfying explosion, leaving us with the minor problem of extinguishing the wreckage. Sometimes, however, nothing would happen and we would have to douse the dying embers to cool down the cartridge case. But occasionally the cartridge would explode just as we approached, bucket in hand, and this really grabbed one's attention. Brian, excitable chap that he was, would either throw the bucket or push me – if I happened to be holding the bucket – into the fire. It was remarkable that neither of us got injured.

There was a grand firework display in the town on 8 May 1945 to celebrate VE Day – Victory in Europe. As children we did not see any great change when the war ended; our little world was obviously much safer, but rationing remained and we were only vaguely aware of the turbulence as industry slowly returned to a peacetime footing. Dad bought an automobile repair business in Paignton where I would spend hours either watching the mechanics at work or tinkering with some antique component retrieved from the junk pile behind the garage. It was excellent mechanical experience.

After Brian's family moved away I took up with Vincent Toffolo. He was two years older, and there was definitely an element of hero worship on my part. We made a great team, exploring the local woods and searching the caves for an entrance to the tunnel that was rumoured to connect Bridgetown with Berry Pomeroy Castle. We never found it; since Berry Pomeroy was at least four miles from Bridgetown I doubt that such a tunnel ever existed. We also used to dig for fossils. During one holiday we simply dug foxholes in Vincent's back garden and threw rocks at one another – which says a lot for our intellectual development but was great fun. Then, on 13 June 1949, Vincent was struck down with polio. I watched from our garden as he was carried on a stretcher to the ambulance. I can still remember the grey pallor of his face. Vincent died a few hours later, and I was the altar boy at his funeral.

The combined efforts of the teachers at the church school and Mrs McKenna paid off when I took the scholarship. Afterwards, I was able to describe in detail the decor of the examination room, although much to Mother's despair I could not recall any of the questions. She need not have worried – I passed the examination with flying colours.

2
Grammar school, the Air Training Corps and into a proper job

Four hundred years ago, on 30 June 1553, less than a week before he died, King Edward VI granted to the mayor and citizens of Totnes the right to use a derelict building that had previously been owned by a Catholic priory for the teaching and instruction of boys. History records that the school then consisted of one room. There were twenty pupils and, by a special arrangement with the mayor, the boys were permitted to use the open space in front of the Guildhall for recreation. However, I suspect there was precious little of that. The school's alumni included many eminent scholars: Charles Babbage, the inventor of the computer, plus a governor of Newfoundland and a shoal of bishops.

The school was still short of accommodation in September 1947, when I joined Form 2B. Our form master, Mr Hawk – or 'Arry Awk' as he was known to the boys – marched us off every day after assembly to the Co-operative Hall for lessons. I never got the hang of Latin and French, but was reasonably proficient in all the other subjects. It would be fair to say I was one of the school's less distinguished boys; although I enjoyed my school days I was never a brilliant scholar, and the only prizes I ever won were for gymnastics – which, much to Mother's irritation, were always the last to be presented on speech days.

Soon after I started at the grammar school I teamed up with John Rowlands and Dick Irwin. We were a close-knit trio, 'thick as thieves' as the saying goes, and never at a loss for things to do. At this time I also took out hire purchase on a bicycle, a drop-handlebar sports model, and was obliged to find a job. Dad was employed at Boyer's, a local newsagent, so delivering papers seemed the obvious answer. But there was a problem: the health visitor at school decided that I was seriously underweight, and I remember having to report to the welfare clinic every week for a check-up. Not that this was particularly onerous: I would stand on the scales, the nurse would record my weight and give me a bottle of creamy pink medicine with instructions to take one tablespoonful twice a day. Well I *did* try, but the medicine, which tasted strongly of cod liver oil, was revolting. Be that as it may, the nurse seemed quite happy as long as I gained weight. So, on check-up days I took the precaution of concealing the weights from Mum's kitchen scales in my blazer pockets – a cunning wheeze, because I could add to my weight by small, easily identifiable increments, the smallest weight being two ounces and the heaviest 5 lb. Fortunately these health checks lasted for only eight weeks. By then seven bottles of El Pinko had gone down the drain, the nurse was ecstatic because I had apparently put on 8 lb, and my blazer pockets had a distinctly baggy look. I was declared fit to deliver newspapers, and I continued with morning and evening rounds during the weekdays and one round on Sundays for the next three years. I managed to pay off the debt on my sports bike, and I even had some cash left over for pocket money.

John, Dick and I were keen aero-modellers. We started with simple gliders and graduated to diesel-engined free-flight models. It was an absorbing hobby; during the winter we built models, either from kits or our own designs, and we flew them during the summer. The local club ran competitions, and I remember on one occasion Dick and I were joint favourites to win a 1.0 cc-engined free-flight contest. The scoring was based on the total time of flight less the number of seconds spent under power. A steep, powered climb followed by a long, shallow glide would win the contest. Dick Irwin's entry was a Kiel Kraft Slicker, a model specifically designed for high performance, powered by an Amco 0.87 cc engine, with its wing mounted on a pylon. My model was a Kiel Kraft Bandit, a more conventional high-wing monoplane powered by my 1.0 cc E.D. Bee engine. The Amco's fuel tank was made of perspex, so Dick could see exactly how much fuel was available, whereas the E.D. Bee's tank was metal and the fuel quantity was largely a matter of guesswork. There were other entrants, but on previous form we reckoned they didn't stand a chance.

Dick launched first. The Slicker climbed like a homesick angel for five seconds, but as soon as the engine cut the model went into a suicidal spiral dive and ended in a splintering crash a few yards from the point of launch. Dick's total flight time was less than ten seconds. The other contestants had no better luck; they all crashed with engines still running. The contest was in the bag – or so I thought. I tweaked up the E.D. Bee to maximum revs and launched the Bandit into the wind. But I too had miscalculated the trim, and instead of climbing in a wide orbit the Bandit made a beeline for the distant horizon beyond the river. On and on it droned, until the judges disqualified me because no one could hear when the engine cut or see where the plane landed. Dick, with his pile of wreckage, was declared the winner, although the moral victory was eventually mine when a pair of grinning urchins returned my Bandit, all in one piece, an hour later.

By the age of fourteen a number of factors had convinced me that my future lay with the Royal Air Force. In 1947 a compulsory two years' National Service was introduced. Of course, memories of the Second World War were still fresh when the Korean War started in June 1950 – so a period of military service seemed natural. But I remember thinking, If I am obliged to fight, then I had better make sure I am in a machine that will compensate for my weedy physique. Soldiering did not appeal, nor did the Navy; since I was interested in aircraft the RAF seemed the logical choice. But I was determined to break free from the average mould – I wanted to be different. Thus arose my ambition to be a fighter pilot.

'Beefy' Owens, the headmaster, said I would never make it. 'Some of the best boys in the school have been turned down by the RAF, and you are not in the same league,' he told me. Others voiced similar opinions. But nothing ventured nothing gained, I told myself. According to the newspapers the RAF was losing two Meteor pilots every week, and I was a willing volunteer.

Still, success at school was a prerequisite, and I knew I would have my work cut out. I remember all the masters who laboured against the odds to get me through O levels: 'Shell' Foster, who taught mathematics; 'Ghandi' Ray, who taught geography and started each lesson with a test on our previous work; Mr Phelps, the English master who thought I showed promise; and many others – Phillips, Guy, Farrell, Booker, Caldwell and Knight. . . .

I made the wise decision to apply to join the Air Training Corps – No. 339 Squadron ATC – based at Paignton. While other boys busied themselves with scouting and field crafts, I studied the principles of flight and Morse code. After joining, from fellow cadets I picked up all manner of useful tips: how to bull one's shoes with liberal applications of spit and polish; how to run the edge of a bar of soap along the inside of a crease to ensure that it stayed razor sharp, at least until it rained. Before long I had the sharpest creases – and the cleanest knees – in the whole squadron. At that time there were few opportunities to get any flying, but 339 Squadron managed to procure a Link Trainer – an early type of flight simulator – which was a reasonable substitute. In fact the Link Trainer had motion simulation which could reproduce a fairly convincing spin, especially when the opaque cockpit canopy was closed. I was taken on as Flying Officer Drew's assistant on the Link, and I spent hours practising basic instrument flying techniques.

The family returned to Lymington in February 1952, and in order to continue with my school studies I moved into lodgings in Bridgetown. Mrs Osborne, my Irish landlady, was a kindly soul, but she must have taken cooking lessons from the nuns because it was back to the boiled fish and potatoes. That year I cycled to Lymington to spend Easter with the family and reluctantly returned to Totnes for my final term at school. I took five O levels, which may seem feeble by today's standards, but the school's science curriculum was limited. As I remember, the papers were quite straightforward, and I passed all five subjects. I could have stayed on and attempted A levels in the sixth form, but my parents could not have afforded the boarding fees. Besides, I had other plans.

So that particular chapter of life was closed, and now I could not wait to get away. The relief of finishing exams and leaving school made light of the miles as I cycled back to Lymington. I regretted having to say goodbye to the Paignton ATC Squadron, but was grateful that they had arranged for me to transfer to No. 1308 ATC Squadron in Lymington.

Like teenagers the world over, the thought of earning a living appealed to me. My parents wanted me to learn a trade – 'You must have something to fall back on, Tony' – which was not exactly what I had in mind, but at sixteen I was too young for pilot training. In any case, I needed parental consent to join the RAF. Thus I was packed off to the Labour Exchange to find a job. Not any old job, of course – it had to be an apprenticeship.

I eventually got a job as an apprentice engineering draughtsman at Wellworthy's. The pay was low, but I was training for a career – what more did I expect? I started on the print lamp, producing copies of drawings for the machine shop, with the prospect in mind of moving on to the drawing board within six months. But unfortunately there was no spare board in the office when my turn came round; after a further six months and still no board, I realised that promotion in this line of work was pedestrian to say the least. Besides, my heart was not really in it.

But if life at Wellworthy's was beginning to drag, my progress in the ATC had really taken off. Flying Officer Mullins, the CO of 1308 Squadron, welcomed me with open arms. As luck would have it, he needed a cadet sergeant, and as I had just been promoted before leaving Paignton I had fallen on my feet. Furthermore, it was easier to get flying experience in Hampshire. As cadets we cycled for miles to scrounge trips, either in Ansons at Hamble or in Sunderland flying boats at Calshot.

On 6 September 1952 the squadron visited the Farnborough Air Show. There were many new aircraft types on display including the V bombers – Valiant, Victor and Vulcan – but I was more interested in the high-speed aircraft such as the Swift, the Hunter and the de Havilland DH 110. Speed was all important. At this time the Americans and the Russians were way ahead in high-speed research, and the race was on to produce a British fighter that could match, hopefully even outclass, the Sabre and the MiG 15. In those days, if an aircraft was capable of flying faster than the speed of sound, if only at high altitude, then it was customary to do so at Farnborough. It was most impressive to deliver the characteristic double sonic boom on the airfield, then within seconds appear over the runway very fast, with vapour enveloping the wings.

At this show the DH 110 flown by John Derry delivered a thunderous sonic bang and streaked low across the airfield before turning left through 270° to face the crowd. Then the aircraft pitched up violently, its twin tail booms disintegrated like torn silver paper, and the engines burst free from its belly. It was all over in split seconds: what was left of the fuselage and cockpit crashed beside the runway, the engines arched high over the heads of the spectators, and plummeted into a crowded hillside. Thirty people were killed – including John Derry and Anthony Richards, his observer – and a further sixty-three spectators were injured.

Within minutes Squadron Leader Neville Duke, flying a Hunter, delivered another thunderous sonic boom over the airfield. It was a brave show but by then most of the spectators had had enough.

Our spirits were somewhat subdued on the journey home; perhaps for the first time it really hit home that flying obviously involved an element of risk, as the events of that afternoon had tragically demonstrated.

In March 1953, Flying Officer Mullins put my name forward for a flying scholarship. This splendid scheme enabled a small number of cadets to be trained up to Private Pilot's Licence (PPL) standard at a local civilian aero club. The selection and medical examination procedures were done at Pucklechurch, and the scholarships awarded on a competitive basis. As far as my future intentions to join the RAF were concerned it would not have mattered if I was not selected at this stage, but I was still worried because this was the first opportunity I had had to be medically assessed for flying. So many people had told me I would never get through I was beginning to believe them.

We were not given our results immediately, but three weeks later news came through that I had been accepted. I could hardly believe my luck. In those days dual instruction – flying with an instructor – cost £7 per hour, whereas solo flying was slightly cheaper at £5 per hour. Inexpensive by modern standards, but I certainly could not have afforded to pay for the thirty flying hours required to qualify for a PPL. My flying kit – Sidcup flying suit, fur-lined boots, leather helmet and gloves – was delivered to the ATC Squadron in Lymington, and in April I reported to Mr Langridge, the chief instructor at the Hampshire Aero Club, based at Eastleigh in Southampton.

At first sight the de Havilland Tiger Moth, with its fabric skin, struts, bracing wires and balloon tyres, appeared too fragile to hang together in the air. But this stringy little biplane, with a maximum speed of just 109 m.p.h., was well capable of surviving the sort of abuse meted out by the average novice pilot. Voice communication between the cockpits (via Gosport speaking tubes) was rudimentary to say the least, and much of the instruction had to be covered in detailed pre-flight briefings before take-off. The great advantage of learning to fly in the Tiger Moth was that it taught co-ordination of hands, feet and eyes. It was classic 'seat of the pants' type of flying: left to its own devices the Tiger would wander all over the sky, but the open cockpit and exposure to the elements soon encouraged the pilot to maintain balanced flight. An icy draught across the cockpit was an instant reminder that the rudder wasn't properly applied. Like all good training aircraft the Tiger was fully aerobatic, although it was more responsive in vertical manoeuvres, such as loops and wing-overs, than in roll. You had to be really hamfisted to lose control, but if that happened, then it was easy to recover from the ensuing spin. Though the Tiger Moth was fairly easy to fly, it required considerable skill and concentration to fly accurately: five miles per hour too fast on the final approach and the aircraft would float for ever. If you foolishly allowed the wheels to touch the ground too soon, then the Tiger would balloon back into the air before bouncing even harder on the second and subsequent contacts with Mother Earth. And of course the Tiger Moth had no wheel brakes; you had to rely on the rudder and tail skid for steering on the ground.

My first flight lasted only thirty minutes. I was petrified, and bit through my bottom lip; it was like riding a motorcycle with no visible means of support. After a final lumpy landing, Mr Langridge commented, 'And we come to rest in a series of short, birdlike hops, by the grace of God and Mr de Havilland.' By the second flight I was overconfident, but must have shown some early promise, as according to my log book I went solo after just 6 hours and 35 minutes' flying time. Perhaps Mr Langridge could not stand the strain of flying with me.

I was only able to fly at the weekends, and between flights I spent my time browsing around the hangar, which contained many fascinating aircraft including one of the original Supermarine S6Bs, the outright winners of the Schneider Trophy for Britain in 1931, and a beautifully maintained Gloster Gladiator – the last of the biplane fighters. I spent hours sitting in the cockpits daydreaming.

The final land-away navigation exercise was from Eastleigh to Bristol, thence to Thruxton Airfield for a landing, before a return to Eastleigh. The first half of the flight was uneventful, but on landing at Thruxton I was confronted by a rope fence strung between iron stakes.

I gave the Tiger a quick burst of power, hopped over the obstacle and finally stopped opposite a hessian enclosure with a 'Gents' sign pinned to its entrance. A truck arrived, and the driver explained in fairly colourful language that they were preparing the airfield for motor racing the next day, and would I please leave. I agreed, provided someone lowered the rope fence to make room for my take-off. There were one or two red faces when I got back to Eastleigh, but nothing more was said.

It took two months – effectively eighteen flying days – for me to complete the scholarship. I got my Private Pilot's Licence in May 1953, which entitled me to hire the Tiger Moth and carry non-fare-paying passengers. Few volunteered – and I can't say I blamed them; I only knew enough to be dangerous. But Mr Skelton, a reporter on the *Lymington Times*, did come along for a ride, for which we shared the cost of the fuel.

When I was not flying, or dreaming about flying, I was wholly involved in the ATC. I attended the Coronation Parade in London on 2 June and stood with many other cadets in front of Buckingham Palace to cheer the newly crowned Queen Elizabeth II. In August the squadron spent three weeks' summer camp at RAF Colerne. I was given a flight in a Bristol Brigand light bomber, and cadged a dual sortie in an RAF Tiger Moth.

Up to this time my parents had opposed my plans to join the RAF, but in September they came home from the Hearts of Oak public house one evening and said that, if I was still keen on the RAF, they would not stand in my way. I didn't need a second invitation; Mother's final caution was that it was a hard life in the service, and perhaps I should think again. But this was not the time for the faint-hearted – within a couple of weeks I was called forward to RAF Hornchurch for aircrew aptitude tests.

The selection process was nerve-racking; one could fail for any number of reasons, and I was still worried about the medical. Compared to the sixty or so other applicants I was painfully thin and I wheezed a bit – the aftermath of childhood asthma. The medical orderlies ostentatiously closed the windows when I walked in: 'We wouldn't want you to blow away, would we, sir?'

I had applied for the RAF College at Cranwell, so from Hornchurch

I went on to Daedallus House to be tested with a fascinating series of problems: bridging apparently unbridgeable gaps with an assortment of planks and ropes that were all too short. Then it was over and I returned home to await the results.

Two weeks later a letter arrived informing me that I had not been accepted for Cranwell. No reason was given – which was fairly demoralising – but within a few days a second letter arrived offering me a Short Service Commission to train as a pilot in the RAF.

The volunteer instructors of the ATC, many of whom already had distinguished service careers, deserved much of the credit for my being accepted into the RAF. Without the help of Flying Officers Drew and Mullins, to name but two, I would probably not have had sufficient drive to carry me through. I would certainly not have qualified as a pilot at the age of seventeen. The moral must be: if you have a clear idea of what you want out of life, then go for it, and use all the help you can get on the way.

3
Induction into the RAF and flying training in Canada

I was attested at RAF Cardington on 11 November 1953. According to the diary I was obliged to keep it was a solemn occasion, and difficult to believe that at last I had made it. But I could have said so much more: the room was sparsely furnished, with highly polished brown linoleum on the floor, and the brick walls were painted cream and green; a black cast-iron coke stove in one corner generated heat and noxious fumes in equal measure. Twelve of us were sworn in at a time – I suspect the size of the group was limited by the number of bibles. But none of this mattered – I was over the first and probably the most difficult hurdle. I was in the RAF.

We were kitted out for initial training and given eight drill sessions on the parade square, to teach us how to march, how to salute, and generally how to conduct ourselves when dressed in uniform. Then we were posted to RAF Kirton-in-Lindsey for Initial Officer Training. The IOT course was a blend of academic study, practical ground combat training and projects designed to develop leadership. My entry group consisted of sixty cadets, most of whom were on Short Service Commissions, but there were a few National Servicemen who were of sufficiently high calibre to be accepted for aircrew training – provided they agreed to serve for an additional two years. In fact many recruits who started as National Servicemen stayed on to complete distinguished careers in the service.

RAF Kirton-in-Lindsey was no holiday camp. As usual with recruit training there was a wealth of petty discipline. The standards expected of us were high, but it was not difficult to hit upon a survivable routine. Inevitably people were given nicknames, more as a mark of affection than anything else: John Edwards became 'Jim' after a well-known comedian, and Jim first coined the name of 'Bugs' for me

– because of my front teeth and big ears. I didn't mind; it could have been worse – a fellow named Poole was instantly christened 'Cess' – but for me it was 'Bugs', and the name stuck. The coursework was fine, although at one stage I was worried about mathematics, which was strange because that had always been one of my strong subjects.

By June 1950, responding to the threat of communist expansion, the Western powers had embarked on a massive rearmament programme. The RAF's aircrew requirements consequently increased by a factor of ten and, just as they had done with the Empire Air Training Scheme during the Second World War, the Canadian government offered to provide training facilities for pilots and navigators with the Royal Canadian Air Force. Twenty cadets, including Jim Edwards and myself, were lucky enough to be selected for the Canadian draft. The war had restricted foreign travel for my generation, and I remember being thrilled at the prospect of going abroad.

The final examinations at IOT were easier than expected, although six students failed and a further nineteen were placed on review. Those of us destined for Canada were given three weeks' embarkation leave. I suspect my parents were a little surprised that I had survived the course.

I was on cloud nine throughout that leave. As a full-blown officer cadet with a tin trunk for hold baggage, a Revelation expanding suitcase for my uniforms and one set of civilian clothes, nothing could stop me. But on 13 March 1954, the crucial day of departure, the taxi to take me to Brockenhurst station failed to turn up. I missed the train I had planned on catching, and came within an ace of missing my connection to London. Eventually I arrived at Waterloo just twenty minutes before the boat train was due to leave Euston Station. Throwing caution to the winds I promised the cabbie a five-pound tip if he could get me to Euston on time. We set off, scattering pedestrians, barrow-boys and old ladies before us. I made it through the Euston platform gates with seconds to spare.

My pulse slowly returned to normal during the journey to Liverpool, and I vowed never again to allow travel arrangements to go so badly awry.

The *Empress of France* weighed in at 11,500 tons – surely, I thought, a ship this big would be as steady as a rock. Don't you believe it. The *Empress* had a flat bottom and no stabilisers; among the crew she was affectionately known as the *Drunken Duchess*, on account of her sedate, rolling gait. I watched the Royal Liver building as we left port. A dirty grey drizzle had set in.

During boat drill we were advised to eat well before the Atlantic swell took its toll, so we really tucked in that first evening at dinner. The standard of food aboard was excellent. It was hard to believe the waiter's confident prediction that the restaurant would be relatively quiet for the first two days – but sure enough, very few passengers turned up for breakfast next morning. Jim Edwards was there, albeit a bit green. I lasted until the poached eggs arrived, then discretion persuaded me to seek fresh air. After barking at the waves and gazing at distant horizons for an hour or two I retreated to my cabin and took a couple of Qwells, which I promptly brought up in the sink. A fellow traveller advised me that the best way to cope with seasickness is to get plenty of fresh air and lie down as close as possible to the centre of the ship. Unfortunately, on anything larger than a municipal park paddle boat, these two requirements were mutually exclusive: the library was fairly close to the centre of the *Drunken Duchess*, and there was an abundance of fresh air on the upper decks, but the March temperatures were bracing to say the least. So it was the library for me. I sat for hours listening to the creaking, shuddering hull. 'That's a good sign,' commented a passing sailor. 'It means the ship is alive.' But I didn't need to know that; the wretched ship was so lively it was making me ill.

After a couple of days of queasy discomfort the passengers slowly drifted back to the restaurant and the social life on board blossomed. Many of those aboard were heading for a new life in Canada and there was a carnival atmosphere on board. For the first and only time I made a killing at bingo, recouping the expenses of my panic-stricken dash across London.

There were forty officer cadets on board, all desperately trying to appear as men of the world, but most of them greener than grass. On the last two days of the voyage, sea conditions became very yo-ho-ho – the crew tied down the tables and chairs and rigged safety ropes – but by then we were all seasoned travellers and the wild lurches of the ship simply added to the fun. The farewell ball on the last night was a great success, the human tide of revellers washing back and forth across the dance floor as the *Drunken Duchess* rolled on through the night.

Next day we docked at Saint John, New Brunswick, amidst sleet and snow. Canada looked fairly solid to me, but the world continued to lurch for a couple of days. We travelled by train to London, Ontario for three weeks' Canadian acclimatisation: popcorn, candyfloss and ice hockey. Jim and I bought cameras to record our progress – I splashed out on a Paxette 35mm, which I put to immediate use during a bus excursion to Niagara Falls.

The acclimatisation at London was more for the benefit of the French Air Force cadets, who were given three months to brush up on their English before starting flying training. For the basic flying training course, half of the RAF contingent were posted to RCAF Centralia, not far from London; the other half – which included Jim Edwards, Ralph Clough 'Cess' Poole and me – went west to Moose Jaw, Saskatchewan.

It is only by surface travel that one can truly appreciate the vast size of Canada. Spring had not yet arrived, so the ground remained frozen and there was still plenty of snow. The Canadian Pacific trains were built for comfort rather than speed, with a caboose at the rear where one could sit in armchair luxury and watch the scenery roll by. And what majestic scenery it was: to Toronto, then north around Lake Huron and Lake Superior, through Sudbury, White River and west across the great plains. Mile after mile the train rumbled on; every so often it would slow to walking pace, either to drop off a box of fish in the snow to await collection, or to pick up a bag of mail. Occasionally I caught a glimpse of an isolated log cabin way back among the trees. Despite the scenery, it was a cold, desolate country. Once or twice a day the train would stop at some one-horse town to take on water and we would stretch our legs. There was little to see, often just a few stores with raised, Western-style sidewalks. All the time we were obliged to wear uniform, which aroused some interest amongst the local people.

On the third day the train rumbled into Winnipeg and we were met by a group of ladies who handed out free packets of cigarettes and sweets – another relic from the days of the Empire Air Training scheme. The good ladies of Winnipeg were under the impression that anyone from England was a half-starved refugee – and it would have been churlish to discourage them. We took photographs in front of an historic locomotive outside the station, and having bade farewell to the girls we boarded the train for the last lap: to Moose Jaw.

There was a reception in the students' mess for Course 5402 when we arrived, and we learned that our first duty was to attend a funeral service in the town for those who had died as a result of a mid-air collision between a civil airliner and a Harvard flown by an RAF student. The collision had occurred in broad daylight over the town – thus, needless to say, the RAF was not very popular. Hardly the best start, but it didn't dampen our enthusiasm for the challenges to come.

We spent two weeks in ground school studying the Harvard's aircraft systems and learning about the Canadian weather. This was followed by several hours in the cockpit learning the checks. For the benefit of those not familiar with the business of flying, the checks insure that the aircraft is serviceable and properly configured for the next manoeuvre. For example, it is essential to make sure the undercarriage is down before attempting to land. There are checks before climbing into the cockpit, before starting the engine, before take-off and so on, until the shut-down checks before finally vacating the aircraft. The checks were designed to reduce flying risks to a minimum.

The RCAF Harvard had been in use as a trainer since 1936; indeed, some of the aircraft at Moose Jaw had been flying before I was born – a sobering thought. I was immediately struck by its size. With a 600-horsepower Pratt & Whitney Wasp engine up front, the Harvard was an impressive beast, made even more daunting by its raucous snarl in the circuit, as the propeller tips exceeded the speed of sound.

We were each issued with a parachute, hopefully to sit on rather than use. A pillow was stitched to the back of my harness, so that I would be able to apply full rudder. In the hangar, my instructor – Flying Officer Topper – showed me how to abandon the aircraft in case of an emergency. It was just a case of pulling back the hood, releasing the seat harness and stepping over the side. No problems – I got out in just over five seconds; of course, it might prove to be more difficult in the air. We were obliged to repeat this bail-out drill every month.

The Harvard was awkward to control on the ground; the big radial engine obstructed forward vision, and it was necessary to taxi in a zig-zag fashion to clear the way ahead. (We were taken to see the wreckage of an aircraft that had been chopped up one night because a student pilot had not followed rules: the student's propeller had severed the left arm of an instructor sitting in the rear cockpit of the aircraft in front. We were unlikely to forget the gruesome spectacle.) But the plane was a reformed character in the air, firmer on the controls and obviously more powerful than the Tiger Moth. It was a joy to fly. It was also fairly easy to land – although once on the ground, due to its wide undercarriage, the Harvard had a perverse tendency to spin around as though on a treacherous skid-pan. This uncontrolled manoeuvre was known as a 'ground loop'. The instructors drummed it into us that with the Harvard you could not afford to relax until the chocks were in place and the engine was switched off.

The stall – that was the sudden loss of lift that occurred when the airflow over the top of the wing became turbulent – was straightforward; but in the Harvard the spin was less predictable. The aircraft would spin when one wing stalled before the other, which induced a rotation about all three axes. Normal control movements were ineffective and the aircraft rapidly lost height. Personally I never cared much for spinning, but knowledge of the correct spin recovery was vital, and that required practice. To induce a spin, speed was reduced by raising the nose and, just on the point of stall, full rudder and opposite stick were applied. With this treatment, the Harvard would flick into a rapid, nose-down rotation, the airspeed would remain low, the rate of descent high. It was easier to spin the Harvard to the right rather than to the left, because the combined engine exhaust/cockpit heater induced turbulence along the top of the starboard wing root.

The action for recovery was to apply full opposite rudder (hence the need for my pillow), with the stick held fully forward and the ailerons neutral. As soon as the rotation stopped the rudder had to be centralised, otherwise the aircraft would flick into a spin in the opposite direction. The same thing could happen if the pilot attempted to recover too quickly from the ensuing dive. These secondary spins were flatter and potentially far more dangerous than the initial spin. Again, the lesson was brought home quite forcibly to us: shortly after we arrived at Moose Jaw a student was killed after failing to recover from a secondary spin. Out of morbid curiosity four of us drove out to see the crash site. One look at the crushed and twisted cockpit, with unmentionable grey gunge spilling from the sheared stump of the control column, was enough to put us off spinning for life.

The excellent weather permitted maximum continuity, and my

flying hours quickly mounted: twenty-five hours in May, thirty-five in June and twenty-six in July. We were totally absorbed in flying.

During those early months there was little else to distract our attention. Moose Jaw was a quiet, agricultural town; grain elevators marched across the horizon, tracing out the line of the Canadian National Railway. The town boasted a number of buffalo – a small remnant of the once mighty herds – which was exotic, although not to everyone's taste. When the weather was hot, there was nothing better than a refreshing dip in Moose Jaw Creek. The water trapped behind the wooden dam was cool, deep and green. No one caught anything unpleasant, but the creek lost much of its charm as a bathing hole when we found we shared it with a number of fat leeches.

Later on, when we had time to spare, the warm hospitality of the local population more than compensated for Moose Jaw's lack of amenities. Several families – or rather several daughters – adopted us, and you can't beat home cooking, wherever home may be. However, we were a bit limited by the lack of transport, and this was no place for a loner: to date a girl when no one else was around might create the wrong impression.

In an attempt to ease our transport problems Jim Edwards persuaded John Hilliard and me to contribute towards buying a car. Jim had his eye on a bargain. Trouble was the vehicle in question had only three wheels – the fourth wheel and the spare had been stolen. Long after the vendor had disappeared over the horizon, we discovered that there was a serious shortage of car wheels in Saskatchewan. Spares couldn't be bought for love or money. We never did get that car on the road, nor did we get our money back.

On 19 August we started our mid-course leave. Ralph Clough headed west to do some climbing in the Rocky Mountains, while Jim and I teamed up with four of our Canadian buddies to tour the west coast of the United States in Garth Macrae's father's late-model Packard. We set off south across the border, through Montana, Idaho and Washington State to Seattle, then south to Portland, Oregon, through giant redwood country and across the Golden Gate bridge to San Francisco. We lapped it up. We could not afford motel accommodation every night, so a couple of the guys would book in with the car and the rest of us would sneak in through the back door. One motel room between six was not luxurious but it was just about affordable. The trick was to get out unseen the following morning.

San Francisco, with its steep roller-coaster hills, trolley cars, Nob Hill and Fisherman's Wharf, was surely one of the most attractive cities in the States. Jim paid two dollars to a Chinaman on a street corner for some fire crackers. It was another pay-in-advance deal – the man disappeared with the money and we figured that Jim had been conned – but he eventually returned with six plaster cylinders, about the size of a shotgun cartridge, painted silver with green string fuses – obviously he had seen Jim coming.

In the meantime Garth hailed a taxi; he wanted to find some women. We piled in like lambs to the slaughter. First we were driven to a deserted warehouse, where the yellow cab was swapped for an unmarked black saloon – shades of Mickey Spillane. From there our journey took us out of town across the Oakland Bay bridge. The bridge itself was almost eight miles long and those of us in the back decided to hide our money in our shoes, just in case we were mugged. At last we pulled up at a motel apartment. The door was opened by a blowzy tart of mature years who greeted us in broad cockney – ''Allo, Dearie'. There were two girls on duty that night. It turned out they had emigrated from England a few months before. Not very exciting, although the girl I was with was a bit surprised when I had to fish around in my left shoe for the money. The return fare to San Francisco was marginally more expensive. We were sitting in the motel room drinking beer and retelling the events of the evening when a stunning explosion ripped through the apartment: Jim had let off one of his fire crackers in the shower cubicle. The plastic curtain was in tatters and the tiles were smoke-blackened up to eye level. We repaired the damage as best we could and quietly slipped away the following morning.

Next stop Los Angeles. For eighteen hours we took in the sights: Hollywood, Sunset Boulevard, Graumann's Chinese Theatre and Beverly Hills. We even had time to get a new exhaust fitted to the car. Then we headed inland for Nevada and Las Vegas.

After nine days on the road we needed a break, and Las Vegas, the gambling town in the middle of the desert, was a tempting oasis. With a temperature in the shade of over 100°F it was far too hot for the one-room routine, so we checked into the Kit Carson Motel, which had air conditioning and the added attraction of a swimming pool. Gambling is legal in Nevada, and Las Vegas catered for all tastes: blackjack, craps, roulette, baccarat and the ubiquitous one-armed bandits – they were all there, poised ready to separate the fool from his money. Compared to European casinos, the odds were biased slightly more in favour of the house. There was a zero and a double zero on the roulette wheel, and the blackjack cards were regularly shuffled to foil the seasoned gambler. There was no need for the casinos to cheat. With beautiful cocktail waitresses on hand to serve free drinks, and no clocks or windows to distract, the gambler could stake his or her bets, and usually lose in the long run. In downtown Las Vegas we watched old ladies feeding silver dollars into slot machines – one old soul kept six machines going at the same time and became very tetchy if anyone disturbed her routine – then we cruised along the Strip to check out the big casinos: the Desert Inn, the Thunderbird, the Sands, the Stardust and the Flamingo. In these clubs gambling financed the very best of light entertainment.

Provided one steered clear of the tables, Las Vegas was not expensive. For the price of a drink one could be entertained all evening at a lounge show. Dinner shows were slightly more expensive, but that included the cost of food. If all else failed one could celebrate by getting hitched in a wedding chapel: the Wee Chapel O'The Heather or the Chapel of the White Stars – several were available for business most of the day. The honeymoon suite at the nearest motel would be included as part of the deal . . . It was another world; one could win or lose a fortune, get drunk, fall in love and get laid or married – all in the same evening. Being below the legal age for drinking and being short of cash, Jim and I could not take full advantage of Las Vegas. Which was probably just as well – our Canadian buddies lost their money within hours of hitting town.

Before moving on, we drove thirty miles to Black Canyon to see the Boulder Dam. The wild Colorado River, untamed for millions of years, has carved its way through the surface of the earth to form the Grand Canyon. Before the dam had been built, every spring, when the high snows melted, great floods would sweep down the river, destroying everything in their path, regularly inundating Southern California. The flood waters destroyed crops and eroded rich farmlands.

Then, in the late 1920s, it was decided that a dam should be built to harness the Colorado. The project would also assist in the recovery from the Depression. Construction was started in 1930 at Black Canyon, and the dam was completed in just five years. It is a truly impressive structure; a quarter of a mile across between canyon walls, 750 ft high from foundation rock to crest, weighing seven million tons and holding back thirty million acre feet of water in Lake Mead. Garth Macrae, who had had a few beers, reckoned that if you were fast enough you could run around the inside rim of the dam without falling off. I could see what he was on about – it was like an enormous wall of death – still, thank God he didn't try.

Next day we headed north to Salt Lake City. We bathed in the Great Salt Lake and visited Yellowstone National Park to see Old Faithful, the famous geyser. Then it was non-stop through Montana and across the Canadian border to Moose Jaw. Over four thousand miles in sixteen days: the trip of a lifetime. We were more exhausted when we got back than when we had started out.

I was pleased to get back to flying, but the pressure was on and the less competent students were soon having difficulties. Sadly, Ralph Clough was among those who fell by the wayside. But there was still the occasional gem of humour. One night as I taxied out for take-off a lone Harvard approached to land. The student pilot was obviously too high and too fast, which was confirmed a few moments later by the following exchange on the R/T:

'Moose Jaw tower, this is Delta six-four – I have just overrun the runway and gone through a hedge. Over.'

'Roger, Delta six-four. Is your engine still running? Over.'

'Delta six-four – affirmative.'

'Roger, Delta six-four. Can you taxi back to the line? Over.'

(After a long pause) 'Moose Jaw tower, this is Delta six-four. Do you want me to come back through the same hole in this hedge? Or should I make another hole? Over.'

(With a note of profound resignation) 'Delta six-four, this is Moose Jaw tower. Switch off your engine. We will come and get you!'

In November we were introduced to close formation, one of the essential military flying skills. It was rather like learning to ride a bicycle – not difficult, but it did require concentration. Formation positions were fixed by lining up parts of the leader's aircraft. For example, in echelon starboard, the number two would fly level with the leader's tailplane, lining up the leader's starboard wing-tip and front cockpit. Other standard formation positions were similarly defined; all the formatting pilot had to do was hold the briefed position. Nothing to it, really – but for the novice pilot, slow to recognise relative movement and unsure on the controls, that first close formation sortie was very demanding. Initially the student was apt to thrash the controls around the cockpit to no good purpose, and finish the sortie drenched in sweat. Eventually the penny would drop: many small corrections were better and smoother than great handfuls of power. What was all the fuss about anyway? Well, you have to try hanging on to some chap's wing, approaching to land in black, turbulent weather, with insufficient fuel to go around again, to fully appreciate the skills required.

By mid-November I was fairly confident of graduating, and it was now just a question of whether I would be considered good enough for jet training. My last flight in the Harvard was on 1 December; the following week we handed in our kit and waited to be debriefed.

I had enjoyed the basic flying course at Moose Jaw; no doubt my Tiger Moth experience had given me a head start, but the Canadian instructors were first class. In eight months I had flown 185 hours, which was about average for the course. We would not qualify for the coveted pilot's wings until we completed our advanced training.

The other students were debriefed in alphabetic order, but for some reason my debrief was delayed. I was the last student to be called in, and by then I was a gibbering idiot. But far from failure, it turned out that I had won the Hawker Siddeley Trophy, awarded to the best student pilot.

Along with the others I was posted to RCAF Gimli to complete my advanced training on the Lockheed T-33 Silver Star. But before we left Moose Jaw our civilian friends threw an early Christmas party for us. The evening was tinged with sadness at having to say goodbye. I dare say the odd girlish tear was shed – not for me, of course – although Mrs Shuttleworth, a charming lady with two attractive teenage daughters, exchanged letters with my mother for several years. But we had to be moving on.

The weather got colder as we drove east to Manitoba. Gimli was a summer holiday resort on the shore of Lake Winnipeg, but in December the lake was frozen solid and the roads were hemmed in by banks of snow. The town had that seedy, run-down appearance of a seaside resort in the off-season. Most of the stores were boarded up for the winter. Business was slow – so slow, in fact, that one local barman allowed us to drink without asking for proof of our age. Not that the experience was particularly uplifting. As I remember, we had to remain seated at a table; in Canada it was against the law to stand and drink at the bar. And we had to add salt to take the gas out of the beer.

But we were not at Gimli to admire the scenery, or to sample the local brew. It was straight into ground school to learn about the T-33 and other items of jet-age equipment. This was the first time I had seen an ejection seat, let alone sat in one; the seat would fire the pilot clear of the cockpit and automatically deploy his parachute. He would survive, provided he initiated ejection at least 500 ft above the ground. We watched films on winter survival in northern Canada and were given lectures on aviation medicine. We were taught to recognise the difference between hypoxia – the lack of oxygen – and hyperventilation, or in other words 'over-breathing'. Since either condition led to loss of consciousness, it was important to make the correct diagnosis. On 29 December, eight students at a time spent an hour in a decompression chamber to become familiar with the T-33's oxygen equipment and practise emergency procedures. Finally, to simulate the loss of the cockpit canopy at high altitude, we were explosively decompressed. There was a loud bang, instant fog, and we belched and farted in unison, as the chamber's relative altitude rocketed from a comfortable 18,000 ft to a frigid 40,000 ft in less than three seconds.

After the hype of ground school, the transition to the T-33 promised to be exciting. Still, I fully expected my reactions to be too slow. I flew the first dual sortie with Flying Officer Robinson on 5 January 1955. Although things happened faster than I had been used to, the T-33 was remarkably well mannered. The controls were precise and the aircraft had none of the capricious habits of the Harvard. The RCAF T-33s were fitted with wing-tip fuel tanks, which gave a useful flight duration of one and three-quarter hours. We climbed to 40,000 ft, from where the winter landscape became a flat tapestry of grey forest and white, frozen lakes – a bleak world, far removed from the pressurised comfort of the cockpit. It was an exhilarating experience.

An hour and a half later we were back on the ground, debriefing. After four more dual sorties in as many days, I found myself airborne in sole charge of a jet aircraft for the first time. The Canadian version of the T-33 was fitted with a Rolls-Royce Nene 10 engine, which gave a lively performance but, like any other jet engine, was slow to accelerate from low power settings. Speed control – both on the approach to land and in close formation – required greater anticipation than in the Harvard. The T-33 was fully aerobatic, although it was not cleared for spinning because it tended to tumble end over end. This was the only limitation of an otherwise superb trainer.

In addition to general handling and formation sorties, the course included twenty hours' simulated instrument flying from the rear seat. To fly in cloud, or at night, the pilot has to scan six basic flight instruments: the artificial horizon, the airspeed indicator, the altimeter, the vertical speed indicator, the turn and slip gauge and the compass. In an emergency, one could get home without the artificial horizon and the electronic compass – in RAF parlance, flying 'limited panel' – but that is strictly back to basics. Unusually for a modern aircraft, the T-33's essential flight instruments were distributed around the cockpit in a haphazard fashion, making the instrument scan very awkward.

Not that we were much affected by adverse weather at Gimli: it was either gin clear or so bad no one would wish to get airborne. The chill factor – even in a modest breeze, when the temperature was a mere minus ten degrees – was most uncomfortable, and one had to guard against frostbite. The extreme cold could produce other unusual effects: the lowest temperature I experienced at Gimli was a raw –35°F, and at that sort of temperature the first aircraft to take off in the morning would lay a carpet of ice fog along the runway, as the engine added just enough heat and moisture to disturb the delicate balance of the cold, soaked air. The contrails produced by high-flying aircraft were similar. But as I said, the weather was not a problem for us at Gimli. In three winter months, traditionally the worst months of the year for flying, I few eighty-seven hours in the T-33 and logged only ninety minutes' actual cloud time.

On 17 March we were given a token check-out at night – just two sorties, one dual and one solo. It was a beautiful night with no cloud and unlimited visibility – perfect flying conditions. The dual sortie consisted of a triangular cross-country at high level, followed by circuits and bumps. At high altitude, the glow of Winnipeg's lights to the south was unmistakable, and Gimli's radio beacon was coming in loud and clear – no problems.

After debriefing I had a quick cup of coffee and prepared for my solo sortie. The route was different, but otherwise the procedures were identical. I dimmed the red cockpit lights to preserve my night vision and launched down the runway. After take-off I eased into the climb and turned on to the outbound heading. I checked the oxygen at 10,000 ft and thereafter every 5,000 ft, levelling off at 31,000 ft. After seven minutes I retuned the radio compass to make good my first turning point. The night sky was brilliant, with more stars than I had ever seen before. A green light, high and to the right, was another aircraft on a reciprocal heading inbound for Gimli. Suddenly a bright flash from somewhere behind lit up the canopy – what the hell was that? Everything was normal in my aircraft, and there was nothing to be seen when I turned to look back. On the radio someone reported an explosion to the east of Gimli. Air Traffic called the individual aircraft to check in: only Foxtrot two-four, one of the student pilots, failed to answer.

By the time I landed, Foxtrot two-four, George Fradey – a young French air-force cadet – was long overdue. He could have ejected, of course, but since he had not declared an emergency that was unlikely. If he had ejected his problem would be one of survival – but nothing could be done until daylight.

At first light a search aircraft found a hole in the ice on Lake Winnipeg. The hole had refrozen, but from the wreckage on top of the ice it was obvious that George had crashed at high speed. There was speculation of course, but no one could be sure of what had happened. It was a sad day – George was a popular lad, he had been with us from the start, and he had come within an ace of graduating.

I flew my last T-33 sortie on 28 March 1955, and two days later we paraded in one of the hangars to be presented with our RAF pilot's wings by the station commander. It was a proud moment. In just over a year we had progressed from being raw recruits to qualified pilots. For hard work and sheer enjoyment, there was nothing to match military pilot training.

We travelled by train to Montreal, and there I took the opportunity to visit Mick and Kathleen Darney, who had recently emigrated to Canada. They were living with their three children – Jean, Michael and Cushla – at Lachine, a suburb of Montreal. I had to admire their spirit; it required courage to start life in a new country, but then Uncle Micky had always been one of my heroes. We chatted about Canada, and I said I intended to return when I left the RAF. At the time, I thought that was so.

We sailed for England on the RMS *Ascania.* The ship was hardly the size of an Isle of Wight ferry and had only one funnel – could this tiny vessel really cross the Atlantic? But, unlike the *Empress of France,* the *Ascania* was fitted with stabilisers and the voyage was quite comfortable. We were men of the world now; we could hold our drink and we could fly . . . Surely the girls would not be able to resist our charms. Well, they could and they did. There were few shipboard romances and frankly the competition was too hot for me.

After a virtuous five days we docked at Liverpool. I remember it was raining as I boarded the train to London – some things never change.

4
Rehabilitation training in the UK and conversion on the Hunter F1

I was at home on disembarkation leave, waiting for formal posting instructions, when a letter arrived ordering me to report to RAF Thorney Island. This was unwelcome news: at Liverpool we had been told we would be posted to RAF Chivenor to fly Hunters, but Thorney was an advanced flying school for multi-engined training, using piston-engined Varsity and Valetta aircraft. After the exhilaration of jet flying, the prospect of slow, cumbersome transport aircraft did not appeal.

But life at Thorney was better than I expected. The officers' mess, which was situated on the far side of the airfield from the rest of the station, was comfortable, the food was good and I had a room to myself. Jim Edwards, Mick Letton, John Hilliard and Dennis Carruthers – all Canadian trained – were also posted in.

It was explained to us that there was a backlog of pilots waiting for Hunter conversion, and our course at Chivenor had been delayed. We were assigned for copilot duties on the Varsity pilot conversion squadron. Being members of the permanent staff we enjoyed a more relaxed lifestyle than the students attending the course, which was a welcome change. The Varsity was a powerful twin-engined aircraft equipped with nose-wheel steering. At a pinch it could take off on one engine, but that was not recommended. The right-hand seat had to be filled and, although it was not exactly what we had hoped for when we stepped off the boat in Liverpool, it would be an interesting challenge. The great advantage was that we would remain in flying practice prior to further jet training, and that was invaluable. The students on the course could claim first pilot hours, the equivalent of solo, when they flew with us, and we got the kudos of being the only staff pilot on board the aircraft for their first solo flights and much of their conversion flying. The initial solo sorties were usually uneventful, but on subsequent sorties, as the students relaxed, the level of risk increased. One student feathered the wrong engine – in other words he switched off both engines while practising single-engined circuits – and instantly converted a perfectly serviceable aircraft into a fat, overweight glider. Apparently the activity in the cockpit was positively frantic while the local air traffic controller activated the crash alarm. Fortunately the crew managed to restart one engine and they eventually recovered control with less than 200 ft to spare. We made sure no one repeated the same mistake.

Another incident, in which I was personally involved, was amusing rather than dangerous. Some of the students had great difficulty getting to grips with captaincy – the art of being in command – and Flight Lieutenant Bloggs (not his real name) was one such fellow. Even in the crewroom he came across as a rude, abrasive sort of chap, and no one enjoyed flying with him. During the pre-flight checks for his third solo, Bloggs pompously reminded me not to touch any switches or controls until he ordered me to do so – which was fair comment, but his authoritarian style was hardly in the interests of best crew co-operation. Typical of Bloggs, but not worth arguing over. The approved drill on take-off in the Varsity was for the copilot to hold the control column forward, thus ensuring that the twin nose-wheels stayed on the ground, while the captain in the left-hand seat opened the throttles and controlled direction with a small steering wheel mounted on the port console. As speed increased and the rudder became effective, the captain transferred his grip to the control column and smoothly rotated the aircraft into the climb.

But to get back to Bloggs. There was a frosty silence in the cockpit as we taxied out, which was only broken by the clipped jargon of essential checks. The tower cleared us for take-off; Bloggs grasped the nose-wheel steering and opened the throttles. But he had forgotten to order me to hold the control column forward, so it came as no surprise – to me at least – when, at 50 knots, the nose reared off the ground. Unfortunately Bloggs had not locked his seat properly in position and, as the aircraft's nose went up, so his seat slid back. In a desperate attempt to arrest his rearward progress, he grabbed the control column which coaxed the nose even higher. There we were, climbing at a ridiculously steep angle, at minimum airspeed. Bloggs was severely inconvenienced, at full stretch, bum firmly strapped to the seat, his eyes standing out like chapel hat-pegs. He was unwilling to release his grip on the controls lest his wayward seat carry him out the back of the aircraft. To make matters worse, he had switched off his microphone before starting the take-off and could not tell me to take control. I let him stew for a bit, much to the alarm of both Bloggs and all who watched from the ground, before I levelled the aircraft. Bloggs mellowed somewhat after that flight.

We did a lot of flying that summer, much of it at night. It was fairly routine, but one peaceful night, with the aircraft in darkness except for the subdued cockpit lighting and just two of us aboard, cruising along the south coast at about 2000 ft, there was a loud bang from the rear of the aircraft. The student captain asked me to investigate. I unstrapped and was about to step back when I looked down and saw, through a gaping black hole in the floor, the lights of Worthing drift by. The escape hatch just behind the front seats had operated of its own accord. Obviously that had caused the bang. I had almost taken an involuntary high dive without a parachute. We immediately returned to base. As a reward for our work as safety pilots, we were each given a few hours' dual instruction. I eventually went solo in the Varsity in August, with Jim Edwards acting as my copilot.

Aside from the flying, for the first time since enlisting, I had an opportunity to catch up with life outside the service. I travelled home most weekends. For some while I had been embarrassed by the fact that, while I was a qualified pilot, I had not yet learned how to drive a car. I booked driving lessons in Chichester, but I needed a vehicle in which to practise. That was easier said than done: with a bank balance only just in the black, and a monthly income of £30 out of which I needed £5 a week living expenses, I had precious little left over for motoring. Thus a new car was out of the question – but one of the rogues in the Hearts of Oak pub in Lymington offered to sell me a 'special' for just £50. You don't see many cars of this type nowadays – the annual Ministry of Transport test killed the market – but in the mid-fifties, 'specials' were all the rage. Venus – that's what I christened her – had started life as an Austin Seven. The Seven stood for seven horsepower. Her original sit-up-and-beg coachwork had been replaced by a low-cut, topless, slingback, powder blue, aluminium shell. She was registered as a sports car and, as if to prove her pedigree, she had wire (spokes to the uninitiated) wheels. But then, so did all the other Austin Sevens – Venus's wire wheels were a sign of advanced age rather than sparkling performance. The man who sold her said she had a Coventry Climax engine, but it needed some work done on it. Being a gullible fool I actually believed him, and I bought the car. He was right about the engine needing some work: the pistons rattled around in the cylinders like demented maracas; the compression was nonexistent, and the bearings – both big and small – were shot. The brass plate on the side of the engine, which I had naively assumed bore the maker's name, was actually a patch covering a gaping hole in the crank case. Dad rebuilt the engine with new bearings, pistons and rings, and when he had finished the engine purred like a well-oiled sewing machine. Needless to say, it was not a Coventry Climax engine – just a lowly Austin Seven.

Venus held many surprises on the road. The passenger seat was not properly anchored to the floor, which occasionally resulted in the unfortunate occupant being tipped back into the rear seat. In those days, if I remember rightly, the feminine fashion was for frothy net petticoats – the sights were often charming. At the other end of the scale, any sudden braking would cause a geyser of hot, rusty water to erupt from the top of the radiator, giving Venus's occupants, and the car in front, an unsolicited shower. Venus was not fitted with a heater but she was a very warm little car. I always assumed it had something to do with the exhaust pipe being too close to the floor, until one evening I noticed that the stockings of the girl I had just escorted home glistened in the lamplight. An inspection the following day revealed that a gasket on the gearbox cover had blown, allowing a mist of warm oil to escape (Venus's heating was based on the circulation of warm oil). Needless to say the system never caught on with the general public.

Despite all her idiosyncrasies, Venus was an enjoyable diversion. There was always some work to be done to keep her on the road. With her Heath Robinson mechanics, crash gearbox and other quirky habits, driving her was an acquired skill. After practising in Venus, the driving test in one of the driving school's vehicles was a doddle.

In September we were posted to RAF Feltwell for a short, single-engine refresher course on the piston Provost; from there we went on to RAF Swinderby for jet refresher training in the two-seat Vampire T11 and the single-seat Vampires F5 and F9. On the morning we arrived, the aerobatic display pilot misjudged a loop and fatally crashed a mile from the end of the runway.

It seemed as though the industrial fumes from the East Midlands were permanently trapped beneath a blanket of low cloud, leaving the dull, grey scenery bathed in a damp, corrosive drizzle. Our first dual Vampire T11 sorties terminated with practice bad weather circuits. I remember thinking, If this is for practice I would hate to be doing it for real. It would have been far safer to make GCA instrument approaches, but that would not have given us much landing practice.

The weather conditions in the UK in winter can be very murky indeed, and the RAF demands high standards of instrument flying. Every RAF pilot has to pass an annual instrument rating test (IRT). In those days the IRT on fighter-type aircraft was a test of basic instrument skills. Each manoeuvre was flown to precise limits – plus or minus five knots here, twenty feet there, within two degrees of the desired heading, and so on. It was flown either under a canvas hood or with an opaque visor, to ensure there was no cheating. The IRT, which usually lasted an hour, required skilful flying and total concentration. There were three recognised skill levels: the white card for inexperienced pilots; the green card for pilots with 400 hours' first-pilot time on type; and the master green for pilots with more than 1400 hours on type. With fighter sorties averaging less than one hour, it took several years to achieve a master green. I qualified for my White Card on the Vampire on 6 December 1955.

The RAF's instrument-rating scheme enabled pilots to gain experience in marginal weather conditions while ensuring that no one was knowingly permitted to fly in conditions beyond their ability. For example, a white-rated pilot was permitted to recover to land at an airfield when the cloud base was no lower than 500 ft and the visibility was at least two nautical miles; a green-rated pilot was permitted to recover down to airfield minimums – say 300 ft and one nautical mile. The master green landing limits were similar, but a master green pilot was allowed to take off in any weather. As an additional safety measure the RAF regulations specified that sufficient reserves of fuel had to be maintained to enable the aircraft to divert to an appropriate alternative airfield. Flying was suspended if there were no suitable diversions.

The Vampire was designed during the war, but it was still impressively agile and at high altitude it could out-turn most jet aircraft. It was even possible to pull up for a loop at 30,000 ft with a fair chance of getting over the top, provided you were not too fussy about which way the aircraft was pointing on the way down – which was an excellent confidence booster. But the thick, high-lift wings that gave the Vampire its superior manoeuvrability also generated a great deal of drag. At low level the Vampire's maximum speed was in the order of 460 knots, but this reduced with altitude as the compressibility of the air – associated with increasing Mach number – became the dominant factor. The speed of sound varies with temperature and pressure: at sea level it is approximately 660 knots, but this reduces with height, and at 36,000 ft the speed of sound is nearer 560 knots. The Mach meter automatically compensates for these variations and shows the aircraft's speed in comparison to the local speed of sound. Mach 1.0 always represents the local speed of sound, an indicated Mach of 0.5 is half the speed of sound, and so on. The indicated Mach number was vitally important on aircraft such as the Vampire and the T-33, because their handling characteristics were adversely affected by compressibility.

At high altitude the Vampire was limited to Mach 0.84 – roughly equivalent to 500 knots true air speed. But this could only be achieved in a dive. At Mach 0.78 shockwaves began to form on the Vampire's wings and tailplane, causing slight airframe buffet and lateral wing rock. As the speed increased the aircraft became unstable in pitch, and at Mach 0.84 the elevator control was not powerful enough to hold the nose down.

In comparison to the T-33, the Vampire was a much earlier and less sophisticated design. The aircraft at Swinderby were not even fitted with ejection seats. To ensure safe separation from the twin-boom tailplane, the recommended procedure for bailing out was to roll inverted, open the canopy and release the seat harness. The Vampire T11 was a good trainer, but I much preferred flying the F5 or the F9, which were much lighter on the controls. They were also the first true single-seat aircraft I had ever flown; I was on my own. Flying solo in a dual-capable aircraft was never quite the same again.

In February we got our long-awaited posting to No. 229 OCU (Operational Conversion Unit) at RAF Chivenor in Devon. By that time, the fellows I had trained with in Canada had been well dispersed, and there were only four of the original group on No. 12 Hunter Course. The OCU was the halfway house between flying training and the operational squadrons.

At Chivenor the relationship between the staff and the students was quite different from anything we had experienced before. For the first time we were actually encouraged to mix with the staff. It soon became clear that fighter pilots were an extrovert breed – it seemed to go with the job – and there was no shortage of characters at the bar, willing to accept a beer or two in exchange for pearls of wisdom. Inevitably, the more beer they consumed the bigger the pearls. A lot of it was rubbish, but along with all the line shooting there were gems of vital information – information that might one day save our skins. So we bought the beer and we listened. It must be said that the best talkers were often among the best pilots, or so they would have us believe. I well remember 'Spike' Jones, Fred Hartley and Mike Calvey, each of whom held court in Chivenor's bar on many occasions.

The Hunter F1, which had been in service for barely a year, was proving difficult to maintain, so much of our operational training was done in the Vampire – no great hardship. The Vampire had arrived too late to see any action during the war, but it was a potent little fighter, equipped with four 20 mm cannon – although only one gun was used for academic practice against the flag. Air gunnery could be quite exciting in the Vampire F5, because the vibration of the gun tended to unlock the cockpit canopy, allowing it to open in flight. It was a known fault. The canopy closing handle was fitted with a string lanyard, which limited its rearward movement but still allowed it to open a couple of inches in mid-firing pass, which disturbed one's aim and was downright unnerving at high altitude. Fortunately, the cockpits of the single-seat Vampires were not pressurised, or the disturbance would have been even greater.

After five weeks at Chivenor we went back to ground school to learn about the Hunter. Designed by Sir Sydney Camm in the early fifties to meet the RAF's requirement for a single-seat day interceptor, the Hunter combined a powerful jet engine with a sleek, swept-wing airframe. After years of apathy on the part of the post-war governments towards research into high-speed flight, the Hunter's design broke new ground for British aviation. Of course, there were other British swept-wing aircraft – the Supermarine Swift and the de Havilland DH110 – but neither of these matched the elegant lines of the Hunter. There is a saying, 'If an aircraft looks good, it will fly well,' and the Hunter looked very good indeed. It was not a complex aircraft, although some degree of sophistication was inevitable. It was fitted with power controls – rather like powered steering on a car – and a system of springs provided artificial feel to compensate for the lack of feedback to the pilot. The incidence of the tailplane – the angle of the horizontal stabiliser relative to the airflow – was variable, which served the purpose of an elevator trim and improved pitch control at transonic speeds. The aircraft was fitted with a Martin Baker 2H seat, with a minimum safe ejection height from straight and level flight of 200 ft above the ground – which was a marked improvement on the seat fitted to the T-33.

We were issued with protective helmets – Bone Domes – and oxygen masks of the same type we had used in Canada, and were given another session in the decompression chamber, which included an explosive decompression. We were also fitted with anti-g suits – nylon corsets with leggings – which inflated as g (gravitational acceleration) was applied, and so delayed the pooling of blood in the lower half of the body. It was still necessary to tense stomach and leg muscles to combat g, but with the benefit of the g-suit the Hunter pilot could stand higher acceleration forces. The British g-suit was designed to be worn under the flying suit, but Mike Calvey wore it, in the American style, as an outer garment, looking for all the world like some latter-day Wyatt Earp.

In the midst of all this, the sound of Rolls-Royce Avon starter cartridges followed by the low rumble of idling jet engines could be heard from the flight line. In this highly charged atmosphere, we needed little encouragement to memorise the slim volume of *Hunter F1 Pilot's Notes.*

The following weekend Mike Calvey's badger attacked the cook. Mike had rescued the animal from the local pub, where it had been taken after a baiting atrocity of some kind. He was keeping the animal in a disused air-raid shelter alongside the mess, where Brock thrived on scraps from the mess kitchen and was generally well behaved. Or he was until the Sunday when Mike was away, when he decided the cook was more appetising than the kitchen leftovers. Literally a case of biting the hand that feeds you. The cook bolted without closing the shelter door, and was next seen making a spirited attempt at the four-minute mile around the officers' mess, with Brock in hot pursuit. On his third lap, the cook – by this time visibly flagging – was offered sanctuary through the front door. He made it, but only just. The badger eventally went back to the shelter. No one had appreciated how fast an irate badger could move. Clearly the badger could fend for himself, and Mike was persuaded to release him into the wild.

On the following Tuesday I flew my first Hunter sortie. Much has been written about the Hunter and it would be inappropriate for me to attempt to do it justice in this book, but after some 1500 hours in the aircraft I can claim to have a reasonable working knowledge. At that time there was no flight simulator and no equivalent dual aircraft to prepare you for your first flight in the aircraft. So when I walked out to Hunter WT634 my mood was a mixture of excitement and trepidation. In psychological terms I was in a highly aroused state, every sinew poised for action. The curious thing about arousal though is that, while it sharpens one's reactions, it is like living on the edge of a cliff – one step too far and you tend to fall off. But that was not going to happen to me – I was ready for anything. Which was just as well, because there was no room for error on this flight.

Fred Hartley was detailed to see me off – air-force jargon for making sure that I got the engine started. The pre-flight and the 'left to right' cockpit checks with Fred looking on from the ladder were straightforward. He removed the face blind safety pin from the ejection seat, clapped me on the shoulder, and with a quick 'Enjoy the ride' he was gone. From then on I was on my own.

Starter master-switch – on; high-pressure fuel cock – on; press the starter button . . . The aircraft juddered slightly as the cartridge fired and the engine bounced up to 1500 r.p.m. before slowly accelerating to 2750. The jet pipe temperature stabilised within limits.

Now for the functional checks, helped by the ground crew: flaps, air-brake, trim, power controls – this was new – the doll's eye indicators obediently flipping from white to black as I switched on the aileron and elevator power controls. A hydraulic pressure of 3000 p.s.i. would now assist me on the controls.

Checks complete. Select the radio to the airfield local channel:

'Chivenor. Banjo two-four request taxi clearance.'

'Roger, two-four. You are cleared to runway two-eight, QNH one zero-zero-niner.'

The runway was identified by the first two digits of its magnetic heading rounded up to the nearest ten degrees, so the westerly runway was in use. I set 1009 millibars on the altimeter's barometric sub scale and the altimeter registered 10 ft, which was close enough for government work. I waved the chocks away, saluted the ground crew and released the brakes.

In other jet aircraft I had flown it was usually necessary to add power to get moving, but the Hunter needed no such encouragement, as much as to say, 'I am going flying and you are welcome to come along for the ride.' Steering on the ground was simple: just apply the appropriate rudder and squeeze the brake lever on the stick. Turning to the right, needle to the right, ball to the left, gyro horizon steady, compass indication increasing . . . I checked the instruments again in a left turn. In future, I would complete the vital actions while taxiing, but there was no point rushing on the first sortie. So I stopped short of the runway. Trim – set one and a half degrees nose down; fuel – contents sufficient, transfer pressure OK; flaps – up; instruments – checked; oxygen – on, contents sufficient, 100% selected, mask connections checked; hood – closed and locked; hydraulics – pressure steady at 3000 p.s.i.; power controls – engaged.

I checked that the approach was clear:

'Chivenor. Banjo two-four line up.'

'Banjo two-four, you are cleared to line up and take off. Wind two-niner-zero at ten. Climb out on three-four-zero.'

I rolled on to the runway and held the aircraft on the brakes for the engine checks. Throttle up to 7200 r.p.m. The brakes were holding, but only just – an indication that the engine was producing sufficient power. Jet pipe temperature, 650° and increasing. So this was it; there was no turning back now.

I released the brakes and applied full power. With 7500 lb of thrust, the Hunter's acceleration was impressive. As the instructors would say, I had set in motion a chain of events over which I had little control. I should have checked the engine instruments again during take-off, but the airspeed was already surging past 90 knots. Lift-off was at 135 kts. A quick dab of the brake to stop the main wheels rotating and I selected 'undercarriage up'. The three red lights – one for each leg – had to be out by 230 kts or the undercarriage would not retract. At 225 kts the last remaining red – the nose-wheel – extinguished. Where had the runway gone? I turned right on to 340° and changed to approach frequency for the climb out. The initial climbing speed should have been 430 kts, but I was willing to accept anything between three-fifty and four-fifty, just as long as the aircraft was climbing. Passing 13,000 ft I transferred to the Mach meter and held Mach 0.85.

Three minutes after take-off, passing through 20,000 ft, I actually caught up with the aircraft. Next time I would make a determined effort to fly more accurately.

Much of that first sortie was taken up with exploring the effects of the controls and worrying about getting back on the ground in one piece. I practised the circuit pattern at 15,000 ft – to get a feel for the trim changes that occurred when the undercarriage and flaps were selected. Off my own bat I also attempted a loop. With 450 kts on the clock I pulled back on the stick; the g forces pushed me down into the seat and my suit inflated, but I had not pulled hard enough and the aircraft flopped over the top at minimum airspeed. It must have been the laziest, slowest loop on record, but it impressed the hell out of me. I made a note in my logbook.

We celebrated our first Hunter sorties by downing a few beers in the Three Tonnes pub in Barnstaple, and at least one member of the party over-indulged. After the pub closed he was collared by the police relieving himself in an alleyway – conduct clearly unbecoming an officer and a gentleman – and was promptly dubbed the Liberal Peer of Barnstaple.

The fourth conversion flight was at high speed – a boom run – as it was essential for us to find out how the Hunter handled at supersonic level. The brief was simply to climb to 40,000 ft over the Bristol Channel, maintain full power and roll into a steep dive pointing out to sea. I followed the briefing to the letter: the Mach meter inched up to

0.98 and, after a moment's hesitation, it lurched up to Mach 1.12. Nothing to it, really. The absence of sound was uncanny, but the altimeter was unwinding at an alarming rate and it was time to pull out of the dive. That was easier said than done. Even with the engine throttled right back and the airbrake out, for a few dreadful moments – probably less than three seconds – the aircraft refused to respond to the controls. Then, very slowly, the nose began to rise. Above Mach 0.97, due to the formation of shockwaves on the tailplane, the Hunter's elevator was relatively ineffective. Furthermore, the air loads on the elevator were sometimes too high for the power-control hydraulic jacks. I could have pulled out more rapidly by trimming back on the tailplane, but there was always a risk that, as the speed reduced and the elevator became more effective, the aircraft might pitch up. I levelled out at 20,000 ft, less than fifty seconds having elapsed since I had initiated the dive.

Hedley Molland, who had attended a previous course, was less fortunate. Subsequently it was believed he had 10° of flap-down when he did his boom run, which prevented his plane's recovery from the dive. Hedley became the first RAF pilot to eject at supersonic speed. He survived – although he was badly injured by wind blast, and it was many months before he returned to the cockpit.

For me, the next sortie also proved to be exciting, but for very different reasons. The aim was to practise flying in manual – that is, without power controls. Again the sortie profile was straightforward: climb to 15,000 ft and switch off the power controls. After flying around in manual for a while, reselect power and return for an instrument recovery. So much for the plan. We had been warned that in manual the ailerons were heavy – which was no exaggeration. At speeds above 350 knots I could not move them at all. In manual, rolling the aircraft was a two-handed job, and pitch control was little better. No matter; manual was a get-you-home option in case of a hydraulic failure, so all I had to do was reselect power and chalk up another success. The elevator immediately clunked back into power, but when I selected the ailerons, the doll's eye stubbornly stayed white. Worse still, the stick was clamped solidly in the central position. I had what was known as a double false anchorage.

Without going into great detail, for proper operation the aileron hydro-boosters had to be locked on to control shafts attached to the airframe. Two palls (mechanical latches), one in each aileron hydro-booster, engaged in slots on their respective control shafts. But after flying in manual for any length of time a hydro-booster could drift to the extremity of its control shaft, and when hydraulic power was re-applied the pall would clamp in the wrong position. On the Hunter F1 this false anchorage could only be cleared by forcing the stick hard against the restriction until the pall re-engaged in its slot. The instructors in ground school had joked about what would happen if false anchorages occurred on both left and right ailerons at the same time. No one took them seriously, but this was exactly what had happened to me, and it was no laughing matter. For the next ten minutes I beat the stick from side to side attempting to clear the restrictions. Of course I could have switched off the power controls and landed in manual, but this was only my fifth Hunter sortie and landing with power controls engaged was exciting enough for me. After what seemed an eternity I managed to beat the ailerons back into power. I landed, a quaking ball of sweat, with minimum fuel. Beware the practice emergency that turns out to be worse than the real thing.

The Hunter was not difficult to fly, but some care was necessary at low speed. Compared to most straight-wing aircraft, the plane gave less warning of the stall, and its post-stall behaviour was more violent. Nothing particularly dangerous in that – most aircraft were unpredictable after stalling and the Hunter's handling characteristics were well known. Indeed, we thought we knew all there was to know about the Hunter at low speed – until an accident was to prove otherwise.

It was a fresh, blustery April day with glorious sunshine – the sort of day when flying was especially enjoyable. The Hunter had sufficient power and agility to barge through low-level turbulence and play tag with the fluffy white cumulus clouds. The only reason for caution – and even then the risk was thought to be slight – was the cross-wind in the circuit which was tending to tighten up the final turn. Such conditions were part and parcel of normal flying and were not dangerous, provided proper allowance was made on the downwind leg to correct for drift and the bulk of the final turn was completed early. Usually the worst that could happen was for the aircraft to drift through the runway centre line before the final turn was complete – which was embarrassing for the pilot, but no harm done provided he took immediate action to go round again for another circuit. Unfortunately, one lad on our course misjudged the cross-wind and attempted to salvage his approach by tightening the final turn. It was poor airmanship by any standards. He might have got away with it in a Vampire, but the Hunter flick-rolled at 500 ft and crashed inverted in the Taw estuary. The pilot had no chance to eject, and was killed on impact. A timely reminder that one never stops learning about flying.

The Hunter was not a dangerous aircraft, but neither was it a machine for the beginner. Certainly the F1 had two fundamental shortcomings: it was critically short of fuel, with a total capacity of 330 gallons and an engine capable of burning twenty gallons a minute, thus it was obvious the aircraft could not stay airborne for long; secondly, the engine tended to surge (in other words become unstable and lose power) when the guns were fired – which was clearly unacceptable for a fighter aircraft. These defects were resolved on subsequent marks of the Hunter, but the F1 was a delight to fly. Most pilots completed the Hunter syllabus at Chivenor with just twelve hours (twenty-four sorties) on the aircraft, but it was enough. We could safely continue our work up on operational squadrons.

We were given our posting instructions before we left Chivenor. Mick Letton and I had the good fortune to be posted overseas to No. 67 Squadron – equipped with Hunter F4s – at RAF Bruggen in West Germany. Who said I would never make it?

5
Tours in RAF Germany; Nos 67 and 4 Squadrons (Hunter 4 & 6)

RAF Germany was a popular posting for any aspiring fighter pilot in 1956. It was overseas, it was in the front line and Soviet forces were just across the border – what more could one ask of a first squadron tour? There were twelve Hunter squadrons based in Germany. Their primary role was air defence, which was reflected in their monthly flying task, but they also had a limited ground-attack capability. The squadrons were also tactically mobile, they had their own motor transport and sufficient field kit to operate from semi-prepared bases. To assist in the squadrons' mobility, the junior pilots were qualified to drive Magirus Deutze four-ton trucks. But unlike the tactical fighter squadrons during the war, which could operate from any reasonable field, the Hunter needed 1800 yards of runway.

No. 135 Wing based at Bruggen consisted of four Hunter squadrons: Nos 67, 71, 112 and 130. No. 71 was known as an Eagle Squadron because it had been formed, during World War II, with American pilots who volunteered to fly with the RAF. The Bruggen wing had recently exchanged its North American F-86 Sabres for Hunter F4s. This change of aircraft had not been universally welcomed by the pilots. After all, the F-86 had been proven in combat during the Korean War, whereas the Hunter was as yet untried in battle. Furthermore the Hunter's introduction into service had been dogged by poor serviceability.

As far as I was concerned, the F-86 was a fine aircraft, but the Hunter was better. With its four 30 mm cannon, the Hunter's firepower was greatly superior to the Sabre's. The Hunter F4 was a marked improvement on the F1; it carried an additional 600 lb of fuel and the Avon 115 engine was now surge-free. But gun-firing trials had highlighted yet another hazard: the ammunition links, which served to feed successive rounds into the guns and were designed to be jettisoned overboard after use, were being sucked into the engine intakes, with catastrophic results. This was solved by fitting two link collectors – colloquially known as Sabrinas (after a certain well-endowed film star) – to the gun pack. The Hunter F4 had other minor refinements, but in terms of handling it was similar to the F1.

Of course, this was my first introduction to an operational fighter squadron. The CO of No. 67 Squadron – Squadron Leader Harry Walmsley – was a much-decorated fighter pilot who had learned his skills in the hard school of combat. There could be no better boss to supervise our operational work-up. Harry Walmsley was a refined English gentleman, a charming man respected by all who knew him – so it seemed rather out of character, in those days of post-war enlightenment, that he should still hate the Germans. But then few people knew of the underlying reasons. In April 1945, during the closing months of the war, Harry Walmsley had commanded a Belgian squadron deployed at Celle, an airfield some twenty miles north-east of Hanover. One day an RAF foraging party had stumbled upon the vast concentration camp at Bergen-Belsen. The SS guards had fled, but the inmates – those that were still alive – were too weak to move, much less escape. The scale of aid needed at Belsen was clearly beyond the capabilities of a fighting unit, but the wing at Celle had deposited a truck-load of potatoes inside the camp gates. When they returned the following day, the potatoes had gone and so too had many of the inmates. Over the next few days the former prisoners returned. Some died because they had gorged themselves on the unaccustomed food, but many more had succumbed to typhus. Photographs of Belsen, with close to ten thousand unburied corpses, mass open graves and skeletal survivors, were subsequently published – I remember seeing them in the *Picture Post* – and the world at large finally learned of the appalling atrocities committed in Nazi Germany. One of the pilots on Harry's squadron, whose wife had been transported to a Nazi concentration camp, went completely berserk. So it was that Harry was unimpressed with the Germans – and who could blame him?

I was assigned to 'A' Flight, led by Flight Lieutenant Pete Cornell. Flight Lieutenant Bruce Wingate commanded 'B' Flight, and Ted Hines had 'C' Flight – in charge of the ground crew. As junior pilots,

Mick Letton and I were immediately given secondary duties: Mick inherited the aircrew coffee bar from Jock Beatson, who had held the job for almost a year and was delighted to be rid of it; I took over an inventory of miscellaneous equipment from an officer returning to the UK: 'Sorry about the short notice, old boy. I haven't managed to get the holder's copy updated. But no sweat, its just a few sticks of office furniture.' Actually the miscellaneous inventory ran to some thirty-four pages of equipment, and its notable deficiencies included: one Rolls-Royce Derwent jet engine, which had not been seen since the squadron was equipped with Meteor aircraft in the late forties; and nineteen galvanised buckets. With hindsight, I should have refused to accept the inventory, but the fellow handing it over was a smooth talker and he managed to convince me that it was just a question of the paperwork not catching up with the actual state of affairs. Besides, I felt it was rather small-minded to get all steamed up about an inventory, when my immediate priority was to become operational in the Hunter F4.

Some tasks in the air are best accomplished by single aircraft, but when it comes to fighter operations, one aircraft on its own is of limited value. The single fighter is vulnerable to attack simply because the pilot cannot see directly behind – the fuselage creates a blind spot that is difficult to clear. At least two aircraft are necessary for effective self-defence; many more might be required for offensive operations. The modern battle formations evolved from tactics used by the Luftwaffe during the Spanish Civil War. The size and shape of the formation varied to suit both the task and local conditions. The separation between individual aircraft also varied, from close formation – which might be necessary during cloud penetration – out to a distance of several miles, in order to gain tactical advantage. For example, at high altitude and in clear conditions, it was prudent to fly with wide lateral separation to afford maximum cover to the rear. But if the formation was at low level, avoiding bad weather or in mountainous terrain, it was more practical to adopt a swept-back arrow formation, permitting maximum manoeuvrability.

We had much to learn. In those days a first tourist pilot would spend three months or more flying as a wingman – No. 2 or No. 4. After that he might be allowed to lead a pair of aircraft, but he had to train for a further three months before he was given the chance of leading a four-plane formation. The flying was not difficult; at least, I did not find it so. In theory all a wingman had to do was stick to the leader, search for other aircraft and report – but that concealed a wealth of practical knowhow. Much more was involved in sticking than just hanging on to another fellow's wing. You had to know the right position, taking into account the leader's intentions, and you had to anticipate manoeuvres to avoid being left behind. In the air there were quicker, more effective ways of closing distance other than simply opening the throttle. More importantly, every pilot had to develop an awareness of the air picture – a mental, three-dimensional map of his position in space, relative to other aircraft – without which a young man could kill himself and take others with him. In the Hunter we had to rely on visual lookout, but even visual search techniques could be improved with training. In a relaxed state, the human eye tends to focus at about eighteen inches and, particularly at high altitude, a conscious effort is needed to refocus the eyes regularly on some distant object. Sharp eyesight is vitally important in the air, even at cruising speeds – approaching aircraft can close one mile every three seconds. While the human eye is good at recognising relative movement, it is far less adept at picking up objects that simply grow larger in size. For this reason, aircraft on a collision course, which have no relative angular movement, are often not seen until the last few seconds.

Visual contacts are reported using a clock code. To understand the system one has to imagine the reporting aircraft being at the centre of a huge, horizontal clock-face: straight ahead is twelve o'clock, ninety degrees to the right – over the right shoulder – is three o'clock, directly behind is six o'clock, and so on. By simple interpolation it is possible to identify the line of sight of any object. Its position can be further refined by estimating its range and elevation relative to the horizon. For example, Green four might transmit the following sighting report: 'Green four, left eight o'clock high, two bogeys, range six – closing fast.' From that one brief call all members of the formation are alerted to an approaching threat, and each pilot knows where to look. It is then up to the formation leader to take appropriate action. In fighter tactics, maintaining visual contact on the threat is more than half the battle. Of course, many of these skills are an essential part of basic pilot training, but in a constantly changing tactical situation their application requires constant practice.

In those days the great advantage of fighter training in RAF Germany was the presence of a wide variety of aircraft, flown by many different national air forces: Belgian, Dutch, French, Danish, USAFE and RCAF, and from 1957 on even the reformed post-war Luftwaffe – all were ready to do battle. Transport aircraft were invariably given safe passage, but all other military aircraft were fair game. From the moment the wheels were tucked into the wells until they were lowered again on the final approach to land, there was a constant threat of being bounced. No shots were fired, of course, but much ciné film was taken and it was bad for one's reputation to star prominently at the wrong end of the gun camera.

After I had been on the squadron for about four months, Flight Lieutenant Lee Jones – one of the flight commanders on 112 Squadron who had recently graduated from the Fighter Leaders' School at RAF West Raynham – was authorised to lead a sweep, commonly known as a 'wing ding', against the USAFE fighter squadrons in 4 ATAF. It was quite usual for the Bruggen squadrons to operate as a wing; we conformed to the same standard operating procedures – or SOPs, as they were called. And we were often tasked as a wing during major exercises. But this time it was different: Lee had telephoned the USAFE base at Bitburg and had thrown down the gauntlet, so to speak, telling them that the Bruggen wing would be overhead at 1500 hrs, and that they – the USAFE – could do nothing about it. Needless to say, the Yanks had other ideas – 'Who is this crazy Limey anyway?' – and they made plans.

The Bruggen squadrons eventually produced twenty-four aircraft. I was programmed to fly as Blue four – the last aircraft in the formation – but at least I had been selected for the home team, which I took as a compliment.

The weather was perfect, eight eighths blue – not a cloud in the sky. The start-up and radio checks went without a hitch:

'Gold, check in.'

'Two.'

'Three.'

'Four.'

'Silver, check in.'

'Two.'

'Three.'

And so on, until the twenty-four Hunters were lined up on the runway. It was hot and turbulent at the back end during the engine checks.

At last we were ready for take-off, in pairs at five-second intervals: the first pair pulled high, the next stayed low, the next high, and so on. In that way successive pairs avoided the turbulent wake of the aircraft ahead. Lee Jones climbed in a wide spiral to allow Bruggen Combine to join up.

Contrails started at 25,000 ft; from the briefing we knew that they would be persistent above this altitude. The Americans could see us coming almost from the top of the climb, but for fuel conservation we had to stay high, as the Hunger F4's radius of action was limited. Bruggen Combine made a brave sight, though, as it headed south.

About twenty miles from Bruggen, a lone Meteor F8 crossed our path and in clipped R/T; Lee directed Blue three and four to take care of the bogey at eleven o'clock low. My adrenalin started pumping; this was going to be exciting. The Meteor was certainly no threat to Bruggen Combine, but one never questioned the leader. Blue three acknowledged the call and we changed radio channels to avoid cluttering the formation's frequency. Our bogey was probably a Belgium Air Force Meteor; at least, he was heading in that direction, but the pilot had seen what was going on and had wisely decided to run for cover. We chased him but he had too much of a head start and he disappeared in the industrial haze at low level, north of the Ardennes.

We climbed back up to high level, hoping to rejoin Bruggen Combine, but they were long gone. Instead we found a geriatric USAF B-45 bomber, cruising sedately by at 15,000 ft. It would have been churlish to ignore him, so we each made a quarter attack and took gun camera film to back up our 'splash' claim – that was the simulated destruction of the B-45. Then we set course for home.

We were the first pair to land, but the rest of Bruggen Combine was not far behind. Jones called for the debriefing in 112 Squadron's crewroom.

He opened the proceedings by asking the members of the

formation to state their claims. There was a painful silence, then the whole of Bruggen Combine, to a man, announced, 'I got a B-45.' We were all claiming the same aircraft. The B-45 pilot must have been flattered by so much attention – at one stage the Hunters had been queuing up on the perch, waiting to have a go.

Then the sorry tale unfolded. Following Lee's phone challenge, Bitburg had called for assistance from the other USAFE bases; someone had spoken to the Canadians – who were always game for a scrap – and they had roped in one or two French squadrons. As for Bruggen Combine, after Blue three and four had left, Lee had continued to fritter away sections of the formation: a pair here to take out a French Air Force Vautour; a pair there to chase four Dutch F-84s; and so on. The only members of Bruggen Combine to arrive overhead Bitburg were Lee Jones and his No. 2. They were met by forty plus American, Canadian and French fighters. Lee had been hard pressed to hold the initiative. Fortunately he had a height advantage, and after circling high out of reach for a while, he and his wingman had gone down through the middle of the pack and high-tailed it for home with half of NATO snapping at their heels.

But not every brush we had with the USAFE and the Canadians was that one-sided. The F-86, particularly the Canadian soft-edge version – so called because its wings were fitted with high-lift leading edge slats – was certainly more manoeuvrable than the Hunter, but we could cruise quite happily above 45,000 ft, which usually gave us a height advantage. The secret was to choose the right moment to attack, then drop like a bird of prey, take a quick burst of ciné and zoom back to altitude. It was tempting to stay in with the mêlée – 'Just five seconds more tracking and I'll nail him' – but if you delayed, someone else would surely latch on to your tail. The Hunter was heavier than the F-86, which meant that it accelerated faster in the dive, and it could store greater potential energy. Cruising at Mach 0.9 the Hunter could zoom through several thousand feet of altitude and still have enough airspeed left for manoeuvre. Many an F-86 pilot had been caught unawares, when he thought he was safely out of reach.

At that time, few frontline fighter aircraft in West Germany could match the overall performance of the Hunter – we were the scourge of the skies. But our advantage was to be short-lived. With the arrival of the F-100 Super Sabre, the first of the American century series aircraft, the USAFE regained the initiative, at least in terms of speed.

Battle Flight – our operational air-defence commitment – came around one week in every six. The Hunter squadrons held the alert state from dawn to dusk (the night and all-weather commitment was covered by Venom and Meteor NF11 squadrons based at Ahlhorn and Wahn). The Hunter was designed for rapid reaction. At Bruggen two aircraft were held on the operational readiness platform (ORP) at the end of the runway, with pilots strapped in, listening to the Sector Operations Centre on the telebrief. When ordered to scramble, these aircraft could start engines and be airborne within two minutes. A second pair of aircraft was held at a ten-minute alert state on the Aircraft Servicing Platform (ASP) in front of the hangar, but in this case the pilots were allowed to stand by in the crewroom. Air defence involved a great deal of waiting, but reaction had to be swift and sure when West German airspace was infringed. One never knew if it was simply a case of a pilot straying from his planned route or something more sinister. This problem of identification is the crucial weakness of a missile-only defence system; no one in their right minds would wish to shoot down an unarmed civilian transport aircraft, no matter how far off track it might be.

In those days the Battle Flight commitment in RAF Germany was not particularly onerous: we were permitted to hold the state while airborne and we were often scrambled from the ORP to exercise the system. We did occasionally fly at night, but it was only the bare minimum to maintain currency. There was a feeling among day fighter pilots that flying in the dark was somehow dangerous.

One night in August, Lieutenant Mike Maina, our Royal Navy exchange pilot, was taking off in a Hunter XF290 when the engine caught fire. Mike pulled up and ejected at 600 ft, and the aircraft crashed off the end of the runway in the middle of an RAF Regiment field exercise. The arrival of eight tons of burning wreckage must have added an unusual degree of realism to the exercise, but the 'rock apes' appreciated that sort of thing. Mike was back in the bar within the hour, none the worse for his experience, but the accident confirmed our belief that night flying was inherently dangerous. Besides, the Hunter squadrons did not have a night role.

On another occasion we were told that two other stations would also be night flying: RAF Jever in the north with Hunter F6s; and RAF Fassberg, equipped with de Havilland Venoms, close to the East German border. No problem – there was plenty of airspace, and it was comforting to know that other fools were similarly occupied. I was halfway around my cross-country when a highly agitated voice broke the silence on the radio:

'Mayday! Mayday! Mayday! This is Ladybird two-five, a Venom, approximately thirty miles south of Wunsdorf. My engine has flamed out. Request an immediate homing for a glide approach to land at the nearest suitable airfield.'

This was high drama indeed; landing 'dead stick' was tricky enough by day, but by night it was downright suicidal.

The Venom pilot came on the air again, much calmer now, and in a voice several octaves lower he explained that he had managed to restart his engine. At that point his tone switched back to a high falsetto: 'It's gone out again!'

Whenever the Venom pilot transmitted a radio call, a spoke of light would flicker across the direction-finding cathode ray tube in front of every approach controller tuned into that frequency. By plotting two or more bearings, Ladybird two-five's position could be pinpointed.

The Wunsdorf controller came on the air. He could afford to be cool; after all, he was not sitting in the hot seat of a bent Venom. 'Roger, Ladybird two-five. You are eighteen miles south-west of Wunsdorf. Steer zero-four-five. Request your present height?'

The Venom pilot was calm again, having restarted his engine. 'Roger, Wundsdorf. Two-five is descending through angels two-two-zero. My engine now appears to be OK, but—' The voice cracked: 'It's gone out again!'

At this point voices from all over Germany chipped in: 'It's gone out again! It's gone out again! It's gone out again!' Wunsdorf's air traffic control was not amused, and neither was the Venom pilot. The extraneous transmissions were screwing up the D/F bearings. Ladybird two-five was having a hard time.

His engine flamed out at least five times before he calmly reported: 'Ladybird two-five, finals.' Then, in a squeak: 'Three greens.'

I guessed that his engine had gone out again, but he was too busy to report it.

We were given a well-deserved rocket for poor R/T discipline when we got back. It was later confirmed that Ladybird two-five had landed safely at Wunsdorf. The pilot was subsequently awarded a Green endorsement – an official pat on the back for a job well done.

We enjoyed a comfortable standard of living in RAF Germany. The exchange rate was twelve Deutschmarks to the pound, but the standard currency at military units was the British Armed Forces Voucher, the BAFV, which was directly equivalent to one pound sterling. We could buy petrol at concessionary rates, and cigarettes and alcoholic drinks were duty-free in the mess. The only cloud on the horizon was the shortage of eligible young women. There were the school teachers, of course, but even here the choice was limited. Unfortunately the teachers had their sights set on marriage, which was not exactly what most young pilots had in mind. Besides, the service's attitude to marriage was stuffy to say the least. Officers were not entitled either to draw marriage allowance or to live in married quarters until the age of twenty-five. The young married officers on 67 Squadron – Terry Filing, Ian Forrester and Bob Honey – preferred to live across the border in the Dutch town of Roermonde, where the cost of living was cheaper. I thought the official service line on marriage was unfair, although I doubt it made any difference to me.

It was frustrating, though. I only managed to date a girl once while I was at Bruggen. She was a dumpy little teacher known throughout the mess as Peardrop on account of her figure. Peardrop liked her booze and was usually to be found propping up the bar in the officers' mess. She was a great talker; in fact she never stopped talking, even at meal times. Peardrop was best avoided at breakfast, especially if you had a hangover.

I had just purchased a second-hand BMW 501, which was a great improvement on Venus, and to mark the occasion I invited Peardrop out to dinner at a local lakeside restaurant. It was very romantic; Peardrop became more attractive and more desirable with every sip of wine, and I could sense that this was going to be my night. We lingered over the coffee and liqueurs . . . by now she was really quite beautiful.

Back in the car I tried to steal a kiss, but that was when Peardrop lowered the boom: 'Mother wouldn't like that,' she snapped.

I must confess I had not included Peardrop's mother in my plans.

Covered with confusion, I let the clutch out with a bang and smartly accelerated back into the lake. Fortunately, the water was not deep at that point, and with Peardrop pushing I was able to drive the car out. Next morning, in the cold light of dawn, I realised that the stories about Peardrop were all true – she was a tease and I was her latest victim.

So I resigned myself to a life of celibacy at Bruggen. Still, there was always the flying – at least that was going well. In October I qualified as a fours leader.

Early in November, following President Nasser's nationalisation of the Suez Canal Company, the RAF was heavily committed in Operation Musketeer – the British/French/Israeli invasion of Egypt. Several squadrons, including two Hunter squadrons from the UK, were deployed to Cyprus. The Bruggen wing would have liked to be involved but the RAF Germany Hunters were committed exclusively to NATO. Anyway, as history records, Operation Musketeer was called off after a few days, due to pressure from the Americans.

The Squadron deployed to Sylt in mid-November for an armament practice camp (APC) – we were programmed for two APCs a year. Sylt is one of the North Frisian Islands, to the west of the Schleswig-Holstein Peninsula in northern Germany. In summer, the island attracted the health and strength fanatics from Hamburg, who defied the elements and stripped down to the altogether in the hopes of getting an all-over tan. The island was well known for its nudist beaches, but in winter the beaches were deserted, leaving mile upon mile of desolate sand dunes. The weather left much to be desired, but as long as the conditions were clear at high altitude for gunnery practice, we were kept busy.

In those days the target for air-to-air firing was a flag or banner measuring twenty-four feet by six, towed behind a Meteor at 180 kts. The typical gun quarter attack started with the fighter in a perch position 2000 yards line abreast of the target, and stepped up 1000 ft. From there the fighter turned hard in and reversed his turn to track the target in a smooth curve of pursuit. The Hunter's radar ranging equipment, designed to feed precise range information to the gyro gunsight (GGS), was not yet operational, but the GGS could be manually ranged (using a twist grip on the throttle) to match the target's wingspan against an expandable circle of diamond-shaped symbols reflected in the gunsight. For obvious reasons, manual ranging was not possible against the flag, so the GGS was pegged at 350 yds and we opened fire when the depth of the flag was three times the size of the aiming pipper. Using this technique, the GGS only presented the correct deflection for 350 yds; firing at greater or lesser ranges would cause the rounds to miss, either behind or ahead of the aiming mark. And with closing speeds in the order of 200 kts, the effective firing bracket for each pass lasted for less than one fifth of a second.

Two fighters shared the firing pattern for twenty minutes at a time and a total of six aircraft, each firing ammunition dipped in different coloured paint, could fire on the flag before the Meteor had to return to base to refuel. You could never be certain that you had hit the flag until after landing. Sometimes the last pair would formate on the flag to see if it had been a good shoot, but the accurate scores could only be calculated when the flag was delivered back to the squadron and the number of hits for each colour was compared to the number of rounds fired. Using pegged range, a score of 25% was considered reasonable, although on a good day, when everything was right, it was possible to get into the high forties.

It was also important to fire at a reasonable angle off – in other words, from the side. At 18° angle off or more, the flag appeared elongated and the attacking pilot had to pull hard to track the target; at 15° the flag looked square; 12° was the minimum acceptable. At angles lower than that you only had the back end of a flapping rag to aim at, and if you shot the flag off – which was a distinct possibility due to over deflection – the flag and its associated ironmongery could well come back and join you in the cockpit. Alternatively, you might shoot holes in the towing aircraft – and the tow pilots were sensitive about that sort of thing. Even if you avoided such misfortune, the evidence on the flag – long streaks of colour instead of neat round holes – was plain for all to see.

It had happened before I joined the squadron, but on one occasion Pete Cornell thought he had shot down the towship – a Hawker Tempest – flown by Tony Goadby. During air-to-air gunnery the tow pilot acted as the range safety officer, positively clearing the fighters in, whether for live firing or for ciné only. Two-way radio contact was essential and, in the days of piston-engined towing aircraft, the tow pilot had the facility to fire a red Very flare to warn the fighters if he had suffered radio failure. But to get back to the story – on this particular day Pete Cornell was having difficulty achieving the necessary angle off. Tony cleared him in for his last attack. By Sod's Law, this time Pete's aiming pipper stayed glued on the flat all the way in. The angle off was still a touch low, but you can't have everything. Pete fired off a long burst and called clear, switches safe. Tony Goadby should have acknowledged that call, but he remained silent – and, worse still, an ominous trail of white smoke issued from the Tempest's cockpit. Something had gone terribly wrong and Pete had an uncomfortable feeling that in some way he might be responsible. The Tempest was a war vintage, piston-engined fighter bomber and, in those machines, fire in the air was a serious emergency. Pete redoubled his efforts to raise Tony Goadby on the radio, but there was still no reply. Clearly Tony was still in control, because he had jettisoned the flag and was heading for home. The only thing Pete could do was to warn Sylt that the towship Tempest was on fire and returning to base, apparently with a radio failure. He toyed with the idea of confessing that his last firing burst might have hit the towship; he even thought about bailing out himself, but in the event he did neither. The Tempest limped back and landed at Sylt, where it burned out on the runway after Tony had scrambled clear.

Incredibly, no one came to hear what Pete had to say, and he was left to make judicious inquiries of his own – without giving anything away of course. He need not have worried. After clearing Pete in for his final attack the Tempest's radio had failed, and Tony had decided to fire a red flare. For reasons best known to himself he had assumed that the Tempest's Very pistol stowage incorporated a flare tube down through the fuselage, as it did on the Harvard, and that all he had to do was load the appropriate coloured cartridge in the pistol and pull the trigger. But the Tempest was different. When Tony pulled the trigger he fired a red flare on to the floor of the cockpit, where it skittered around burning everything in its path. So, while Pete Cornell was agonising over how he was going to earn his living after being drummed out of the RAF, Tony Goadby was desperately trying to extinguish a mammoth-sized, self-inflicted hot-foot.

In winter, the flying programme at Sylt was frequently disrupted by bad weather. On one such occasion, after being grounded for a week of continuous fog and low cloud, the boss decided that the aircraft engines should be run up to dry out the electronics. This was a reasonable precaution; the Hunter rarely performed well after standing idle on the ground for days on end. The Hunter F4's starter motor was powered by a large, slow-burning cartridge, which drove a high-speed turbine connected to the main engine via a clutch and reduction gears. The starter breech held three cartridges but, to avoid an excessive build-up of temperature in the starter turbine, there were strict time limits between successive attempts to start.

I walked out to the flight line with Bob Foulks, who had been assigned to the aircraft immediately to my right. We each went through the pre-start checks. The high-energy igniters, used only on jet engines for starting, either on the ground or in the air, crackled loudly – so far so good. I gave my ground crew the wind-up signal, pressed the starter button and the engine rumbled into life. Bob was obviously having problems, though. His starter cartridge had failed to fire on the first attempt, so he had to wait thirty seconds before making a second attempt. When he pressed the button again, there was a loud explosion and fuel poured from the Hunter, igniting in a pool of fire beneath the aircraft. It was all very quick. Bob, who was an RAF Germany skiing champion, leapt over the windscreen arch and ran down over the nose, across ten yards of concrete, and up over a thirty-foot-high safety embankment. Meanwhile, things were beginning to get warm on the line. I attempted to taxi forward, but the ground crew had departed leaving a chock in front of the nose wheel, and I had to apply full power to get moving. A junior engineering officer who chose that moment to run behind my aircraft collected 7000 lb of hot air in his left ear and was completely bowled over. My aircraft eventually jumped the chock, but by that time the fire had spread, blocking off the taxi track so that I could only turn left to point directly at the ready-use weapons store less than twenty yards away. The armourers, who knew my guns were fully loaded, hastily abandoned the building with their hands up.

Bob Foulks's aircraft was completely burnt out – a total write-off. Two starter cartridges had fired simultaneously and the starter motor had disintegrated, shedding red-hot turbine blades, some of which had penetrated the Hunter's main fuel tanks. We sure as hell dried out the electronics on that aircraft!

The squadron returned to Bruggen on 18 December in time for Christmas. It was decided that the bachelors would mount a team effort and attend the New Year's Eve fancy-dress ball in the mess as a band of marauding Vikings. It seemed appropriate; after all we had just returned from the frozen north. According to one of the chaps there was plenty of sackcloth waste in stores that could be fashioned into rough shirts, and there was an ample supply of yellow fluffy material that would serve nicely as fair Nordic hair.

We finished flying early on the 31st to allow time to prepare. Although I say it myself, I was quite pleased with my efforts. With a cardboard shield and a helmet sprayed silver, a sackcloth shirt and leggings laced on with string, I had a certain rustic charm. But the yellow cotton wool stuck around my chin and tucked under my helmet really completed the picture. I was a right little marauder – all set for a lecherous if somewhat itchy evening in the bar.

The others looked good too. We downed a quick pint to ease the strain of fancy dress. Oakey Oakford, dressed in green overalls with a red cushion sewn to his backside and carrying a broomstick – supposed to be a stuffed olive – would surely deserve the prize for the most original costume. The party was barely under way when I attempted to light up my first cigarette of the evening. For a few fleeting moments I was aware of a searing pain as my head was enveloped in a ball of fire, then I passed out.

They told me afterwards that it had taken several pints of beer to put me out – frightful waste. The yellow 'hair' was actually cotton wool soaked in paraffin wax – a highly flammable mixture. I came to lying on a settee in the ladies' lounge, with a pimply faced schoolboy – complete with short trousers, gaudy blazer and school cap – standing over me. Slowly it dawned: it was the station commander, Group Captain Dudgeon, and the strange woman standing next to him was the station medical officer in drag. They were relieved that I had recovered consciousness, although I was not sure it was such a good idea.

The brain tends to block one's recollection of pain, but even now I can remember the soothing effect of the cold night air as a team of volunteers carried me back to my room. The doc pumped me full of morphine and I drifted off into an uneasy sleep with my head floating in a barrel of jelly. There had to be a better way of celebrating the New Year.

Next morning the batwoman screamed and, dropping the cup of tea, fled. I looked in the mirror and thought, Oh shit, Bugs, you've really screwed it up this time. I was never one of the world's beautiful people, but now my face was a mask of raw flesh, blisters, black ash and leaking sores. This was going to be a challenge for the medical staff.

Peardrop blanched visibly as I sat down in the chair opposite for breakfast. For a change she seemed lost for words, and she didn't even stay to finish her scrambled eggs.

They cleaned me up at sick quarters. The damage was not as bad as it had first appeared – the burns were mostly second degree, meaning blistering, although the crispy edges around my right ear suggested something more serious. The doc dusted me with M & B powder and let nature take its course. The latest treatment at the time was to leave the burns uncovered. I looked like something out of a horror movie, but it worked well. After a week my face fell off and I was back flying again.

In March I flew a total of twenty-six hours on Hunters, which was good for those days. During the first week of April, Squadron Leader Gordon Tricker arrived to take over from Harry Walmsley, and a few days later all Bruggen officers were assembled in one of the hangars to briefed on the Duncan Sandys 1957 White Paper on Defence. This extraordinarily ill-advised document declared, among other things, that missiles would in future replace manned military aircraft. The Lightning, which was still some years ahead, would be the RAF's last manned fighter. We were appalled. The need to establish positive identification of intruders had not been properly considered, neither was it recognised that there would still be a role for tactical aircraft in support of the army. But for the moment the missile lobby had won the day and the four Hunter squadrons at Bruggen were the first of many in the RAF to be disbanded.

Surplus to requirements. No longer required. Disbandment was a sure way of destroying a squadron's morale – but we had little time to dwell on it. Other than for essential air tests, flying stopped immediately and all our energies were directed towards winding up the squadron by the end of the month – just two weeks away. My involvement was simple, or it should have been – all I had to do was hand over my inventory. But there was a problem. It was difficult enough rounding up the kit to check just one inventory – when all the equipment on the station had to be accounted for at the same time, the task was next to impossible. Every inventory holder at Bruggen was wheeling and dealing to find the necessary equipment. The checking officers were sent in by command headquarters. Even discounting the story – no doubt apocryphal – of the enterprising young flying officer who successfully converted his 'One hangar – aircraft' into 'One hanger – coat', there were some remarkable deals. Equipment that had already been checked changed hands at the dead of night and was rechecked against another inventory next day.

Over the previous year I had managed to get the Derwent engine struck off and reduce my galvanised bucket deficit to nine, but that was it. The checking officer was not too impressed by my tentative suggestion that the nine missing buckets had been stored at the precise spot Mike Maina's aircraft had ploughed in, but he did accept that the aircraft had been carrying a full set of navigation equipment – which was equally unlikely. Of course these were minor problems. The wholesale disbandment meant that the pilots faced a double threat: premature repatriation to the UK and probable posting to a ground tour.

The round of farewell parties was never-ending. On the final dining-in night the assembled officers, led by the AOC – affectionately known as the abandoned earl – were forced to retire from the dinner table before coffee was served, amidst the smoke and fog of a barrage of fireworks. Word went around that those who had recently purchased a car would not be repatriated to the UK until they had served sufficient time in Germany to qualify for the import tax concession. There may have been some truth in this, but I doubt that it was the only factor to be taken into account by the personnel staff.

When 67 Squadron was finally disbanded on 30 April, after one of the shortest command tours on record, Gordon Tricker returned to RAF Wahn. Mike Letton, 'Tinkle' Bell and I were among the lucky few to be posted to No. 4 Squadron, equipped with Hunter F6s, at RAF Jever in northern Germany.

There were actually four Hunter squadrons on No. 122 Fighter Wing at RAF Jever, but of these only 4 Squadron would survive Sandy's axe. Jever had been a Luftwaffe base during the war, and it had a different atmosphere to the post-war bases west of the Rhine. Apparently, the Luftwaffe officers had preferred to live off the station, so the building used for the RAF officers' mess, which was indeed luxurious, had previously been German NCO accommodation.

Some of the officers at Jever were even wilder than those at Bruggen. When I first walked into the mess, a dazed young man by the name of 'Bodger' Edwards was standing at one end of the bar, with a beer bottle balanced on his head, playing Aunt Sally for three other lunatics armed with empties at the other end of the bar. A large officer by the name of Olaf Bergh surveyed the scene benignly from the sidelines. Fortunately for Bodger the empties all missed their mark. He probably wouldn't have noticed anyway, but I shudder to think what would have happened if any of the missiles had hit Olaf. He was a tough character, and I learned that he had spent many months in solitary confinement as a POW in North Korea.

Life at Jever was never dull. A group of budding musicians from the station formed a jazz band called the Jade (pronounced Yarda) Basin Five plus One, which was in great demand in the local area. Dave Watt was on the piano, Stanford Howard played trumpet, Maurice Gavin the clarinet, Dennis Crew the trombone, Dave Fowler the drums, and the plus one was a Dutchman by the name of Willi de Graaf, who played the guitar. They were good; the beat was solid rhythm and blues, and the young German audiences loved it.

With a more powerful engine – 10,000 lb of thrust – the F6 was livelier than earlier marks of Hunter, and it climbed faster. Several other improvements had been incorporated: the unpredictable starter cartridges had been replaced by a liquid-fuelled AVPIN system, and two fuel-low-level (Bingo) lights were fitted in the cockpit. These did nothing for the Hunter's limited internal fuel capacity, but they did provide an accurate warning of the fuel remaining.

We read through *Pilot's Notes* and, after a simple quiz, we launched into the blue. Within a week of arriving at Jever I was doing my share of Battle Flight. It was the same commitment we had held at Bruggen, but it came around more frequently as successive squadrons were disbanded.

Soon after we arrived at Jever, Andy McNae, a junior pilot on the squadron, was taxiing a replacement aircraft out to the ORP when Battle Flight was scrambled. The No. 2 aircraft, already on the ORP, failed to start his engine, and Andy immediately volunteered to go in his place. It was exactly the sort of initiative expected of a keen young fighter pilot – in this game you had to think fast – and Andy was cleared for immediate take-off. In the mean time the original No. 2 had managed to start, so there were two No. 2s accelerating down the runway. That should not have caused a problem, except that one of the aircraft still had its cockpit ladder fitted. In a desperate attempt to salvage the situation the local air traffic controller transmitted, 'No. 2, you still have your ladder fitted,' but which aircraft was he talking to? The original No. 2 aborted his take-off and juddered to a halt with smoking brakes at the far end of the runway; the other aircraft, flown by the keen young Andy, launched into the air complete with the ladder. Not being designed for that sort of thing, the ladder soon blew off. It was an embarrassing cock-up, although not as expensive as the occasion at a Belgian airfield when Air Traffic had transmitted, 'Jake, you are on fire – get out!' Jake, who was taxiing past the tower, had stopped his aircraft and jumped out – which was reasonable, since the aircraft was clearly on fire. Unfortunately, another Jake, who was airborne in the visual circuit at the time, had ejected from a perfectly serviceable F-84.

In August the squadron deployed to Sylt for an APC. We were still using pegged ranging, still in the realms of trick shooting, but practice was beginning to pay off, and my average over seven consecutive shoots improved to 32%. Bill Maish, the squadron's pilot attack instructor, and Bush Barrey, the C Flight commander, were better marksmen, but they had had more practice. In fact, Bush had originally trained during the war as an air gunner in Fairey Battle aircraft. One day his pilot had lost control in cloud and bailed out, whereupon Bush had crawled along the wing-root to the front cockpit, climbed in, and flown the aircraft back to a safe landing at base. One can imagine the erstwhile pilot's surprise when he returned, parachute bundled under his arm, to find the aircraft he had so recently abandoned safely parked on the flight line. On the strength of this, Bush was offered pilot training and went on to fly bombers. After the war he converted to jet fighters. Bush was a rough Australian diamond, ever popular with the ground crew, and a great asset to the squadron – good on you, Dig.

But at this time of the year there were other attractions at Sylt besides air gunnery. With these in mind, John Dobson once elected to take his new car on detachment. I shall never forget the first time we persuaded him to drive us to the beach. Dobson was by nature a shy man, and he would blush furiously from head to toe at the first hint of anything saucy. So it came as no surprise when he announced before setting out that, while he intended to swim, under no circumstances would he strip to the buff. Most of the beaches at Sylt were, in the RAF vernacular, 'bare arse'. We explained to Dobson that he would be the odd man out, but he was not to be persuaded – Dobson was definitely not into skinny-dipping. Of course, that did not apply to the rest of us.

We took a stout spade to dig the communal sandpit, and piled into Dobson's Beetle. (I should explain that Sylt's beaches were exposed to the cool North Sea breezes and, in the absence of clothes, some protection was essential – the answer was to dig a hole in the sand. The Germans tended to dig deep, whereas we Brits preferred a shallower depression with a clear, unrestricted view.) The car park was separated from the beach by a range of sand dunes. There were no hard and fast rules, but clothes were usually worn between the car park and the beach, so Dobson was fairly relaxed as he set off in the lead at a cracking pace. I was next in line. All went well until we came in sight of the beach, when the strain on Dobson – of staring fixedly ahead, so as not to see all the naked bodies – began to tell. His neck stiffened and his jaws clenched, but he resolutely strode on.

Dobson might well have come through totally unscathed if *she* had not appeared. Coming towards us along the narrow path behind the beach was this gorgeous, nubile young woman, blonde and stark naked. Dobson could not avoid this one. She smiled sweetly at him as she squeezed by, and I thought Dobson would burst a blood vessel. He turned to watch her as she passed. He was transported – nothing else mattered – still walking backwards, he blushed redder. Then he tripped over the single strand of wire separating the path from the beach and fell headlong into a deep hole occupied by a German family: father, mother and two teenager daughters, all stark naked. There was nothing we could do, and it would have been churlish to join the party uninvited, so we left the bright-red, acutely embarrassed Englishman stumbling around the hole, shaking hands, bowing and wishing '*Guten tag*' to each member of the family.

Further along the beach, we were digging our hole prior to stripping off, when a great cry – 'Banzai!' or words to that effect – went up as Dobson streaked by naked on his way to the sea. And there he stayed, despite the frigid sea temperatures, for most of the afternoon.

Dobson shed his inhibitions along with his clothes that day, and we couldn't keep him away from the beach after that – but sadly we saw no more of the stunning blonde beauty.

Sylt's night-life was limited, but there was a gambling casino in Westerland – the main town – and there were several other nightclubs and bars. We preferred to drink at the Copper Kettle, which was an up-market bar with soft lights and sexy music. Strange to think that the Copper Kettle had originally been a wartime bunker. One evening, the doorman refused to let us in because he said the place was over-crowded. We would have accepted this with good grace, but then it became obvious that the embargo did not apply to German customers. We were used to the sullen, uncooperative attitude of some of the local population – in fact Westerland was well known for its extreme right-wing politics – but blatant discrimination was rare. So for us, gaining entry became something of a challenge. We knew there was a back-door-cum-fire-exit in the cellar bar, but on this occasion it appeared to be bolted on the inside. One of the chaps suggested that, if I was lowered through the skylight in the gents' toilet, I could slip the bolts on the back door and let everyone in. It seemed to be a reasonable plan. I was by far the slimmest member of the group and, since the Copper Kettle was mostly below ground level, it was a simple matter to scramble on to the turf-covered roof.

We eventually found the skylight we were looking for. Fortunately the toilet was unoccupied and two of the chaps held up the glass while I swung my legs over the sill. This was going to be easy. At that moment the door below opened and in walked an overweight frau. Bloody hell, I thought, we've picked the wrong toilet. She looked up, let out a startled shriek and backed out of the toilet wailing loudly, whereupon my buddies dropped the skylight and scarpered, leaving me trapped in the roof. Obviously I had to get out of there within the next few seconds, or face some very awkward questions. The skylight was a heavy wrought iron and glass affair, far in excess of my top lifting weight, but it is amazing what one can do with a stiff shot of adrenalin. With a great heave I lifted the window enough to roll clear just as the heavy mob came in through the toilet door.

We met up back at the car. After a respectable delay we slowly cruised out of the car park. Dark figures with flashlights were still searching on top of the bunker. Next time we visited the Copper Kettle they let us in, no questions asked.

In mid-September the Jever wing deployed to Schleswigland in northern Germany for exercise Brown Jug, a tactical air exercise involving the Danish defence forces. The airfield was what was known as a 'bare base' – in other words, the facilities were limited and we lived under canvas for two weeks. A fighter reconnaissance squadron equipped with Supermarine Swifts and a specialist ground-attack Venom squadron were also deployed. Our Hunters were fitted with two 100-gallon wing tanks. The purists deplored the reduction in performance but most of us welcomed the extra fuel, which gave us a comfortable ninety minutes in the air. The tanks could always be jettisoned if maximum performance was essential, although that was unlikely in exercise conditions. Besides, it was emphasised that even though they were drop tanks we were expected to bring them back.

I think we were all impressed by the Recce pilots – they were the experts at low level – but we could not say the same for the Swift. It was fast but its manoeuvrability was poor, especially above 10,000 ft.

The exercise tasking was flexible: one day we would be tasked with low-level attacks against land or sea targets, and the next we would be providing air defence for the Danish forces. The Danish civilians were thrilled by all the aerial activity; it was not unusual for us to find our targets marked by large white tablecloths and cheering crowds – a marked contrast to our experience in Germany.

The weather here was superb, and perhaps it was inevitable that some of the tactics went over the top: Danish warships would occasionally launch surface-to-air rockets at us – hopefully of the cardboard kind – as we flew over the top, and the mock dogfights were sometimes a trifle hairy. Towards the end of the exercise two Venoms crashed after their main wing spars failed; it was probably a case of metal fatigue.

On 21 September 1957 I was recommended for appointment as an instrument rating examiner (IRE) by Flight Lieutenant John Sutton – the command IRE. I like to think that the selection was due, at least in part, to the superior standard of my instrument flying, but the immediate effect was that I got more flying – albeit in the Vampire T11. It also crossed my mind that being an IRE might improve my chances of getting another flying tour when I left RAF Germany.

Posting to a ground tour was always possible. The personnel staffs claimed it was essential to have a balanced career, but if the truth were known few of us wanted to do anything other than fly. The policy had recently changed in that officers could now apply for a permanent commission (PC) – that is to serve to the age of fifty-five. Prior to this, one's CO had to initiate action and recommend officers for a PC. I was enjoying service life, so I decided to apply. I did not appreciate the fact that, if anyone further up the chain should choose not to support my request, the application would go no further. The applicant had no right of appeal and – even less satisfactorily – he might not even be told that his application had been turned down.

I waited for a couple of months and, hearing nothing, I eventually spoke to the boss – Squadron Leader Tim McElhaw. He told me that I was too young to be considered for a PC, which was incorrect, and that he had quashed my application. It was a bitter disappointment; I had barely four years left to serve in the RAF, and then I might have to look for another job.

Replacement pilots from the UK always travelled out by boat and train from Harwich to the Hook of Holland and on to the nearest railhead. We knew precisely when they would arrive at the officers' mess, and it was a simple matter to arrange a reception to give them a chance to meet the station's executive officers. At least, that was the theory. The dress on such occasions was invariably best blue, because that was the appropriate uniform in the mess after 1800 hours. But it was common practice to exchange tunics before the new pilots arrived. Don Riley – or 'Skinhead' as he was known, on account of his bald pate – would borrow a dog collar from one of the padres and become a very convincing man of the cloth. 'Bless you, my son,' he would say, as he accepted successive pints of beer and launched into yet another bawdy tale. The erstwhile padre, sporting pilot's wings, would hold forth on the evils of the flesh and confess, confidentially, that flying scared him half to death. Fresh-faced young men would appear as much-decorated war veterans, while the crusty old flying officer, crying in his beer over in the corner of the bar, was actually Wing Commander Ops. By the end of the evening the newcomers were thoroughly pissed and utterly confused. Next morning they would struggle into met briefing nursing thunderous hangovers, their discomfort becoming even more acute when they realised the true identity of those with whom they had shared confidences the previous evening. They need not have worried; no one took the slightest notice of what had been said.

Occasionally an incident occurs in the air that cannot easily be forgotten. On 28 March 1958 I was leading two aircraft on a high-level battle formation sortie. My official report on what happened read as follows:

> During the climb I noted that all oxygen indications were satisfactory, the flow was normal and 100% oxygen was selected. Shortly after levelling at 37,000 ft we split for air combat. The next thing I remember was regaining consciousness at 7,000ft, descending, with the throttle closed, air brakes out, and oxygen selected to emergency. We continued the sortie below 10,000 ft; I made a normal approach and landing at base.

Alan Pollock, my No. 2, was able to fill in some of the details. From the very beginning he was surprised by the ladylike gait of the dogfight. After a couple of turns I reported that I had an oxygen problem. Apparently my voice sounded normal, but then my aircraft rolled inverted and went into a steep spiral dive. Al asked if I was OK, but my reply was unintelligible. In desperation, using my name instead of the official callsign, Al managed to talk me into a controlled descent. I must have been at least semi-conscious, because I followed his instructions. At 10,000 ft I cut in on the R/T and resumed the lead.

I was met at the aircraft by the station medical officer. After discussing what had happened he took a blood sample to check if I had inhaled any toxic fumes. In the absence of long-term ill effects, it seemed likely that I had been anoxic – possibly due to a disconnected oxygen supply. At that time the tube from the pilot's oxygen mask was attached to the aircraft supply by a push-fit connector, which was designed to detach easily during an ejection. Unfortunately the connector could just as easily become disconnected in flight. At high altitude, air is not an adequate substitute for oxygen, but the effects of anoxia are so insidious that a break in the oxygen supply could easily go unnoticed. Fortunately, Al Pollock was on the ball. With that kind of problem, pilots of single-seat aircraft were seldom given a second chance.

Some months later a safety valve was fitted to the oxygen connector which prevented the pilot drawing breath through the mask when the tube was disconnected. This modification provided a positive warning of inadvertent oxygen disconnection.

My last few months on 4 Squadron quickly passed. In an effort to improve RAF relations with the local community, the station commander announced plans for an Anglo/German Week. A programme of events was arranged for the first week in May. All good stuff, it was generally agreed that West Germany would eventually take over its share of NATO's defence commitments and, with this in mind, it was sensible to start building bridges. But some of the older pilots felt that a whole week of Anglo/German festivities was going too far, too fast. On a bright, cloudless day, high above the airfield, an unknown pilot traced out a huge cock and balls in persistent contrails against an otherwise clear blue sky – a silent gesture of dissent, plain for all to see as it drifted slowly in the direction of Wilhelmshaven. There was no doubt the RAF were responsible, but the aerial artist remained anonymous.

The protest made no difference, and the Anglo/German Week went ahead as planned. During a soccer match between RAF Jever and a team from the local town, the German goalkeeper collided with his goalpost and died. Instead of casting a blight on the rest of the week, this tragic accident served to draw the communities closer together.

The grand finale was an air display involving many different types of aircraft, and of course the Hunter squadrons at RAF Jever provided much of the flying. No. 93 Squadron's formation aerobatic team put on an impressive display, and Ken Goodwin's solo Hunter aerobatics – which included negative-g manoeuvres, outside loops, inverted turns and such like – greatly impressed the spectators, professional and amateur alike. The week was a resounding success, but I was relieved to get back to normal squadron flying.

Then in July I came to the end of my tour. I much regretted having to say goodbye to my mates on the squadron, but that was part and parcel of service life. Every two or three years one had to move on and give someone else a chance. I had applied for an extension but had been turned down. Besides, I had served in Germany for twenty-six months, which was not far short of a full tour, so I had little cause for complaint. By any standards I had had a successful tour. I had flown more than 400 hours in the Hunter, had been assessed as an above-average day fighter pilot, and I was an IRE. But I was concerned about the future. With so little time left of my existing service engagement, the chances of getting another squadron tour seemed remote. It was even possible that I might not fly again in the RAF.

I was wrong on both counts. On reporting to the Air Ministry at Adastral House in London I was informed that I was posted to No. 66 Squadron – equipped with Hunter F6s – at RAF Acklington in Northumberland. The squadron needed an IRE – I could hardly believe my good fortune.

6
Tour on No. 66 Squadron (Hunter 6, T7 & 9)

I spent my disembarkation leave at home. Little had changed in the two years I had been away. Henry, my youngest brother, had taken up aero-modelling and was working on a home-made rocket. His mixture of weed-killer and sugar, packed into a short length of copper pipe, sounded an unlikely combination to me, but I had learned caution from my misspent youth – especially when it came to pyrotechnics. We observed the test firing from the far end of the garden. Even Henry would have to admit that the weed-killer and sugar mixture was not the greatest rocket fuel, but it made an impressive explosion that afternoon.

In the evenings I did the rounds of favourite drinking haunts with my parents. Visiting the many unspoiled country inns in the New Forest – and Dad knew most of them – was a pleasant enough way of passing the time. But then I met Claire. She was one of Theresa's friends, and the most attractive girl I had seen in a long while. Claire was keen on the theatre; indeed, she was determined to make a career on the stage. I was quite happy to tag along, although her parents did not really approve. No doubt they saw me as a threat to their daughter – and they were probably right. But we thought we could make a go of it.

When my leave finished, Claire sallied forth to London to attend the Royal Academy of Dramatic Art (RADA), and I headed for the other end of the country. We promised to keep in touch.

It was early August when I drove north. RAF Acklington was a typical World War II airfield, with wooden-hutted accommodation and black corrugated-iron hangars. This was coal-mining country: a grey slag-heap brooded menacingly to the south-east, and below ground there was a honeycomb of old, uncharted mine workings. Like many roads in the local area, the airfield was liable to subsidence. Which was no great cause for concern, until the night one of 29 Squadron's Javelins sank up to its wheel axles through the hangar floor. The Javelins were quickly redeployed to RAF Leuchars. In May 1958 No. 66 Squadron had been withdrawn from its UK air defence commitment and given forty-eight hours' notice to deploy to Cyprus, with the task of reinforcing the island's air defences during a crisis in the Lebanon. They were still there. With no resident squadrons, Acklington had a deserted, run-down look about it, a veritable sleepy hollow.

Barry Stott, a brash young pilot fresh out of Chivenor, was also waiting to join Sixty-Six. Stott's heart was in the right place – he was a boisterous lad, desperately anxious to please, full of fun – but not quite house-trained. He also talked a lot, and much of what he had to say was rubbish. No doubt he would learn, but I made a mental note to distance myself from young 'Stotters' when we met up with the rest of the squadron.

It was touch and go as to whether we would deploy to Cyprus or wait for the squadron to return, but on 14 August Stott and I boarded a Beverley at RAF Abingdon *en route* for Nicosia. The Beverley was the RAF's tactical transport workhorse. Designed to meet the Berlin Airlift, with a cruising speed of 150 knots, the plane was ideal for lifting twenty tons of freight and ninety passengers over a distance of 250 miles. But UK to Cyprus was a much longer haul. We refuelled at Orange Caritat in the south of France, and staggered on to Malta for a night stop. Next day we flew to El Adem – a hot little airfield in the Sahara south of Tobruk – then on to Nicosia. The journey was downright tedious, fifteen hours' flying time even with the benefit of a tailwind.

The airfield at Nicosia was bulging at the seams, with three fighter squadrons, a Hastings transport squadron, a Beverley detachment and assorted civil airline traffic all vying for space. We lived in tented accommodation, although all the modern creature comforts were provided for by the officers' mess. Cyprus had once been a notorious black spot for malaria, but that had all changed with the introduction of modern insecticides. The current problems were entirely man-made.

The Greek Cypriots – roughly 80% of the population – and the

Turkish Cypriots were at each other's throats, and both sections of the community distrusted the British. But it was the Greek faction, led by Archbishop Makarios and General George Grivas, who spearheaded the EOKA terrorist campaign against the British. EOKA's political aims were to achieve independence from the British and to unify Cyprus with Greece. The Turkish Cypriot population wisely aligned themselves with the British. It was a dirty little campaign, with indiscriminate bombings, murder and mayhem. On base the terrorist risk was minimal, although precautions were necessary to protect the aircraft and passengers. The rule was never to leave a packed bag unattended before a flight. Outside the station a curfew was occasionally imposed; it was safer to travel in pairs and advisable to carry side-arms. Being newcomers, Stott and I found the conditions exhilarating, but the detachment had long since lost its attraction for the married members of the squadron. The squadron had deployed at short notice, supposedly for a few weeks, but that had been extended to three months and, despite the odd false alarm, there was still no date for its return to Acklington.

The CO, Squadron Leader P. E. Bairsto AFC, was known throughout the RAF as the Bear, although to those of us on the squadron he was either 'sir' or 'the boss', depending on the occasion. The previous CO had been relieved of his command, and Peter Bairsto had been given three months to sort out the squadron. He had a reputation for being a hard man. At my arrival interview, with voice raised high, he said, 'I expect twenty-three hours and fifty-nine minutes' work out of you in any twenty-four-hour period, and if you are not prepared for that, then I can find five hundred pilots who would willingly change places with you.' Not exactly the friendly chat I had expected, but I gathered by now that the boss demanded total commitment – which was fine by me. All the same, Peter Bairsto gave you the uncomfortable feeling that you had already failed. The pilots' crewroom was just next door, and as I left the office one wag commented that 'Dinger' Bell (not to be confused with Tinkle) was the only man on the squadron not to have been bollocked that week. The remark was intended to be heard by the boss. When Dinger arrived he was immediately summoned. He emerged some minutes later, thoroughly bewildered – both by the severity of the rocket and the raucous laughter of those in the crewroom. Evidently the Bear also had a sense of humour – offbeat, perhaps, but one could live with that.

I found it easy to settle in. One or two faces were familiar, including Ian Madelin from 4 Squadron days. But all that really mattered – the standard by which new pilots were judged – was how competent they were in the air, and I was fairly confident on that score. Two days after arriving in Cyprus I flew the essential day-and-night dual checks with the boss in a Vampire T11.

Within a week I was sitting in a fully-armed Hunter F6 at the end of Nicosia's runway, holding Battle Flight. That was what it was all about.

Because of the heat, the permanent staff at Nicosia worked from seven o'clock in the morning until two in the afternoon; but more was expected of Sixty-Six. Our flying programme started early, went on all day and extended well into the night.

Looking down from high altitude I was struck by the beauty of Cyprus. It was a jewel in the blue Mediterranean, and from here the violence and misery wrought by man did not show.

As a result of a recent terrorist murder, the walled city of Nicosia had been put off limits to military personnel. Which posed a problem for Flying Officer Ken Hayr, who had been instructed by the boss to purchase a quantity of blue and white caps for the squadron. Blue and white were the squadron's colours, but they were also the colours worn by supporters of EOKA. The incongruity of it all was of no concern to us, but in Nicosia the sole distributor of blue and white caps was a merchant at the far end of Ledra Street – otherwise known as Murder Mile – and that was tricky. It was a toss-up as to which would cause the greatest heartache, either incurring the boss's wrath or running the gauntlet of Ledra Street. No contest really – the boss would know, but EOKA's hit men might never find out. It was best not to enquire too closely as to how Ken resolved the problem. Flying Officers Preece and Dickin certainly helped out – but the caps duly appeared.

At the weekends, those of us not on duty would borrow one of the squadron's Land Rovers and drive to Kyrenia, a picturesque fishing port on the north coast. It made a welcome break from the dusty heat of Nicosia and our first priority was a cool dip in the sea from 'the Slab' a secure bathing spot much favoured by the Brits. About four o'clock in the afternoon, when the heat of the day was spent, we would start back to camp. There was a mysterious quality about the Kyrenia range of hills. It was intriguing to think that, back in 1191, Richard Coeur de Lion, who had stayed at St Hilarion castle with his new bride, Berengaria of Navarre, while *en route* to the third Crusade, may have had similar thoughts. I imagine Queen Berengaria was suitably impressed with her first married quarter.

But to return to 1958. It was rumoured that George Grivas was actually holed out in these hills, and it was not difficult to imagine terrorist gunmen concealed in the lengthening shadows, waiting to strike. The road between Kyrenia and Nicosia was much used by military vehicles, but the risk of attack in broad daylight was low. Nevertheless, it was a relief to move into the more open country south of the Kyrenia Range. The flags fluttering over isolated villages proclaimed their ethnic allegiance, which was a matter of vital importance in Cyprus. Only recently, on this very road, a gang of Greek Cypriot lads from Nicosia had gatecrashed a dance at Geunyeli – a Turkish Cypriot village. Apparently the boys had made a nuisance of themselves with the village girls, so they had been rounded up and sent back to Nicosia by bus. Harmless fun so far – but then the Greek youths had returned to Geunyeli and had disappeared. Next day, a military patrol had found a severed arm in a field. A house-to-house search of Geunyeli had turned up the dismembered remains of the rest of the gang. The menfolk of Geunyeli did not make idle threats.

The squadron eventually returned to the UK in mid-September. The Hunters, cruising at almost nine miles a minute, made short work of the trip, but the journey took far longer for those of us returning in the Beverley. We made good progress until Orange Caritat, but strong headwinds over the south of France severely reduced the Beverley's ground speed. Then the No. 1 engine (port outer) developed an oil leak and had to be shut down. That was not a problem – the Beverley could cruise quite happily on three engines – but we were forced to descend to 4000 ft, and from that altitude cars could be seen overtaking us as they headed north. I was visiting the flight deck with Ian Thomson, a fellow squadron pilot, while all this was going on. The Beverley captain handled the incident with practised skill – the loss of an engine was a common enough occurrence on the Beverley – but he suggested that it would be best not to mention the oil leak lest it alarm the other passengers. He could have saved his breath. The huge, stationary propeller was plain for all to see, and by the time we got back to our seats the other passengers – all experienced squadron tradesmen – were craning their necks, checking on the progress of the black streaks of oil oozing back along the engine cowling. Our flight time from Orange to Acklington was extended by an hour, but no one complained. Sixty-Six was home at last.

The first month or so back at Acklington was a period of considerable turbulence. Seven pilots were posted out. Some were due to leave anyway, having come to the end of their tour, but others were moved on as part of the boss's sweep-clean policy. Among the replacement pilots was an American exchange officer – Captain Richard Oliver Bruce, affectionately known as 'the Captain'. He was an impeccably smart bachelor, a perfect gentleman and an all-round, straight-arrow credit to the United States Marine Corps. The Captain became the butt of a constant stream of good-natured ribbing from the rest of the squadron, but he gave as good as he got. And he completely outsmarted his tormentors when he bought a brand new Jaguar XK 140. Few RAF officers could afford such expensive, high-class motoring.

In the reshuffle of secondary duties I was given the task of writing both the official and unofficial diaries for the squadron. It will be of little solace for readers to know that my skills as a writer have improved since then. The unofficial diary provided a useful reference for this chapter.

In 1958, due to the performance limitations of contemporary aircraft, the Soviet manned bomber threat to the UK would have had to come from the east at high altitude. A chain of powerful ground control interception (GCI) radars kept watch on the approaches to UK airspace. If an intruder was detected, fighters would be scrambled from ground alert for a close-controlled interception. This ground alert procedure optimised the use of the available fighters and offered the best chance of successfully intercepting high-flying targets. Alternative broadcast control procedures were employed when the GCI radars or radio communications were disrupted by jamming. In these conditions a running commentary on the intruder's position was broadcast and the fighters would self-navigate to make good their own interception. In the unlikely event of the GCI radars being completely jammed out, pairs of fighters would be scrambled to maintain standing air patrols some fifty miles off the coast. We trained on a steady diet of practice interceptions (PIs) and took part in frequent exercises to test the efficiency of the system. The UK's air defence procedures were probably the best in the world – but then Fighter Command had a wealth of practical experience.

We regularly practised air gunnery on the flag. The Hunter's radar ranging was sorted out early in 1958. Given precise range information, the GGS accurately predicted the gravity drop and deflection on any target tracked in the gunsight between 200 and 800 yards. A bolt-on radar reflector was also developed for the flag, so we were no longer limited to pegged range procedures for academic shooting, and the squadron's air-to-air scores rapidly improved.

However, aircraft serviceability – or rather the lack of it – was still a problem. The Hunter was not a complex aircraft, but it certainly required more work on the ground per flying hour than previous fighter types. On some squadrons this was accepted as a valid excuse for failing to meet the monthly flying target of 400 hours, but the boss maintained that this target was a minimum requirement. The ground crew worked long and hard to produce serviceable aircraft, but then everyone on Sixty-Six was highly motivated. With Peter Bairsto in command, anything less would have been unacceptable.

We had several unique advantages. Acklington was a Master Airfield, which meant that it remained open twenty-four hours a day. And being the only frontline squadron on the station, we had the airfield all to ourselves. We could fly whenever we wished. In fact the station's primary role was to support Sixty-Six. In one month I flew fifty-three sorties – more than fifty hours – which in those days was an exceptional achievement on jet fighter aircraft.

But it was not all hard graft. One Friday in November I borrowed a Hunter to fly down to RAF Odiham. I planned to spend the weekend in London with Claire, and one hour in a Hunter was far better than nine hours behind the wheel of a car. Alas, the best laid schemes of mice and men . . . *En route* to Odiham the hydraulics failed. The first I knew of it was a red warning light, rapidly followed by falling hydraulic pressure and the flying controls reverting to manual. It was too late to turn back.

After landing at Odiham it became obvious that my aircraft had suffered a massive hydraulic leak. Thinking I would have more time to spend with Claire, I was quite pleased, but when I called the squadron to tell them the good news, they suggested – well, it was more of an order, really – that I was to work on the aircraft until it was repaired and return to base as soon as possible. You can't win them all. Even with the assistance of Odiham's duty ground crew, it was Wednesday before the leak was repaired. Sadly, I did not keep my date with Claire that weekend – she was not amused – but I did learn a great deal about the Hunter's hydraulic system.

Acklington could be difficult during the winter months because of the lack of suitable diversion airfields. We continued flying until the weather was down to the limits, but even Master Green-rated pilots earned their flying pay landing back when the cloud base was 200 ft and the visibility down to half a mile. Occasionally we would fly for diversions; in other words we'd take off knowing that we would probably have to land elsewhere. But we would conserve sufficient fuel to practise one approach at Acklington before diverting, and if the conditions permitted we would land off the approach. We seldom broke the rules, although we may have bent them occasionally, and in the process we sharpened our instrument skills. Even the haar – with its treacherous combination of low cloud, drizzle and fog that could hang around the north-east coast for days on end – did not stop us. One aircraft would remain in the GCA pattern, keeping a check on the weather, while others in the air would be ready for immediate recall, should the sea-fog start to roll in. We were confident in our ability to handle bad weather. We flew the GCA approach 10 knots slower than other Hunter squadrons, because that gave us a better chance of landing off the first approach. To 66 Squadron's pilots, Acklington's short, uneven runway never appeared as short as it did to other visiting Hunter pilots.

Early in January, after much ice and snow, I was detailed to lead a flight of four aircraft to RAF Leuchars, to take advantage of forecast better weather. The intention was to return the following day, but Acklington's runway remained snowbound. For the next seven days we drifted from one airfield to the next, avoiding the worst of the weather and steadily clocking up the flying hours, and showing the squadron flag at most of the Fighter Command airfields. The aircraft stood up surprisingly well. Initially we were well received socially, but as the week wore on our hosts noticeably stayed upwind – which may have had something to do with the fact that none of us possessed a change of socks. There were some powerful men on that particular round robin. By the time we got back to Acklington we had added sixty hard earned flying hours to the monthly total, while the other squadrons in Fighter Command had barely turned a wheel.

Later that month we fitted four underwing tanks to our aircraft, instead of the usual two. With the extra fuel the Hunter's endurance was extended to over two and a half hours – a far cry from the frantic thirty minutes of the Hunter F1 – and the problem of finding suitable weather diversions was greatly eased.

Then there was the saga of the squadron's mascot. It all started when the boss casually commented, 'This Squadron has no reason to be proud – it doesn't even own a mascot.' It was common knowledge that the boss's former unit, 43 Squadron – 'The Fighting Cocks' – kept a pair of bedraggled bantams at Leuchars. But that was beside the point. The boss was not that keen on livestock, it was just his way of keeping young pilots on their toes. But his comment was taken as a challenge, and a few days later an ad appeared in the *The Times*: 'Rattlesnake wanted, as mascot, dead or alive. Box No——'. (The squadron's badge was a rattlesnake, coiled and ready to strike, with the motto 'Cavete Praemonui' – Beware, you have been warned.) Response to the advertisement was fairly slow in coming, but on 20 February at a formal dining-in night, Colonel A. T. Sampson, USAF, presented the squadron with a stuffed rattlesnake on behalf of the Ross Allen Reptile Institute in Florida. This was followed by a further offer, again from the United States, of a live Western Diamondback. We could hardly believe our luck. Opinions were divided about whether it was a good idea to keep the snake in the crewroom; self-appointed experts were worried the creature might escape and overrun Northumberland, but that seemed unlikely. Besides, there was no law against keeping mascots in crewrooms. The station medical officer procured a supply of antivenin, which was extracted from horse's blood and almost as toxic as rattlesnake venom (in other words, make sure the victim has actually been bitten before you use it). The station carpenter put together a snake tank – a free-standing glass-fronted case with an electric heater and a light built into the lid, to simulate the sun. We were ready for our mascot!

Actually the squadron was deployed in Denmark for Exercise Topweight when the snake arrived at Heathrow Airport. So there was some delay before Ken Hayr drove down to collect it. Since the snake had been in transit for the best part of two weeks, we all assumed it was already dead. The staff at Heathrow were inclined to agree; to the best of their knowledge the reptile had not been fed since starting out, and the box was beginning to smell. But back at the squadron, no one was prepared to take any chances. The boss drew a .38 Smith & Wesson service revolver from the armoury. We were not sure what he intended to do with it – although the gun would have been useful mercifully to dispatch anyone unfortunate enough to be bitten. It also added an appropriate flavour of the Wild West to the proceedings. The crewroom windows were opened wide for ventilation and/or to facilitate rapid egress should the need arise. Although, by the smell of things, the snake had been dead for some time and was fast decaying.

The source of the pong was a robust plywood box, approximately 24 × 18 × 6 inches, with air holes at the side and a firmly screwed-down lid: obviously it was not a large snake, which was rather disappointing. An envelope containing instructions was attached. Inside the box we found a soiled cotton bag with a coil of string tied around the neck and a similar length of string attached to one of the bottom corners. According to the instructions, the rattlesnake could inflict a lethal bite through the bag, so the drill was to lift the bag by pulling on the strings. Once the bag was safely inside the tank, the string around the neck could be cut, thereby releasing the snake.

There was no sign of life from the bag, but we decided to follow the instructions to the letter. Two officers were detailed to pull on the strings. The bag had just cleared the box when the snake began to rattle. In the quiet confines of the crewroom, the effect was bloodcurdling. What we had thought was a shroud rapidly transformed into a writhing, struggling strait-jacket. Surely it was only a question of time before the bag gave way. Discretion was definitely the better part of valour, and the steely-eyed fighter pilot spectators bailed out of the crewroom by the nearest available exit, leaving the boss, who was showing an unaccustomed degree of flap, and the two terrified string holders to sort out the problem. Mike Chandler attempted to record the episode on film. We never saw the photographs, but apparently the boss demonstrated a near-perfect vertical take-off when the first flash-bulb fired. Fortunately the bag remained intact, and when the string around the neck was cut, a seven-foot rattlesnake burst out. As the Americans would say, he was meaner than hell. Can't say I blame him. To add insult to injury, he was christened Ponsonby Forsdyke-Psmith, which was a ridiculous name for a rattlesnake.

There was nothing remotely attractive about Ponsonby. Indeed, while he was shedding his skin, which happened every six weeks or so, he looked like the devil incarnate. But visitors to the squadron were intrigued. They would stoop in front of his tank to get a closer look. Ponsonby would give a brief warning rattle and lunge out – leaving a splash of venom on the inside of the glass. His intended victim would rear back, hair standing on end, the single pane of reinforced glass appearing all too flimsy. One shocked air traffic controller somersaulted back across the crewroom table in his effort to get away. After striking, Ponsonby would recoil, ready to have another go. We read that after three strikes the snake would need time to recharge his venom sacs, but no one volunteered to test that little gem of information.

As snakes go, Ponsonby was remarkably active. At four o'clock each afternoon he would slither around his tank, take a drink of water and lever himself up against a log to inspect the lid. If the lid had ever been left open Ponsonby would certainly have escaped, but Ken Hayr, the officer appointed i/c snake, was very careful about security. He had our full co-operation, although we were fairly sure that no one in their right mind would attempt to kidnap Ponsonby.

We were all enrolled as members of the International Association of Rattlesnake Hunters, based at Okeene, Oklahoma, which specialised in 'catching man-killing rattlers alive'. I still have my membership card, but you wouldn't catch me within a country mile of Salt Creek Canyon, the scene of their annual rattlesnake roundup. The squadron was given a supply of genuine rattlesnake tails. We modified the boss's electric call bell; with gong removed and a rattle attached to the striker it sounded very like Ponsonby, which guaranteed the undivided attention of many an unsuspecting visitor.

The weekly pilots' meetings were held in the crewroom on Friday afternoons. Old hands knew it was best not to raise any contentious issues, because they had a nasty habit of backfiring. So when Bill Jago, who had been with the squadron for only a few months, said he was going to complain about the working hours, the opportunity for some fun, albeit at Bill's expense, was too good to miss. Bill's moan was that, at tea time, the toast and sandwiches were always eaten up before he got back to the mess. The fact that dinner was served an hour later was immaterial; after all, Bill was a growing lad – a rugby player, to boot – and he needed regular meals. We could hardly believe our ears – where had this man come from? But we heartily agreed and urged him to raise it at the next pilots' meeting. Bill should have realised he was being set up. The following Friday the meeting was delayed – it usually was – and Bill was certain to miss out on his tea yet again. At last, with routine business complete, the boss asked if there were any other questions. Ponsonby gave a warning rattle (his timing was immaculate), but, undeterred, Bill rose to his feet. He deserved full credit for initiative, but I thought his suggestion that the squadron should knock off work early in time for tea was a little thin. The boss looked around the assembled company and said in elevated tones – his equivalent of Ponsonby's rattle: 'Does anyone else share this view?' Well, of course we didn't, and the silence was deafening. Bill searched desperately for support – none of which was forthcoming. We suspected that Bill would shortly be hearing about the boss's five hundred pilots who would give their eye teeth for his job. Bill never forgave us, but if he couldn't stand a joke, he shouldn't have joined.

Aside from Bill's tea problems, the food in the mess was excellent, and we could always supplement our diet with goods purchased at knock-down prices in Alnmouth. A local poacher, who used to hang out in the Red Lion pub, would surreptitiously offer game or the odd salmon, but his supplies were irregular – in more ways than one. Crabs and lobsters were usually available at the fish quay, and a short way up the coast at Craster they produced the finest kippers in the world. The married officers living in Alnmouth were well placed to take advantage of the good life, although their wives may have had mixed feelings. Ian Thomson came home one evening to find the diminutive Daisy – armed with a wooden spoon – doing battle with an irate lobster which was determined to escape from a pot slowly heating on the stove. Daisy was a game girl, but judging from the state of the kitchen it had been a damned close-run thing.

At the other extreme, Ponsonby refused to eat anything. We tempted him with run-of-the-mill field mice and white-coated delicacies from the pet shop, but he was simply not interested in food. According to the experts, that was not unusual for a captive rattlesnake. He survived for three months, but one morning we found him dead in his tank. Ken Hayr arranged the corpse in a lifelike pose on a patch of grass by the door of the Squadron. Barry Stott – the first unsuspecting officer to turn the corner – took it very badly. Like Zebedee in *The Magic Roundabout* Stotters spun around three times and disappeared. We had him skinned – the snake, that is, not Barry – and his hide, mounted on green baize, was hung on the crewroom wall.

In May we learned that the squadron had qualified for the final shoot-off for Fighter Command's gunnery competition – the prestigious Dacre Trophy – due to be held in June at RAF Horsham-St-Faith. Apart from air gunnery, the competition included a ciné phase against evading aircraft at high altitude and an operational turn-round (i.e. the rapid rearming of an aircraft between sorties). All the Hunter squadrons in Fighter Command competed for the Dacre Trophy but, by a process of elimination, only one squadron from each group qualified for the finals. In 1959 the final line-up was: 66 Squadron from No. 13 Group; 65 Squadron from No. 12 Group; and 54 Squadron from No. 11 Group. Naturally the boss led the 66 Squadron team, comprising Mike Chandler, Maurice Chapman, John Dickin, Pete Gatrell (the squadron engineering officer) and a ground support party. For two weeks prior to the competition we concentrated on weapons training. Pilots not directly involved with the team towed flags and flew as targets for the ciné sorties. The armourers practised operational turn-rounds until they were rearming Hunters in their sleep.

The Dacre team deployed to Horsham on 14 June. Each pilot was tasked to fly six sorties – three against the flag and three ciné evasion. All sorties were taken into account, and pilots were disqualified and scored zero if they either fired too close or at too low an angle off. When the results were added up, the 66 Squadron air-to-air average was 51%, and they had won every phase of the competition by a substantial margin. Maurice Chapman covered himself in glory by achieving the highest individual score. The team returned to Acklington in high spirits on 18 June.

Winning the Dacre Trophy was a great boost to squadron morale. In just twelve months, Sixty-Six had risen from the bottom of the league to become the premier air gunnery squadron in Fighter Command. Of course much of the credit was due to the team and their efforts at Horsham, but the whole squadron had worked throughout the year to get them there. So we thought we had just cause to celebrate. The squadron was congratulated by Air Vice Marshal Earle – the air officer commanding No. 13 Group. The boss was obviously pleased, though he refused to show it.

Some weeks later the squadron was host to a Fighter Command team preparing for NATO's AIRCENT fighter weapons meet, due to be held at Cazaux in France. Once again the team was led by Peter Bairsto, with Tammy Syme, Dennis Caldwell, Harry Davidson and Tony Park – four talented rogues imported from other squadrons – in support. The visitors cut a broad swathe through the local night-life, such as it was, and blotted Acklington's copy book at more than one establishment. The station's membership of the local golf club was withdrawn after Caldwell and Co. engaged the tweed-clad captain of the ladies' golf team in a dubious joke about what she would do if he gave her two hot half-crowns. With some reluctance the lady eventually admitted, 'I would drop them', and was acutely embarrassed by the punch-line, which was delivered in a drunken giggle: 'What, for five bob?' Tony Park was the quietest member of the group, that was until he had had a few beers.

They redeemed themselves at Cazaux, though, by coming second, against stiff opposition, with a gunnery average of 72%.

The social life on Sixty-Six was slightly more refined. My affair with Claire had cooled during the year. I had visited her once or twice in London and she had come up for a ball in the officers' mess. I even bought an engagement ring, but when it came to making any firm plans we found that we had little in common. Claire was determined to act and I had my RAF career, and neither one of us was ready for marriage, so we agreed to go our separate ways. I was somewhat relieved, and teamed up with John Walker, a fellow pilot, to play the field at various local nurses' homes. What with formal mess functions, squadron and private parties, seldom a week went by without some kind of thrash. We had the wheels and the money and, by and large, the girls appeared to appreciate our company.

In June, the squadron laid on a farewell dinner at Beadnell Hall to say goodbye to Mike Chandler, Ray Passfield and John Davis. It was a memorable evening with the usual farewell speeches. John Davis composed an ode, poking fun at the rest of the squadron. Of course we were sorry to see them go, but we managed to drown our sorrows. On the way home, Bill Jago – aided and abetted by Barry Stott – rolled his Morris Minor. The car was a total write-off. As usual, Barry walked away without a scratch, but Bill, much the worse for wear, was admitted to Newcastle General Hospital for a face-lift. Bill's injuries did not slow him down though; while he was recovering in hospital he met Freda, a charming young nurse, whom he eventually married.

John Sutton was posted in to replace Mike Chandler as the operations officer. John had been my flight commander on 4 Squadron, and since then he had served with the Fighter Combat School at RAF West Raynham. Flight Lieutenant 'Dickie' Dicken came to us from Group Headquarters. He was a qualified flying instructor (QFI) and an experienced fighter pilot. Alan Garside also joined us, straight from the OCU.

Ray Passfield had been the squadron's solo aerobatic display pilot. Since watching Ken Goodwin at Jever I had been itching to have a go, so I volunteered to take on the commitment. The boss finally agreed. The Hunter was a splendid display aircraft: powerful, robust and highly manoeuvrable, even at low speed. Manoeuvrability was essential for display flying; after all, it made for an extremely dull show if the aircraft covered three counties and disappeared from view every time the pilot turned about through 180°.

After practising at medium altitude, I was given clearance to perform over the airfield. One of the advantages of solo aerobatics, as opposed to being a member of a formation team, was that I could practise my routine at the end of any standard training sortie. The boss witnessed every practice, as did the station executive officers and the other squadron pilots. It was not just because they were interested; it was a known fact that anyone who witnessed an accident could not be called upon to serve on the subsequent board of inquiry. My first display in front of the public was at Colwyn Bay on 29 August 1959.

For convenience, I usually flew my display with the external wing tanks fitted, though I made sure the tanks were empty before throwing the aircraft around. Loops, rolls, wing-overs and such like were easy to perform in the Hunter. Stalling was not permitted, which precluded flick rolls and true stall turns, but it was possible to cheat a bit and perform an impressive high vertical wing-over. A senior staff officer from Group Headquarters once tried to tell me that the half loop I was using immediately after take-off to reposition in front of the crowd was dangerous. He insisted that the aircraft would stall at the top of the loop. I knew that was unlikely. Under zero-g conditions, an aircraft would neither stall nor spin. Left to its own devices, the Hunter would drift over the top of a loop quite safely, at a remarkably low airspeed. I suggested to the staff officer that, to lose control at that point, the pilot would have to be extremely ham-handed, which seemed to upset him. Next day the boss called me into his office. Apparently the self same staff officer had once lost control while looping a Hunter and had had to bail out. I rested my case. The boss accepted that the manoeuvre was safe and I did not have to change my display sequence.

I included an inverted loop and an outside break in my show, mainly for the benefit of regular aircrew who could appreciate the finer points of that kind of flying. The uncomfortable moment was when the aircraft first inverted and one fell away from the seat – there was always some slack in the harness, even when the ground crew had helped me tighten the lap straps. All manner of doubts flashed through one's mind at that moment. Would the straps hold; would I still be able to reach the controls; or would I finish up sitting in the cockpit canopy? Minus 3½ g was considered to be the practical human limit. Which may well have been true. I had regularly experienced the pink flood of vision, signalling the onset of red-out – the opposite of blackout. I'd thought no more of it until after a display in Cyprus, when an RAF doctor had confirmed that my eyes were bleeding internally – proving, if nothing else, that the bleary-eyed, bloodshot appearance of some negative-g display specialists was not solely due to the demon drink.

Inverted flight could spring other unpleasant surprises. On one occasion, due to a fault in the aircraft's fuel system, the engine flamed out as I pushed up at 600 ft for an inverted loop. Everything went very quiet. Fortunately the engine responded immediately after I rolled upright and pressed the relight button, but from then on I made a point of checking each aircraft at a safe altitude before using it for a display.

At 360 knots, which was the basic airspeed I used for my show, the Hunter's pitch control – that was the aircraft's response to fore and aft stick movements – could be improved by judicious use of flap. At full power, with ten degrees of flap selected, the Hunter could be hauled around in a seven-g turn – without losing airspeed – which was impressive. But it was essential to raise all flaps before attempting any rolling manoeuvre, otherwise the aircraft tended to dish out. On one occasion I was distracted during a Derry turn and mistakenly rolled under with the flap still down. The aircraft dished, losing a hundred feet or so of height and, more by luck than good judgement, I just managed to avoid the control tower. At low altitude there was little margin for error.

Display flying was tightly controlled in the RAF, but the display pilot's self-discipline and his ability to analyse his own performance were equally important. After all, the pilot was the man on the spot and he had to take appropriate action before the situation got out of hand. It was fine to appear as though one was having to pull out all the stops to recover from a vertical dive – indeed, that added to the thrill of the show – but it was foolish ever to allow oneself to be trapped in that position. Then again, a fractional loss of altitude during a hesitation roll might not be critical on the day, it might even go unnoticed by the crowd, but at low level, any unintentional loss of height was potentially dangerous.

I thoroughly enjoyed display flying in the Hunter, though I must confess it was physically exhausting. It was the element of risk – a sort of living on the edge – that probably appealed to me. Many of the squadron's ground crew also enjoyed being involved. There was no shortage of volunteers to prepare my aircraft, and one particularly amiable giant made sure he was always on hand to assist with strapping me in.

In August, an all-ranks party was organised at a local working men's club, and I was treated to a different version of 'It's not you, sir, it's all the other orficers I 'ate'. I was pinned in a corner by one beer-sodden character poking me in the chest. 'The other orficers are alright, sir. Wot the 'ells up with you?' They were a great bunch of fellows though. At the same party a happily sozzled young airman fell down the stairs, knocking himself out. We called for an ambulance and packed him off to the local hospital with two of his mates.

As we watched the ambulance drive off, a rabble rouser in a flat cap launched into a long diatribe about how the officers always abandoned their men when things went wrong. I thought that was out of order, and suggested that he should mind his own business. He was all set to pursue the argument by more physical means, when a large hand gently eased me aside and the owner (I think it was one of our armourers) politely enquired, 'Shall I hit 'im now or later, sir?' Before I had time to answer, the flat-capped gent had turned smartly about and was scuttling up the road.

In September the officers were hosts at a 66 Squadron reunion in the RAF Club in London. This was an opportunity for ex-members of the squadron to get together, dine, have a few drinks and reminisce. We knew most of the Hunter pilots but on this occasion an old-timer, Wing Commander Maud, who had served on Sixty-Six in 1918, told us the fascinating tale about the time Lieutenant Alan Jerrard won the Victoria Cross. The squadron had been deployed to Italy, and Maud was sharing a billet with Jerrard. The morning of 30 March 1918 dawned cold and foggy. Jerrard, who had got up late following a party in the mess, borrowed Maud's tunic before taking off on the first patrol in a formation of Sopwith Camels. It was on this patrol that Jerrard shot down three Austrian aircraft, for which he was subsequently decorated, before being shot down himself. He spent the remainder of the war in a prison camp.

On 1 April 1918 a note signed by Jerrard and addressed to No. 66 Squadron was dropped on the airfield by an Austrian aircraft: 'Please send my own tunic,' with a postscript, 'Also some tobacco and some tennis balls. I am playing tennis with the Austrians.' The items mentioned in the note were acquired with some difficulty – tennis balls were in short supply at the time – but a suitable parcel was eventually made up and delivered by air, in the same way as the original note.

Nothing more was heard until the armistice, when Jerrard returned to the squadron. He thanked the CO for sending his tunic but he had been surprised to receive the tennis balls and tobacco, since he neither smoked, nor played tennis. The truth of the matter finally came out: Jerrard had asked Linkey Crawford and his brother to deliver the note to 66 Squadron. The two Crawfords were Austrian fighter aces at the time, and both were keen tennis players. Linkey had added his own shopping list to Jerrard's note. Unfortunately the day after Linkey delivered the note he was killed in a dogfight, so the tobacco and tennis balls were never claimed.

In October the boss recommended me for a permanent commission, and I was called forward for an interview with the AOC. I had been promoted to flight lieutenant in July, having belatedly passed the required promotion examination, and with the boss's support the result of the interview was almost a foregone conclusion. I was only too pleased to commit myself to serve until the age of 55; I had even invested in a formal mess kit.

On 23 October the squadron deployed with ten aircraft to El Adem, for Exercise Sambar. The deployment was intended to be completed in one day, but we were behind schedule and elected to stay the night at Luqa. Dickie Dicken, who had served as an NCO pilot on squadrons in the Middle East and claimed that he knew all the best night spots, kindly offered to show us around Valetta. According to Dickie, Valetta consisted of 'Straight Street' and 'The Gut'. Fortunately the Fleet was not in port and the ladies of the night were desperate for attention. 'Welcome, you air-force boys in blue khaki, big cock, two watches and no money . . .'

After numerous doubtful invitations, we wandered into the Egyptian Queen and were immediately surrounded by a host of diminutive bar girls. The drill was to buy the girls a drink – a bright green concoction – with each round. The girls received commission on the number of drinks they sold. We had to leave when 'Fingers' Jennings showed signs of falling in love. Our next port of call was the New Life – same deal, different girls – but here there was an added twist. Susie was eight months pregnant and the other girls were doing their bit to support her while she was temporarily inconvenienced. An extra drink for Susie had to be included in each round – which was a small enough price to pay, for when Susie sat on your lap you were getting two for the price of one, so to speak. But Ian Thomson, being a canny Scot, refused to subsidise Susie and was set upon by the lady in question. The squadron retreated after thirty minutes or so of good-natured banter, but the captain came within an ace of losing all he held dear when they were grabbed from behind by one of the girls.

That was about all we saw of Valetta's night-life. Unfortunately, the Sparrow – according to Dickie, Malta's hostess with the mostest – had married an American sailor and gone to live in the States. As the taxi driver said, the town was dead without the Navy.

The following day, during my pre-flight inspection, I found a broken bracket in the starboard wheel well, and my departure for the final leg was delayed for twenty-four hours. We expected El Adem to be dry – Dickie told us it never rained in the desert in October – so an extra supply of water was included in the aircraft survival packs, just in case we had to bail out. But the gods must have been laughing. Within two days, the heavens opened and dumped five years' worth of rainfall on the airfield. The deluge uncovered anti-tank mines that had been buried since World War II, and washed great quantities of sand across taxi tracks and runways, putting the airfield out of action for forty-eight hours.

Most of us took the opportunity to visit Tobruk. It was a squalid little town. The shacks alongside the road were made from flattened five-gallon jerrycans, while away in the distance we could occasionally see the black tents of the Bedu. It was a desolate country, a land of extremes – from the abject poverty of the streets to the opulence of the King's Palace. The peaceful order of the British and Italian cemeteries contrasted sharply with the noisy squalor of the Arab souk.

Back at El Adem, Exercise Sambar never really got off the ground, and the squadron returned to Acklington on 28 October.

On 23 December, just as the squadron was about to stand down, a formation of four Hunters from 43 Squadron flew over and dropped a shower of toy rattlesnakes on the airfield – Christmas greetings with a difference. One had to admire their spirit, but I doubt that the 'Fighting Cocks' had properly thought it through. The boss immediately advised air traffic control that one of the snakes appeared to have gone down the intake of the No. 4 aircraft. The formation leader was informed and, since he could not afford to ignore such a warning, No. 4 was ordered to land at Acklington. Needless to say, the unfortunate pilot – Chris Golds – was given a warm reception, with an ambulance, stretcher and a yard of lemonade to quench his thirst. Chris was sent on his way in a suitably zapped aircraft, with a silver cup from Woolworths inscribed, 'To the World's Biggest Charlie'. OC 43 Squadron took it very badly.

Dick Bruce and I stayed at Acklington over the Christmas grant. With just four days off it was not worth travelling south. But there was no shortage of hospitality. The year closed with a Vamps and Tramps Ball in the mess, and to keep the pot boiling, on 2 January Anne and Dickie Dicken threw a party in their quarter. It was a simple question of topping up the alcohol content. The Captain chatted up the girls and dispensed liberal quantities of his love potion cocktails. Quite early in the evening a rotund air traffic controller by the name of George Preston nosedived into a corner while attempting to stub out a cigarette. He would have stayed there all night had not some of his friends noticed an uncharacteristic lack of conversation. But it was only a temporary reprieve: George was found next morning, fast asleep behind the settee. One of the girls lost her sweater during a treasure hunt, and shortly thereafter the wives debagged Captain Bruce. Whether the two incidents were connected it was difficult to say, but it certainly didn't slow the captain down. Displaying patriotic Stars-and-Stripes boxer shorts, he coolly observed that his love potions seemed to be working. I woke up at one stage with Daisy Thomson coaching me in broad Scots, 'It's a braw bricht moonlicht nicht the nicht.' Aye, Daisy, it was that. The boss spent most of the evening wearing Anne Dicken's pink lace-up corsets, which were found next morning hanging from a tree in the garden. The party folded at four a.m. Fortunately New Year's Day was a stand-down.

The first weeks of January were taken up with preparations for a squadron detachment to RAF Akrotiri in Cyprus. I was given the task of leading a mixed formation of three aircraft – the Hunter T7, a Meteor T7 and a Meteor F8 – on the deployment. It was an interesting exercise. We flew a couple of trial long-range cross-country sorties around the UK. Fuel was not really a problem, but we obviously had to fly at the best range speed for the Meteors and at a fairly low altitude – in the order of 25,000 ft – because the Meteor's cockpits were unpressurised. The planned route was the standard – Orange Caritat, Luqa (for a night stop), El Adem, Akrotiri. According to the boss, French cuisine was not to be trusted, and we should be careful over the choice of lunch at Orange. As a perk, Chief Technician Roberts came with me in the right-hand seat of the Hunter T7 and Pete Gatrell flew in the back seat of the Meteor T7 with Dickie Dicken. We took off at 0900 on 12 January, and landed two hours later at Orange in brilliant sunshine. We had planned on having a leisurely lunch in the balmy south of France, but we had not taken into account the icy mistral, which was blasting in from the north. Despite the sun, the outside air temperature was several degrees below zero.

In the next hour the wind increased to 60 knots, blowing directly across the runway which was well above the Hunter's cross-wind limits for take-off. We were effectively grounded for the next four days. On the first night, the temperature dropped to a chilly –10°C, with a light dusting of snow. Blasted by the high winds, the aircraft had migrated into one corner of the dispersal, where they huddled together in an intricate jigsaw of machinery. Incredibly, there was no damage. Everyone turned out the following morning swathed in blankets or anything else we could find to keep warm, to secure the planes.

It was simply a question of waiting for the weather to improve. 'John' Dickin, the squadron's resident card-sharp, produced a deck of cards and it was eyes down for poker. John was something of an expert when it came to poker, and it was best to fold early when he was on a winning streak. On the other hand the boss, who could be read like a book at the card table, was not easily intimidated. During our second session at the table he raised the ante – obviously he had a good hand – and most of us got out. Only John Dickin hung in there. After much raising and counter-raising, John paid to see the boss's hand. A full house – queens on tens – which was good. The Boss reached for the pot, but his hand was not quite good enough to beat John Dickin's four jacks. In one fell swoop the boss had lost the entire stake he had set aside for the whole detachment. I swear the air temperature dropped another ten degrees.

On 14 January our hosts laid on a bus to take us to a local Chateauneuf-du-Pape wine cave. The proprietor had the right idea when he greeted us with a stack of balloon wine glasses. We sampled every vintage back to 1927. As Ian Madelin observed, they were all good, and the last one tasted even better than the first. We offered to sell our Gallic friend a Hunter, and he gave us two dust-encrusted bottles of ancient wine to go with our dinner. Fortunately, we didn't complete the Hunter deal – the ancient wine was corked and tasted like vinegar. Still, the food in the transit mess at Orange was excellent, and there were no complaints from the squadron's groundcrew.

The Beverley, which carried them and all our baggage, was stranded for four days at Nice Airport. Before leaving we had a whip-round for the mess staff at Orange. They seemed quite touched, and lined up to wave *au revoir* to us on 16 January.

Pete Gatrell got the bends *en route* to Luqa. Basically the condition is similar to the bends suffered by marine divers when they come up too fast, due to the release of nitrogen bubbles in the bloodstream, and was a fairly common occurrence in an unpressurised cockpit. Fortunately, in the case of flying, the bends seldom cause permanent damage, but as Pete was experiencing some pain I set up a long, slow cruise descent into Malta.

The squadron eventually arrived at Akrotiri on 17 January, and twenty minutes after landing the first two Hunters were armed and placed on standby.

The Cyprus detachment was an outstanding success. Morale was high, the weather was superb, and we easily achieved the flying target and took the opportunity to practise some of the skills more usually associated with ground attack. Air-to-ground gunnery and rocketing with the vintage three-inch rocket – affectionately known as the three-inch drain, on account of its slow acceleration and horrendous gravity drop. We made mock attacks on military targets using an air contact team – the forerunner of forward air controllers (FAC). The squadron was also included in the programme to welcome the commanding general of the Turkish Air Force – General Ariburum – to Akrotiri, and I had to provide some out-of-season solo aerobatic displays.

The social life at Akrotiri was slow, until the boss took the initiative and invited all resident officers and their ladies to a squadron party in the mess. Two hundred guests turned up. Fortunately the booze was fairly cheap – although most of the guests were legless after two glasses of a special cocktail mixed by Officers Sutton and Dickin. The squadron party marked a watershed: from then on we seldom had an evening to spare. One of the most memorable occasions was a cocktail party held at the Cape Gata mess, when two pilots commandeered a large diesel roller and left it in the car park. The same thing happened to a bulldozer some days later, when the boss indulged in a little unsolicited landscaping. Then the nurses got in on the act and threw their own party for Sixty-Six. Captain Bruce demonstrated his skill on the dance floor by performing what someone unkindly described as the King Penguin Stomp, and I fell asleep in a flower bed.

On 20 February the squadron launched ten Hunters in support of a flypast to celebrate the birth of His Royal Highness Prince Andrew. Only six Hunters were involved with the formation, with six Canberras from Akrotiri. After showing the flag the boss led a tail chase with all ten Hunters over the air headquarters at Episkopi. Numbers nine and ten swapped positions over the top of the final loop, which was not part of the brief but no one seemed to notice. On the strength of the squadron's showing, we were all invited to dine in the mess at RAF Episcopi.

Sadly, I had to return to the UK on 27 February, to attend the Day Fighter Combat School at RAF West Raynham. The DFCS course, which covered the whole spectrum of fighter operations, was a prerequisite for being appointed flight commander on any fighter squadron. Much emphasis was placed on leadership in the air, and most of the sorties involved simulated air combat.

In March the squadron arranged to fly me back to Acklington for the boss's dining-out night; Captain Bruce was also being dined out. We were sad to see them go, but that was RAF life. Squadron Leader Pete Pledger took over as CO on 1 April. On 4 April the commander-in-chief Fighter Command sent a letter congratulating No. 66 Squadron on its superb record for the past year. In the next post, a second letter arrived informing the new boss that his squadron would be disbanded by December 1960: RAF Acklington was due to close as a fighter airfield and, since squadrons were still being disbanded in accordance with the Sandys White Paper, the Air Ministry had decided to kill two birds with one stone. It was difficult to argue with the logic of the decision, but it marked the end of Sixty-Six as a fighter squadron.

In the meantime I was having to concentrate on the finer points of the DFCS course. The Hunters were painted with distinctive red or yellow tail fins, the theory being that we could thereby distinguish between friend and foe in any set-piece air combat engagement. In practice, the distinctive markings ensured that every pilot in Fighter Command recognised DFCS aircraft, and we were considered to be fair game. Nor was this gratuitous opposition left purely to chance. Details of our targets and routes had been phoned through to other fighter squadrons before the student-led formations had actually taken off. It was quite usual to see defensive fighters swarming around the target from some distance away, but we were not permitted to vary our time on target. The chances of getting through unscathed were nil.

On one occasion I evened up the odds by agreeing with the other student members of my formation outside the briefing that, instead of passively sitting there, we would take the initiative. At an agreed signal, Nos 3 and 4 would break away and attack the welcoming committee. It was all done maintaining radio silence, and the plan was extremely successful. The opposing fighters scattered in disarray, leaving the way clear for me and my wingman to attack the target. Nos 3 and 4 followed us in. Of course, the permanent staff, who had no prior knowledge of my plan, cried foul – students on DFCS were not supposed to win.

The final sortie was a fighter escort sweep to RAF Gutersloh in West Germany. Four Javelins from the all-weather fighter course acted as the bomber formation, and eight Hunters, led by yours truly, provided the fighter escort. Dutch, Belgian and RAF Germany squadrons provided the opposition. The rendezvous with the Javelins went as planned, except that one extra aircraft – a Hunter with Belgian markings – attempted to join up with the formation. We were still over Norfolk at the time. The 'bogey' was quickly disposed of, but from then on the outbound flight was one long continuous dogfight. My ciné film showed that I had tracked ten different aircraft in the gunsight, and other members of the fighter escort made similar claims. The claims were hardly realistic – the Hunter only carried eight seconds' worth of ammunition – but as I pointed out, when one was only shooting ciné film, the fellow in front was not to know the state of the ammunition. In any case it was better to have one's adversary in the gunsight than the other way around.

We graduated on 3 June 1960. I had enjoyed the DFCS experience, but it was a relief to get back to routine flying at Acklington, even if it was only to be for a matter of weeks.

Despite its uncertain future, Sixty-Six was in good spirits. As always, the threat of a ground tour loomed large with the pilots, but those who already knew their next posting were reasonably satisfied. I had over 1000 hours on the Hunter, but now it seemed appropriate to move on. The Hunter was beginning to show its age as an interceptor, and many of the bomber aircraft currently in service, even the jet transports then being introduced, could fly beyond the reach of a simple gun-armed fighter. Of course, the Hunter was still supreme at low altitude and was much in demand in the ground-attack role. Many of the Hunter F6s were being converted to fighter/ground attack – Hunter FGA 9s – but that was not really my preferred option. Besides, the English Electric Lightning was about to enter service, and I rather fancied my chances. I had actually been nominating the Lightning as my first preference since RAF Germany days. I was therefore delighted when my posting came through to take over a flight on No. 111 Squadron. Treble One had a unique reputation as the RAF's premier Hunter aerobatic display team – the Black Arrows – but the squadron was due to be re-equipped with the Lightning. Before that, I was ordered to spend six months on the Air Fighting Development Squadron (AFDS) at RAF Coltishall, participating in the Lightning acceptance trials.

I departed from Acklington on 16 July with mixed emotions. I had learned a great deal over the previous two years. No. 66 Squadron had been a happy combination of the right people in the right place at the right time. Peter Bairsto would be the first to admit that he had a good team working for him, but then he was a brilliantly successful commander. Even those who disapproved of his methods assumed a similar style of leadership when they eventually achieved command. Subsequently, Peter Bairsto, Ken Hayr, John Sutton and John Walker all reached air rank and all received knighthoods.

No. 66 Squadron disbanded on 30 September 1960. It reformed again in 1963, equipped with Bristol Belvedere helicopters. Pete Pledger went on to command another Hunter squadron.

7
Trials flying, Flight Commander on No. 111 Squadron (Lightning)

Initial design studies for the English Electric P1 – the prototype of the Lightning – started in 1948. The previous year, Colonel Chuck Yeager, USAF, flying an experimental rocket-propelled aircraft, the Bell X-1, had exceeded the speed of sound. The Bell X-1 had very thin, straight wings, but research data on the behaviour of the airflow at or beyond the so-called sound barrier was very limited. This was still a high-risk area.

Taking note of work done by German aerodynamicists during the war, the design team at English Electric opted for highly swept-back wings and tailplane. The P1's wing section was a compromise: thin enough to reduce drag at high speed to a minimum, but also capable of producing sufficient lift at low speed to give a good take-off and landing performance. Unlike previous conventional designs, the P1 had no separate elevator; the complete horizontal tailplane (or stabiliser) was pivoted to provide an extremely powerful pitch control. Opinion was divided as to the best position for the horizontal stabiliser. Experts at RAE Farnborough believed that it should be mounted high on top of the fin, clear of any disturbed airflow from the wings. This high-tail option was adopted for a number of contemporary aircraft designs – it had certain advantages – but many of these aircraft proved to be unstable at low speed. In contrast, English Electric mounted the P1's tailplane low on the fuselage – below the level of the wings. It was a wise decision. The P1, and in due course the Lightning, were highly manoeuvrable and remarkably stable throughout the speed range.

The P1 first flew on 4 August 1954, with Wing Commander R. P. Beamont at the controls. It was immediately apparent that the aircraft had exceptional potential. Three years later the design standard for the Lightning F1 was finalised. The Lightning was fitted with Rolls-

Royce Avon 210 engines with variable staged reheat. Reheat, or afterburner as it was known in America, was the burning of raw fuel in the jet pipe to produce extra thrust. The total thrust available on the Lightning F1, with full reheat selected, was 29,000 lb. Since the aircraft, fully loaded with fuel and weapons, weighed only 34,000 lb, its power-to-weight ratio was far better than any previous British fighter. In just ten years, English Electric had recovered the ground lost during the late forties, as a result of the government's moratorium on research into high-speed flight.

I reported to the Air Fighting Development Squadron (AFDS) at RAF Coltishall in mid-July 1960. No. 74 Squadron, the resident front-line squadron and the first to re-equip with the Lightning, was due to receive its aircraft in August. But the AFDS – the trials unit responsible for developing new fighter tactics and for the operational evaluation of armament – had already taken delivery of four Lightning F1s. The Lightning presented a major challenge. It was the RAF's first supersonic, night/all-weather interceptor. In speed alone it doubled the performance of the Hunter. But more than that – with its combination of AI 23 (airborne interception radar) and Firestreak air-to-air guided weapons – the Lightning had a genuine interception capability against high-performance bomber aircraft. The F1 was also fitted with two 30 mm Aden cannon, mounted at shoulder level aft of the cockpit. Alternative weapons packs, consisting of additional guns or unguided air-to-air rockets, could be fitted in place of Firestreaks. At that time opinion within Fighter Command was sharply divided as to the need for gun armament on modern fighters. Missile aficionados claimed that only guided missiles would be effective in future air combat, while those who supported the gun – rightly, in my opinion – insisted that it was still the best short-range, multi-shot weapon available. But for the time being, the main thrust of the Lightning weapons development was limited to the Firestreak.

With the introduction of the Lightning, air defence was at last being given an appropriate degree of priority. Many fighter experts thought this was long overdue.

My Lightning conversion on the AFDS was a one-off case. First I had to attend the Aeromedical Training Centre at RAF Upwood to be fitted with the necessary high-altitude partial-pressure clothing; the

Lightning could easily exceed 60,000 ft, which fully justified specialist equipment. Much research had been done on the medical aspects of flight at high altitude. As a general rule, the cockpits of modern military aircraft were pressurised to a nominal maximum of 25,000 ft. But the pilot also needed protection in case of pressurisation failure. The simple pressure-demand oxygen system fitted to the Hunter gave protection up to 45,000 ft. Above this altitude, even breathing pure oxygen, the partial pressure available to the lungs was insufficient to sustain consciousness – even for an emergency descent. For adequate protection, oxygen had to be delivered at increased pressure. This pressure breathing effectively reversed the normal pattern of respiration: oxygen was forced into the lungs and a conscious effort was needed to exhale.

In the Lightning, external support for the pilot's body was provided by a combination of the g-suit and a partial-pressure jerkin. The g-suit was similar to that used in the Hunter, but in the Lightning it also served as the lower half of a partial-pressure garment, while an inflatable jerkin, which balanced the increased oxygen pressure, gave protection to the chest and trunk. The wearing of an air ventilated suit to combat heat stress was optional. I was fitted with the latest type of protective helmet and a 'P' type oxygen mask. On the Lightning, to simplify strapping-in procedures, all connections between the pilot and the aircraft were achieved through a single personal equipment connector which mated with the ejection seat. Finally I was measured for a Taylor helmet – a close-fitting helmet and collar – to protect my head and neck, enabling pressure breathing above 56,000 ft. Now I could begin practical training.

I remember being strapped like a helpless blue beetle in an ejection seat rig, with sensors attached to wrists and ankles, recording my pulse and blood pressure while breathing against ever-increasing oxygen pressures. A positive pressure of 20 millimetres of mercury caused minimum problems, but as the pressure increased, so did the discomfort. At 80 millimetres (equivalent to 1.5 lb p.s.i.) – the maximum pressure bearable without the Taylor helmet – my eyes felt as though they were about to pop out of their sockets and the veins on the back of my hands stood out like knotted purple cords.

One of the known side-effects of pressure breathing is to develop a raging thirst – which was no problem for any self-respecting fighter pilot, but for three days, the combination of pressure breathing and drinking to slake one's thirst was an exhausting process. Then it was into the chamber for an explosive decompression – from a simulated 22,000 ft to 56,000 ft in three seconds. The equipment performed well, but it was a relief when the chamber run was over.

On the way back from Upwood I dropped in to see Claire. She was spending the summer season with a repertory company at Great Yarmouth, not far from Coltishall. We went out to dinner, and she was still bubbling with enthusiasm for the theatre.

Back at Coltishall I spent eleven hours in the simulator before flying my first Lightning sortie. There was no dual Lightning, so the first flight was also a first solo and thus it was very exciting. Even at idling power I had to ride the brakes to curb the acceleration. The main tyre pressures were a rock-hard 350 lb p.s.i., but the long-stroke undercarriage smoothed out the bumps. In the Lightning F1, it was not necessary to use reheat for take-off; even in cold power, nose wheel lift-off at 150 knots occurred well within ten seconds of brake release. As one wag on 74 Squadron was later heard to comment, 'I was with it all the way, until I released the brakes on take-off.'

Once airborne, the critical speeds were not much different from the Hunter. But the acceleration was much faster and I had my work cut out to stay ahead. Care was needed not to exceed the undercarriage limit of 250 knots, but with the undercarriage retracted and with full reheat applied for a maximum-rate climb, the Lightning really lifted its skirts. The initial rate of climb was in the order of 50,000 ft per minute, at an angle of 65°. This would hold the speed at 450 kts, until converting to Mach 0.9 at about 13,000 ft. (Many pilots, on their first Lightning sortie, did not transfer quickly enough to the Mach meter and found themselves surging up through 18,000 ft at speeds well in excess of Mach 1.0.)

The Lightning was very positive on the controls throughout the speed range. After an action-packed thirty minutes at altitude, it was time for the recovery. With the tactical air navigation equipment (TACAN) it was possible to self-navigate back to the airfield, even in bad weather, without assistance from ground control.

The Lightning was remarkably docile at low speed, although the circuit was marginally wider than I had been accustomed to in the Hunter, and the touchdown at 165 knots was noticeably quicker. Once on the ground, the nose wheel had to be positively lowered on to the runway to make room for the brake parachute to deploy from beneath the tail. In the event of brake parachute failure, the standard procedure was to overshoot but, as I gained experience, this kneejerk reaction seemed to be questionable. In theory it was better to avoid having to make a time-critical decision, but there were occasions – for example bad weather or a critical fuel state – when launching back into the air was definitely unwise. In my opinion the decision on whether or not to overshoot was best made at the time, although I usually preferred to stay down. In fact, brake parachute failures were comparatively rare.

The Lightning F1 was extremely short range, and a jettisonable ventral tank carrying an additional 2000 lb of fuel was fitted as standard. Even then the total fuel capacity was only 7500 lb. To put this into perspective, although the Lightning could cruise economically at altitude, consuming a meagre 60 lb of fuel a minute, with full reheat its consumption increased tenfold to 600 lb a minute. The actual transition to supersonic flight was hardly noticeable, but having effortlessly slipped through to Mach 1.3 the Lightning was clearly in its element. On one occasion I was asked to determine the maximum sustainable rate of turn at Mach 1.3, at 36,000 ft, with full reheat selected. I found it difficult to hold the speed down to Mach 1.3 even with 80° of bank applied and increasing g. Obviously this sort of performance could be used to advantage in visual conditions, but it was hardly the sort of manoeuvre a pilot would wish to employ on a dark night with his head buried in the AI radar scope.

The Lightning was superbly agile throughout the speed range. Due to its small fin the F1 was limited to Mach 1.6, but the aircraft was clearly capable of higher speeds, maybe even Mach 2.0. These factors changed many preconceived ideas on fighter tactics.

The Lightning team on the AFDS consisted of the CO – Wing Commander David Simmonds – and Squadron Leaders Frank Babst and Peter Collins. I joined as an additional reserve pilot. My particular project was to report on the Lightning's navigation equipment. TACAN effectively combined radio compass bearings with distance measuring. For the first time the fighter pilot had available an easily interpreted fixing aid, with a theoretical range of 200 nautical miles from the ground-based beacon. The British equipment was pressurised, and for that reason it was claimed to be better than similar American kit. But it soon became apparent that the readings we were getting in the Lightning were wildly inaccurate. On stripping down the equipment the engineers found that the delicate electrical components were soaked in condensation – hardly surprising the readings were unreliable! But it was easily fixed.

By its very nature, trials flying called for a more measured and analytical approach than normal squadron training, and the engineering staff on the AFDS were also finding that the Lightning was difficult to keep serviceable. In four months I accumulated only twenty-three hours in the aircraft. Fortunately the AFDS also had Javelins, a Hunter F6 and a Meteor T7 available, so there was plenty for me to do. I even managed to remain in practice with my Hunter solo display. Of course the Lightning was the centre of attention at Coltishall, but a well-flown Hunter display could still attract an appreciative audience.

I had promised Acklington that I would return to do a Hunter show on their final Battle of Britain display and, with that in mind, I borrowed the AFDS Hunter. Sixty-Six, a shadow of its former self, was due to disband at the end of the month. To add to the gloom, on the day of the display, Acklington's weather was practically unflyable. A sad exit for one of the best squadrons in Fighter Command. I had to do some fast talking to persuade OC Ops that it was safe for me to take off for my second display commitment of the day, at Coltishall. I eventually took off intending to do a high-speed pass on the GCA, but I disappeared into cloud at 100 ft. Fortunately the weather at Coltishall was gin clear.

As the first RAF station to be equipped with the Lightning, the morale at Coltishall was sky high, and the mess provided a lively social centre. The Norfolk Broads are very attractive, with many historic inns; few officers at Coltishall will ever forget the best pint of draught Worthington E in Norfolk, served at the Fruiterer's Arms, just off the market square in Norwich. It was a hard-drinking, high-living, fast life.

The work on the AFDS was fascinating, but I was looking forward to starting my flight commander tour on 111 Squadron. I eventually reported to RAF Wattisham in mid-December 1960. The Wattisham wing consisted of three fighter squadrons: Nos 111 (Treble One) and 56 were both equipped with Hunters, but were due to re-equip with Lightnings, and No. 41 (F) Squadron was equipped with Javelin F9s. Treble One had been withdrawn from its formation aerobatic commitment in September and there had been an almost complete turnover of aircrew. Squadron Leader Dickie Wirdnam was the Commanding Officer, and a USAF exchange officer – Captain Harry De Laney – was the 'A' Flight Commander. I took over 'B' Flight.

The division of responsibilities between the flight commanders on Fighter Command squadrons was fairly flexible. Historically each flight had its own aircraft and handled its share of the operational commitments, but as the size of the squadrons reduced, the division into flights was retained mainly for administrative purposes. Some squadrons openly adopted the American system of having an operations officer responsible for operational commitments and exercises, and a training officer responsible for flying standards. Sixty-Six had adopted such a system in 1959. But the squadrons at Wattisham, although dividing responsibilities into operations and training, had retained the traditional flight commander titles.

There was a fair spread of experience among the pilots: only two of the original Black Arrows team – John Curry and Alan Cawsey – remained; the Squadron IRE was an itinerant New Zealander by the name of Jack O'Dowd, who had been transferred from Javelin night fighters. Most of the other pilots, including Ian Thomson, Bill Jago, Sam Lucas, Pete Ginger, Martin Bridge and Alan Garside, were ex Sixty-Six – so it was very much home from home for me. The squadron's Hunters were still painted gloss black, as they had been in the days of the Black Arrows. Of course, we looked forward to the arrival of the Lightnings, but in the meantime the Hunter was an excellent aircraft for whipping the squadron into shape.

It was a pleasure to get back to normal flying and the camaraderie of squadron life. Dickie Wirdnam was a man after my own heart who considered the monthly flying target to be the absolute minimum. In addition to the standard air defence training, we practised low-level ground attack and air-to-ground strafing. Air-to-ground gunnery was a uniquely satisfying exercise – unlike air firing against the flag, the pilot could see the fall of shot and make appropriate correction on his next attack. The scores were usually higher than for air-to-air gunnery. I scored a 36% and 55% on my first two shoots, which was about average.

We finished the phase with an operational shoot-off at high altitude, which consisted of firing off a full load of ammunition from each aircraft, followed by an operational turn-round. In each one-second burst, the recoil of the four Aden cannon reduced the Hunter's airspeed by 10 kts.

In March, flying with Jack O'Dowd, I qualified for my Master Green instrument rating in the Hunter T7.

Wattisham was sufficiently remote for the mess to be the natural centre of the squadron's social life, but London was within striking distance for the odd bachelor weekend. A room at the RAF Club in Piccadilly was relatively inexpensive and drink was fairly cheap at faded clubs such as the Gremlin, or the Pathfinder, where one could swap stories with like-minded air force types. Go-karting was a favourite weekend pastime at Wattisham. It was strangely exciting to roar around a twisting track on a vehicle with no springs, with less than three inches between one's seat and hard concrete. Being lightweight, I had a significant advantage, until the wives joined in – then there was no stopping them. It was difficult to fall out of a go-kart, although I managed to do just that on a couple of occasions. The first time I wound up in hospital with tarmac ingrained in my left ankle, the second was even more embarrassing, when the go-kart continued unguided across 200 yards of concrete and smashed into my own car. Whilst at Coltishall, I had exchanged my BMW 501 for a brand new (but much inferior) Ford Anglia. It was my first new car and it seemed a wise investment.

The service policy on marriage had not changed, but a higher proportion of officers at Wattisham were either married or had plans in that direction. Those not yet promised bought themselves sports cars and toured the pubs hoping to score with the local talent. We seldom succeeded, of course, but that was all part of the game. Needless to say, compared to the other exotic machinery on show at Wattisham, the little Ford Anglia didn't do much for my image. Especially after the go-kart incident.

No. 56 Squadron received its Lightning aircraft in December 1960, and Treble One's first Lightning F1A – XM185 – was delivered in March 1961. The F1A's performance was similar to the aircraft at Coltishall, but it had several worthwhile refinements. Instead of two ten-channel VHF radios, the F1A was fitted with the latest UHF radio with nineteen preset channels, and with nearly two thousand manually dialled frequencies available. Another valuable addition was a rain-removal system: hot air tapped from the engines could be blown in front of the windscreen to keep it clear of precipitation. The F1A also had the necessary plumbing for flight refuelling, although refuelling probes were not fitted to our aircraft until February 1963.

The black livery of our Hunters was inappropriate for the Lightning, so we had to redesign the squadron markings. There were several suggestions, but my proposal for a stylised bolt of black lightning outlined in yellow was eventually chosen for the fuselage. The boss decided that the motif on the fin, consisting of crossed swords and seaxes superimposed on a yellow Cross of Jerusalem, should be copied from the official squadron badge. As a matter of interest, up to the time of writing, the black lightning flash has since remained in continuous use as a standard marking on all Treble-One aircraft.

The squadron's re-equipment was a long, slow business. Lightning aircraft were delivered at the rate of one a week, so it was mid-July before we reached our full complement of twelve aircraft. The re-equipment was not helped by the loss of XM185 on 28 June. Following a services hydraulic failure, Pete Ginger was unable to lower the undercarriage and, since a wheels-up landing was definitely not recommended, he had no choice other than to bail out. The mark 4BS seat was capable of safe ejection from ground level at 90 kts, but Pete wisely decided to climb to 8000 ft before making a copybook ejection. A few moments later, hanging in his parachute, he was pleased to see that one of the chaps had come to see if he was OK. The pilot seemed to be cutting things a bit fine, though – in fact he was going to pass uncomfortably close. Pete then noticed that the passing aircraft had no cockpit canopy and no pilot – it was the aircraft he had just abandoned. After three more close encounters with XM185, Pete finally landed. His aircraft eventually crashed in a field near Lavenham.

That evening, a group of squadron pilots was having a drink in the

Swan when they overheard one of the local farmhands shooting an incredible line about dropping tools and running to avoid this aircraft before it crashed on top of him. It seemed an unlikely tale, but it was good enough to keep him in free beer for the rest of the evening. Some days later, the RAF salvage team dug up the ventral tank, which marked XM185's first contact with terra firma, to reveal the farmhand's hoe buried beneath it.

For the average pilot, the workup syllabus consisting of twenty-six sorties (about twenty-two hours' flying) presented little difficulty – the Lightning was basically easy to fly. But to apply the aircraft in its role as a supersonic all-weather fighter was a demanding new skill requiring considerable manual dexterity and fast mental reaction. The Firestreak was a heat-seeking missile which could only home on to the hot metal of a jet pipe; we were therefore still committed to rear hemisphere attacks. In common with other AI radars, AI 23's cockpit presentation was a 'B' scope display. Without going into confusing detail, the area of sky swept by the AI radar was electronically modified and presented on a rectangular screen. Using the 'B' scope, most targets flying a straight track would be represented by a curve on the screen. Indeed, if the target tracked in a straight line and the angle off remained constant, then the target was on a collision course. Interpretation of a 'B' scope was an acquired skill, and of course the Lightning pilot had to continue flying the aircraft, albeit with the assistance of the autopilot. In fact it was recognised that the workload in the Lightning, when used as an interceptor, either at night or in cloud, was extremely high.

The workup syllabus should have been completed in two months, but unfortunately the Lightnings were dogged by unserviceability. In those days, few Lightning pilots achieved more than eight hours a month, and many training sorties were rendered ineffective because of equipment failure. Of course, the ground crew also lacked experience with the aircraft, but this was by no means the sole cause of the problem. English Electric blamed the MoD for not making adequate manpower allowances for the increased servicing workload of a sophisticated aircraft. There was no doubt that the Lightning – which had been designed in accordance with 1950s engineering standards – required considerable effort to keep serviceable. On the other hand, the MoD could rightly accuse English Electric, or indeed every other aircraft manufacturer of the day, that too little effort had been made either to ease the servicing workload or to improve equipment reliability. Whatever the cause, the lack of serviceable aircraft resulted in the early Lightning squadrons taking six months or more to become operational. On later marks, aircraft serviceability improved but the Lightning continued to strain engineering resources. To those who flew it, the Lightning was an outstanding aircraft – a joy to fly – but the engineers were less enthusiastic. For them the Lightning generated a heavy servicing burden for every hour it spent in the air.

Fortunately, we were allowed to retain the Hunters until mid-July, which boosted our flying hours, and so I took the opportunity to maintain my solo display.

In June, I was one member of a three-man board of inquiry into a fire incident on an aircraft flown by Squadron Leader John Rogers – OC, No. 56 Squadron. The Lightning's fire and overheat warnings were displayed on a standard warning panel, which also triggered klaxon bells and flashing red attention-getters. There was never any question of missing a fire warning; in fact the pilot's first action was usually to cancel the klaxon bells before dealing with the emergency. Unfortunately the Lightning had gained a reputation for fire warnings, both real and spurious. The fire wire sensors, running through the engine bays and jet pipe areas, would detect any local increase in temperature, caused either by fire or simply by a hot gas leak. When the source of heat was removed, the warning light would extinguish and the system would automatically reset. Attempts to find the cause of a warning often disturbed the engines and, in the process, destroyed the evidence. But in John Rogers's incident the fire had reignited in dispersal, indicating a genuine fire rather than an illusive hot gas leak. An expert investigator from the accident investigation branch at RAE Farnborough eventually proved that excess fuel trapped on top of the ventral tank had been sucked back through fuselage drain-holes on to the hot jet pipe, causing an intense but fortunately brief fire. This positive finding did little to restore confidence in the Lightning's warning system, and we continued to experience fire warnings, often for no apparent reason.

In August Wattisham's runway was scheduled for repair, and the

Lightning squadrons were deployed to RAF Coltishall for two months – we benefited greatly from the concentration of Lightning knowhow at one location.

Soon after deployment, the boss detailed me to attempt a scramble from the ORP at the end of the runway, using the aircraft's internal batteries. The normal Lightning starting procedure utilised an external electrical supply, but this aircraft was cleared for battery starts and it was prudent to test the system in case we ever had to operate from an unsupported base. I strapped into XM186 before being towed out to the ORP. Jack O'Dowd, who was to lead the sortie, started as normal on the ASP. I planned to start my engines as he rolled on to the runway. The No. 1 engine started without difficulty and, since it was poor airmanship to drain the aircraft batteries unnecessarily, I brought the aircraft's generator on line before starting the No. 2 engine. I completed the entire start-up sequence and the post-start checks without difficulty, proving that the Lightning was well capable of meeting a two-minute standby commitment using internal power. The formation take-off was normal, and we went into cloud at 1300 ft. Four minutes later we burst into brilliant sunshine at 32,000 ft – a transformation only those who fly can regularly experience. After checking the IFF (identification friend or foe), which highlighted the aircraft's return on the GCI's radar, we separated for our first practice interception. Jack was to act as fighter on the first run. These were mutual unknown interceptions: as target, all I had to do was select a heading roughly reciprocal to that of the fighter and stay clear of cloud. We did this sort of exercise practically every day of the week. I usually attempted to follow the incoming fighter on my radar, but for some reason on this occasion my AI transmitter would not come on line. No matter – I picked up Jack visually at about eight miles, at one o'clock low. He had not managed to get sufficient lateral displacement for a normal interception, and had elected to salvage his attack by doing a short-range procedure. I remember he crossed two miles in front of me, belly-up in a steep turn. In theory, after completing his turn, he would pick me up again on his radar, nicely positioned for acquisition by his Firestreak missiles. But just as Jack crossed ahead, my No. 2 engine flamed out.

The cockpit went deceptively quiet. There were no startling attention-getters or mind-blowing klaxons – but something was seriously amiss. The No. 2 engine was rapidly unwinding. I attempted an immediate relight, but that failed. Both fuel gauges quickly ran down to below zero. I broke into a cold sweat; if lack of fuel was the problem then I would soon be making a Martin Baker letdown for a freezing – possibly fatal – dunking in the North Sea. Fortunately the No. 1 engine kept going, but I could not maintain height above cloud on one engine alone. Instinctively I turned back towards Coltishall and rolled the wings level on a heading of 180°, just as the aircraft sank into the murk. I remember thinking, Jack's going to have his work cut out finding me now. In the meantime I had my hands more than full with this previously unknown and certainly unpractised emergency.

The cockpit indications made little sense. It was fairly obvious that my aircraft had suffered a major electrical failure, but the only lights showing were the oil and hydraulic warnings associated with the flamed-out engine, and these were very dim. Both the main and standby radios appeared to be dead – although I was later informed that the emergency Mayday call I made on the international distress frequency was picked up by the GCI station. Problem was, no one could get through to me.

The Lightning's main flight instruments and most of the back-up instruments depended on electrical power, whether it be for gyro-stabilisation or simply to provide heat to keep the pressure sensors clear of ice. As successive 'off flags' flicked into view, the full implications of my predicament slowly dawned: I had to get clear of cloud before my instruments failed completely.

By 15,000 ft, still descending in cloud, my main and standby instruments had failed, and I was left with the small E2 magnetic compass and an unreliable airspeed indicator. Provided the pitot head didn't ice up I could control speed by fore and aft movements of the stick but, as any pilot faced with a similar situation will appreciate, the greatest hazard was the lack of roll information. Without a roll reference, the aircraft could easily overbank and enter an ever-steepening spiral dive. And if I did lose control in the prevailing weather conditions, there was not enough height for me to recover below cloud. Fortunately, it was possible to maintain roll control solely by reference to the E2 – it was a trick that I sometimes demonstrated during instrument rating tests. This time it would be put to the test. Briefly, on a heading of 180° a simple magnetic compass is extraordinarily sensitive to roll and will swing away from 180° – either towards east or west – immediately bank is applied. All I had to do was rock the aircraft from side to side, making sure the E2's mean heading remained close to 180°, and in theory I would never have more than five degrees of bank applied. The aircraft's stability augmentation system ceased to function at 10,000 ft – but that was the least of my problems.

I eventually broke out of cloud at 1000 ft, in a shallow dive above a cold, inhospitable North Sea. The visibility was less than three miles, although there was little to be seen – this was before the days of gas or oil rigs. Having safely made it down through the cloud I was now more concerned about fuel. Both gauges had been registering below zero since the start of the emergency. It was also possible that I was too far to the east and I might miss East Anglia altogether. If that was so, the next landfall would be the Belgian coast – although I doubted that I had sufficient fuel for that. For the second time during this emergency, ejection seemed a distinct possibility. I tightened the straps and put my stopwatch away in one of my leg pockets – which was a complete waste of time as the stopwatch would never survive a dunking. After what seemed an age, but was probably no more than five or six minutes, I caught sight of land dead ahead. It was Norfolk right enough, and I coasted in over Cromer golf course. From there it was a simple matter to map-read back to Coltishall for a radio out circuit and landing. The flight had lasted for just fifty minutes, but it seemed like a lifetime to me.

The engineers subsequently found that a fuse between the generators and the aircraft's main electrical circuits had ruptured, probably during engine start, leaving the aircraft batteries to supply all the electrical power. The Lightning's standard warning system, which relied on a reverse current through the generator supply line, could not cope with this type of failure. The batteries had eventually drained flat – the aircraft had effectively suffered a complete electrical failure – with no warning in the cockpit. In due course, the incident was reported in the Fighter Command *Flight Safety Review*. The *Review*'s editor exercised his discretion, and as a result his version and mine were rather different. According to the *Review* I had let down through a hole in the cloud – which was news to me – although to senior staff officers the editor's version was probably more acceptable than my E2 compass letdown. But I was awarded a Green Endorsement for my logbook.

Some weeks later Terry Carlton experienced a similar failure at night. Fortunately the weather was clear, but he had to fly the final approach holding a flashlight in his teeth.

The clearance for internal starts was temporarily withdrawn, and in due course a voltmeter, which continually measured the state of the aircraft batteries, was fitted in the cockpit.

The task of solo Lightning demonstrations at Wattisham naturally fell to No. 56 Squadron, and for the time being my display flying was limited to the Hunter T7. The right-hand seat was not usually occupied during low-level aerobatic displays – indeed the carriage of passengers was actively discouraged – but a dual demonstration was useful experience for any would-be display pilot. With this in mind, Flight Lieutenant 'Plucky' Manning from 56 Squadron asked if he could come along on one of my rehearsals. There was nothing worse than being thrown around in an aircraft at low level, with nothing to do and no control over one's fate, so I asked Plucky to do me a favour by timing the individual manoeuvres. My full Hunter show lasted seven minutes, but display organisers sometimes asked for items to be modified, so it was handy to know precise timings. Anyway, it seemed a reasonable task, and I thought it might take Plucky's mind off what was going on. I gave him my stopwatch, and after briefing him to keep his hands and feet clear of the controls we launched into the blue. After a quick practice at medium level, we rejoined the circuit for a rehearsal at low level. Plucky didn't say a lot, for which I was thankful, but I suspected that he was fairly tensed up. After all, it was unusual to indulge in aerobatics that close to the ground, and somewhat unnerving to be pointing vertically down at 1500 ft unless you knew there was plenty of room to pull out.

After the inverted break I asked Plucky if he had enjoyed it. 'Great,' he said.

Then I asked, 'What was the total time?'

Plucky unclenched his left fist to reveal a severely mangled stopwatch, with crushed glass and twisted hands. My service stopwatch was a write-off. Fortunately, I already knew enough about the timing, but it cost Plucky a few beers.

Mum and Dad brought my brother Ian to Coltishall for the Battle of Britain display on 16 September. It was their first and, as far as I know, only visit to an RAF flying station, and they seemed to enjoy themselves. There was a party in the mess afterwards, and Mother was well looked after. Everyone was anxious to buy her a drink, she seldom refused and she never had an empty glass. Mum would never let the side down. We later discovered that she was stacking the glasses behind a curtain.

When the time came to leave, Dad and I escorted her to the car. Mother happily walked in slow motion between us, which was not difficult, since her feet were not actually touching the ground.

The squadron returned to Wattisham on 16 October. For some reason which I cannot recall we were obliged to fly the Lightnings back with their undercarriages down. The boss decided to do a squadron flypast over Coltishall and Wattisham, just to show the flag. It should have been straightforward – after all, the distance between the two stations was less than fifty miles – but halfway back many of the aircraft were running short of fuel. Perhaps it was not a fair test – the Lightning was certainly not designed for this sort of thing – but it was a sharp reminder to one and all that the F1 was critically short of fuel. The Lightning's range was reasonable at high altitude, but after letting down to low level its airborne endurance was strictly limited. In the event of a sudden blockage of the runway, Lightning aircraft on recovery might have as little as five minutes in which to divert and land.

The problem was not new to us. In Fighter Command it was standard procedure always to nominate a so-called crash diversion within fifty nautical miles, to which aircraft could bolthole in emergency. The most suitable crash diversion airfields for Wattisham's aircraft were the USAF bases at Wethersfield, Bentwaters and Woodbridge, but the Americans were very reluctant to accept the commitment. It was not until we mounted a concerted hearts-and-minds campaign that we discovered the reason: the Americans thought that by nominating them as a crash diversion we would select their airfield as a suitable place to crash. As they said: 'If you guys know you are going to crash, why not do it on your own airfield?' It was explained that that was not the purpose of a crash diversion. And when they learned that our full fuel-load was only slightly more than their minimum recovery fuel, they were only too anxious to help.

Back at Wattisham the squadron settled down (although that was hardly an appropriate description) to routine training. With previous fighter aircraft the difference between the day and night roles was clearcut. Of course, the Lightning could fulfil both roles – but the squadrons did not have enough manpower to work round the clock. On the other hand, by extending the working day it was possible to compensate for poor aircraft serviceability. It was simply a question of finding the right balance. For the aircrew it was reasonably straightforward – maximum crew duty times were clearly defined, and we were not allowed to take off more than twelve hours after first reporting for duty. The squadron ran an early shift for day flying, and a separate night shift. Those pilots programmed to fly past midnight usually reported for duty at 1700 hours. The shifts changed over at the weekends.

The groundcrew was organised along similar lines, although their early shift started well before first take-off and the night shift finished well after last landing. In addition, a small rectification party worked on through the night to recover unserviceable aircraft. The squadron worked throughout one weekend in four.

It was a fairly exhausting routine, and it was difficult to acclimatise to the changing sleep patterns between night and day shifts. Despite all our efforts, the squadron seldom achieved the monthly target – but neither did any other Lightning squadron. At least those on night shift had the chance to improve their golf during the day. Jack O'Dowd and myself spent our spare time on the nine-hole course at Lavenham.

The Lightning squadrons had great difficulty finding enough supersonic targets. We usually had to employ other Lightning aircraft, which was far from ideal. But on one occasion we were tasked against a pair of F-105s transiting the North Sea between Holland and Norfolk, supposedly at Mach 1.3. The Lightning's supersonic attack profile was in many ways similar to a subsonic interception, although the aircraft's speed advantage and the pilot's reaction times were much reduced. Timing was critical: if we scrambled too early we would run out of fuel; on the other hand, if we scrambled too late we wouldn't catch the targets.

I was detailed to lead the first pair against the F-105s. The GCI gave a countdown on telebrief, and when the targets got to a predetermined range we were scrambled. I levelled at 36,000 ft and accelerated to Mach 1.4 – we were now closing on our targets at twenty-seven miles a minute. The maximum range on the AI 23 radar scope was just twenty-eight miles, which left little room for adjustment. As luck would have it, the targets appeared at twenty-five miles with ideal displacement to the left. I called 'Judy' – meaning I had control of the interception – and now it was simply a matter of turning hard left when the target was on the edge of my radar scope.

For some reason the target blips were not behaving as high-speed targets should; my attack was far too hot, and we were overtaking too quickly. As I rolled out behind the targets, the missile acquisition lights flickered on and were immediately followed by compulsory break-away signals. I pulled off to one side and watched as the other Lightnings hurtled by in disarray. The F-105s were actually cruising at a sedate Mach 0.85. I later discovered that they too had insufficient fuel for the planned high-speed dash.

Targets at extreme altitude were much more difficult to intercept. We were limited by our flying clothing, although the Lightning's actual ceiling was governed more by speed. At Mach 1.6 the F1A could zoom up above 60,000 ft. The highest I ever flew was 64,000 ft – twelve miles up – where the sky took on a distinctly darker shade of blue. On that occasion I topped out at Mach 1.1, although the indicated airspeed was only 200 knots – close to the theoretical stalling speed. All of this was fairly academic; the real limitation at very high altitude was the lack of manoeuvrability. The Lightning was superbly agile at 36,000 ft, but the controls were much less effective in the thin air above 50,000 ft. Above 60,000 ft it was virtually impossible to change the aircraft's flight path. Not that the Lightning would swap ends and fall out of control; it would just continue in a ballistic trajectory until it descended to thicker air.

Pete Ginger and Martin Bridge were tasked to fly trials sorties against a USAF U-2 reconnaissance aircraft flying at 65,000 ft. The U-2 pilot was most concerned that the Lightnings should not fly too close, in case their supersonic bow wave overstressed the U-2's wing. As a result of the trial it was concluded that the best technique would be to solve the geometry of the interception at 36,000 ft, rolling out four miles or so astern, then accelerate to Mach 1.6 and zoom climb to the point of missile launch. With Firestreak, this was probably the only method of shooting down a target at extreme altitude, but there was no room for error. And at night it would be impossible to identify the target before missile launch.

Towards the end of the year Brian Cheater got married to Sue, in Pinner, and the squadron officers were invited to attend. As a result, my own love life took a distinct turn for the better. Jean lived next door to Sue's parents, and we started dating. Sometimes, Jean would come to Ipswich by train and stay for the weekend with the Wirdnams. On other occasions I would drive down to see her in Pinner.

Jean was a passenger in my Anglia when the engine blew up. There was a loud bang and an awful clatter from the front end. Jean looked across with frightened eyes and asked, 'Is it dirty petrol?' If it was, the petrol was contaminated with rocks! Actually the drive for the overhead camshaft had sheared and had dropped into the timing mechanism. Sod's Law – it was the day after the guarantee on the car expired. I wrote to Ford explaining what had happened and suggested that, since the car was only just out of guarantee, they might see their way clear to contributing to the cost of repairs. They declined, of course, but soon after that I traded the Anglia in part exchange for a second-hand MGA hard-topped sports car, which was much more in keeping with my bachelor image.

In February 1962 I finally got my chance to work up a solo Lightning display. Les Swart of 56 Squadron and Ken Goodwin of the Lightning Conversion Squadron – who had provided demonstrations in 1961 – had moved on. No. 74 Squadron was still providing the formation aerobatic team, but the solo Lightning slot was now vacant. I always believed that solo demonstration flying required thorough professionalism. Any fool could beat up an airfield in a high-performance aircraft, but it needed practice and precise judgement to put together an impressive demonstration. For display purposes, the Lightning was much less physically demanding than the Hunter – the g limits, both positive and negative, were lower. In fact, at typical display speeds, the Lightning F1A's tailplane had insufficient authority to maintain level inverted flight. Negative-g aerobatic manoeuvres were just not practical; although if one started from very low level, with the nose above the horizon, it was still possible to fly the length of the runway inverted. On the other hand the Lightning's excess power was a distinct advantage. It was possible to rotate the aircraft and climb vertically immediately after take-off – though I seldom used that entry manoeuvre because a lower than expected cloud base could prove embarrassing. I preferred to turn 45° away from the crowd, giving them the benefit of thunderous noise and two fiery jet pipes, followed by a high wing-over, back into the display. By substituting sharp corners in place of the conventional smooth flight path, it was possible to do a square loop. In the Lightning you could descend vertically, with nose held high and with no apparent chance of recovery, until power was applied at the last moment and the aircraft abruptly changed direction. At 350 kts – an ideal display speed – the Lightning could be held in a level steep turn, balancing the induced drag against full power, and never exceed 5½ g. Using this technique, the aircraft appeared to be standing on its tail. It was possible to complete a noisy 360° orbit well within the airfield boundaries. I retained the Derry turn in my display sequence, even though I considered it to be one of the most critical manoeuvres. The harder the pilot pulled back on the stick, the lower the available rate of roll. I had learned while flying the Hunter that the safest technique for the Derry turn was to raise the nose slightly and unload the aircraft before rolling under to continue the turn. The slackening of turn was hardly noticeable from the ground, although one had to be slick on the throttles to get the best out of the Lightning. The Derry turn was not a difficult manoeuvre, although at the minimum base altitude of 500 ft it required co-ordination, and was very unforgiving of mistakes.

It was easy to impress people with the Lightning, but the show had to be repeatable. Maurice Williams, a potential Lightning display pilot on 74 Squadron, once lost control while attempting a Derry turn at 1500 ft over the airfield and flicked into a flat spin. Maurice immediately engaged reheat – there was usually a three-second delay before they lit up – and more by luck than good judgement Maurice just managed to recover control before hitting the ground. The aircraft was so low, the flames from the reheats set fire to the grass on the airfield.

On 7 June 1962, Bob Foulks and Bob Baker, both serving on 56

Squadron, were tragically killed while flying in Treble One's all-black Hunter T7. This was the first fatal accident at Wattisham for over two years, and they were buried with full military honours in the village cemetery. I was one of the pall-bearers. I had attended my share of funeral parties, and none had affected me deeply – that was the advantage of youth, it always happened to the other fellow. But I had known Bob Foulks since we had flown together on 67 Squadron at Bruggen. On the way back to the mess it suddenly struck me: if it can happen to a safe, reliable pilot like Bob, then perhaps it could actually happen to me. The same thought may have occurred to others, because the beer in the mess certainly flowed freely that evening.

Later that month our Lightnings were grounded for a re-work programme on the hydraulic system, to replace the light alloy pipes with stainless steel. It was an essential safety modification, but few welcomed the disruption. For the next three months we had to maintain our flying currency in Hunter T7s and Meteors.

I was more fortunate than most. This was the display season, and I was sometimes called upon to give shows in Lightning aircraft borrowed from other squadrons. The main display that year was to celebrate the fiftieth anniversary of flight, which took place at RAF Upavon on 16 June 1962. The Duke of Edinburgh attended the show. No. 74 Squadron's aerobatic team – the Tigers – was included in the programme, and I was called in at short notice to do a solo display in one of their aircraft. Upavon was a small grass airfield, so the Lightnings were based at Boscombe Down. It was an exhilarating challenge; the Lightning F1 was very like the F1A except that the throttles incorporated a piano-key arrangement for control of reheat, which could be tricky. I flew two rehearsals before the actual display and, by all accounts, the spectators were suitably impressed. After the show, Sam Lucas ferried me back to Wattisham in a Meteor T7.

By this time I was collecting modest fan mail. A gentleman, who obviously knew something about flying, wrote saying that, until he had witnessed my Lightning display at Stansted, he had been convinced the Spitfire was the last true fighter aircraft in service. I was quite pleased about that. Less accurate was the press release that appeared following my show at the American Armed Forces Day at Bentwaters, which reported that the star of the show was a British Lightning aircraft whose pilot had flown the complete display fully stalled. Of course it was not true, but one had to make allowances for the press. The thing I remember most about Bentwaters was Air Traffic Control requesting a USAF colonel leading a formation of thirty-six F-101s, who had just called joining in two minutes, to hold for thirty seconds. The leader of the formation could not possibly comply. In typically colourful language he suggested that Air Traffic Control should make alternative arrangements, because he was coming through on time.

Martin Bridge was due to leave the service at the end of August, and he also announced his intention to get married. He and Maggie had been helping to refurbish a trawler, aptly named *Harmony*, in which they planned to sail to New Zealand. The voyage would be their honeymoon. We all thought Martin was mad, but they had worked hard on the boat and were determined to see it through. Martin was appointed ship's navigator. *Harmony* cast off long before dawn on 7 September, and the boss led a four-plane formation to bid farewell as they cruised down the Channel; I flew in the No. 3 slot. It was the proverbial needle in a haystack. We had only two recognition features to work on: *Harmony* had a light-blue upper deck, and there were two Hunter drop tanks, carrying extra fuel, stored on the foredeck. We actually found *Harmony* more or less where Martin said they would be, and the whole crew waved as we went over. If they were surprised to see us, so too was a Silver City's Bristol freighter, cruising by above us *en route* to France. Martin later wrote to thank the boss for the send-off. Apparently, following our flypast, his standing with the rest of the crew dramatically improved.

September was a busy month. To mark the anniversary of the Battle of Britain I flew displays at Biggin Hill and Wyton. Then, on 18 September, I did a show at Wattisham for the first half of a Royal College of Defence Studies visit. The weather was poor, with a thick layer of haze reducing the horizontal visibility to less than a mile. But, as is so often the case in fog, the vertical visibility was better and I managed to do a complete display. The spectators were hard pressed to keep sight of the Lightning. I landed from a high visual circuit, much to the chagrin of a pair of 41 Squadron Javelins that had been obliged to land off a GCA approach.

Two days later I was scheduled to repeat the performance for the remainder of the course and a visiting group of officers from the RAF College of Air Warfare. No problems with weather on this occasion – there had been a complete change of air mass and it was a much colder day. I usually concluded my show with a high-speed run in front of the crowd. With both engines at maximum reheat, the Lightning's silent approach, followed by a thunderous departure with flames issuing from the jet pipes, all made for an impressive finale. There was just one small problem. In the Lightning F1A, reheat ignition could not be guaranteed at speeds above 350 knots, although once they were lit the reheats were stable throughout the speed range. Because of this, I always started my high-speed run from a high wing-over, engaging reheat at about 300 kts. When the burners lit up I would dive for the runway and level out fifty feet or so above the ground. The Lightning accelerated extremely rapidly. It was not possible to monitor the instruments closely at an altitude of fifty feet, but my speed abeam the tower was usually about 600 kts. On this particular day, because of the low ambient air temperature, the engines were more efficient than usual and the local speed of sound was relatively low. The aircraft was moving very fast as I went past the tower. I thought Air Traffic Control were joking when they called on the R/T to say that they no longer needed air conditioning. But after landing the boss met me at the aircraft and told me to report immediately to OC ops – with my hat on! I was in deep trouble. Apparently my high-speed run had caused extensive damage to the tower and surrounding buildings.

Wing Commander Bill Howard's office was in a single-storey prefabricated building alongside the tower. It appeared undamaged from the outside, but that was deceptive. Actually, the roof had been lifted a fraction and the walls had been nudged sideways. All the internal doors were hanging askew, and the pictures hung away from the walls rather than on them. The office was lit by neon tubes, normally suspended from the ceiling on chains, but now all the chains had jumped off their hooks and the lights dangled on the ends of their electric flex. I had to part these pillars of light to get in. Bill was sitting behind his desk, covered in white dust, a ghost of his former self. The only blue thing about him was his hat, which had been in a desk drawer when I flew over.

He looked up as I came in, and, with a perfectly straight face, said with a nasal twang, 'I suppose you think that's funny.' I had to admit that I did. But apologies were in order, and he suggested I start with local control. The tower was a shambles, at least six huge double-plate-glass windows had been shattered and there was a stiff breeze blowing across the controller's desk. The staff, who were busy sweeping up, were taking it all in good spirits.

Next I went to apologise to the duty Met man, whom I found sitting huddled on a stool in one corner of the Met office. The room looked as dusty and dilapidated as Bill Howard's office. The Met man appeared to be suffering from battle fatigue. 'I served throughout the war,' he said, 'and I have never been so frightened in all my life ... And what about my barograph?' He pointed to the sensitive pressure instrument that traces a record of the barometric pressure on a rotating drum. The drum was still rotating, but the pen was bent up against the top stop.

In sympathetic tones I suggested that the queen would probably buy him a new one.

'Maybe,' he snapped, 'but she won't buy me a new raincoat.'

The coat in question had been hanging on the back of the door, but now it was pinned in place by a large splinter of glass.

I apologised profusely and returned to the safety of the squadron crewroom.

It was not long before another message came from on high. I was to change into best blue and be 'on the mat' in the station commander's office, immediately if not sooner. This was getting serious – the station commander, Group Captain Simmonds, was my old boss from the AFDS. I had always got on quite well with him before, but this promised to be a rather one-sided interview.

And so it proved. After a stiff haranguing, which seemed to go on for ever, he ordered me to report to the Air Ministry the following day – the implication being that I would be immediately posted. He finished by demanding, 'What do you think about that?'

Now, a staff tour in London was just about the worst fate I could imagine, and frankly I thought it was uncalled for. So I let fly, pointing out all the reasons for it being unfair.

David Simmonds burst out laughing, and explained that I was being called forward for briefing prior to an exchange tour with the USAF at

Nellis Air Force Base in Nevada.

That evening in the bar they told me how the high-speed run had appeared from the ground. The pilots who had been watching from outside the squadron knew that something was amiss when they saw the grass on the airfield being flattened behind my aircraft. A high-ranking army officer had been heard to comment, as he dusted glass splinters from his uniform and surveyed his badly cut toe-caps, 'I will say this, when the Air Force put on a show they don't spare any expense.'

In addition to the damage sustained by the tower, two other prefabricated buildings alongside were rendered unfit for habitation.

Of course, there had to be an official board of inquiry, and OC 56 Squadron – Squadron Leader Dave Seward – was appointed president. According to Queen's Regulations, immediately it becomes apparent that any person might be held responsible for an accident, he has to be formally warned – and he is entitled to remain present for the remainder of the inquiry. He is also permitted to cross-examine the witnesses.

I was advised of my rights from the outset of the inquiry, which was only to be expected. It soon became apparent that one member of the board – a less-than-friendly officer from another station – was determined to find me guilty of gross culpable negligence. He spent a great deal of time trying to establish the level at which my display had been authorised.

Within reason, a pilot was not usually considered blameworthy if he stayed within his flight authorisation. The visiting member asked me who had authorised my show, and I answered quite truthfully that my squadron commander had done so.

Dicky Wirdnam was called in and confirmed that he had authorised the sortie, 'but of course Bendell's show was also cleared by the station commander'.

Group Captain Simmonds was called in, and confirmed that he too had indeed cleared my display, but it had also been approved by Air Officer Commanding No. 12 Group.

It was inappropriate to call for the AOC's attendance in person, so a phone call was made. We could hear the gist of the conversation, in which he confirmed that, yes, he had approved Bendell's display, 'but of course the display was also cleared and approved by the Commander-in-Chief Fighter Command'.

The question of authorisation was quietly dropped.

The board eventually concluded that the damage had been caused by localised shockwaves which had formed on the aircraft at very high subsonic speeds. I wouldn't argue with that. The question of negligence was also dropped, although at the end of the month I was presented with a bogus mess bill, charging me £1,800 for broken glass.

Overnight I became something of a celebrity among the local schoolboys, who would point me out. 'That's Bugs – he's the guy that broke all those windows . . . '

Some weeks later I was invited to cut the ribbon formally re-opening 41 Squadron's line hut, which had been closed for structural repairs since the fateful day.

In October the squadron deployed four aircraft to Laon air force base in France to participate in a flypast over Paris, marking the end of SACEUR's tour of duty. Dickie Wirdnam, Bill Richardson and myself spent the first weekend in Paris, doing an on-site recce – at least, that was our story. We stayed in a hotel close to the Gare du Nord. The night-life was fascinating – a young man could get into a lot of trouble in Paris. The American squadrons at Laon were equipped with the F-101 Voodoo, which was a fairly capable aircraft although not a patch on the Lightning. With its high-set tailplane, the Voodoo was inclined to be unstable at low speed, and even among American pilots it was known as the 'pitch-up artist'. Pilots are generally proud of the aircraft they fly, and the Americans at Laon took this to extremes – in fact they seemed to be labouring under the impression that America held a monopoly on fighter aircraft design. They were entirely dismissive of the Lightning – until the boss got permission for me to do a practice display.

The boss watched from the tower, and later confessed that for one awful moment he thought there was going to be a repeat of the Wattisham window incident. My high-speed run really rattled their cage. The American spectators were suitably impressed.

But world affairs soon intervened, and as a result of the Cuban missile crisis SACEUR's tour was extended and the Paris flypast was cancelled. We departed from Laon with a spectacular reheat climb, bursting into contrails over the end of the runway. Back at Wattisham, I found that someone had sewn a 'Voodoo Medicineman' badge on the back of my flying suit.

I stayed in the mess over Christmas and the New Year. A barrel of beer was laid on in the anteroom for the benefit of the livers-in, and I remember having a fairly boozy time of it. Then, early on the first of January, the station commander called to congratulate me on the award of an Air Force Cross. It was a total surprise and, of course, a great honour.

From then on the telephone didn't stop ringing. My parents were among the first to offer their congratulations, but the call that really stopped me in my tracks was from Jean. We had drifted apart some seven months before, but Jean said she would like to see me again, and I hastily arranged to visit her in Pinner.

The last months of my tour on Treble One passed quickly. I flew several aerobatic practices in January, in preparation for a visit by the new SACEUR, General Puryear. True to form, the Lightning gave me one final shot of adrenalin. I was leading a tail-chase just east of the airfield when my No. 2 reported that I appeared to be venting an excessive amount of fuel. The Lightning was not prone to fuel venting, so I assumed it was probably a leak. Fortunately the weather was clear and, looking down from 8000 ft, I knew I was well positioned for an emergency straight-in approach. The starboard fuel gauge rapidly decreased below zero, but that appeared to be my only problem. For no particular reason – although it was probably an automatic reaction – I shut down the No. 2 engine.

Less than two minutes later I touched down. The airman in the runway caravan reported that my aircraft was still dumping a lot of fuel, and Air Traffic Control repeated the warning. I remember having a short discussion with the tower about where to park the aircraft, and it was decided that I should taxi towards the fire trucks, which were already on their way.

We came to a halt facing each other on a short section of disused runway. A fireman, axe at the ready, ran towards me, while I busied myself unstrapping and inserting the seat pins. When I next looked up the fireman had dropped his axe and was running hell-for-leather back to the crash vehicles. I was ready to abandon ship, but without a ladder specifically designed for the purpose that was easier said than done. The entire fire crew prepared for the expected conflagration, while I stood on the ejection seat yelling for assistance. A ladder eventually appeared and at last I could see what was happening at the back end. The aircraft, leaking like the proverbial sieve, was standing in a pool of fuel: streams of AVTAG spurted from every drain-hole in the fuselage. One jet of fuel hosed ominously on to a hot wheel brake, giving rise to a cloud of steam. This was distinctly unhealthy. The jet fuel we used – AVTAG – was not as flammable as aviation gasoline, but it would burn readily enough. Like the firemen, I retreated to a safe distance.

The aircraft never did catch fire. On stripping it down the engineers found that a large-bore fuel transfer pipe made up of three or four sections had come apart, allowing fuel to flood into the upper engine bay. The tidemark on the engine casing showed that the No. 2 engine had been half immersed in neat fuel. Apparently the only reason the aircraft hadn't blown up was that the fuel/air mix had been too rich. More by luck than good judgement, by shutting down the engine I had reduced the temperature and removed the most likely source of ignition.

On 26 January Jack O'Dowd took the plunge and got married to Sylvia, the station commander's secretary. Jack had been mooning around the squadron for days on end, so we'd known something was up, but it came as something of a shock to learn that the Kiwi ladykiller had finally popped the question. He apologised that he could not afford to invite all squadron officers to the wedding – as usual he was short of cash. He even had to sell his golf clubs. Jack did his best to play it low-key by booking the church some miles away at Fulborne, but it would have been a sad day if such an occasion had been allowed to go unnoticed, and so we made appropriate arrangements. Jack and Sylvia came out of church to be greeted by their own guard of honour – six officers with drawn swords. From there we all went to the reception, held at a pub in Fen Ditton.

On 5 February I went to Buckingham Palace for an investiture, and was presented with the AFC by Her Majesty Queen Elizabeth the Queen Mother. I can't for the life of me remember what she said, but Mum and Dad, who were also there, were suitably impressed.

Later that month the squadron started flight refuelling training on the Valiant tanker. For me, air refuelling was a unique experience. In simple formation flying the pilot must at all times avoid the other aircraft, but with flight refuelling he deliberately makes contact. I flew one sortie on the Valiant, which was all useful experience for my forthcoming tour in the States, but the bulk of the training was reserved for the other members of the squadron who were due to deploy to Cyprus.

In March I flew tactical checks with the pilots on 'B' Flight. The Squadron's first two-seat Lightning T4 had been delivered in October, and had since been involved in acceptance checks. My last flight on Treble One was a dual low-level aerobatic demonstration for the benefit of Alan Garside, who had volunteered to take over the solo aerobatic slot. Some months later Alan was tragically killed during a display.

My tour on Treble One had lasted twenty-seven months; during that time I had accumulated barely 270 hard-won hours on the Lightning. On any other aircraft this would have accounted for little, but Lightning flying was special. The experience I gained on Treble One would stand me in good stead throughout the rest of my flying career.

There was the usual round of farewell parties. Jean and I made up for lost time. If I had been staying in the country we would probably have got married, although she was very young and to be honest I was not yet ready to settle down. Instead I bought a ring and we got engaged.

The dining-out night from the mess was fairly riotous, but Wattisham had a reputation for wild evenings. Not for me the thunderflash in the feather pillow or the balloon filled with hydrogen with a lighted toilet paper fuse. (The last time that was tried the balloon had caught fire in Derrick Hitchins's hands, giving him a nasty case of sunburn.) Of course I had plenty to drink, and I thought that was it until I was grabbed by the boss and an unruly mob, who proceeded to give me a crew cut in preparation for my exchange tour. I have never placed great store by my physical appearance, but that haircut was a disaster.

Next day I visited the hairdresser in Stowmarket. The barber was shocked. 'Where did you get your hair cut, sir?' he asked.

'Oh, some fellows in the mess did it, but they were drunk at the time.'

'They should have their licences revoked,' opined the barber.

Jean was not amused.

8
Exchange tour with the USAF, instructor on the Republic F-105D

The briefing at the Air Ministry had given me a fair idea of what to expect in the States. The Nellis exchange was intended to be a married accompanied tour, although single officers were not excluded. I had also received, by post, a comprehensive package of material about Nellis Air Force Base and the nearest city – Las Vegas . . .

I had a distinct feeling of *déjà vu.* Little appeared to have changed in Las Vegas since those halcyon days of leave in 1954. The southern Nevada climate was hot and dry, but the standard RAF desert kit of khaki drill shorts and shirt was not considered appropriate for an exchange posting in the States. I visited a military tailor in London's East End to be measured for two sets of silver-tan best uniforms and a white mess jacket.

The two weeks' disembarkation leave gave me ample time to sort out my affairs. Jean must have thought it a cruel twist of fate – we had just got back together, and I was about to depart overseas for two years.

A passage had been reserved for me on the RMS *Queen Elizabeth,* sailing from Southampton on 21 March. I went through the familiar routine of packing. The silver-tan uniforms and my golf clubs went into the tin trunk labelled 'Not Wanted on Voyage'; the rest of my kit was easily contained in three 'globe trotter' suitcases. Disposing of the MG (which I wanted to hold on to until the last moment) might have been a problem, but Peter Rowley, my brother-in-law, offered to take it off my hands for £400.

Southampton was just eighteen miles from home, and the family turned out in force to see me off. I disliked lingering farewells, but if one had no choice, then saying goodbye aboard one of the great Cunard liners was a superb setting. I was travelling cabin class, and had been allocated a single berth, well above the waterline, on the port side of the ship. The sun shone through the porthole, lightening the final moments before departure. Mum and Dad tactfully withdrew, leaving me to say goodbye to Jean. She was very upset, but for me at least, the anticipation of what lay ahead dispelled much of the gloom.

The Cunard ships called briefly at Cherbourg to pick up passengers before heading west. I relaxed in the unaccustomed luxury and took the opportunity to visit the hairdresser, hoping that he might transform my moth-eaten locks. But it was all to no avail; it takes time to cultivate a decent crew cut.

After a leisurely voyage the ship docked in New York and I continued by train to Washington DC to be briefed by the embassy staff. The RAF accountant officer advised me that a fixed monthly allowance of three hundred and sixty dollars – the equivalent of sixty quid – would be paid into my account at the First National Bank of Nevada, starting on 31 March 1963. I was briefed on how to order duty-free booze – the hard stuff, of course – from the embassy. The minimum order was by the crate, although being a beer drinker I was unlikely to make much use of the concession. As an exchange officer I was required to submit an interim report halfway through my tour and a final report at the end. Finally I was warned that, due to the close proximity of Las Vegas, I should expect frequent staff visits.

Next day I continued my journey by air, arriving at McCarran Field, Las Vegas's municipal airport, early in the evening. Flight Lieutenant Tim Barret, the man I was due to replace at Nellis, was there to meet me.

Actually my posting was not a straightforward replacement. Tim had served his tour as an instructor on the Fighter Weapons School, flying the F-100 Super Sabre, but I was assigned to the 4526th Combat Crew Training Squadron to fly the F-105 Thunderchief. Tim had done the decent thing by meeting me, but he knew very little about my posting. He suggested that we stop off at the Aku-Aku, a popular Polynesian restaurant on the Strip, where we could talk. After sinking several smooth rum cocktails I lost track of the conversation. I don't even remember arriving at Nellis – but by that time I could have slept on a clothes-line.

I woke up the next morning in a very civilised bachelor officer's quarter – BOQ to the uninitiated – no more than fifty yards from the officers' club.

Tim eventually turned up, in rude health as always, to show me around the base.

Nellis Air Force Base was far larger than any RAF station I had known; the ramp had parking space for well over three hundred fighter aircraft, and the airfield had two parallel 10,000 ft runways. Nellis was home to the 4520th Combat Crew Training Wing, which was primarily tasked with training F-105 pilots, but its other commitments included: an F-86 training squadron for foreign students; the Fighter Weapons School, and The Thunderbirds – the USAF's premier aerial demonstration team, also equipped with F-100s. The base was an acknowledged centre of excellence for tactical air training, although the inscription above the entrance to the Fighter Weapons School – 'Through these portals pass the world's finest fighter pilots' – may have been slightly over the top. But the staff were fiercely proud, and justly so, of the wing's reputation.

I completed the usual arrival procedures. At the Personnel Services section they typed out my number, rank, name, initials, blood group and religion on two metal discs, which were threaded on to a chain. I was advised to wear these 'dog tags' when on duty.

Finally I reported to the 4526th Combat Crew Training Squadron, known as the Forty-five Twenty-sixth, to learn that there was a minor glitch with my assignment. Tactical Air Command had recently introduced a management control system, by which the efficiency and cost of all activities on the base were assessed. The overall budget was tightly controlled and points were awarded for every approved task. In my case, although I had the necessary orders assigning me to the 4526th CCTS, signed on behalf of General Curtis E. LeMay no less, no application had been made for me to attend the F-105 instructor upgrading course. It was a simple administrative cock-up, but sorting it out was totally beyond the capabilities of the local management.

Fortunately, Colonel 'James' Bean, the feisty don't-confuse-me-with-facts CO of the 4526th, and a much respected Thunderchief pilot, was no great supporter of management control, and he arranged for me to fly a dual land-away cross-country to Davis Monthan AFB in a T-33. It was good to get airborne, and a pleasure to renew my acquaintance with the T-33.

The route followed the line of the Grand Canyon. Even from high altitude, which tends to diminish natural relief, that great scar in the desert was clearly recognisable. But that was the only flying I managed to get during April.

While waiting for upgrading, I sorted out a few administrative details. A car was essential – everyone on the base had a car – so I invested in a second-hand 1959 Fairlane Ford automatic, complete with powered steering and air conditioning. I drew a full set of flying clothing from stores; the flying at Nellis was mostly at low level, so there was no requirement for pressure breathing equipment. The USAF kit was comfortable to wear, although the boots and gloves were not up to RAF standards. I was also issued with a parachute, which really took me back to my flying days in Canada. (In British aircraft, the parachute was usually integral with the ejection seat.) Finally I signed for an F-105D-1, the aircraft's weighty operating manual, together with the inevitable stack of outstanding amendments. At least I could make good use of my spare time.

Born as a private venture, the Republic F-105 Thunderchief was subsequently selected by the Department of the Air Force to meet one of the most exacting general operational requirements ever written. TAC wanted an aircraft capable of delivering a nuclear bomb over long range at high speed and at low level in all weathers. At one stage the Thunderchief had even been considered for use by the RAF. For the Republic Aviation Company, the F-105 was the logical next stage of development following their highly successful F-84F, which had been widely deployed in Europe. For all practical purposes the F-105 was a completely new design. Alexander Kartveli, Republic's chief designer, had used a thin wing to minimise drag, but the F-105's wing section could be modified with flaps on both the leading and trailing edges to improve lift at low airspeed. The wing and horizontal tailplane (in American parlance the horizontal stabiliser) were only moderately swept back at 45°. To further reduce transonic drag the F-105 was area ruled, giving the fuselage a distinctive Coke-bottle appearance. The wing root air intakes were sharply swept forward and were fitted with automatically controlled plugs which varied the size of the ducts, thereby ensuring a smooth, subsonic flow of air to the Pratt & Whitney J-75 jet engine.

The F-105D was primarily designed to carry a nuclear weapon in a

15 ft long internal bomb bay; alternatively it could carry up to six tons of conventional stores, ranging from additional fuel tanks to iron bombs, rockets and guided weapons. The F-105 also had an internally mounted 20 mm Gatling type M-61 Vulcan cannon, with a cyclic rate of fire of one hundred rounds per second. The aircraft was also fitted with TACAN, Doppler navigation equipment, a bombing computer and a low-level-terrain avoidance radar. By any standards, the F-105D was an extremely complex aircraft and, as experience in Vietnam was later to prove, it was also remarkably rugged.

When I arrived at Nellis the standard F-105 conversion course consisted of two weeks' ground school and thirty hours' flying. The majority of the students were already operational on the F-100, so it was just a question of checking them out on the aircraft and teaching them to use the F-105D's specialist equipment. The course was usually completed in two months. The instructor upgrading course covered the same syllabus, although it often took longer to complete, simply because no MCS points were awarded for upgrading. As an exchange officer I was subject to other minor and sometimes irritating limitations. My standard RAF security clearance allowed me full access to the F-105D manuals, I was even allowed to release a dummy nuclear weapon, but I was not permitted to see either the bomb or its dummy shape fitted in the bomb bay. Then there was the nonsense of training films. Soon after I arrived, an all-British film about army tactics employed during the terrorist emergency in Malaysia in the 1950s was due to be shown. The film was compulsory viewing for the squadron's American pilots but, because some anonymous department within the Pentagon had stamped NOFORN on the label, I was not allowed to see it. The British Army had devised the concept of fortified villages in Malaya, both to protect the indigenous population and to deny support to the terrorists. Later a similar concept of 'strategic hamlets' was tried in Vietnam, but the ethnic circumstances were different and the plan failed. The Americans also considered that such tactics were an infringement of personal liberties and were therefore not acceptable.

After a delay of three weeks, clearance finally came through for me to start the F-105 course. The two weeks in ground school also included four sorties in the T-39 Sabre Liner to familiarise the students with the terrain avoidance radar. This was fascinating flying, the first time I had seen the harsh landscape from low level, from desiccated desert to rugged mountains. On the final sortie we descended into the Grand Canyon. It was bumpy as hell but I managed to take some very blurred pictures of the Havasupai Indian reservation at the bottom of the canyon. There was no dual trainer to prepare students for the F-105, but a cockpit simulator provided valuable hands-on training for the state-of-the-art F-105D equipment. Cockpit checks were easier to understand and memorise when the student could operate the controls for himself with an instructor at his side telling him what to look for. The simulator also reproduced the feel of the aircraft at various stages of flight and, perhaps more importantly, it gave an opportunity to work with the integrated flight instrumentation. Instead of clock-type instruments, the main panel included two tape displays which were fed accurate barometric information from a central air-data computer. In place of the standard artificial horizon, the aircraft was fitted with an attitude director indicator (ADI), which combined the functions of an artificial horizon with an ILS display. The ADI and the horizontal situation indicator (HSI) – in other words the compass – were driven by a master reference gyroscope, which permitted full freedom in pitch and roll without toppling the instruments. The HSI was also used to present information from the Doppler, the TACAN and the ILS.

The Doppler measured minute differences of frequency between four narrow radar beams projected beneath the aircraft, and gave readouts for ground speed and drift (i.e. the angle between the aircraft's heading and its track over the ground). This raw information, presented on the HSI, was also fed through a navigation computer to constantly update the aircraft's latitude and longitude. The same computer gave distance and bearing to selected destinations, or way points. On the F-105 the Doppler could be updated, either visually or by use of the radar. The Doppler was a first-generation, self-contained navigation system. It was simple to use and reasonably accurate. Overland, errors of less than a mile per hour were common, although the system was less reliable over the sea.

The integrated instrument layout was designed to reduce the pilot's workload, thereby enabling him to attend to other tasks. So much for the theory. At first the students were confused by the sheer flexibility of the system, but after a few hours in the simulator the advantages became self-evident. By the end of the course, no F-105D pilot ever wished to revert to conventional instrumentation.

I eventually got airborne in the F-105 on 7 May, courtesy of the 4523rd CCTS – the sister squadron to the 4526th. The initial conversion exercises were flown in pairs, with the instructor flying chase in the No. 2 position. For me the F-105D inspired immediate confidence; the powerful J-75 was held in check while taxiing by a thrust decay system, which enlarged the jet efflux and reduced idling thrust. But there was no lack of power on take-off. With full afterburner the engine produced 24,500 lb of thrust. This could be boosted by a further 2000 lb, with water injection, although we seldom needed this at Nellis.

I have to say the F-105D's take-off performance was pedestrian compared to that of the Lightning. The nose wheel lift-off and the take-off speeds were roughly the same, but they occurred further down the runway. Of course the F-105D was a much heavier aircraft – it was scurrilously reported that Republic had initially intended to make the F-105 out of concrete until they found that metal would be heavier. Even during the initial conversion the take-off weights were often in excess of 44,000 lb – roughly one third of that being fuel. Republic aircraft had a reputation for lengthy take-offs. It was a standing joke amongst pilots: 'If a runway was built around the equator, Republic would design an aircraft that would need it all to get airborne.'

But once in the air, with the undercarriage up and flap retracted to the cruise and manoeuvre setting, the F-105D became far more lively. The first sortie involved general handling at medium altitude, followed by work in the landing pattern. I couldn't resist the temptation to try a few aerobatics – the aircraft responded well, there was a solid, sure-footed feel to it, but I could well understand why pilots had christened it 'the Thud'. It was certainly not an interceptor.

The high point of the sortie came when the chase pilot called for A/B. Not being familiar with this abbreviation for afterburner I mistakenly selected air brakes. The chase pilot correctly applied full afterburner and promptly took the lead. He was not amused when I commented over the R/T, 'I thought you were supposed to be following me.'

The second conversion sortie, which I flew next day, included a Mach 2.0 run at 38,000 ft. The initial acceleration was quite brisk, I retracted the cruise and manoeuvre leading-edge flaps at Mach 1.3, and the duct plugs in the variable air intakes started motoring forwards at 1.5. The aircraft eventually reached Mach 2.0, but only after an extended run. In contrast, the Thud's performance at low level was much more impressive, and it easily achieved its limiting speed of 810 kts – in the order of 1,400 miles per hour. Obviously this machine was in its element at low level.

At that time the main aim of the F-105D course was to prepare pilots for the nuclear strike role. This involved practice weapons delivery and long-range combat profile missions, flown blind, using the terrain avoidance radar and the bombing computer against a variety of radar targets. The Nevada bombing and gunnery ranges covered more than three and half million acres. It was a new world to me: low toss, high toss and over the shoulder – all different ways of delivering 'the bomb' designed to give the pilot safe separation from its nuclear blast. The syllabus also covered conventional weapons delivery: high-angle dive bombing; skip bombing; rocketing, and air-to-ground strafe.

At the end of this close-air-support phase, one or two sorties were flown using live ordnance against tactical targets in the desert. The air-to-air tactics phase included gun attacks against towed 'Dart' targets and a Sidewinder air-to-air guided missile firing.

In the case of air-to-air refuelling, the F-105D was capable of taking on fuel from both drogue and boom equipped tankers. We practised on both the KB-50 and the KC-135 tanker aircraft.

On my final standardisation and evaluation check by the wing staff, on 8 July, I scored a creditable 93%. And, with a good deal less accuracy, it must be said, I was assessed as being a highly qualified F-105 instructor. I could now be let loose on the students – I was allocated an instructor callsign of Cobra Jaguar.

There was little relief from the heat during those summer months; the midday temperatures were often well over 100°F in the shade. The BOQs were fitted with swamp coolers which lowered the temperature by ten to fifteen degrees, but also increased the humidity, so any relief was short-lived. It was probably due to these unaccustomed conditions that I developed a painful sore throat. Aircrew were warned not to resort to self-medication because of possible side-effects, so I reported to the base hospital. The junior flight surgeon listened sympathetically to my problems and was about to render appropriate aid when he found that Nellis had no medical records for me. Apparently my records were held by the embassy in Washington, which was not much use to doctors at Nellis. What had started as a simple consultation instantly became a full-blown medical examination. I was poked and prodded for most of the day, then my footprints were taken – for crash identification purposes – and I was booted out through the rear door. Bureaucracy had triumphed, and the official priorities had been satisfied; I was alive and I had records to prove it. But nothing had been done for my throat.

I went round to the front desk to complain, and the fellow said, 'You only reported sick this morning – you must give these drugs time to work.' What drugs?

TAC's early experience with the F-105 was similar to the problems encountered during the introduction of the Lightning. The aircraft, or more precisely its sophisticated sub-systems, were difficult to keep serviceable and the situation at Nellis was not helped by TAC's 66-1 consolidated maintenance programme – the engineering equivalent to the MCS. The 66-1 programme was centralised servicing on a grand scale. The engineering staffs thought it made best use of resources, but they were reluctant to recognise that it also damaged morale. It is a fact of life: the larger the organisation, the more difficult it is to maintain one's identity. Fortunately, the crew chief system, whereby a senior NCO was made personally responsible for each aircraft on the flight line, was retained at Nellis. These men were the salt of the earth. They knew all there was to know about their own aircraft and they took great pride in their work. But many of the crew chiefs at Nellis missed the camaraderie of squadron life and were generally dissatisfied with their lot. The 66-1 system was universally disliked by the aircrew, there was never any question of flexible programming to make best use of scarce resources. Late programme changes were not permitted because they did not score MCS points and they made it difficult to maintain engineering control. At times the rigidity of the programming, where pilots were allotted aircraft by tail number for the following day's flying, seemed deliberately to exacerbate the F-105's maintenance problems.

There were three other exchange pilots at Nellis, two from the RCAF: Ed Stone, who was instructing on the 4523rd, and Buster Kincaid, an instructor on the Fighter Weapons School. And there was Lieutenant Don Riggs, a United States Navy pilot who was also instructing on the 4526th. Don was married to a delightful lady called Pat, who would willingly cook up a feast of Navy beans and cornbread for the odd hungry bachelor. As exchange officers I guess we all held similar views on the USAF and we would often compare notes, but I found a kindred spirit in Captain Gary D. Barnhill. Barney, as he was known on the squadron, had been pre-selected as the stand-by solo pilot for the Skyblazers, 4 ATAF's official aerial demonstration team in Germany, equipped with F-100s, while I had been doing my bit with the Lightning on Treble One. Sadly for Barney, the Skyblazers were disbanded before he was called upon to perform – on the team that is. He was the archetypal American bachelor, and he owned the supreme status symbol: a white Porsche 356 sports car.

Barney took it upon himself to introduce me to the local night-life. There was plenty of variety, but the lounge shows at the hotels on 'the Strip' were still the best value for money. But contrary to popular belief, Las Vegas was not a bachelor's paradise – there was a general shortage of eligible young women. It was an education to listen to Barney's line of chat with the cocktail waitresses, although I swear he only took me along to keep them occupied. They would gush, 'Gee, Bugs, I just love the way you talk,' while he figured out a way to take them to bed. Mind you, Barney was not always successful. The average cocktail waitress did not finish work until two in the morning, and even then she was expected to spend an extra hour at the tables encouraging the players. On one occasion, Barney, mindful of an early-morning briefing, asked a vivacious beauty if she really had to do that. She shrugged and drawled, 'Well, honey, it's not compulsory, but I have to be careful not to catch my ass in the swing doors as I leave.'

Of course the main purpose of the entertainment was to attract gambling money. Firm self-discipline was required not to dally at the tables; even the drinks were free if you were gambling. With a disposable income of barely one hundred dollars a month, I simply could not afford to take any chances. In fact, very few officers based at Nellis actually gambled – it was a foolish pastime. That did not apply to the weekend visitors. A dozen or so aircraft would arrive at Nellis on Friday and the crews would stagger off on Monday, broke and generally the worse for wear. Vegas's population quadrupled at the weekends with an influx of players from the West Coast. The optimists who believed that some day they would strike it lucky were attracted like moths to a flame. One or two won their fortunes, but the majority didn't. And a few – those for whom gambling was an all-consuming passion – lost everything.

Barney also introduced me to water-skiing. I have never been particularly keen on water sports – for me, swimming was more a question of staying alive in the water – but the roasting-high summer temperatures at Nellis made the idea of cooling off in the clear waters of Lake Mead very appealing. Besides, Barney had all the necessary gear, including his own power boat, which was parked on a trailer behind the BOQs. It took only a matter of moments to hook up the trailer, collect a couple of six-packs of beer and hit the road.

It must be said, my initial attempts at water-skiing were a source of considerable amusement to Barney. Thank heavens for the life belt. No sooner had I shouted 'Hit it' to the grinning Barnhill than I was pulled out of my socks into a headfirst imitation of a high-speed submarine. Not to worry – I was a fast learner. The first essential lesson: remember to let go of the tow-rope. My second attempt was a little better – I did manage to rise out of the water before keeling over again. Coach Barnhill instructed me to keep my knees bent, and my next attempt was more successful. This time I came up on the skis and motored around Lake Mead at about twenty knots, bum bouncing off the waves like an under-powered seaplane. I eventually got the hang of it. In the meantime Barney, who was attempting to progress to 'mono' (i.e. a single ski), had troubles of his own.

In August I received a 'Dear John' letter from Jean. She had met someone else while on holiday on the Isle of Wight, which was probably no better than I deserved. For a while I attempted to play the field in Las Vegas, without much success. I was basically a 'one-gal guy,' which didn't cut much ice in Vegas. Nevada girls may have found my accent attractive, but that was as far as it went. Obviously I didn't have Barney's gift of the gab. Maybe I just didn't fit the popular image of a swinging bachelor. Whatever the reason, I was beginning to lose confidence – when I met Betty. I had noticed her before, in the company of Colonel Bean in the officers' club. She was a stylish, good-looking woman but what chance had I? She would never be interested in me – or so I thought. Then one Saturday, at a lunchtime party, I got involved in a heated discussion with a visiting pilot about the relative merits of the F-105, and was pleasantly surprised when Betty weighed in on my side. In retrospect, she might just have been supporting the local team, but it seemed only natural to invite her out for dinner. One date led to another, and before long we were going steady. Like many women in Las Vegas, Betty was a divorcee. Her former husband had been in the USAF, and the marriage had broken up while he was based at Nellis. Betty was left with two charming daughters: Michele, a pretty but solemn eight-year-old, and Sanita, a mischievous and so very appealing young lady of three and a half. Betty and I enjoyed each other's company, and shared similar interests. At weekends we would sometimes take family picnics, either on the shores of Lake Mead or halfway up Mount Charleston. And of course Betty was my ever-attentive companion at the various social events. Our affair was gentler and more fulfilling than any I had known before, and as time went by we talked of marriage; Betty seemed keen enough, but I was reluctant to commit myself. After all, my previous romantic diversions had ended in two broken engagements. I was very fond of her, of course, but I wasn't yet ready to take the plunge. In any case, there was no need to make a hasty decision.

Nellis opened its gates to the local civil population at least once a year on the occasion of the USAF Armed Forces Day. These open days were hugely successful, and there was much to be seen. The stars of the show were always the formation aerobatic teams: the Thunderbirds, with their red white and blue F-100s, and the United States Navy team, the Blue Angels. Both teams had well-deserved reputations for flying tight, highly polished displays. Individual solo aerobatic displays were rare in the USAF, but at Nellis in 1963, a retired air-force pilot by the name of Bob Hoover gave a quite superb demonstration in a World War II vintage P-51 Mustang fighter. For a while I pondered on the possibilities of a solo F-105 demonstration, but discarded the idea almost immediately. The Thud was not really suited for low level-aerobatics; besides – and I took some consolation from the thought – the centralised system of management at Nellis would never cope with that kind of initiative. There was usually an interesting collection of aircraft in the static display, and in 1963 this included the all-black, rocket-propelled X-15, capable of Mach 6.0 on the fringes of space, at that time the fastest and highest-flying piloted aircraft in the world.

Nellis pursued an active public relations programme with the local community. On one occasion, I was actually roped in to speak at a business luncheon in Las Vegas. At the other end of the PR programme, after formal dining-in nights, the officers at Nellis were encouraged to visit the casinos on the Strip while still suited up in formal mess dress. This was thought to be an effective way of raising the awareness of the Vegas night-birds to their military neighbours. After one particular dinner night, a crowd of us visited the Dunes to catch the lounge show. It was standard practice to take a seat, order drinks and pay before leaving – if I remember rightly my particular poison was brandy and American Dry ginger. The drinks duly arrived, but we then discovered that no one had brought any cash. No immediate problem – we could continue drinking on the tab, but sooner or later the bill would have to be settled. Almost unnoticed, Ed Wayne, a buddy of ours on the 4523rd, excused himself. We discussed the various options, and had agreed that someone would have to collect some cash from Nellis when Ed returned with a fistful of dollars. He had spent the previous half-hour outside the main entrance, parking cars for appreciative customers. For the good name of the USAF, I like to think that Ed had removed his USAF mess jacket before filling in, so to speak – but whether he had, or had not, he surely saved our bacon that night. Of course, genuine parking attendants were expected to retrieve the owners' cars on request. Certainly Ed had produced an impressive collection of keys, but we thought the Dunes would prefer to continue the good work. We paid our bill, deposited Ed's keys on the table and left.

In August I flew forty-four hours in the F-105D, which included ten hours ferrying aircraft to and from Republic Aviation's airfield at

Farmingdale. At that time Republic was involved in a major modification programme named 'Look Alike', aimed at standardising the F-105D fleet. With its short runway and steep approaches, Farmingdale was not the best of airfields. It was even rumoured at Nellis that you were not permitted to land there unless you had been there before. Actually, the approach to Farmingdale was not that difficult. The trickiest part came when you attempted to leave. Being fifty miles to the east of New York, at certain times of the day Farmingdale's air traffic conflicted with transatlantic airline traffic, and one could sit with the engine running for hours on end, waiting for departure clearance. These delays occasionally caused hurried recalculation to ensure you didn't run out of fuel. Obviously, the Look Alike programme was necessary, but in the short term it led to a serious shortage of aircraft at Nellis.

On 8 October I was leading two students on a practice nuclear weapon delivery sortie on Target 3-4, about eighty miles north of Nellis, when one of the students reported falling oil pressure. The J-75 was a remarkably reliable engine, but there had been cases where the oil supply to a bearing deep in the heart of the engine had failed, causing the engine to seize and disintegrate. Thus oil pressure failure was rightly considered to be a serious emergency. But on this occasion the student seemed remarkably cool. He explained that the same thing had happened the previous day in this aircraft, and the oil pressure had stabilised above the allowable minimum. I silently cursed the unknown engineer who had declared the aircraft fit to fly. There was an airfield at Groom Lake, fairly close to Target 3-4, which we all knew existed, but it was a hush-hush research and development base, and we were only cleared to use it in dire emergency. I was mulling over the possible options when the student reported with a great deal more urgency that he now had a pressure failure light. The oil light was taken from a different part of the system, so this was a sure sign of a genuine emergency. I sent the other student home – he was a bird colonel, so it was a fair bet he would make it – while I led the man with the oil problems to Groom Lake.

It was customary to seek clearance before joining an airfield's visual circuit, but Groom Lake did not respond to my calls on the international distress frequency. We certainly had the right base – the runway stretched for more than ten miles across a dry lake bed, and an aircraft that looked like something out of a science fiction movie was parked off to one side. We made one orbit and, despite the lack of radio contact, I told the student to land. I overshot and transmitted blind, announcing my intention of returning to Nellis. At that moment Groom Lake came up on the R/T requesting my nationality. At the same time a pair of F-101s with smoke-blackened gun ports drew up on my left wing. I got the distinct impression that it would have been acceptable if I had said I was Canadian, but when they learned I was British they suggested I too should land at Groom Lake. And they said, 'While you are at it, don't look to the left.' Fat chance! But I could well appreciate their reasons for wishing to keep the 'Star Wars' machine under wraps. It was a large, black, batlike delta wing, with two massive engines, each having a dorsal fin which canted inwards. The cockpit was buried in a long, flattened nose. Even from a distance it was obvious the aircraft was designed for high speed and high altitude.

On landing I was greeted by a USAF colonel who climbed the ladder to the cockpit and seemed reluctant to let go of my hand, even for the brief moments I needed to shut down the aircraft. Then I was driven off at great speed for individual interrogation in a darkened room under bright spotlights – a sort of benevolent third degree. I guessed the student was being questioned elsewhere. There were three of them in my team, and they seemed desperately anxious to establish my identity as a bona fide exchange pilot. Although how they thought anyone could pitch up in a USAF F-105 without some kind of official sanction defeated me. They kept asking me who I knew in Las Vegas. Apart from Betty I could only remember Fifi Lamour – the lead dancer at the Tropicana – which didn't seem to impress them much. But the atmosphere loosened up a little when I mentioned that I also knew Group Captain Bird-Wilson, who had been my station commander at Coltishall while I was on AFDS. The fact that I knew 'Birdy-Wilson' made all the difference. I refused to sign a prepared statement which opened with the words, 'As a citizen of the United States of America I swear . . .'. Even my interrogators agreed this was not appropriate, but I gave my word as an RAF officer that I would remain silent. That didn't seem to impress them much either. My account of what had happened in the air was accepted without question, presumably

[above] A DH 82 Tiger Moth similar to the aircraft on which I trained at Eastleigh in 1953.

[right] Boarding a Harvard – note the essential seat adjustment pillow.

[left] My instructor at Moose Jaw – Flying Officer B. Topper

Flight of three Harvard 4s

Lockeed T–33A over the Rockies

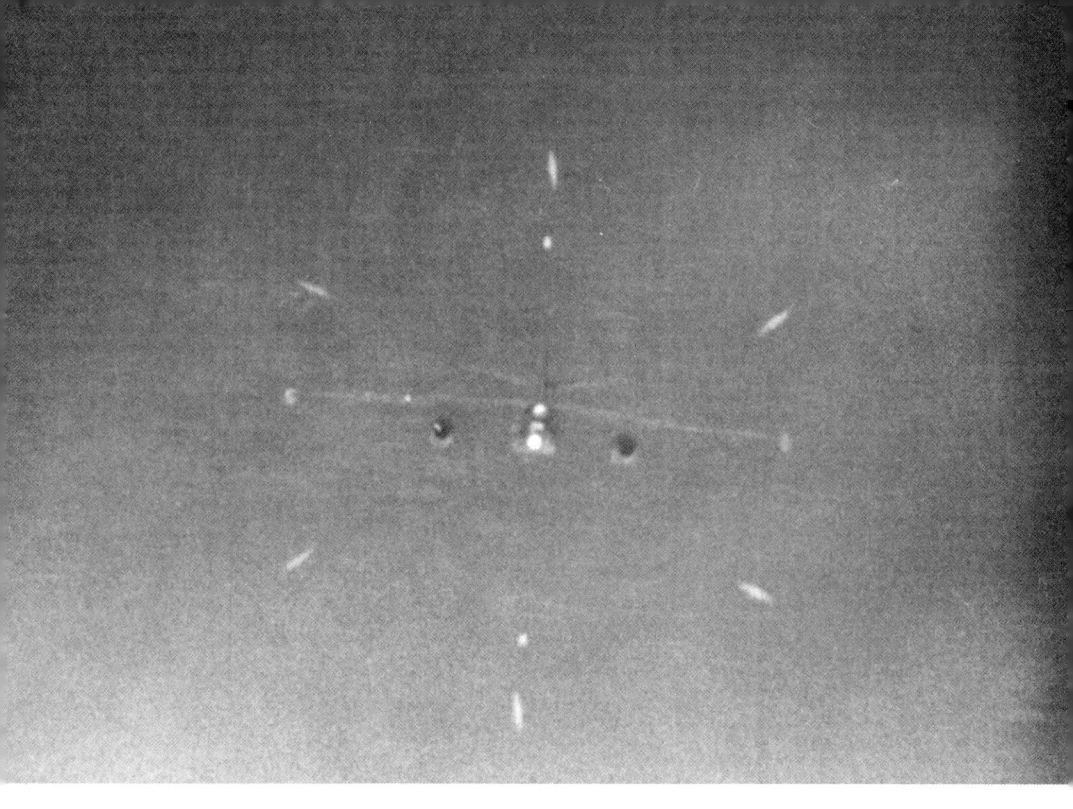

Hunter F4 of No 67 Squadron RAF Bruggen

The pilots of 67 Squadron in 1956

The starter motor from Bob Faulke's Hunter at Sylt.

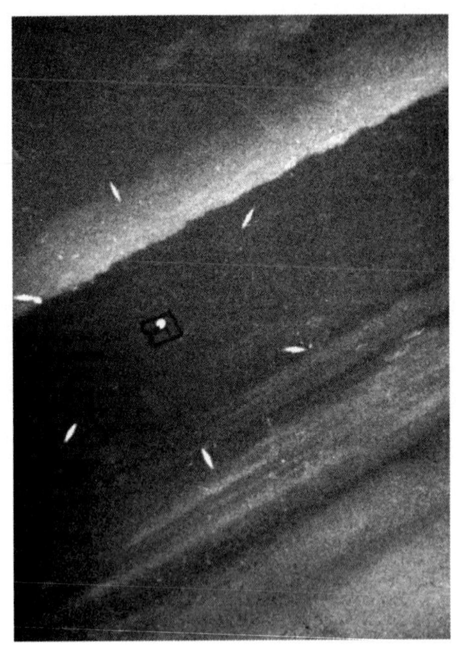

Ideal sight picure for opening fire on the flag

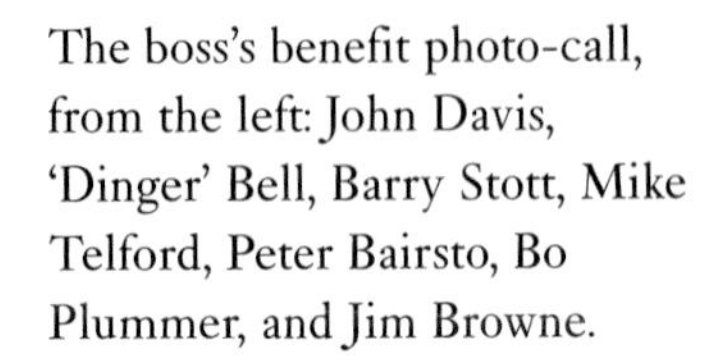

The boss's benefit photo-call, from the left: John Davis, 'Dinger' Bell, Barry Stott, Mike Telford, Peter Bairsto, Bo Plummer, and Jim Browne.

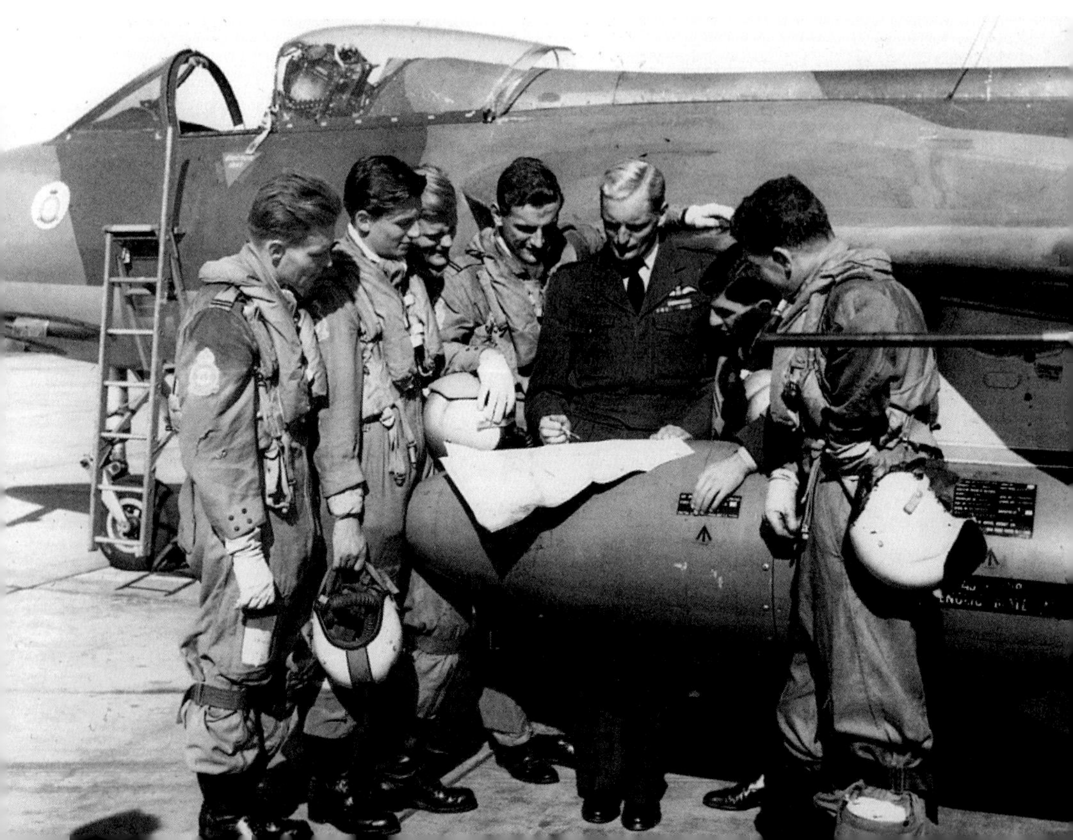

[above] No 7 Course at the Fighter Combat School RAF West Raynham

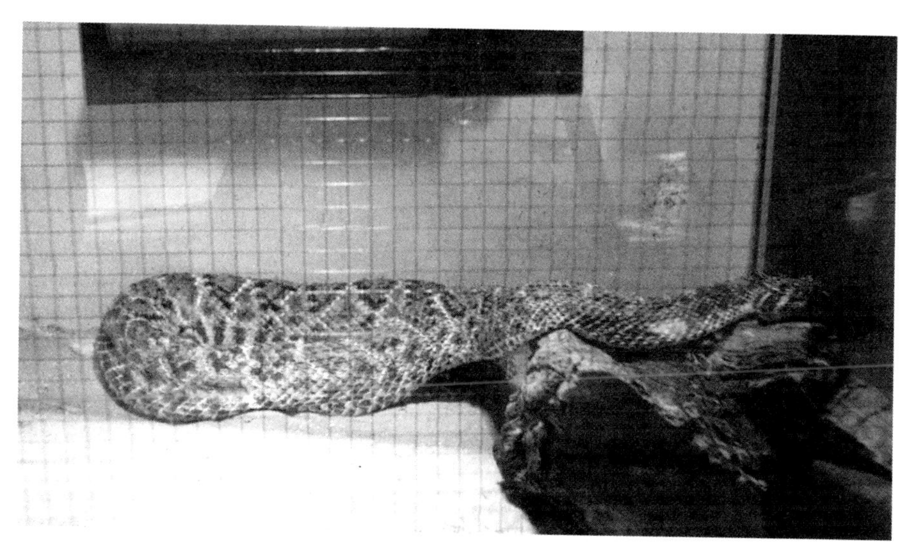

Ponsonby-Forsdyke-Psmith, a seven foot
Western Diamond-back rattlesnake

[left] The author at Acklington 1959

Squadron party to celebrate the arrival of our first Lightning, April 1961

Meatball Black formation

Going down – the
second half of a loop

The author with two lads from an Ipswich Foster-home

F-105D

Captain G.D. 'Barney' Barnhill at Takhli Air Base, Thailand, in October 1965

Loaded up and vertical – Phantom FGR2 with: wing tanks; SNEB pods; Vulcan gun pod and three Sparrow missiles

Ripple SNEB firing in Cyprus

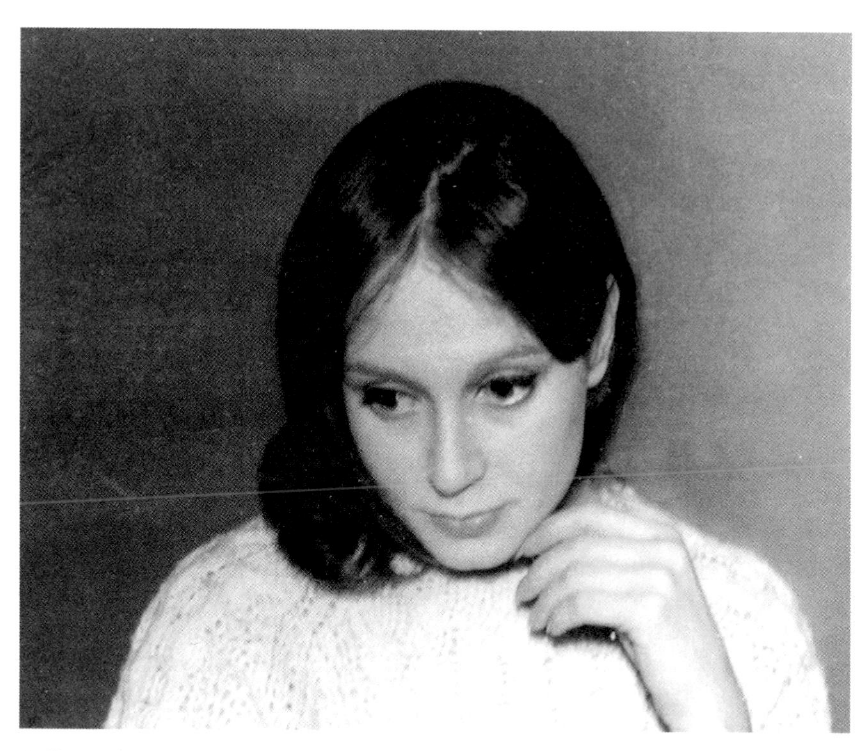

Juliet Helen Dunn, November 1965

The VIP Stand at the Cyprus Firepower Demonstration. The photographer (circled) took the picture below

The photographer is photographed – the author and Dougie Boyd at 450 knots

[left] Jules

[below left] Stuart Anthony Bendell

[below right] Emma Joanne Bendell

[above and right]
The tarmac laying
continued on 'Bravo'
Dispersal

The official reception
for our first aircraft

Exiting a HAS for an early training flight

Flight Lieutenant Norman Browne – an outstanding Phantom Navrad

Airborne photo-call 19 Squadron aircraft armed to the teeth

Wing commander Tim Gauvin takes over 19 Squadron – May 1978

The Duke of Gloucester's visit to Wildernrath

because it matched the student's debrief, but they were still suspicious about my reasons for diverting to Groom Lake. Obviously these people didn't know much about the F-105.

Then came the tricky problem of how to get the aircraft off the base. It was eventually agreed that I would ground-run the student's aircraft, if the oil pressure remained steady, and we would swap aircraft and return to Nellis as a pair. Much to my relief, after running the engine for ten minutes the oil pressure began to fluctuate and the Groom Lake engineers had to accept that the aircraft was unserviceable. I flew my original machine back to Nellis; the student returned later in a passenger aircraft.

Our Groom Lake diversion caused quite a stir at Nellis. I was informed that the base commander, General Boyd-Hubbard, was unhappy about a foreign national diverting to Groom Lake, but Major Foss – then commanding the 4526th – pointed out the inconsistency of having one rule for American airmen and another for the rest. I dodged the other instructor's questions by claiming, with malicious glee, that everything I had seen at Groom Lake was strictly NOFORN. The student, on the other hand, was so overawed by the experience that he refused to talk to anyone about anything at all. Even after two weeks, it was difficult to get a civil 'Good morning' out of him.

After comprehensive checks the student's aircraft was flown back to Nellis by a maintenance pilot, and he suffered yet another oil pressure failure *en route*. This time the oil system was completely stripped down and the remains of a large, commercial-standard paper towel were found in the oil tank. The towel, which had probably been left in the tank during manufacture, had started to disintegrate and was clogging the filters. A complete and catastrophic pressure failure could have occurred at any time. My decision to divert had finally been vindicated.

As for the 'Star Wars' aircraft: some six months later a photograph of America's latest research aircraft, designated the A-11 and claimed to be capable of Mach 3.0 at altitudes in excess of 70,000 ft, was released to the press. I recognised it as the aircraft I had seen at Groom Lake. The same aircraft, or rather a derivative of it, was subsequently introduced into the USAF as the Lockheed SR-71 Blackbird.

During November the 4526th was between courses, so Barney and I were able to take time off for golf. We preferred to play at the Craig Ranch Country Club, which was conveniently close to Nellis and much cheaper than the exclusive courses along the Strip. Barney was an enthusiastic beginner and when on form he could hit the ball a great distance, but his directional control was a trifle erratic. On one occasion we were waiting to tee-off, taking the usual practice swings to loosen up, when Barney asked if he could try out my No. 3 wood. Barney had more than enough problems with the long irons and he didn't possess any woods of his own. After a few tentative waggles to get the feel of the club, he wound up for a full-blooded, agricultural lunge at an imaginary ball. It was almost inevitable that he would misjudge the length of the club. He gouged out a foot-long divot of turf which flew for all of thirty feet and landed, soil side first, in the face of a waiting golfer. Covered with embarrassment, Barney apologised profusely – not to the man chewing the divot sandwich – but to me, for abusing my wood. The other fellow was too timid to complain, but his troubles were not yet over. It was customary at Craig Ranch to team singletons up with other players and as luck would have it he found himself playing with Barney and me. By this time Barney had done his best to restore good relations, and purely in the interests of reducing pressure he and I drove off first. Then our new-found playing partner stepped on to the tee. Unfortunately he topped his shot and his ball skittered barely fifty yards up the fairway. 'Oh, bad luck,' said Barney. 'We'll call that a Mulligan' – meaning we won't count that stroke, have another go. Whereupon the fellow angrily slammed his club back in the bag and exclaimed, 'That was the best shot I have ever hit off the tee.' The game seemed destined for failure, but he stayed with us for three more holes. However, his heart wasn't really in it.

Barney and I played another round of golf that November, and got back to the officers' club in time to hear the shattering news from Dallas that President John F. Kennedy had been shot. The whole nation was stricken with grief. I had always assumed that Las Vegas was basically a rough, tough frontier town, but I was surprised by the depth of emotion shown by the inhabitants. Grown men wept on the streets. Of course, Jack Ruby then shot Lee Harvey Oswald before he could be tried for the assassination. The public's reaction to all of this was fairly ambivalent. Some said that Lee Harvey Oswald deserved to die

– a sort of throwback to the old-fashioned lynch law – but others thought not. There was little doubt that Oswald was guilty of murder most foul, but most of us at Nellis would have been more comfortable if the case had been properly proven in a court of law.

That year Barney kindly invited me to spend Christmas with his family at Tonkawa, Oklahoma. I jumped at the chance. People were always saying Las Vegas was different from the rest of America, so it would be interesting to meet 'normal' folks from the mid-west. The trip would also fit in well with our plans to attend Ed Wayne's wedding in Albuquerque immediately after Christmas. I didn't know it at the time, but Betty was disappointed – she had been hoping we would spend Christmas together. But she was consoled by Donna, a friend of hers from Nellis who was having similar problems with Buster Kinkaid. Donna worked in the 'Procurement Office' at Nellis, which was not as spicy as it sounds.

We set off in Barney's Porsche on 19 December, across the Boulder Dam and south-east to Kingman to pick up Route 66 for the long climb over the Rockies. In those days Route 66 was a good road which passed tantalisingly close to the Grand Canyon National Park. But we had to be in Tonkawa by 21 December to attend the Barnhill family reunion, so there was no time for sightseeing on this trip. Instead, Barney provided a running commentary on points of interest: 'That road off to the left leads to the famous viewing point on the south rim of the Canyon.' And further on: 'That road on the right leads to the mile-wide meteor crater – the largest known to man.' And further still: 'The area off to the left is the petrified forest – the wood is so old it has turned to stone.' And later still: 'That was the Continental Divide – sorry, pal, you missed it!' Barney was a veritable mine of information, a well-informed but woefully behind schedule tour guide. The road was empty of traffic, and the mind-numbing speed limit of sixty miles per hour, for hour after hour, was an insult to the little Porsche. Eventually, after eleven and a half hours' driving, we breasted a rise and saw Albuquerque, a glittering jewel in the high desert, still some twenty miles away. Albuquerque was on the Rio Grande, another of the great rivers in North America, which flowed south-east to the Gulf of Mexico. We were halfway to Tonkawa and sorely in need of a good night's sleep.

Next day we continued our journey east on Route 66. For the first two hours we skirted around impressive snowbound peaks south of the Sangre de Cristo (Blood of Christ) Mountains – the central spine of the Rockies – before starting the slow descent to the Great Plains. We left the spectacular landscapes of Arizona and New Mexico behind and descended to the dry, dusty grasslands of middle America. Early explorers had believed this area incapable of cultivation, but they were wrong – although it still looked unpromising. Even Barney dried up. The towns along the route had romantic Spanish/Indian names: Santa Rosa, Tucumcari and Amarillo. Shortly after Amarillo we saw a Texas longhorn bull. It was probably due to the unexpected excitement of seeing this living legend of the West that we failed to maintain our lookout. Barney must have allowed his speed to drift up to seventy-five, because a state trooper immediately sprang from behind a bush and presented him with a speeding ticket. I was much impressed by the efficiency of the system: the trooper radioed ahead and Barney was invited to report to the court house in the next town for his case to be heard. Since the penalty for not doing so was an immediate jail sentence, Barney thought it wise to comply. It really was a one-horse town, but there nothing slow about the due process of law. The court was in permanent session and doing a roaring trade. Barney was fined $25, and we were back on the road again within thirty minutes.

The Barnhill reunion was the first occasion the entire family had been together for seven years, and it was most kind of them to include me in their celebrations. I spent much of the evening talking to Mrs 'Retta' Bidwell, a grand old lady who, as a young woman, had taken part in one of the Great Oklahoma Land Rushes at the end of the last century. She had lined up with her horse in the city square, and at the sound of a gun had ridden off across the plains to stake her claim. Unfortunately she had been claim-jumped before she could register it at city hall, which, apparently, was a common occurrence. Grandma Retta also offered to make me a cup of tea – a skill which seemed to have died out in America since the Boston Tea Party.

On the Monday we drove 240 miles north to Russell, Kansas, to spend the rest of Christmas with Barney's sister, Margaret Roberts. Her husband Bud was in the oil business and there was much evidence of oil around Russell. Every house, it seemed, had an oil pump nodding away in the back yard. Bud explained that the oil wells in this part of Kansas were relatively shallow and the reserves were limited, but in the meantime life was fairly comfortable. He owned a twin-engined Beachcraft, which he proceeded to run up in the hangar – much to Barney's and my concern. This was high living indeed. Bud cooked lunch on the barbecue, even though there was snow on the ground, and there was a plentiful supply of lobster in the deep freeze. I don't remember much about the social round, but it was certainly lively, and on one occasion I found myself stoutly defending the British National Health Service. Not that I cared much about the National Health Service, but someone had to speak up for the British. I met some charming people, including the Shields family and a future senator for Kansas and presidential candidate, Robert Dole. Dick Shields had flown B-17s with the US Army Air Corps during the war. He was now in the oil drilling business. It seemed to me that the folks from middle America were genuinely hospitable people, just like the normal folks in Las Vegas; but of course, that made no allowance for the wild majority.

We were well refreshed by the time we set off for Ed Wayne's wedding. The bride-to-be – June – was a delightful girl, already a widow in her early twenties; her former husband of just a few weeks had been killed flying a B-57, the American version of the British Canberra. It seemed entirely appropriate that she should find happiness with another airman. Barney and I figured that Ed was a lucky man. After the ceremony, in time-honoured fashion, June threw her bouquet and garter to the assembled throng, and for some reason I found myself clutching the bride's garter. Barney claimed my catching skills would have done credit to a professional baseball star, but I prefer to think of it as a happy coincidence. Ed was due to be posted to Germany, to an F-105 wing in 4 ATAF, so the reception also served as a farewell party.

Barney fell in love with one of the bridesmaids and elected to stay on at Albuquerque, but he kindly allowed me to drive his car back to Nellis. I really didn't mind – the Porsche was fun to drive, and I had to be back for the flying programme.

Betty welcomed me with open arms, and after a hot bath I fell into bed. Maybe marriage was not such a bad idea; one of these days, I thought, I would have to make on honest woman out of this girl.

In January the newly arrived dual-capable F-105F was assessed prior to its introduction into the training programme. The aircraft's performance and handling were identical to the 'D' model, and most of the essential controls and instruments were duplicated in the rear cockpit. On the face of it, the F-105F was an ideal training machine, but due to its very restricted forward visibility from the back seat, it could not be landed by an instructor seated in the rear. The aircraft was therefore of limited value during the initial conversion. Certainly none of the instructors at Nellis, myself included, relished the idea of sand-bagging in the back seat while some ham-fisted student attempted his first solo landing. Not that the Thunderchief was difficult to land. The normal approach speed was in the order of 170 knots, but some students flew their approach at higher than recommended speeds, in the mistaken belief that they were improving the safety margin. Far from improving safety, they were just making it more difficult to kill off their excess speed. And that led to other problems. If power was reduced too quickly on the final approach, the Thud would fall out of the sky like a streamlined brick. It sometimes hit the ground much sooner than expected, still going too fast. I remember watching one misguided student crunch down well short of the threshold, bounce fifty feet in the air, and still fail to stop on the available 10,000ft runway.

I put together a simple presentation which explained the need to balance engine power against airspeed, which was well received. In fact I was directed to give my presentation to all subsequent courses. The F-105F was eventually used during the conversion phase to give the students back-seat familiarisation flights, so-called Dollar rides, before their first solo in the 'D' model.

But the F-105F rapidly proved its worth when it came to training for all the other roles. The combat profile mission phase (i.e. the nuclear strike role) was my particular responsibility. In theory, the F-105D and F were designed specifically for this task, but the pilot's workload was extremely high. Technology had not yet reached the stage of development where a single man could accomplish the strike mission, blind and at low level. Every system in the aircraft – autopilot, Doppler navigation system, terrain-avoidance radar and the bombing computer – had to be fully serviceable, otherwise the pilot quickly became overloaded. In the F-105F we were able to demonstrate the best use of the equipment, and most of the students achieved an acceptable level of competence by the end of the course. But even as a dyed-in-the-wool single-seat pilot, it struck me that certain roles were better accomplished with a two-man crew. Of course the true value of the F-105F only became apparent later – when it was flown with great valour by the pilots and their back-seat Electronic Warfare Officers (the so-called Bears) in the Wild Weasel electronic counter-measures in Vietnam.

But to return to 1964 – it was largely due to the work I had done during the previous six months, to improve the training on the Thunderchief's terrain-avoidance radar, and my landing presentation, that I was nominated as the squadron's outstanding instructor. The award was presented by Major General John C. Meyer – Commander of the Twelfth Air Force – on 24 January. I had, at last, arrived. Life couldn't have been better.

Betty spent the afternoon and evening of 30 January at Nellis. Having been a USAF dependant, she was entitled to use the base facilities. She left the girls in the care of the family creche while she did her shopping. Prices in the PX – the American forces equivalent of the British NAAFI – were significantly cheaper than in local civilian stores. I was tied up with the flying programme all day, and in the evening I had to study for the 'Q' – the qualifying examination for the RAF staff college. Not that I had any burning desire to attend staff college, but the 'Q' examination was due to be replaced by a two-year individual studies course, so it made sense to attempt the examination while I had the chance. Betty dropped into my room shortly after ten o'clock to ask if she could borrow the car to take Michele to an appointment with an eye specialist the following day. I was sorely tempted to drive them all home and stay the night, but I was due to report first thing in the morning to the small-arms range to renew a pistol qualification. Betty took the car and we arranged to meet at the weekend. The tender trap was closing in, but I was not complaining; the thought of spending the weekend with Betty and the girls was very appealing. The wretched 'Q' would have to wait.

The official USAF aircrew side-arm was the Smith & Wesson .38 revolver, but in a country that prided itself on the individual's right to bear arms there was always an interesting collection of weapons at the range. Many preferred the heavy Colt .45 automatic, which was guaranteed to stop a man in his tracks – provided you hit him, of course. Pistol shooting was not one of my fortes. It was difficult enough to hit a target with the Smith & Wesson; I would probably have been lethal, although not very selective, with an overweight .45 calibre cannon. But I was on form on that particular day, and scraped in with a qualifying score. The range session was almost complete when word came through for me to return immediately to the squadron.

Captain Willard Gideon met me at the door, and I knew something was wrong. He sat me down in one of the briefing rooms and told me in quiet, measured tones that Betty and Sanita had been killed in a car accident. After ten years in the air force, I thought I was hardened to violent, untimely death but the awful news shook me. How can one describe the shock and pain of suddenly losing two very dear loved ones? What a tragic waste of two innocent human souls. Will Gideon was clearly upset; both he and his wife, Barbara, had been good friends of Betty's.

The rest of the morning was filled with inconsequential trivia. Clearly Michele, who was lying badly injured in hospital, needed my help, but it was difficult to concentrate. The nightmare reality of what had happened kept coming back. Friends on the squadron rallied around. Barney was away at the time, but Paul McClellan kindly lent me a car until I could straighten things out. I called the Southern Nevada Memorial Hospital to enquire about Michele. The staff seemed genuinely relieved that someone knew the family. Of course I could visit her, they said, but would I please first report to the reception desk?

The doctor in charge of the case explained that Sanita had died instantly in the crash, while Betty and Michele had both been admitted to hospital the previous evening. There had been some delay locating their registered doctor, and in the meantime Betty had succumbed as a result of an internal haemorrhage. Michele had numerous fractures and she was still in some discomfort, but her condition was stable. She had not yet been told about her mother and sister, and the doctor was concerned that she might overhear careless talk by the hospital staff. Since I was a close friend of the family, he asked me to break the sad news.

It was a harrowing experience. This fragile little girl was already desperately hurt, and here was I, adding to her misery by telling her that her mother and baby sister had gone to heaven. Her eyes filled with tears. I wanted to hold her tight, to comfort her, but she was in too much pain, so we just held hands and talked. I did my best to answer all her desperate questions, but the words seemed cruelly inadequate. We both grew up fast that afternoon in hospital.

Over the next few days I managed to piece together what had happened. After she'd left my room, Betty had picked up the girls and started to drive home. About two miles from Nellis, at a minor crossroads, the driver of another car had ignored a stop sign and ploughed into Betty's car. The force of the collision had shunted the big Fairlane sixty yards off the highway. Betty had managed to flag down a passing truck driver, who'd alerted the police. Under normal circumstances, once the victim of a road accident was admitted to hospital, their chances of survival were much improved. But in Nevada there was another crucial factor: through a mixture of human greed and abuse of the legal system, medical staffs were only insured to treat registered patients. From previous experience, I knew that even qualified nurses would refuse to give aid to road accident victims in case they were subsequently sued for medical malpractice. I had simply thought this lack of care was strangely out of place in a civilised community. But now I was angry. Betty may well have died solely because no one was prepared to take appropriate action to save her life.

News of the accident spread, and caring friends of the family started to visit Michele. I called Betty's sister, Mrs Margaret Anderson, in Washington DC, to tell her what had happened. The Andersons were not even aware that Betty had been divorced, which complicated matters: 'Who are you? And how are you involved?' I did my best to explain. At that stage they were the only next of kin available, and I urged them to fly out to Las Vegas. Michele's father eventually turned up at the hospital, and stricken with grief he promised to take care of her. It was none of my business of course – as an unrelated foreign national I had no say in the matter – but I was concerned. Because of the unique pattern of life in Las Vegas, many children – particularly those from single-parent families – became latch-key kids, arriving home from school as their parents were leaving for work. Thus I was not sure that Michele would be properly cared for if she remained with her father in Las Vegas.

After their initial uncertainty, Jim and Margaret Anderson were wonderfully supportive. They arrived in Las Vegas within hours of my call and immediately took over the task of sorting out Betty's personal affairs. After a few days they too recognised that Michele needed a stable family environment, and they managed to persuade her father that she should return with them to live in Washington. All that remained for me to do was to say my last goodbyes to Betty and Sanita in the chapel of rest.

They were both placed in the same coffin. A sad end to a tragic episode.

The office of the District Attorney prepared a case charging the woman driver of the other car with involuntary manslaughter. But Michele was the only surviving witness, and the case eventually had to be dropped through lack of evidence. It was probably all for the best – the unfortunate woman had neither money nor insurance. The knowledge that she had caused a fatal accident would be on her conscience for the rest of her life; it would serve no useful purpose to have it all dragged up in court, and it spared Michele the trauma of having to testify.

Grieving for a loved one was an entirely new experience for me, and I found it difficult to come to terms with Betty's death. Oh, I had lost grandparents of course, but in the grand scheme of things that was to be expected. This was entirely different. This was a very private, lonely agony. My friends at Nellis – Barney, Buster and Donna, Don and Pat Riggs, and the other instructors – did their best to console me, but I fear it was hard going. One afternoon while I was having a cool beer with Buster and Donna, my eyes filled with tears. I had been brought up to believe that men weren't supposed to cry, but it didn't seem at all inappropriate. I was among friends. I used to lie awake at night tortured with the same pointless 'if only' regrets: if only I had delayed Betty for a moment longer; if only I had driven them home . . .

Letters from home were a great comfort, particularly one written by my sister Paddy, who offered some hope for the future. I sought solace in religion, which alone held out the promise that someday we might all meet again. It was a slow, painful process. At times I doubted that I would ever get over Betty's death.

After the guilt came the crushing loneliness – but gradually I came to realise that, while one should never forget, the pain of bereavement eventually diminishes.

Like countless millions before, I buried myself in my work and I was back in the air within the week. The great advantage about the flying at Nellis was that it demanded total commitment.

A new group of students had just arrived and the flying task kept me fully occupied. As part of the air combat phase, each student had to fire a Sidewinder air-to-air missile. The Sidewinder was an infra-red heat seeker which homed on to the hot jet pipe of the target aircraft. It was a relatively cheap but highly effective missile. We used to joke that we were about to fire a Cadillac, because they cost the same.

The missile firing sortie was very simple and the instructor normally chased in a second F-105D. All the student had to do was climb to 20,000 ft, raise the aircraft's nose high above the horizon and launch a target rocket. After a count of ten, while listening to the audio acquisition signal (a growl through the earphones) of the Sidewinder, and tracking the flares on the back end of the target, the student was free to launch his missile. If things went according to plan, the target would just be descending below the horizon about three miles ahead when the Sidewinder would streak off. The missile would snake from side to side searching out its target. The warhead was fused to detonate as the missile passed alongside its target.

At least, that was the plan. But in their highly aroused state, the students often counted to ten faster than expected. Sometimes they would launch the Sidewinder when the target was a mere 500 yards ahead, and at that range the detonation of the warhead was quite impressive. It was impossible to avoid the dirty brown smudge which marked the explosion of the Sidewinder's 10 lb blast/fragmentation warhead. The safest option was to fly through the centre of the burst, hoping you didn't pick up any debris. For the instructor, slightly displaced off to one side, it all added to the thrill of the chase.

Early in 1964 the USAF increased pilot training to compensate for an expected shortfall later in the decade. At Nellis there were plans to inrroduce a standard sixty-hour course – for experienced crews – and a 120-hour course for pilots just out of advanced training. The quality of some of the students was to give cause for concern. It appeared as though every pilot in the USAF, regardless of their previous experience, was being pushed through the F-105 programme. The first sign that anything was amiss usually appeared in the landing pattern. We had a certain amount of sympathy for any ex-Strategic Air Command pilot having to speed up his reactions to cope with a fighter type circuit, but students having difficulty with this basic skill stood little chance of successfully completing the course.

I remember discussing the relative lack of aptitude of some of the students with a USAF colonel who also had experience in the RAF. He agreed that perhaps too little account was taken of the pilot's previous experience in the USAF selection system, but pointed out that the USAF was a large organisation, and the majority of pilots would be able to achieve average results in the F-105, which was all that was required. He also said that America would always win a war of attrition, simply because it could afford to commit greater resources than any likely enemy. Which was fair comment, I have to say – most of the students were extremely competent in the air.

Of course, we had no way of knowing that within thirteen months American pilots would be fighting for survival in the skies over North Vietnam. And before the decade was out, American military staffs would have reason to question their policies.

I had intended to spend some leave with the Andersons and Michele in April, but instead I had to attend the annual RAF Week at the USAF Air Warfare College at Maxwell in Alabama. There was no way I could excuse myself; it was the only occasion the exchange officers got together during their overseas tour. The programme of lectures was fairly relaxed, but the social round was daunting. I was not yet prepared to live it up, but I did take the opportunity to explain to the RAF embassy staff why I wished to cancel my application to sit the 'Q' examination.

Tragedy struck at Nellis in May. The Thunderbirds had recently re-equipped with F-105Bs. In those days it was important that the premier aerial demonstration team flew the most up-to-date fighter type. The 'B' models had been lightened and modified to improve their performance at display speeds. The Thunderbirds' F-105 display was certainly impressive. It covered more sky than their F-100 show, but that was more than offset by the sheer spectacle of four large, colourfully decorated aircraft wheeling around in tight formation. After six public shows, on 9 May 1964, while joining the circuit to land at Hamilton AFB in California, Captain Gene Devlin's aircraft suffered a massive structural failure and disintegrated. It was the first fatal accident on the Thunderbirds for many years. Four days later one of our students – Lieutenant Hebert – flying an F-105D, lost power soon after take-off and crashed into a housing estate in North Las Vegas, killing six civilians including three children. Hebert also died.

Take-off is always a critical stage of flight, particularly in a heavily laden single-engined aircraft. We all had our theories as to the reason for Hebert's apparent loss of power, but nothing was ever confirmed.

Of course there was no connection between the two accidents. The fact that they both occurred within a week was pure coincidence – these things do happen. But the reputation of the F-105 sank to an all-time low. The Thunderbirds re-equipped with F-100 Super Sabres. A plan for them to return to the F-105 was never followed up. In due course, many of the world's top formation teams reverted to advanced training aircraft. Checks were made on the structural integrity of the Thud. Actually the loss rate of F-105s – running at 7.5% per year – was comparable to other single-engined jet aircraft.

The only undue excitement I experienced in an F-105D occurred during a 600-knot run-in at 500 ft, for a practice weapons delivery, when the stability augmentation system malfunctioned and applied a series of full alternate rudder deflections. Fortunately the wing tanks were empty, otherwise they would certainly have been torn off. Despite its wild gyrations, my aircraft safely gained height, but clearly it was not designed for that sort of thing – and neither was I.

Nellis quickly recovered from its misfortunes. In my case, the double tragedy brought some sort of cathartic release. I was not the only one with cause to grieve, and the sooner I got to grips with living life the better. In time I would have other loves, although no one in Las Vegas could ever replace Betty.

Humour is a great salve for the human spirit, and there was plenty of that at Nellis. We were due for a commanding general's inspection at the end of May. As usual on such occasions, the day was to start with a full-blown parade. Aircrew generally preferred to leave marching and foot drill to other mortals, but the base commander decided that the instructing staff, including the exchange officers, should form an all-officer squadron in the centre of the parade. Several rehearsals were planned, to make up for our lack of expertise. The exchange officers, who obviously had not spent hours at a USAF boot camp, had a minor problem with American foot drill. Marching was straightforward, but parade orders – delivered at maximum volume – were sometimes incomprehensible. And troop formations with men marching six abreast, shoulder-to-shoulder, were completely new. Even the simple about turn – about face in American military jargon – would leave British and Canadian officers standing one full pace out of line. But that apart, we were a reasonably well co-ordinated body of men.

After the first rehearsal it was decided that everything would be fine if marching and drill manoeuvres were reduced to a minimum and the exchange officers were carefully concealed in the middle of the officer squadron. The next rehearsal also went surprisingly well, until we marched on to take up position on parade. It must have looked impressive, with a guidon bearer in the lead followed by the parade squadron commander and a body of eighty or more officers, all in step. The guidon bearer, who had obviously done this sort of thing before, was twirling his guidon staff with gusto.

As we approached our appointed position on parade, the squadron commander turned round to face his troops, presumably so that we would more clearly hear his orders. He continued marching backwards, of course, otherwise he would be out of position. 'SQUAAAADRON,' he roared, in preparation for the halt. In the meantime, the guidon bearer had worked up to a frenzy, the penultimate movement of which was to thrust his guidon staff, pointed end first, vigorously backwards . . . which jabbed the squadron commander squarely in the arse.

The final order sounded more like a startled squawk: 'HAOOOWLT!'

Someone sniggered, the CO minced off clutching his buttocks, and in seconds the whole squadron had collapsed, helpless with laughter.

That was the last time the exchange officers at Nellis marched on parade. On the big day, we were lined up safely behind the saluting base and the guidons were positioned before the squadrons marched on. The general was suitably impressed.

Then there was the unlikely tale of the magical 'snifter bags'. It all started on one of those days when high winds at Nellis whipped up the sand and dust and made life uncomfortably gritty. The CO's secretary, a long-legged Southern Belle from Georgia, also named Betty, came into the crewroom and asked what caused those little piles of sand in front of the aircraft on the ramp.

There were many hydraulic pipes and unions in the nose-wheel bay of the F-105, and it was not unusual to have a slight hydraulic leak in that area. The drips of fluid on the dust dry concrete retained fine particles of grit, which rapidly built up to form tiny but perfectly symmetrical pinnacles of sand.

To the uninitiated it appeared as though the sand had fallen from the aircraft – and quick as a flash Will Gideon said, 'Those are caused by leaking snifter bags.'

Betty was intrigued – so was I.

Perfectly dead-pan, Will went on to explain, 'The F-105 really doesn't want to fly . . .' That much must have been obvious from Betty's office as she watched the twenty-five-ton tricycles thundering down the runway. 'So when the speed is right the pilot pulls a switch in the cockpit, which drops sand on the nose-wheel, fooling it into believing that it has run out of runway and it is time to get airborne.'

Betty, bless her, a lovely girl but easily conned, swallowed it hook, line and sinker.

We managed to keep the tale of 'snifter bags' going for several days.

I eventually got away on leave at the end of June. The USAF had a splendid scheme whereby uniformed personnel were entitled to travel free on military transport aircraft, provided there was space available. I managed to hitch a ride, albeit by a roundabout route, to Andrews AFB near Washington DC. The Andersons were expecting me. They lived in an elegant house on Hillcrest Drive in the suburbs to the south-east of the city. They had a teenage son and daughter, Tom and Karen, who were much older than Michele, but I was pleased to see that she had been warmly absorbed into the family. As usual at that time of the year, Washington was oppressively humid, but Michele was determined to show me the sights and I was given the grand tour. Jim Anderson generously loaned me his car – a Cadillac, no less – to get around. We did all the usual things, visiting the Lincoln Memorial and the Washington Monument, driving past the White House and visiting the Smithsonian Institute's Air Museum, where I saw John Glenn's Mercury space capsule, in which he had become the first American to orbit the Earth. And of course we visited Betty's and Sinita's grave, a small, insignificant plot beside the cemetery path. I also took Karen out one evening; we dined on lobster, and afterwards went on to the theatre to see *Camelot.* Karen was a charming companion, young and full of life. I felt slightly shop-soiled and positively seedy in comparison.

After an enjoyable week with the Andersons I headed back to Nellis. I got as far as Salt Lake City via military transport, but then bought a commercial air ticket to Las Vegas – a small price to pay for a round trip of more than four thousand miles.

Back at Nellis the F-105 wing was beginning to reap the benefit of the Look Alike programme, and the maintenance men were at last getting to grips with the aircraft's engineering problems. By September we had three different courses running concurrently and an average student population of twenty-eight. The instructors were fully stretched. Not that I had any complaints – during the latter half of 1964 I flew more than 180 hours in the F-105 and it was all high-quality flying. One of the advantages of the new system was that instructors and students were paired up on a one-to-one basis for the initial ten sorties. Any problems were quickly sorted out and the students benefited from the continuity. The instructors also derived maximum job satisfaction. Among my many students, I flew some thirty hours checking out Colonel Chairsell and Captain Ed Stanford on the F-105. They both went on to serve with distinction in Vietnam.

Fortunately we could still relax at the weekends. In the unbroken sunshine of Nevada, the offer of a day's water-skiing on Lake Mead was almost irresistible to the sporting girls of Las Vegas, and Barney was only too willing to oblige. I was usually invited along to make up the crew – at least two people were needed to launch the boat. I have to say, some of Barney's guests were impressive. I remember one statuesque young lady who didn't have much to say, but turned up with her own ski – just the one – complete with its own shammy-leather bag. The lake was unusually choppy that day, and Barney and I were discussing the skiing possibilities when the girl dived over the side – obviously she wasn't put off by the conditions. In no time at all she had fitted her ski, grabbed the rope and yelled 'Hit it'. She rose from the waves like a bronzed godess, and for the next thirty minutes she gave a faultless exhibition of 'mono' skiing. It was perhaps fortunate that the outboard motor quit before either Barney or myself could demonstrate our own meagre skills.

About that time, Buster Kincaid completed his tour of duty and escaped to Canada, leaving Donna alone and blue at Nellis. But Buster's bachelor days were numbered. Seven weeks later he called Donna, reversing the charges, and proposed. The next we knew was a card announcing their wedding at Cold Lake, Alberta, on 8 August 1964. Like the Mounties, Donna had chased her man north, finally got him and presented him with the phone bill.

The embassy's warning about visitors proved to be correct. Although I only had one official visit during 1963, many of the RAF exchange officers trickled through Friday's 'happy hour' drinks in the Stag Bar prior to hitting town. I never realised I had so many friends. But by 1964 word had got round that there was something worth seeing at Nellis. By this time work on the UK's new all-weather nuclear strike aircraft – the TSR 2 – was well advanced. Although the TSR 2's radar equipment was very different from that used in the F-105D, the concept was more or less the same. Officially the main interest was the F-105D, but any visitor worth his salt arranged to spend a few days, including a weekend, in Las Vegas, and of course they all preferred to be booked into one of the hotels on the Strip. Among the early visits was a group captain from the RAF's operational requirements directorate at the Ministry of Defence in London; he was followed by a small team from the British Aircraft Corporation. Since the loss of the Fairlane, I had purchased a clapped-out 1957 Ford, and I usually gave my visitors a guided tour of Las Vegas.

Then in August, I received a letter from Wing Commander Bill Howard, ex-Wattisham, who had been posted to the embassy in Washington, advising me that he was escorting a team of officers from the Central Fighter Establishment on a fact-finding tour of the USAF. They planned to arrive on a Friday evening, spend the weekend in Las Vegas and depart from Nellis on the Wednesday. I noticed that Air Commodore Bill Tacon, Peter Collins, John Rogers and several other old friends from Hunter and Lightning days were on the team. As Bill

Howard said, all I had to do was make reservations for one air commodore, six wing commanders and two squadron leaders at a select, but reasonably cheap hotel on the Strip, arrange to keep them occupied during off-duty hours and escort them around Nellis.

This called for specialist assistance, and I immediately roped in Barney. If I remember rightly, they stayed at the Flamingo. For the Saturday afternoon I managed to organise an official tour of the Boulder Dam, and I went with them. At that time, one of the most popular shows in town was at a minor night-spot called the Pussycat-a-Go-Go, which presented a fast-talking comedian and a couple of scantily clad dolly birds, suspended in guilded cages above the bar, gyrating their way through the latest hot dance numbers. It was almost impossible to get a seat at the Pussycat on a Saturday night, but Barney somehow managed to get us in. Not only that, but we were met at the door by the owner and escorted to the best seats in the house. That night the comedian seemed to have a fixation about Middle Eastern gentlemen, which had a minimal effect on the RAF visitors, but the go-go girls really grabbed their attention. As we left the club, Barney explained that he had told the *maître d'* that he was escorting a party of high-spending Egyptian generals – which, no doubt, accounted for our welcome at the door and the comedian's repertoire. That was just the start of a riotous evening. The CFE team later acquitted themselves well during the official visit to Nellis; at least, their USAF hosts were suitably impressed. As a parting gesture, they treated Barney and me to an excellent supper at the Aku-Aku.

Leiutenant 'Harley' Hall, United States Navy, joined the squadron in November to replace Don Riggs. It was a pity Don and Pat had to leave but, like any other exchange officer, Don was anxious to return to his own service. Harley was an experienced fighter pilot and easily coped with the upgrading course. Being an easygoing bachelor with debonair good looks and a gleaming red and white, two-tone Thunderbird, Harley was bound to succeed. We figured the ladies of Las Vegas would find him irresistible, and we were right. We could have done without the competition, but he was a good lad to have on the team.

Early in December, Air Commodore Bird-Wilson visited Nellis. I didn't bother to mention my interview with his friends at Groom Lake.

The Christmas stand-down started on 23 December. Barney and I had been invited to join the Roberts and the Shields for a skiing holiday at Breckenridge in Colorado. It was good to seem them all again. On the first day I was limited to the nursery slopes, where I was constantly upstaged by Lynn and Sue Shields – who were clearly born with skis, but at least it made them laugh. In the following days they encouraged me to go higher and higher up the mountain, from where I descended in every-increasing abandonment. Trouble was, I could only turn to the right; whenever I tried to go left I would get halfway round and accelerate to destruction straight downhill. If we had stayed there another six months I am sure I would have mastered it.

A week later, on our drive back to Nellis, Barney called in at Vail to visit June Wayne. Barely six week after their wedding, Ed had been killed attempting to recover a stricken F-105D into Wheelus air base in Libya. Poor June – twice widowed, yet a wife for less than three months. According to Barney she was coping well.

On 1 January a signal arrived from Washington advising of my promotion to squadron leader. The promotion was a complete surprise. Even more unexpected, I was immediately elevated to the post of operations officer (i.e. deputy commander) of the squadron. By this time the 4526th was actually commanded by Major Walter E. Carson II. Frankly I could have done without the honour – other members of the squadron were far better qualified for the post – but that was the American way. The job was no more demanding than I had done on Treble One, although, as I later found out, I was also responsible for writing the annual effectivness reports on all the assigned instructors – and that was a pain.

Of course, annual reports are essential, but I always feel vaguely uncomfortable assessing my fellow officers. The ERs served the same purpose as the RAF's Form 1369. The officers' personal attributes were numerically assessed, and this was followed by a narrative report. At that time, the problem with the USAF effectiveness report was that the numerical assessments had been grossly devalued. Applying normal standards, on a scale of one to nine, five was a good average, but because I thought the instructors on the 4526th were above average, I used seven as the baseline. My initial reports were returned with the comment, 'If you mark these men down like this, their careers are finished.' After a few more rejections it became obvious that only the nines would do, and the only square on the ER with any meaning was the answer to the question, 'Has this man got a degree? This exaggerated the importance of the narrative; apart from it being almost impossible to match up the two parts of the report, I was quickly at a loss for superlatives to adequately describe my peers.

On a separate issue, I later found that the USAF's confidential reports submitted on the RAF exchange officers were automatically downgraded by the British Embassy staffs.

About this time, Barney volunteered for service in Vietnam. In February 1965 he was posted to an operational F-105 wing at McConnell AFB. F-105 squadron detachments to Thailand had first become involved in combat over Laos in August 1964, and we were soon getting feedback from the operational squadrons. Nuclear strike was still the predominant role for which we trained, but the emphasis was slowly shifting towards visual low-level navigation and conventional attack. The hounds of war had been loosed, and several pilots from 4526th, including Oscar Brooks and Paul McClellan, had actually volunteered for airborne forward air controller duties in South-East Asia, flying the sturdy A1-E piston-engined trainer.

On 12 January I managed to get a back-seat ride in an F-100F Super Sabre from the Fighter Weapons School, on a Dart target sortie for air-to-air gunnery. The F-100 was unique among jet fighters, in that the rudder was the predominant control for all turning manoeuvres. Which explained some of the problems ex-F-100 pilots had when they converted to the F-105. But otherwise the F-100 was pleasantly light on the controls.

Harley Hall duly qualified as an instructor and took over the usual tasks. He was good, but like many of the best fighter pilots he was inclined to be overconfident. You learn to live with that sort of thing if you are one of the same breed, but Harley really pushed his luck. Whenever he went out to fly he would call 'Check Six,' implying that everyone should watch out otherwise they were liable to be waxed by one Harley H. Hall. But Harley had not served his apprenticeship in Europe, and one day I got my chance. I was flying with a student in an F-105F, and Harley was leading a pair of F-105Ds against the same target just ten minutes later. Halfway round the route I set up an ambush. It was a classic 'bounce' – Harley must have been asleep, but fortunately for him we had no gun camera. We approached from deep six and passed between the two Ds with well over two hundred knots' overtake. I called 'Check Six, Harley,' and fire-walled the throttle. He took it all in good part, but it surprised the hell out of his student.

A hundred miles or so up the road towards Tonopah – commonly known as Widowmaker Highway – lay the Nevada Nuclear Test Facility. By this time all testing was done underground. A shaft, shaped like a huge, inverted walking stick, was sunk 2,000ft deep, the nuclear device was mounted round the curve of the handle, and the shaft was filled in with concrete. The heat and blast generated by the nuclear explosion were fully contained, although the surface would heave slightly. The desert's rocky crust would then subside after the explosion, leaving a wide, shallow depression. We were forbidden to overfly the area, and special procedures were published in case 'the Concrete Cork' ever blew. These were never invoked while I served at Nellis, but one morning, after returning from a standard weapons sortie on one of the radar targets, my aircraft was surrounded by armed guards. The touch-down might have been a trifle firm, but I didn't think it was that bad. I was escorted to the base commander's office: it turned out that one of my radio transmissions had interrupted the countdown to an underground test, which was being witnessed by the new breed of airmen – the first team of American astronauts. The countdown had gone something like: five, four, three, Jaguar Lead at the IP, in hot . . . It wasn't my fault; no one in the flight had heard anything of the countdown, but I was not the most popular flavour of the month. After various tests, it was found that the radio on my aircraft was transmitting both on the correct channel and on a harmonic frequency, which happened to coincide with the nuclear test frequency.

Flight Lieutenant 'Jock' Heron, my replacement, arrived during the last week in March. I had mixed feelings about leaving. It would be nice to get back to the familiar surroundings of the RAF, but the Nellis tour had been a high point of my career, and I was reluctant to give it all up. In two years I had flown well over 500 hours in the F-105 and had gained a wealth of valuable experience. Never before had I known such extremes of emotion, both high and low – it was as though I had lived life at double the normal speed. I also knew that my next tour would be at the Ministry of Defence in London, which was distinctly unwelcome. But the evil day could not be put off for ever. I flew my last sortie at Nellis on 25 March with Captain Hugh Milton in an F-105F.

There was the usual round of farewell parties, the squadron gave me an inscribed, silver-plated brandy snifter, and Harley presented me with miniature US Navy wings mounted on a brass plate, with the inscription 'Bugs – "Check Six" – H^3'.

I introduced Jock around the base and helped him to settle in, although I could give little assistance with the domestic arrangements. Jock was accompanied by his family, and they really needed married accommodation. He did buy my car, though, and when I eventually left the base early in April, Jock had been promised a married quarter within the week.

I reported to the embassy in Washington for my final debriefing and learned that they were a bit upset about not being informed of my diversion to Groom Lake. But as I pointed out, no one had told me that the gathering of military intelligence was part and parcel of my duties as an exchange officer. I also took the opportunity to say goodbye to Michele and the Andersons. I think they were sad to see me go – I had kept in fairly regular contact with Michele – but the tragedy of Betty's and Sanita's deaths had now passed, and it struck me that maybe I was just another unwelcome reminder. Now it might be appropriate to fade discreetly from the scene.

I had a day in New York, and took in the Empire State Building and Times Square before embarking on the RMS *Queen Mary*, bound for Southampton. It seemed a fitting end as I watched the Statue of Liberty slowly disappear astern. Then I went into the bar and found an ex-girlfriend from Las Vegas also bound for England. Hell's teeth – I'd thought I had left all that behind me, but obviously she hadn't got the message.

My friends at Nellis went on to greater things. I can hardly do justice to the crucial role the F-105 played in the Vietnam War, but neither am I prepared just to leave it at that. In contrast to all the problems during its initial introduction, the F-105 performed extremely well in South-East Asia, and mainained remarkably high serviceability states. The 'Rolling Thunder' series of air strikes against targets in North

Vietnam started on 2 March 1965, and from then until August 1972 the F-105 bore the brunt of the American air offensive against the North. Unfortunately, President Johnson's policy of gradually increasing the pressure, in the belief that the North Vietnamese would quickly break, was a mistake. In fact the North Vietnamese easily kept pace with the slow escalation of the war, and rather than pursue the cause of peace they blatantly used the periodic bombing halts to re-group their forces. The American generals were treating Vietnam as a conventional war of attrition, but the North Vietnamese and their allies – the Vietcong – were bent on fighting a very different kind of war. Knowing that time was on their side, they were prepared to accept disproportionate losses.

Until the Tet Offensive in 1968, the Vietcong preferred to avoid direct confrontation, adopting tactics which tended to neutralise the superior firepower of the American forces. American operations were tightly controlled from Washington DC. For the first two years of the war, large sanctuary areas – within which offensive air operations were either prohibited or severely curtailed – were established around Hanoi and the vital port of Haiphong. Prior to April 1967, American pilots were not even allowed to attack targets of opportunity, such as active North Vietnamese military airfields. The transit routes to and from the target areas were also subject to strict central control and seldom changed, which enabled the North Vietnamese to deploy their gun and missile air defences for maximum effect. American commanders in the field were subjected to constant political interference and were not allowed to use their own initiative.

To the independent observer it appeared as though the American giant was trying to fight the war with one arm tied behind its back, a paradoxical evening up of odds between the sophisticated American war machine and the downtrodden Communist peasant army – but this would be naive. So was the simplistic view that Vietnam was part of the continuing communist threat of world domination. Of course the North Vietnamese and the Vietcong were communist inspired, and they were provided with weapons by both China and the Soviet Union. But rather than be part of a larger scheme of world communist expansion, the North Vietnamese were primarily motivated by nationalistic sentiments to liberate South Vietnam from the occupying

American Forces and to unify the country, albeit under communist control. By 1968, in their attempts to support the corrupt, unstable South Vietnamese government, America had committed over 540,000 troops on the ground.

Despite the tactical strait-jacket, the F-105 pilots pressed home their attacks with great courage. In the circumstances, no other aircraft could have done the task more effectively, and no other aircraft could have better survived the punishment – but in seven years the USAF lost 382 F-105s, mainly to radar-laid anti-aircraft guns. Although the F-105s were never used in the pure fighter role, in the course of self-defence its pilots accounted for no less than twenty-eight MiG 17s.

Barney served with distinction in South-East Asia. He completed the prescribed combat tour between August and December 1965, flying with the 562nd Tactical Fighter Squadron out of Takhli in Thailand. During the course of his spell he was awarded a USAF Distinguished Flying Cross for his part in the first hunter-killer sortie against a heavily defended SA-2 Guideline SAM site. They destroyed the site, but the flight leader – a US Navy commander – was killed over the target; Barney's aircraft took thirty-seven hits before he limped back for an emergency landing at Da Nang. On another occasion, while refuelling from a KC-135 tanker prior to an attack, Barney's aircraft developed a massive fuel leak and he ejected split seconds before it exploded. He volunteered to extend his tour at Takhli, but at that time consecutive operational tours were not permitted. Barney returned to McConnell to train other F-105 pilots for Vietnam.

In 1967, Major Leo Thorsness, another contemporary of mine on the 4526th, was recommended for the Congressional Medal of Honor for an action-packed mission flying a Wild Weasel F-105F, during which he shot down a MiG 17. Unfortunately, Leo himself was shot down eleven days later and he had to wait six years before he collected his award. Many other Nellis pilots, including Captain Willard Gideon and Colonel Bean, spent long years as prisoners of war in North Vietnam.

Others, including Harley Hall, were less fortunate. After completing his tour at Nellis, Harley converted to Phantom F-4s and led the US Navy's Blue Angels aerial demonstration team. He subsequently served in Vietnam and was shot down in 1973 – barely two hours before the cessation of hostilities. Ever since then Harley Hall has been listed as missing in action.

Vietnam was a war that America could never have won by conventional means, but the American military forces surely deserved better support, both from their political masters and from the great American public. By the time it was over, American casualties – either killed or missing in action – exceeded 58,000.

9
Staff tour at the Ministry of Defence

It took a while to shake off the girl from Las Vegas, but the *Queen Mary* was a big ship. After a day or so of playing hide-and-seek between decks the siren transferred her attentions to the ship's purser. I didn't feel at all guilty – after all, she was doing the chasing – but good luck to the purser. This left me free to play the field, which was how I met Christine, a petite English rose. I could have fallen for that lady in a big way; right from the start we had an easygoing, light-hearted relationship. She had spent the previous two years working for a civilian airline based in Los Angeles. Sadly, for me at least, Christine's family was due to emigrate to Australia within weeks of arriving back in England, and she would be going with them. So our encounter was destined to be all too brief, but we arranged to see each other in England before she departed.

Mum and Dad met me at Southampton docks. In the two years spent in the States I had acquired a strong American accent and a proper crewcut, which must have been hard on Mother, but as I later found out she was more concerned about my state of health. She could not have known that the haggard, dissipated appearance was largely due to the hectic social life aboard ship. Still, it was good to be home again.

For the first time since joining the RAF, I had no great desire to report to my next place of duty. The Ministry of Defence was a far cry from anything I had known before in the air force and, to be brutally frank, a desk job in London did not appeal to me.

But now I was entitled to three weeks' disembarkation leave and I needed some form of transport. I had saved a few hundred pounds in my UK bank account and, with Dad's help, I found a very reasonable second-hand Jaguar 2.4. The Jaguar was a great deal more luxurious than my old MG. It was not really a sports car at all, but I figured the hard top would be welcome protection against the UK's weather. Besides, the metallic blue car, with real leather upholstery and polished walnut dashboard, appealed to my maturing tastes.

After a week at home and the inevitable round of pubs with my parents, I set out to restore my contacts with the RAF. There was no point in going back to Wattisham – the pilots I had flown with on Treble One had long gone – but I learned that Terry Carlton had taken over a squadron on No. 226 OCU (the Lightning conversion unit) at Coltishall, which was as good a place as any to start. Lightning flying hours were still difficult to come by, so there was no chance of my grabbing a quick ride in a T4, but it was a pleasure to get back to something resembling an RAF squadron. When I arrived, one of the staff pilots was practising his aerobatic routine in a Lightning F1A over the airfield. In my day, this would have been obligatory viewing for every available pilot on the base, but the young students on the OCU chose to continue their card game in the crewroom. I found this very strange. Terry explained that the new students were academically highly qualified and, generally, they were more interested in their future security than they were in honing their flying skills. I had always assumed that the two were inextricably linked; without a modicum of skill, there was no need to concern oneself overmuch with long-term security. Thus I got the distinct impression that the RAF's recruitment policy had gone awry.

It was good to see Christine again. She was staying with a friend of the family in a village just south of Stamford, and I booked into the officers' mess at RAF Wittering. After a few days sightseeing around the local area we drove north to York for more touring. I also took the opportunity to call in at the Central Fighter Establishment, which was then based at Binbrook. As luck would have it, the team that visited Nellis was away in France, but I cadged a quick instrument-rating test in a Hunter T7 from Dickie Dicken, my old mate from 66 Squadron. It had been difficult to accumulate actual cloud time at Nellis, so it seemed sensible to renew my instrument rating while I was still in current flying practice. I could have saved myself the effort, but I was not to know how difficult it would be to get any sort of flying while serving at the Ministry.

Then I drove south to Bentley Priory, the home of Headquarters

Fighter Command, to book living accommodation for my tour at the MoD.

RAF Uxbridge was the administrative headquarters for RAF personnel assigned to the MoD, but there was no specially designated mess. It was a matter of personal preference as to where one lived, although costs alone ruled out the ideal solution of a bachelor flat in town. The MoD paid the commuting fare, but it was still important to reduce the daily journey to a minimum. For me, the mess at Bentley Priory was a happy compromise. It was conveniently close to Stanmore, the last stop on the Bakerloo underground line, and the journey of an hour and a quarter, door to door, was reasonable. Besides, I liked the company at Bentley Priory.

I have to say, after the action-packed life at Nellis, my posting to the gloomy corridors of the MoD was a severe culture shock. The first six months of commuting into London were probably the most tedious. In the real air force I was quite prepared to remain on duty eighteen hours or more a day, but I was not keen on the three hours per day wasted on commuting. More to the point, I resented having to swap my flying kit for a grey suit and an umbrella.

Truth to tell, I was ill-prepared for employment at the MoD. I had no formal staff training; indeed, I usually preferred to keep staff work at arm's length. My previous brush with politics and their effect on defence had been in 1957, when Sandys had decimated the frontline Hunter squadrons. The situation in the mid-sixties was not much better. The national economy had been weakened, partly as a result of Labour winning the General Election in 1964. In a typical example of political carping, Labour claimed they had inherited seriously overstretched and dangerously under-equipped defence forces. Amid much criticism of the previous Conservative administration, Prime Minister Harold Wilson set in train a series of studies on defence, which would culminate in a review of the UK's Defence Strategy. Wilson's avowed intention was to reduce defence expenditure, but those in the military were under no illusions that this really meant budget cuts.

There was little room for manoeuvre for reducing British defence commitments. The UK's national security depended on NATO and we contributed appropriate forces, but Britain also had major defence commitments elsewhere overseas. In 1965, the most onerous of these was 'Confrontation' – a trial of strength to preserve the integrity of Malaysian territory against incursion by Indonesian terrorists. All three of Britain's military services were committed, together with forces from Malaysia, Singapore, Australia and New Zealand. Since the UK's overseas commitments could not easily be abandoned, the government was more likely to save money by cancelling high-cost equipment programmes. In fact, shortly before I reported for duty, the TSR 2, which was intended to replace the ageing Canberra and was one of the few aircraft projects to survive the Sandys debacle of 1957, was cancelled. Another aircraft project, the P1154, the so-called supersonic Hunter, had previously been cancelled by the Conservative government on grounds of cost and timescale, but in this case an option had been taken out to purchase the McDonnell Phantom F-4 aircraft from the States.

In fact the TSR 2 project had been fraught with difficulty almost from the outset. The initial problems stemmed from a politically inspired move to force British aircraft manufacturers to amalgamate. The contract to develop the TSR 2, which was the first attempt in the UK to design an integrated aircraft weapons system, was awarded to a conglomerate of Vickers-Armstrong and English Electric, collectively known as the British Aircraft Corporation (BAC). Significantly, no one was appointed as having overall design authority. Everyone from the government down – the Ministry of Defence, the Ministry of Aviation and the aviation industry in general – wished to be involved in the action. But no one exercised proper financial control. Finally, the MoD staffs were not prepared to accept compromise and costs spiralled out of control.

With this deplorable lack of direction it was surprising that the TSR 2 ever got off the drawing board, but in September 1964 it actually flew. The first flight tests were promising, but even within the Ministry of Defence there was powerful opposition to the aircraft. The Chief Scientific Advisor – Sir Solly Zuckermann – and the Chief of Defence Staff – Lord Louis Mountbatten – vehemently opposed the TSR 2. Of course, being a Royal Navy man, Mountbatten wished to protect his partisan Naval interests by earmarking funds for replacement aircraft carriers. He would have preferred the RAF to adopt the cheaper but far less capable land-based version of the Buccaneer. Mountbatten was also primarily responsible for undoing attempts to sell the TSR 2 to Australia. While on tour there, he intimated that the aircraft was unlikely ever to enter service. James Callaghan – the Chancellor of the Exchequer – drove the final nail in TSR 2's coffin on 6 April 1965, when he announced the decision to scrap the project. An option was immediately taken out to purchase the General Dynamics F-111 aircraft from the United States.

Not that I was ever involved in such weighty decisions, but the sorry tale of the TSR 2 was fairly typical of the negative internecine squabbling that went on at the MoD in the early sixties. Executive staffs of the three armed services had been co-located at Whitehall since April 1964, but that had done little to improve inter-service co-operation. Junior staff officers of the different services at best kept their distance, while senior officers, even at the highest level, were suspicious and basically unwilling to co-operate. Meanwhile the government, working on the principle of divide and conquer, exploited every opportunity to reduce the defence budget.

I took over as ops F1A from David Vass, with whom I had served on the AFDS. The Directorate of Air Defence & Overseas occupied offices on the fourth floor of the main MoD building in Whitehall Gardens. The director, Air Commodore 'Micky' Mount, was a charming man. In mufti, which was *de rigueur* at the MoD, the director looked rather nondescript – a visitor once mistook him for the office cleaner. Even among his peers he was affectionally known as 'Scruffy', which hardly did him justice. In fact, Micky Mount was a much-decorated war hero, and on the few occasions he was obliged to wear uniform he seemed to grow ten feet tall. Next in line, as Group Captain Air Defence, was 'Freddie' Rothwell, who at one time had commanded a Lightning station. My immediate boss as ops F1 (the F stood for fighter) was Wing Commander 'Pete' Anson. I shared an office with Squadron Leader 'Peter' Menzies, who was responsible for air-to-air missiles. I was the resident Lightning expert, despite the fact that my knowledge of the aircraft was at least two years out of date. But for all that, the working arrangements within the directorate were reasonably effective.

My daily working routine started when I caught the tube train at

Stanmore, at a quarter to eight, to be in the office by nine. I took one hour for lunch, and if I was lucky I could catch the tube home at six fifteen to be back at Bentley Priory by seven thirty in the evening. No doubt there were some interesting jobs at the MoD – the Operational Requirements chaps could at least get out and about – but for sheer drudgery the life of a squadron leader in one of the ops directorates was difficult to match. The MoD was too far removed from the sharp end of the air force for my liking. The appropriate command staffs were responsible for the operational flying squadrons; matters were only referred up the line to the MoD when there was a conflict of interests or the situation threatened to get out of hand.

About a week after starting work I took time off to drive Christine to Tilbury Docks to embark for Australia. It was a sad parting of our ways. Of course we promised to keep in touch, but we both knew it could not last. With Betty's death, my attitude to life had changed. I had matured, and casual romantic affairs were no longer enough for me. I was ready to accept a long-term commitment – even marriage. One might almost say I was looking for the right girl. But Christine was sailing to the other side of the world. We would meet again, but under very different circumstances.

David Vass admitted that the Lightning files were in a bit of a mess, and suggested there was not much point in trying to read through them all. 'Best wait and see what turns up in the mail, and research each subject as required,' he said. He was certainly right about the files. At least one of my predecessors had opened up a new file for almost every letter he received. He had been followed by a chap who put all the correspondence on one very large multi-purpose file. Either way, the Lightning filing system was a nightmare and it took me best part of three years to sort it out. It was in the course of searching for previous correspondence on tactical fighter operations that I came across a paper on the F-105. The paper had been written before the introduction of the 'D' model and therefore was somewhat dated, but at least it showed that the RAF had indeed considered the Thunderchief, which explained my exchange tour with the 4526th. Now, with the cancellation of the TSR 2, it looked as though my experience at Nellis would not be put to immediate use.

By this time the major deployment plans for the Lightning were well advanced. Two Lightning F2 squadrons, Nos 19 and 92, had been formed at RAF Leconfield and would later be deployed to RAF Germany. The F2 was powered by similar engines to the F1A, but with improved, fully variable reheat systems. The aircraft was also fitted with a standby turbo generator to produce DC power in the event of a major electrical failure of the kind I had experienced in the F1A. The radar had also been improved. But the main Lightning re-equipment programme, starting in 1965, was the formation of six F3 squadrons. The F3 was fitted with the more powerful Avon 301R engines, each developing, with reheat, 16,360 lbs of thrust. This gave the Lightning F3 a power-to-weight ratio of almost 1:1. The weapons system had also been upgraded to carry either Red Tops – collision course missiles – or Firestreaks. The RAF was still in a quandary about the value of guns, with the result that the F3 had no gun armament. Most fighter pilots, myself included, believed this to be serious omission. But the F3's most critical limitation was its lack of fuel. The F3 carried the same fuel load as the F1, even when flown at the most economical altitude, so the average sortie length was in the order of thirty-five minutes, which was hardly adequate for an all-weather fighter in the UK. This crucial fuel shortage was finally remedied in 1966 with the introduction of the Lightning F6.

The F6 was fitted with a long, ventral tank carrying 600 gallons of fuel, instead of the 250-gallon capacity of the original ventral tank. For ferry purposes the F6 could also be fitted with additional overwing fuel tanks. The final Lightning development, at least in RAF service, was the introduction of two Aden cannons in the front section of the F6's ventral tank. Many of the improvements introduced on the F6 were later incorporated in the Lightning F2 – upgrading it to the F2A.

Within the MoD, responsibility for new marks of aircraft was retained by the Operational Requirement Staffs until the aircraft was formally released to service. Thereafter, responsibility was transferred to the operations staffs. My main involvement was with the never-ending modifications programme. For those not familiar with RAF engineering policy, any change of aircraft equipment has to be approved by an appropriate modifications committee. I was the ops staff's permanent representative on the Lightning airframe modifications committee, which used to meet every month in the Ministry of Technology at St Giles's Court. The meetings were chaired by a peppery group captain engineer, who ruled over the proceedings with a rod of iron. By this time the Lightning had generated over three thousand separate modifications, although only fifty or so were being staffed at any one time. Some were just simple changes of material specification, which were quickly dealt with, but other changes required lengthy (and inevitably more costly) programmes. The Lightning's fuel system was still inclined to leak, and fire in the air was a fairly common occurrence. Indeed, fire protection gave rise to extensive modifications. The staff work resulting from the Lightning improvement programmes kept me well occupied.

After four months, the daily commuting journey had settled down to a dull grind and I was beginning to get to grips with the job. Not that I was finding the work any more enjoyable, but I was more familiar with the office routine and I had established useful contacts. In those days the sole advantage of a tour in the MoD was that the staff were usually free at the weekends, which gave me the opportunity to re-establish some sort of social life. By this time my correspondence with Christine had dried up and, even in the swinging sixties, London was as lonely as any other city. I eventually managed to get in touch with Claire, having vague thoughts that we might get back together. Claire invited me to a party at her flat, but she was surrounded by a young arty set of friends and I felt totally out of place. Then one day I invited an attractive young lady, who worked in an office on the third floor, out to dinner. She refused, because she was about to go on holiday. Perhaps another time. Her name was Juliet, but she preferred to be called Jules, and she lived with two other girls in a flat above the fire station in Basil Street, Knightsbridge – not far from Harrods.

Jules could not resist the chance of a free supper, and we eventually kept our dinner date. She was suitably impressed by the Jaguar – which I had christened Josephine. Over the following weeks we attended various parties and visited friends together. We went to the cinema one night and got back to find the flat had been broken into. Not that there was much worth stealing – none of the girls was well off – but the thief had made off with clothes and trinkets of jewellery. The loss was all relative, but Jules, who was the only one staying in the flat that weekend, was distraught. The police took our statements. Apparently several of the flats above the fire station had been done over. The chances of getting anything back were remote, but the police suggested that she might find some of her belongings on sale in Petticoat Lane.

In November I took leave and drove down to Barton-on-Sea to stay with my parents. Jules and I had become closer over the weeks; maybe she was the girl for me, although I was still not sure – I had been this way too many times before, and I needed time to think. Jules planned to come down by train at the weekend and I arranged to pick her up from Brockenhurst station. In true Bendell tradition, Jules first met my parents in a pub, the Fleur-de-Lis in Pilley. As usual, she charmed the company. The evening was well advanced when she announced that her eye had fallen out. Actually it was her contact lens, but most of the occupants of the public bar, including Mother, thought she had lost a complete glass eye and proceeded to look for something similar to a large marble. Jules eventually found the lens. Mother was somewhat relieved to learn that it was a contact lens and the local gravedigger – Tickle – was amazed that anything so small could replace normal spectacles.

Later that evening I parked the car on Barton cliffs overlooking the Solent. The Needles on the Isle of Wight were clearly visible in the moonlight, and I popped the question. Mindful of my previous affairs, I warned Jules that I would ask her only once. Fortunately she accepted. Next day we all drove to Southampton, where Jules chose a ring. We broke the news to Mum and Dad over lunch.

At the end of my leave I visited Frank Babst, my previous flight commander on the AFDS, who was then commanding Cambridge University Air Squadron. Frank recognised a friend in need and was quite happy to let me fly the Chipmunk, nominally as safety pilot while the students practised their instrument flying, although eventually I was checked out to fly solo. Thanks to Frank Babst's generosity, I managed to get eight hours in the Chipmunk, but that was the only flying I got in the three years I spent in London. No wonder the MoD was a thoroughly unpopular posting!

About this time the Royal Navy and RAF staffs at the MoD were engaged in a fierce debate on the future requirement for replacement aircraft carriers. The problem was, the Navy's existing carriers were approaching the end of their useful lives, and replacing them – if indeed that was necessary – would be extremely expensive. Such a programme would certainly reduce the funds available for other items in the defence budget. The only conceivable role for British carriers was in support of an invasion fleet in South-East Asia. The Navy staffs put forward a scenario of mounting a continuous combat air patrol (CAP) over a convoy, 600 nautical miles from the nearest land base, which they confidently believed could only be fulfilled by carrier-based aircraft.

I was tasked to produce a paper on the feasibility of meeting the Naval scenario using the planned force levels of RAF Phantom F-4 aircraft and Victor air-to-air refuelling tankers. Actually, the case was not difficult to prove. Much experience had been gained in the States using air refuelling to extend the combat radius of fighter aircraft. Even without refuelling, the Phantom in a typical air defence configuration could stay airborne for over two hours, and with tanker support this could easily be extended to ten hours or more. With its eight guided missiles, the Phantom was unlikely to run short of weapons. I can't remember the precise figures but, on paper, the Naval scenario could be comfortably met by land-based aircraft. The Naval staff refused to accept my conclusions, but it was difficult for them to disprove the figures. In any case, with the weakened state of the British economy, the demise of the Navy's carrier force was almost inevitable. Moreover, the Labour government was unlikely ever to commit British forces to a unilateral invasion in South-East Asia.

Wilson's long-awaited Defence Review was published in February 1966, and as expected it concentrated more on cuts than on defence requirements. The government's stated intention was to reduce the defence budget by £400 million – approximately 16% – by 1970. There was to be a relief of over-stretch for British military forces, but there was no indication as to how that might be achieved. Overseas expenditure was also to be reduced, which boded ill for the proposed purchase of American aircraft. Four Polaris missile equipped nuclear submarines would be built to take over the nuclear deterrent role in 1969. In the meantime the existing V-force, equipped with the Blue Steel stand-off bombs, would fulfil the deterrent role. It was confirmed that the existing carrier force would be maintained in service until the mid-seventies, but no new carriers would be built. A new Anglo-French variable-geometry aircraft (that is, swing-wing) would take over the Canberra's light bomber/reconnaissance roles in the mid-seventies and, as an interim measure, fifty General Dynamics F-111s would be purchased from the United States. The foreign exchange costs would be offset by the sale of British defence equipment to America. It was confirmed that Phantom F-4 aircraft and a developed version of the P1127 Kestrel vertical take-off aircraft (subsequently named the Harrier) would take over the Hunter's short-range ground attack and reconnaissance roles in 1969. In the longer term, the Anglo-French SEPECAT Jaguar would take over the tactical strike and ground attack roles, thereby releasing the Phantom F-4 to replace Lightning air defence aircraft. The review provided a welcome measure of stability for the RAF, but the government warned that it would continuously review defence spending.

Jules and I got married at Stanmore on 17 March 1966. It was a quiet wedding, mainly for family and a few close friends, but with generous help from friends and associates I managed to organise a guard of honour. The reception was held in the mess at Bentley Priory. Next day we drove to RAF Lyneham to catch an indulgence flight to Malta. All went well until I was pulled up for speeding in Swindon – the traffic police were not at all swayed by my pleas that we were about to embark on our honeymoon.

We stayed at the Plevna Hotel in Sliema for two weeks. The problem with RAF indulgence flights was that you could not put your name down for the return flight until you arrived at your overseas destination. Which was fine for the single man with flexible leave arrangements, but far less practical for a married couple living on a tight budget. The allocation of indulgence seats was done by RAF movements staffs, who were not renowned for their goodwill towards aircrew officers. We moved into the transit mess at RAF Luqa for the last two days of our honeymoon – I figured the closer we got to the flight line, the better our chances of getting a flight home. And so it proved. Within hours I managed to talk the captain of an Argosy training flight into giving Jules a lift to RAF Benson in Oxfordshire. From there she struggled home by train and tube.

Two days later I almost made it as far as West Germany, as supernumerary crew in a Canberra, but that fell through at the last minute and I had to buy a civil air ticket to London. I have never understood why, in Europe, a single air fare is almost as expensive as a full return fare. I actually flew back on the inaugural passenger flight of a British European Airways Trident – champagne and all the trimmings. Even that would have been acceptable to Jules had I not taken a taxi from the Knightsbridge Air Terminal to our hiring in North Wembley.

Being newly married I had expected difficulty finding somewhere to live, but times had changed. We were offered a married quarter at RAF Hornchurch, to the east of London. But that was too far removed from our friends, so a week before the wedding I had taken over a hiring – that is, property rented by the RAF and sub-let to married tenants – in North Wembley. It was a happy arrangement: we lived in an area of our choice, at a reasonable rent, and we had a chance of making friends outside the service. A week after we arrived back from Malta I received a letter from my bank manager advising that I was £174 overdrawn and asking what I intended to do about it. Everyone else seemed to be in debt – why should we be any different?

Some weeks later Barney dropped in on a visit. It was the first time we had met since he'd left Nellis, and I was intrigued by his news. Apparently the war in Vietnam was deeply unpopular in the States. It was sad to hear that such a proud nation was riven by doubt and suspicion. Barney had volunteered to extend his tour in Vietnam but his request had been turned down and he'd returned to the States. Returning Vietnam veterans were largely ignored. In fact, Barney was so embittered by the shoddy treatment and almost total indifference shown by both the military leaders and the American civilian population to those who were doing the fighting that he resigned from the USAF. He was not alone; many others who fought during the early months of the war followed suit. It was a grand gesture, but it cost these men their pension rights. Subsequently, Barney had joined TWA (Trans World Airlines) and was once again enjoying his flying.

It was probably just as well that Jules and I could not afford the high life. In February I started the two-year Individual Staff Studies course (ISS), the replacement for the 'Q' examination. While I was not that keen on two years' night school, ISS was a prerequisite for staff college, and passing it might even shorten my tour at the MoD.

On 31 March Harold Wilson called for a second general election and increased his majority in the House of Commons to ninety-three – which foretold of further defence cuts. But before the government could take any action, the United Nations Security Council imposed an oil embargo on the newly independent Rhodesia, and the Royal Navy was immediately committed to a standing patrol of the Mozambique channel to prevent oil unloading at the port of Beira. The RAF had been committed to support Zambia – Rhodesia's land-locked neighbour – since December, with the deployment of an air defence squadron, No. 29 Squadron, equipped with Javelin aircraft and with air transport to supply oil. Now the RAF was also tasked to provide Shackleton aircraft for maritime surveillance in support of the Beira patrol. The Beira blockade was intended to put pressure on Mr Ian Smith, and it appeared to be a long-term commitment. More in keeping with the government's intention to reduce commitments, on 11 August 1966 the Bangkok Agreement between Malaysia and Indonesia was signed, marking the end of 'confrontation'. The ending of hostilities in Malaysia would allow at least 10,000 British military personnel to be withdrawn, although that would take time.

The ops staffs at the MoD were often asked to make what I chose to call 'cloud-cuckoo-land' decisions. For example, they had to forecast how much fuel would be required for fighter aircraft operating out of Muharraq – an airfield in the Middle East – in 1971. It never ceased to amaze me how reluctant the planning staffs were to commit themselves. Perhaps that was the answer to being a successful staff officer – never allow yourself to go on record if you could find someone else to carry the can. But some studies were interesting. One I remember, more in keeping with my experience, was on the question of aircraft noise. The Anglo-French Concorde was soon due to fly, and some bright spark had suggested that we test public reaction to supersonic flight overland by mounting a trial with Lightning aircraft over London. There was little information published about the noise footprint of an aircraft flying faster than sound at high level, although it was known from various Lightning incidents – not to mention the Wattisham tower – that the sonic shockwave could cause considerable damage. The severity of the sonic boom was known to be directly proportional to the aircraft's height and weight. Turning manoeuvres caused excessive over-pressures by focusing the sonic pressure waves. Anyway, I consulted the scientists and drew up a map which showed the area likely to be affected as being a corridor some twenty miles wide – which covered most of London. Fortunately, we didn't proceed with the trial; the public outcry would have been overwhelming. In fact the USAF had done a similar trial in America in 1964. It was hoped that the civilian population would get used to the disturbance caused by supersonic flights, but the USAF found that people actually got more angry as the trial progressed. A supersonic trial over London would certainly have provided further ammunition for the government to withdraw from the Concorde project. And they would have done so, had it not been for swingeing cancellation costs.

On a more practical issue, Ops F1 was asked to produce a 'Concept of Operations' for the projected new Harrier squadrons. By November 1965 the tripartite Kestrel Evaluation Squadron, manned by British, American and German pilots, had successfully completed its trials, and the way was now clear for Harrier production. VSTOL (i.e. vertical/short take-off and landing) was a significant breakthrough for military aviation. The Harrier squadrons would not be tied to large, easily targeted, permanent airfields, but could disperse and operate from field sites closer to the front line. Reaction times would be reduced, which was ideal for supporting the land battle, and at the same time dispersed aircraft would be relatively immune to the counter-attack from the air. Of course there were practical limitations, such as fuel and weapons re-supply and the occasional need for deeper servicing. Local ground defence of the sites would also have to be provided. Anyway, I teamed up with Pete Anson and in one afternoon we produced an outline plan for the future Harrier squadrons, consisting of three sub-sites and a larger maintenance/headquarters site. The plan was no more than a snapshot, but it sounded reasonable. I had no further personal involvement with the Harrier, so only time would tell if we were accurate or not.

In June 1966 a contract to provide Saudi Arabia with an entirely British-equipped air defence system, including up to fifty Lightning aircraft, was won against stiff opposition from American industry. While the commercial success of the government-sponsored Defence Sales Organisation was to be applauded, it fell to the RAF to provide much of the initial support, starting with five Lightning F2s and two T4s. These aircraft were immediately converted to Lightning F52s and T54s respectively. That was just the start. The bulk of the Saudi buy was for Lightning F53s and T55s, but in the initial stages the RAF had to provide spares back-up for the Saudi contract. And all of this at a time when RAF Lightning flying hours were circumscribed by a general shortage of spares. The RAF staffs at the MoD were hard pressed to protect the interests of the UK's frontline squadrons.

At the same time it became quite obvious that the BAC's priorities were firmly switched to the Saudi contract. A request had been made by RAF Lightning squadrons for a modification to introduce an expanding frequency card holder. The introduction of UHF radios, with the manual dialling facility, had greatly increased the number of available radio frequencies, and these needed to be available for reference in the cockpits.

It was thought that something like an expanded plastic credit card holder would suffice, but after much delay the BAC presented an excessively complicated proposal. On the grounds of cost I turned it down at the airframe modification committee – obviously the company was no longer interested in the RAF's custom. The need for a frequency card holder was eventually met by a cheaper but perfectly satisfactory modification produced from service resources.

In September I wangled a trip out to the Far East with a liaison team from Headquarters Fighter Command. The purpose of the visit was to prepare the way for the deployment, in 1967, of Lightning aircraft to replace the ageing Javelins. Several modifications had been proposed to customise the Lightning for hot climate operations, and I really needed to check out the local conditions for myself. Besides, I have to say it was a relief to get out of the office for a week. Singapore was hot and sticky but, compared to Nellis, nothing that I saw would classify the climatic conditions as extreme. The airfield at RAF Tengah was well up to modern standards and the team from the UK gave appropriate presentations. I also found time to have dinner with John and Pat Dickin.

After leaving Acklington, John had converted to helicopters and was now flying Bristol Belvederes with the reformed No. 66 Squadron. John Dickin had many an entertaining tale to tell about

'Confrontation'. I bought some dress material and a box of orchids as peace offerings for Jules, and on the return journey by Comet 4 we stopped at RAF Gan, in the Maldives, to refuel. Here I was met by my brother Tim, who was serving as an instrument technician. I hadn't seen Tim for best part of four years.

It was partly as a result of my visit to the Far East that I was able to make a reasoned judgement on the question of the Lightning's brake cooling. Aircraft wheel brakes have to absorb an enormous amount of energy, generating heat which is eventually transferred to the tyres. The Lightning's tyres incorporated fusible plugs, designed to rupture before the tyre exploded. Overheated brakes sometimes occurred in the UK, but according to the BAC, hot brakes were far more likely to occur in the high ambient temperatures encountered in Singapore, so they proposed an extremely expensive modification to introduce six miniature cooling fans on each main undercarriage wheel. In such cases the RAF would normally accept the manufacturer's advice, but there was something odd about this proposal. The cooling fans required AC electrical power and the only way of providing that, while taxiing a Lightning back to the ASP, was to keep one of the engines running at 60% – far more power than was needed to keep the aircraft moving. In effect, pilots would be taxiing against the brakes in order to ensure electrical power for brake cooling. I refused to support the modification, much to the annoyance of the firm's representative. Subsequently, the rep admitted that the company had been hoping to find a use for the electric fans originally provisioned for the TSR 2.

In February 1967 the government announced its intention to withdraw from all military commitments east of Suez by 1971 and, in the same timescale, reduce uniformed personnel by 37,000. Apart from the purely partisan reluctance to accept manpower reductions, this all seemed fairly reasonable. Southern Arabia was due to gain independence by 1968, and the introduction of modern air transport aircraft such as the Hercules C-130 enabled air-mobile forces to be based in the UK, which would save on foreign exchange rates. A voluntary redundancy scheme was introduced. The monetary inducements were very attractive and the scheme became known as the 'Golden Bowler'. Pete Anson chose to take advantage of this scheme and within months he emigrated to Australia. His position at the MoD was filled by Wing Commander Ball.

Much as I would have liked to get away from Whitehall, I was not prepared to throw away my career. Besides there were some interesting developments in the Lightning force.

In March, No. 74 Squadron participated in an aircraft arrester trial. Their Lightning F6s were fitted with simple spring-loaded tail hooks which, in an emergency, could be lowered to engage a wire stretched across the runway. There was nothing new in this, of course; the Navy had used tail hooks for years, but it was something of a breakthrough for the RAF. Up to now we had relied upon the Safeland barrier – a giant tennis net arrangement at the overshoot end of the runway, which effectively stopped aircraft but also caused substantial airframe damage. Now, with equipment known as RHAG – Rotary Hydraulic Arrester Gear – installed on the runway, the RAF had a totally reliable, damage-free arrester system. The arrester trial was completely successful, and tail hooks were retrospectively fitted to other marks of Lightning, becoming standard equipment on all new fast jet aircraft.

In May, No. 56 Squadron, equipped with Lightning F3s, deployed to Akrotiri to take over Cyprus's air defence commitment. Then, in June, 74 Squadron, commanded by Wing Commander Ken Goodwin, my old mate from Jever, deployed to RAF Tengah. The Lightning F6s subsequently operated in the Far East with great distinction until they were eventually withdrawn in August 1971. (The F6's wheel brakes proved to be entirely adequate, without the need for additional cooling.)

I also attempted to get the RAF to adopt the 'Dart', a 30-ft-long air-to-air gunnery target, constructed mainly of wood and cardboard, which could be towed by a fighter aircraft at speeds up to Mach 1.1. The other advantage of the Dart was that it could be manoeuvred up to 5g to simulate typical air combat. I had both towed and fired on the Dart at Nellis, and I knew that it was an ideal gunnery target for aircraft such as the Lightning. The Dart was cheap and convenient, but you either scored a hit or you missed – it was not possible to count the holes – which put it at a grave disadvantage in the minds of some self-styled RAF experts. And of course the Dart was not invented in the UK. Try as I might, I could not convince the powers that be, even those at Headquarters Fighter Command, that the Dart was a valid replacement for the totally inadequate Banner. The RAF's opposition to the

Dart was yet another example of the muddled thinking that had dogged the requirement for gun armament on fighter aircraft.

In due course, all other NATO air forces adopted the Dart target. Indeed the Allied Forces Central Europe gunnery qualification criteria were written around this target system. Even in 1995, the RAF had still not procured a reliable, high-speed air-air gunnery target.

In the meantime Jules and I were well settled into our flat in Elms Lane. We had intended to delay starting a family for a few years, but then Jules met Belinda, the mischievous two-year-old daughter of near neighbours the Harwoods, and our family planning changed. Stuart Anthony, our son, was born on 14 July 1967. Actually the friends we made when we were first married have endured ever since. Peggy Sadler, otherwise known as Gab, was a dear friend of Jules's before we met, and we regularly drove down to Eton Wick for Sunday lunch. Across the way from us, in Elms Lane, lived Stu and Joss Hordern, with their grown-up children Gillian and David. Stu had flown Hurricanes and Typhoons with the RAF during the war, and afterwards he had served with distinction with the Gold Coast Police – rising to the rank of assistant commissioner. He now worked in the Central Office of Information in London, and we occasionally travelled into town together.

John and Cherry Harwood were closer to our generation. John was on his way to becoming a successful director in the wholesale meat trade in London. He too had served in the RAF, as a national serviceman based at RAF Geilenkirchen in West Germany, about the same time as I was stationed at Bruggen.

But to get back to the MoD – the Middle East was in turmoil during 1967. On 5 June, Israel responded to an increasing threat from her Arab neighbours by launching a brilliantly executed pre-emptive air strike against Arab airfields. Within five hours Israeli forces had achieved air supremacy. At the same time, Israeli ground forces launched a series of aggressive armoured thrusts which overran the opposing Arab forces. In six days Israeli forces occupied the Sinai Peninsula, the West Bank of the River Jordan and the Golan Heights. Of course, Britain had treaties with several Arab countries, and therefore we had to maintain a fairly ambivalent stance – but everyone at the MoD, particularly the air staffs, was impressed by the sheer audacity and outstanding professionalism of the Israeli forces.

In accordance with the stated government policy, British forces were in the process of withdrawing from Aden, but on 20 June, the situation there rapidly deteriorated when the civil police mutinied. Order was quickly restored, but the British forces became the target of an ever-increasing terrorist threat. The government decided to pull out of Aden with all possible speed and, by 29 November, all British forces had been withdrawn. One might have expected this to be only of passing interest to the Bendells, but as a result of the withdrawal the owners of our flat returned early to the UK and we were obliged to move out. We moved into another hiring at Ruislip, which had central heating and was actually a better house. The commuting journey from Ruislip was slightly longer, but my tour at the MoD would only last for a further six months at the most.

In November 1967, British sterling was devalued from $2.80 to $2.40, and even dyed-in-the-wool socialists had difficulty swallowing Harold Wilson's assurances that the pound in their pocket was still worth the same. The effect on defence was devastating. £110 million was immediately slashed from the defence budget, the order for the fifty F-111 aircraft from the States was cancelled, and it was confirmed that all British military forces would be withdrawn from Malaysia and Singapore by the end of 1971. The Defence Estimates published in February repeated the government's intention to withdraw into Europe, and confirmed British support for NATO. At this time, Western strategic thinking was moving away from the trip-wire of immediate nuclear retaliation to a more flexible response. If anything, this would require even greater investment in conventional forces, and many officers doubted the government's commitment. For the staffs at the MoD, 1968 was a year of unrelenting damage limitation. All three services shared the pain: the army lost a new secure-communications network; the phasing out of the Navy's aircraft carriers was brought forward; and, of course, for the RAF, the cancellation of the F-111 meant the virtual abandonment of a vital element of air power. At a time when the RAF could reasonably be expected to be operational in the low-level, all-weather nuclear strike role – and would have achieved as much, either with the TSR 2 or with the F-111 – we were left with no replacement for the ageing Canberra. The French had already pulled out of the Anglo/French variable geometry aircraft, which left the SEPECAT Jaguar as the only new aircraft project, and this aircraft did not have an all-weather capability.

It was ironic that, of all the aircraft produced in the sixties and seventies, only the F-111 came anywhere close to matching the promised performance of the TSR 2. The cost of both of these aircraft would have been similar, but of course the TSR 2 would not have been a burden on the exchange rates. The RAF paid dearly for the government's lack of commitment to defence, and all we at the MoD could do was pick up the pieces. Some of those at the sharp end were less sanguine. After a week of formal celebrations marking the fiftieth anniversary of the formation of the RAF, on 5 April, Alan Pollock, the pilot who probably saved my life at Jever, registered his disgust by flying his Hunter under the upper span of London's Tower Bridge. Al certainly made his point, but it was a futile gesture and, sadly, it only served to mark the end of his promising career in the RAF.

I passed my final ISS examination in February. Actually I learned a lot from the ISS; my writing skills and knowledge of current affairs greatly improved, which just goes to show that even an unwilling dunce can benefit from practice.

Ever since returning from the States I had nominated the Phantom as my preference for my next appointment. I accepted that, in its day, the Lightning was a fine aircraft and the best of the breed in RAF service – the F6 and the F2A were arguably among the best short-range, quick-reaction fighters in the world. But in aircraft design there is always a trade-off between all-up weight and performance, and in the case of the Lightning this balance was firmly biased in favour of performance. The Lightning could out-perform most contemporary fighters, but by modern standards it was too lightly armed and too short range. It was in the context of ever-changing operational requirements that the Lightning's fundamental design limitations could not be ignored. The positioning of the AI radar in the nose intake restricted the size of the radar dish, thereby limiting its maximum range. The Lightning's wing planform and undercarriage retraction geometry severely limited the carriage of external stores. The over-wing tanks, which were basically subsonic, could never be regarded as a combat configuration. So, while I shared a certain empathy with those who claimed that the Lightning was the best all-weather fighter aircraft of its generation, by 1968 it was becoming dated and would soon need to be replaced by a more capable aircraft – such as the Phantom F-4. It was not a question of performance (the Lightning was marginally the better flying machine), but the Phantom could carry a far greater payload, both of weapons and fuel, the AI radar was far superior and the aircraft had an inbuilt flexibility the Lightning could never match.

In the five and a half years I had been away from the RAF frontline, the rank of officers commanding operational flying squadrons had been upgraded to wing commander. Under the old system, after two tours as the equivalent of a flight commander and a full-blown staff tour, I could have expected that my next flying tour would be as a squadron commander, but the goalposts had been moved. I was destined for another tour as a flight commander, and in June I was delighted to learn that my next posting would be to RAF Coningsby as flight commander on No. 6 Squadron – the first RAF Phantom squadron.

Squadron Leader Tim Elworthy took over from me as Ops F1A in mid-July. Understandably he was not greatly enthused with the prospect of an MoD tour, but I was over the moon. After thirty-nine months of grinding staff work I was escaping back to the cockpit. There was just one last chore: I had been assigned to attend the junior command and staff school (JC & SS), more commonly known as the Jack-Ass course, at RAF Ternhill. I was not convinced by the claim that attending the JC & SS course was all part of a balanced career. Staff training in the RAF was supposed to follow the pattern of the JC & SS course, followed by the ISS and Staff College. In theory, the officer was then qualified for a staff appointment. I had already done the staff appointment and completed the ISS, so my so-called balanced career was all ass about face. But after five years away from the RAF, Ternhill was a useful reintroduction to the minutiae of station life. The pleasure of getting back to the real air force easily compensated for the delayed return to flying.

In the meantime, Jules and Stuart stayed in Ruislip, while I commuted home at the weekends with Squadron Leader 'Les' Parker – an engineer who had also escaped from the MoD.

There was more pain to come for the armed forces. In July the government declared that by 1972 a further £260 million would be cut from the defence budget and manpower would be reduced by 75,000. As a sop to clamouring air staff demands, there would be a continuing study on the need for an advanced combat aircraft in the mid-seventies. The operational requirement that eventually emerged was similar to that written for the TSR 2 – what price progress?

10
Flight Commander on No. 6 Squadron (Phantom FGR 2)

I reported to the School of Refresher Flying at RAF Manby in September 1968, and in five weeks I had accumulated forty-five hours on the Jet Provost (JP) 4. The excellent flying continuity was exactly right to get me back in the groove. It was a relief to find that the sharp edge of skill I had once taken for granted was not entirely lost. My knowledge of airmanship and basic handling skills quickly returned, but it took longer for me to re-learn the art of coping with more than one thing at a time. The course at Manby was good value, but the subsequent jump from basic trainer straight to an operational aircraft – such as the Phantom F-4 – was more difficult. (In later years this problem was eased by an intermediate tactical weapons course on the Hunter – but even then several previously competent pilots failed their OCU course, which was a regrettable waste of potential.)

We moved into married quarters at Coningsby during the second week of October. The house had been vacant for almost two years, and it showed – but Jules quickly set about restoring order. After the luxury of gas-fired central heating in Ruislip, it was back to solid fuel fires and draughty rooms. And lest there be any doubt, Lincolnshire could be very draughty indeed. It was rumoured that the only wind-break between Coningsby and Siberia was the familiar Boston Stump church tower.

The following Monday I reported for work. It was like stepping back in time. Group Captain 'John' Rogers, the station commander, had commanded No. 56 Squadron at Wattisham when I joined Treble One; the CO of No. 228 OCU, Wing Commander 'John' Howe, had commanded No. 74 Squadron at Coltishall in 1960. And on the first night, in the bar, I bumped into Wilf Ewbank, another old friend from my Lightning days. Wilf was a well-respected Rolls-Royce rep, now employed on the Spey/Phantom project. Clearly the original Lightning team was back in business.

The McDonnell Phantom F-4, which was originally procured for the United States Navy as a carrierborne interceptor and later developed as a ground attack fighter by the US Marine Corps and the USAF, had first flown in May 1958. Two different marks were procured for the UK forces: the F-4K, designated the Phantom FG 1 for the Royal Navy; and the F-4M, designated the Phantom FGR 2, for the RAF. For political reasons, but mainly to off-set foreign exchange costs, much of the ancillary equipment installed in the UK Phantoms was of British design. There were minor differences in specification between the FG 1 and the FGR 2, but in terms of performance they were much the same. The nearest all-American equivalent was the Phantom F-4J.

Delivery of the UK's Phantoms had been delayed by the technical difficulties of installing the Rolls-Royce engines, and so the first OCU course was delayed until December. In the meantime I was able to keep my hand in ferrying various members of the staff around the UK in a Jet Provost. During November I attended a short course on offensive air support, at the Joint Warfare Establishment at Old Sarum.

Our preliminary Phantom training started at the end of November, when the aircrews destined for No. 6 Squadron first gathered for the Sea Survival course at RAF Mount Batten, near Plymouth. There was nothing quite like a dunking in the sea in winter – without the protection of immersion suits – to encourage an immediate and lasting bond. Then it was back to the relative luxury of RAF North Luffenham, to attend the aviation medicine course and be fitted with the Phantom's specialist flying clothing. Both the equipment and lectures on human physiology were similar to the Lightning era, and there was no escaping the pressure breathing sessions, the decompression chamber runs, the anoxia experience and, of course, the explosive decompression.

The Phantom ground school on No. 228 OCU started on 9 December. The Phantom and the Lightning were about the same vintage, but while the Lightning had a certain elegance of line, the Phantom, with its cranked wings and anhedral (i.e. downswept) stabilator, was just plain ugly. The anhedral stabilator was actually an effective alternative to the low-set stabilators of both the Lightning and the F-105, but wiseacres would still claim that either McDonnell's chief designer had got his sums wrong or someone had trapped the tail in the hangar door. The Rolls-Royce Spey engines each developed a nominal 20,000 lb of thrust in reheat – some 2,000 lb more than the General Electric J79 engines in the Phantom F-4J. The more powerful engines were essential to enable the Navy's Phantom FG 1s to operate from the relatively small British aircraft carriers – but at higher levels the hoped-for general improvement in performance was largely offset by a significant increase in aerodynamic drag. The fitting of Speys to the RAF Phantoms was an expensive option which offered little if any real improvement. Compared to F-4J, the UK Phantoms performed better on take-off and they had a longer range, but they were slower at altitude.

The massive tail hook and folding wings were clear evidence of the Phantom's naval pedigree. Less obvious but essential to the aircraft's take-off and landing performance was the use of boundary layer control. With BLC, high-pressure air, bled from the engines, was blown over the leading and trailing edge flaps to improve lift and reduce the minimum approach speeds.

The UK Phantoms were equipped with state-of-the-art ancillary equipment. The cockpit layout was typically American, with standard clock-face instrumentation. I recognised the ADI and the HSI from my F-105 flying, but there was the welcome addition of a radio altimeter. The Westinghouse/Ferranti AWG 12 pulse/Doppler radar more than doubled the range of previous British AI radars, and provided an effective look-down capability. The communications fit was all British. The main radio was a combined UHF/VHF set offering some 28,000 manually dialled frequencies. The aircraft was also fitted with an HF radio for long-range work and a standby emergency radio. The FGR 2 was equipped with a Ferranti Inertial Nav/Attack system (INAS). In the navigation mode, the INAS's gyroscopically stabilised platform measured the aircraft's movement in space, which was then converted to ground speed and drift. This information was processed through a computer to update the aircraft's present position (presented in latitude and longitude) and gave course and distance to a number of preselected destinations. The FGR 2 was the first RAF fighter to be fitted with a self-contained, long-range navigation aid. With a good INAS, the typical error, after one hour in the air, was in the order of one nautical mile. But it took a full year to iron out the problems with the INAS. Understandably our confidence in the equipment was slow to develop.

After two weeks of lectures and a final written test, we were ready for the somewhat arcane procedure of crewing up. Nothing new to the navigators, of course – after all, they would be hard pressed to fly solo in any aircraft – but most of the pilots had previously been on single-seat fighters, and we were not used to sharing. A 'shotgun wedding' party was arranged in the mess, at which pilots and navigators were expected to choose their flying partners. It didn't happen that way for me. At the end of the evening I was left on the sidelines with Flight Lieutenant 'John' Douglas-Boyd, who could hardly be described as a shrinking violet. Dougie's previous experience was on all-weather fighters, and he had just completed an exchange tour with the RCAF on F-101s. With so much in common we were well suited.

It was not appreciated at the time, but the OCU had been set an impossible task. The first course was planned to last five months and produce thirteen crews for 6 Squadron. This in itself did not appear overly ambitious but, to complete the syllabus, each pilot was expected to fly ninety-five hours – the navigators would get slightly less. In practice, insufficient allowance had been made for Lincolnshire's foul winter weather, and no account had been taken of the Phantom's abysmal serviceability – although, in all fairness, the latter would have been difficult to forecast. These problems were compounded by the fact that most people at Coningsby lacked Phantom experience. The OCU staff, the ground crews and of course the students themselves were all learning together. There was simply not enough flying to go around, and the staff naturally awarded themselves the higher priority.

I flew my first Phantom solo with Dougie on 12 January 1969. The standard aircraft configuration at 228 OCU included two 308 imperial gallon 'Sergeant Fletcher' under-wing drop tanks, which more or less guaranteed a sortie duration of ninety minutes. It was easy to overlook this additional fuel load when comparing the Phantom's performance with previous aircraft. Certainly, the Phantom accelerated faster than the F-105 on take-off, and it got airborne at a lower airspeed, but its performance was not as dramatic as the Lightning's and it was not as responsive on the controls. At speeds above 350 knots the Phantom handled well, but more care was needed when manoeuvring at lower speeds with higher angles of attack (AOA). The buffet margin, signifying an approaching stall, was never far away. Someone described the Phantom as wall-to-wall buffet; and after buffet came wing rock, which was a sure sign for the pilot to back off. At high AOA the Phantom was prone to adverse yaw (i.e. yawing away from the direction of turn), and at stalling speeds the aircraft could rapidly depart from normal flight. Intentional spinning was not recommended. Although it was possible to recover from a normal spin, the height lost per turn was in excess of 2,000 ft and there was always the possibility that the spin might become flat, from which there was no recovery. The response of the Spey engine was slow for a fighter aircraft, and at high subsonic Mach numbers the large cross-section area at the tail pipes generated what the boffins called 'boat tail drag'. Unlike the Lightning, at high altitude, the Phantom FGR 2 needed the assistance of gravity to accelerate to supersonic flight. The approved technique was to unload the aircraft (i.e. push the stick forward) into a shallow dive. Once through the high-drag transonic region the Phantom's handling improved, but it was still sluggish compared to the Lightning. In the landing configuration, with the benefit of an automatic aileron/rudder interconnect to compensate for adverse yaw, the aircraft was pleasantly stable. However, if the BLC malfunctioned the Phantom could be difficult to handle. Engine failure on take-off at a high all-up weight also required care and the asymmetric power was quite marked and had to be corrected, but that is true of most multi-engined aircraft.

But despite its capricious handling characteristics the Phantom F-4 was recognised as an extremely flexible multi-role combat aircraft. It was probably the first multi-role aircraft in RAF service since the remarkable de Havilland Mosquito. With their pulse/Doppler AI radar, the UK Phantoms were optimised for air defence, but the FGR 2 was capable of filling many other roles. Initially, pending the arrival of the SEPECAT Jaguar, it was employed for ground attack with conventional weapons, for tactical reconnaissance, and even for tactical nuclear strike. In due course the Phantoms built for British forces replaced the Lightnings in the air defence role.

But to get back to Coningsby. The lack of continuity on 228 OCU was appalling; at one stage we were only flying one sortie a week. The OCU lost one aircraft when John Rooum and Forbes Pearson were returning from a training sortie and suffered a double power-control failure – their only option was to bail out. They both landed safely some eight miles short of Coningsby.

I finished the course in April, with just fifty-seven hours flying in the Phantom: barely ten hours a month – hardly enough to maintain currency, let alone convert on to a new aircraft. It was fortunate that the aircrews selected for the first courses at Coningsby were fairly experienced and were able to build on a generally inadequate level of training. It would be true to say that those destined for 6 Squadron were delighted to get away from the 'prima donna' atmosphere of the OCU and, no doubt, the permanent staff were relieved to be shot of us.

No. 6 Squadron was officially reformed, with Phantom aircraft, on 7 May 1969. We inherited the numberplate, the squadron silver and two standards, from a Canberra squadron previously stationed at Akrotiri. At the time I was otherwise occupied, wrapping up a board of inquiry into damage caused to a row of bungalows during a Phantom solo display at RAF Abingdon. Shades of Wattisham in 1962 – and that was probably why I had been lumbered. There were obvious similarities; the damage had been caused by transonic shock waves at low level, but in this case the display crew, 'Bill' Wratten and 'Bob' Rogers, both members of the OCU, who had put on an impressive solo aerobatic display, had been distracted at a critical moment by conflicting air traffic. I like to think that my experience at Wattisham played its part in them getting a fair hearing.

No. 6 Squadron is the only squadron in the RAF to have two royal standards. In addition to its RAF colour, in 1950 King Abdullah of Trans-Jordan had presented the squadron with his personal standard. The squadron had first served in the Middle East in 1919 in Mesopotamia (now Iraq), but in 1940 it had established firm links with the Jordanian royal family.

At Coningsby we were fortunate to inherit brand new accommodation that had originally been intended for the OCU, but was considered inadequate for their purposes. Their loss was our gain, and we were delighted to take over the building in front of No. 3 Hangar and adjacent to the main ASP. The command structure on No. 6 Squadron was standard: Wing Commander 'David' Harcourt-Smith was the CO; the other flight commander was Squadron Leader 'Bill' Rowe (an ex Bomber Command navigator). As OC 'B' Flight, I was primarily responsible for the squadron's flying training programme. It was a job I had done before, both on Treble One and at Nellis, but with the Phantom's multi-role capability it promised to be an interesting challenge. The Nav/Rad leader was Squadron Leader 'Bill' Hobby. Below executive level, the squadron had a wealth of practical experience: suitably qualified aircrew officers were made responsible for specialist duties such as flight planning, the target library, weapons training, statistics, survival and flight safety, and so on.

The immediate problem facing the squadron was the question of engineering support. The engineering staffs, both at Group and at Coningsby, were fighting tooth and nail to retain the centralised servicing thus far employed to support the OCU. The fact that the system was detrimental to morale and had manifestly failed to produce sufficient aircraft to meet the OCU's task was beside the point. As far as OC Eng Wing was concerned, centralisation was essential for an aircraft as complex as the Phantom. He saw the additional aircraft and manpower provided for 6 Squadron simply as an enlargement of Engineering Wing. He envisaged a central pool of serviceable aircraft, which would be allocated to the flying squadrons on a daily basis. The flying squadrons would have a small team of airmen solely for flight-line maintenance duties. Needless to say this view was not shared by the aircrews of 6 Squadron. Many of us already had experience of centralised maintenance, and were aware of its limitations. We were suspicious of the power – without responsibility – centralised maintenance afforded the engineering hierarchy. And, since many of our commitments would be on the flanks of NATO, far removed from Coningsby, we believed there were compelling reasons why 6 Squadron should have its own ground personnel. Fortunately, David Harcourt-Smith was a forthright leader with a very short fuse. There was never any doubt that we would win in the end – it was just a question of time.

The introduction of the Phantom dramatically enhanced No. 38

Group's offensive capabilities. The Phantom's range and weapons-carrying capacity were substantially greater than the Hunter's. Actually the Phantom FGR 2 was best suited to pre-planned interdiction, where its superior range and navigation equipment could be used to advantage, rather than for close air support. Certainly, compared to the Hunter, the Phantom, even with a partial load of air-to-air weapons, was better able to fend for itself behind enemy lines. Using the AWG 12's ground-mapping mode to let down through cloud in relative safety, we could press home our attack in far worse weather conditions. We used this tactic without a second thought, until we found that due to an obscure technical fault the radar picture could be off-set by as much as 30°.

Dougie and I had one close encounter with Exmoor when, according to the radar, we were letting down over the Bristol Channel. Other crews were similarly alarmed when they found discrepancies in the radar display. But it was a simple matter to crosscheck the radar with the aircraft's other navigation aids.

For all the aircraft's sophistication, the FGR 2's conventional ground-attack weapons system was fairly basic. In the air-to-ground mode, the aiming pipper could be depressed to allow for the various weapons deliveries. The optical sight was effective when using forward-firing weapons such as the gun or SNEB rockets, but at low-grazing angles the radar ranging was not particularly accurate. The sighting problem was more difficult for dive bombing. To maintain a steady dive angle, the sight was allowed to drift on to the target. There was nothing new in this – it was the air-to-ground equivalent of pegged ranging. The sight depression varied according to the ballistics of the bomb, the dive angle, the speed of the aircraft and the desired height of release. But everything had to come together at the moment of bomb release; if any one of the parameters was adrift the bomb would miss the target. And even the minor errors tended to be cumulative. For example, a shallow dive angle would produce an early release sight picture at a lower than ideal air speed, and the bomb would fall many feet short of the target. In retrospect, it was remarkable that we ever scored a direct hit (DH), especially when using an operational profile. The fact that we actually qualified in 20° free-fall dive bombing was a triumph of the old-fashioned seaman's eye – but that needed regular practice. Operational crews had to qualify across the whole range of conventional weaponry, including bombs, rockets and air-to-ground gunnery.

Apart from weapons training we practised simulated attack profiles (SAPs) using tactical formations of two or more aircraft. When short of aircraft, we would switch to singleton reconnaissance sorties using a strike camera mounted in the left forward Sparrow recess. Most of our flying was at low level, because, at that time, low altitude was believed to be the best way of avoiding detection by the Warsaw Pact's air defence radars. It took many months to optimise our tactics to make best use of the Phantom FGR 2's unique capabilities.

Then, out of the blue, Barney phoned to say that he had got married and was bringing his wife Joanie to England on honeymoon. We invited them to the Summer Ball at Coningsby. It was good to see that my old pal had finally met the right girl. Not only was he married, he had also gained a family – Joanie already had a son, Greg, who was a year or two older than Stuart. We talked about the old times: thankfully Barney seemed to have recovered from his experiences in Vietnam. He and Joanie made an ideal couple, and we were happy for them.

Being the first frontline RAF Phantom squadron, we were soon involved with exercise tasking. In June the squadron deployed four aircraft to support an air display at RAF Wildenrath in West Germany. We were actually billeted at Bruggen. The station had hardly changed from my memories of it in 1956. We flew a number of recce sorties over northern Germany. I also took advantage of an offer by an old mate of mine, Flight Lieutenant 'Euan' Perraux, to fly with the Red Arrows during their display over Wildenrath. It was an interesting experience but, given the choice, I would still prefer solo aerobatics.

On our return to Coningsby the squadron was tasked to provide a formation flypast for the investiture of His Royal Highness The Prince of Wales, at Caernarfon on 1 July 1969. This called for twelve aircraft and six full rehearsals. It was a major commitment, and we had to import some crews from the OCU. Up to now Coningsby had rarely produced twelve serviceable aircraft at any one time; certainly very little additional flying was done on the rehearsal days. The boss and Bill Hobby led the formation; I flew as deputy leader, with Dougie in the No. 3 slot. Needless to say, the timing had to be precise, so we took off early and held at an initial point (IP) some twenty miles from the reviewing stand. The flying time from the IP was calculated to the nearest second; all we had to do was leave the IP on track at precisely the right time. Quite straightforward really – although Dougie and I were relieved that we never had to take over the lead. Our minimum altitude over Caernarfon Castle was limited to 1500 ft. Tradition had it that a lone, mounted guardsman stood on the castle battlements – and no one, least of all the officer in question (who had been chosen for his stature rather than his equestrian skills), was prepared to take the risk of the horse being startled by low-flying aircraft. It was rumoured that the horse was actually chained down.

Sod's Law again: the rehearsals went off without a hitch, but on the great day the weather was atrocious. We arrived at the holding area in good order, but at 1500 ft we were between layers of cloud and the ground was hidden beneath a solid undercast. No problem – we were able to pinpoint our position using INAS and TACAN, and Caernarfon Castle was easy to identify on the radar. Six Squadron overflew the investiture on time but blind. Actually the wives back at Coningsby, who were watching the ceremony on the television, caught a fleeting glimpse of the formation through a hole in the cloud. In the prevailing conditions, few other aircraft in service with the RAF could have completed the task.

Four days later, on 5 July, we flew a similar flypast over Cardiff, but this time the weather was perfect.

The squadron was also involved in trials for the Central Trials and Tactics Organisation (CTTO). The RAF's specialist trials organisations, including CFE, had been disbanded in the late sixties to save money. From then on, trials were managed by the CTTO using the frontline squadrons. In my opinion it was a retrograde step – the conflict of priorities between trials work and training was inevitable. On 6 Squadron we were still trying to get to grips with a new aircraft and it was inevitable that the trials flying would suffer. In those early days the normal CTTO sortie called for two operational attacks (i.e. a low-level approach with a pull-up and tip-in dive) delivering either rockets or bombs on a specially instrumented target at Cowden range. All good experience – if you knew what you were doing. Sadly, at that stage most of us were not at all sure. Clearly, the CTTO got something out of the trial but it would be wrong to give much weight to the findings. The CTTO commitment remained a regular feature on the flying programme.

In September the squadron deployed with eight aircraft to RAF Akrotiri for our first APC. For ferry purposes the aircraft were each fitted with an additional 500-gallon drop tank, on the centreline, which extended our range to well in excess of 1500 nautical miles. We staged through Luqa.

It was great to be back in Cyprus. The opportunity for a prolonged period of good weather was most welcome, although the air-to-ground range facilities were somewhat limited. We were permitted to release SNEB rockets and low-angle retard bombs at Larnaca Range, but for the less accurate 20° free-fall dive bombing we had to use a sea target anchored in Episkopi Bay – the target was too distant for land-based scoring and the training pattern was excessively large. But, as far as we were concerned, the most serious limitation in Cyprus was the lack of a scorable strafe target. Larnaca was the obvious choice, but the range was plagued by local scrap metal merchants on the lookout for trade. The trouble was, the Vulcan M61 gun on the Phantom jettisoned four or five live rounds at the end of each firing burst, and for obvious reasons the RAF was reluctant to hand over live ordnance to Cypriot civilians. We eventually fired against a splash target towed behind an RAF safety launch, but this target could not be scored and was therefore of limited value.

The squadron also took part in a firepower demonstration over Episkopi Bay for a group of senior NATO Officers. The setting was ideal for the resident Vulcan squadron – one aircraft dropped a stick of eighteen live 1000 lb bombs, which was impressive by any standards. Our Phantom demonstration, which was limited to practice ordnance, was tame by comparison. To redress the balance, after our final attack, Dougie and I broke away from the target and made a high-speed pass over the spectators on top of the cliffs, capturing them on the strike camera. Which by all accounts was suitably impressive, especially when we presented the visitors with copies of the photograph within the hour.

On 7 October we laid on a simulated attack on RAF Akrotiri. The island was defended by the Lightning aircraft of No. 56 Squadron. Our attack was planned to take place at dusk. It was almost impossible to approach closer than 200 nautical miles to Cyprus and avoid radar detection, but we had one or two tactical surprises for the Lightnings. We flew outbound at high level in a single formation to a position some 250 nautical miles west of the island, before splitting into four independent pairs for a co-ordinated attack from widely differing sectors. We knew we would be detected, but we also knew the GCI controllers would have difficulty keeping track of our height, especially if it was constantly changing. The height profiles were left to the discretion of the pairs' leaders, although our simulated weapons load dictated that the final attacks would have to be mounted at low level. The plan worked well; the Lightnings had to spread themselves thinly, and instead of flying in pairs they chose to operate as single aircraft, which was not the best tactic against a bomber force equipped with an effective counter-air capability. We were able to pick up the defending fighters at long range and, armed as we were with AIM 7E Sparrows, we could legitimately claim an effective air-to-air missile launch at fourteen nautical miles – far beyond the range of the Lightning's weapons. But in the nature of such exercises, old-style, close-range dogfights between Phantoms and Lightnings were fought out some twenty miles west of Akrotiri. Compared to the Phantom the Lightning was superbly agile – although, had it been for real, few Lightnings would have survived to press home their attacks.

Our planned strike on the airfield was delivered on time. At the subsequent debriefing the Lightning's claims and our counter-claims were hotly contested. We all learned a great deal from the experience but, in the end, there was little doubt that the Phantom was the superior aircraft.

The squadron returned to Coningsby in two easy stages, via RAF Luqa, on 13 October 1969. No. 54 Squadron – our sister squadron at Coningsby – had formed on 1 September, and by now it was obvious, even to the engineering staffs, that the operational squadrons needed to be self-sufficient. Centralised servicing was abandoned in favour of squadron maintenance, and we were established with a full complement of ground personnel and twelve aircraft. To mark the occasion we set about designing appropriate squadron markings. Actually, it was more a question of deciding how best to display the official squadron markings on the Phantom.

During the First World War No. 6 Squadron had adopted the red zigzag 'gunner's stripe' to mark its role of spotting for the artillery. Then, during the Second World War, equipped with Hurricane 2Ds, the squadron had gained a reputation as the 'flying can-openers' for their success against Rommel's Afrika Korps. And that too had to be commemorated. We eventually settled on the 'gunner's stripe' across the fin and a red 'winged can-opener' on the forward fuselage. Each aircraft was given an identifying letter and allocated to a specific crew – although this was a slight anachronism. Long gone were the days of only flying one's personal aircraft, but the painting of names was good for morale. I adopted 'J' for Juliet; not only was this good for morale at home, but *Juliet* was actually one of the more reliable aircraft on the Squadron.

Even during the winter months, when weather ruled out low flying, it was possible to get productive training in the Phantom. We could easily revert to practice interceptions at high level, sharpening our skills with the FGR 2's unique air-defence equipment.

During the latter part of 1969 all our crews qualified on flight refuelling, using Victor tanker aircraft.

Then, in February 1970, the squadron deployed to Andoya in Norway, about 180 miles north of the Arctic Circle, to take part in Arctic Express – a NATO exercise. The UK's contribution included Royal Marine Commandos and a close-air-support squadron from 38 Group. The commitment was originally intended to be the first detachment for the Harriers of No. 1 Squadron at RAF Wittering, but their workup had been delayed and 6 Squadron was rushed into the breach. There was just one precondition – the staffs insisted that a portable arrestor gear (RHAG) be installed on the runway at Andoya. This was a reasonable precaution; the RHAGs at Coningsby had proved their worth on numerous occasions, and no one on this side of the Atlantic had much Phantom experience in extreme cold weather conditions.

A team of royal engineers and the necessary equipment had deployed to Andoya on 20 February, but there were doubts that the work could be completed in time. I was detailed to accompany the squadron's advanced party, flying to Andoya in a Belfast on 23 February, to give a pilot's assessment of the conditions. Actually, it was just as well I was travelling as a passenger, as I was feeling pretty wretched with a painful throat infection – but I talked the medical officer into giving me the necessary pills to keep me going.

The Belfast was the RAF's heavy lift strategic transport aircraft, the passengers sat on the upper deck overlooking the cavernous freight bay; there was plenty of room, but it was deafeningly noisy.

The captain called me up to the flight deck as we approached Andoya. The scene ahead, under a darkening overcast, looked ominous: the grey sea contrasted sharply with the frostbitten, snow-covered land; even the runway, picked out by the lights, appeared as a glistening white strip. Andoya had not long emerged from two months of permanent darkness. The daylight now lasted eight hours per day, but even in the middle of the afternoon the light was fading fast.

We unloaded the ground equipment, had a bite to eat in a makeshift combined mess, and I found a bed in an overheated, rancid-smelling wooden hut. (Much later we found the cause of the stench was a pile of reindeer skins drying out in the cellar.)

Next day Andoya was transformed. It was still bitterly cold, but the sun was shining and there was hardly a breath of wind. The scenery was stunning. Andoya is at the northern end of the Lafoten Islands and the airfield nestled at the base of a range of mountains. At that time of the year the place is invariably covered by a thick blanket of snow and ice.

Squadron Leader 'Jim' Chance busied himself preparing the site for the arrival of the squadron, while I went in search of OC Ops. He was a charming fellow who spoke excellent English – as indeed did all the RNAF Officers we spoke to. OC Ops was well clued up on the requirements for fast jet aircraft, even though Andoya was primarily a base for long-range Neptune P2 maritime patrol operations. The Norwegians did not attempt to clear their runways – they simply rolled them and operated from packed snow. The roads were similarly covered, but the Norwegian Air Force was equipped with ideal transport for the conditions in the shape of a Volvo Jeep – the Norwegian driver translated the name into English as the 'Wolwo Yeep'. When I inspected the runway the snow surface was covered with a one-inch-thick layer of hoar-frost.

I had never seen anything like it before – not even in Canada. The braking action, measured by the runway controller's specially instrumented car, was surprisingly good, but caution suggested that there was a world of difference between a saloon car and twenty tons of aircraft. The news from the RHAG party was not altogether encouraging either. The braking units on both sides of the runway had to be mounted on substantial concrete foundations. The concrete had been poured but it would be three days before the braking units could be installed and a further three days before the RHAG could be used. Earlier use would distort the concrete foundations, making them permanently unusable. I was not overly concerned by that possibility. The RHAG was designed to run out approximately 1200 ft, regardless of the speed of engagement. While an approach end engagement (or an aborted take-off) might place maximum strain on the RHAG, far less energy needed to be absorbed at the end of a normal landing run.

The REs eventually installed the braking units on the 25th. On the morning of the 26th, OC Ops confirmed that the runway conditions were the best that could be expected at that time of the year, and I signalled the squadron, recommending that they deploy as planned.

HQ 38 Group dickered over the decision for as long as possible but they eventually gave approval and the squadron launched. Two hours later, I installed myself in the air traffic control bunker alongside the runway to await their arrival. Much to my relief, the Phantoms landed without difficulty; every aircraft got a good braking parachute, and they didn't need the RHAG. Taxiing in proved to be more difficult. The problem was, the heat from the canted-down jet pipes melted the top layer of snow which rapidly turned to ice, and the braking action on ice was nil. One aircraft did a graceful low-speed pirouette, which was exciting for the crew but caused no damage.

By this time my throat was a good deal better, but I was left with a curious sensation of pins and needles on the right side of my face. In the following weeks the pins and needles migrated around the rest of my body. It was mildly irritating. The doctors couldn't give me a reasonable diagnosis as to the cause. It was suggested that it might be due to stress, but that was rubbish – I thoroughly enjoyed flying. With hindsight, I now know that the pins and needles were probably the first symptom of something far more serious.

I got my chance to assess the local conditions first-hand next day, leading a pair for high-level interceptions and sector recce. I have to say the Norwegian terrain was impressive: high, snow-covered mountain peaks dropped vertically down into narrow black fjords. With no sun to lighten the landscape, Norway was a bitterly cold monochrome world of white and grey.

The tasking for Arctic Express started on 2 March 1970. For me the exercise was strongly reminiscent of 'Brown Jug' back in 1957. We were used mainly for close support of the British forces, but we flew many other interdiction and reconnaissance sorties against a wide range of targets, from troop concentrations and armoured columns to fast patrol boats and massive, World War II vintage German naval guns. Dougie and I flew one sortie to the far north, across the Finmark Plain to an air defence radar station on North Cape, which must surely be one of the most desolate places on Earth.

The Phantom coped well with the arctic conditions, although we had to modify our operating procedures. Formation take-offs and landings were not practical, but we found that, if anything, the rolling resistance was higher on packed snow than on dry concrete. We minimised our use of wheel brakes and relied more on nose-wheel steering. Throughout the detachment we had no cause to make emergency use of the RHAG, but we laid on a successful demonstration for the benefit of the REs. It was generally agreed that Arctic Express provided excellent training.

At the end of the exercise we threw a party for the Norwegian officers and their wives. Alcohol is very expensive in Norway, but we had taken the precaution of exporting our own 'duty free' booze from the UK – courtesy of Flight Lieutenant 'Horace' Farquhar-Smith. The squadron arranged to hold the party in the Andoya officers' mess, which was about eight miles from the airfield. We provided the hard licquor, while the mess agreed to supply the soft mixes. Something may have got lost in the translation – and it was probably a mistake to employ the Norwegian servicemen as stewards – the Norwegians, it seems, prefer their alcohol neat and in copious quantities – but in the event there were no mixers, and brandy, Scotch, gin and vodka were doled out by the tumblerful – undiluted! The party was a roaring success – while it lasted. Trouble was, all our guests got drunk very quickly. The traditional exchange of squadron plaques was brought forward by an hour, but that was barely enough.

The Norwegian CO announced that to commemorate the occasion he would sing a song close to every Englishman's heart, and in strong guttural tones he launched into '"It's a long way to Tipperary, It's a long way to go, It's a long way to Tipperary, to the sweetest girl I know . . ."' He would have continued with the subsequent verses had he not been dragged off. By that time most of the Norwegian officers and one or two of their wives were paralytic.

There was a certain irony on the day of our return to UK. The boss was away attending the post-exercise debriefing, and it fell to me to lead the squadron home. After successfully operating for ten days in what could fairly be described as extreme cold in Norway, Coningsby's runway was declared 'black' (i.e. unusable) due to snow. But that was the least of our problems – Andoya was forecasting blizzard conditions within two hours. True to form, HQ 38 Group wanted us to delay until Coningsby was cleared, but that would probably extend the detachment by four or five days. I checked that the weather was clear over the rest of the UK, and advised 38 Group that we should not delay our take-off: if necessary, we would divert to RAF Leuchars. Without waiting for a reply, with cockpits stuffed with frozen salmon and shrimp, we launched. And we were only just in time; the cloud base was already approaching the minimum limits. As expected we diverted to Leuchars where we were welcomed by No. 43 Squadron, the first RAF squadron equipped with Phantom FG 1 aircraft, originally procured for the Royal Navy. The Fighting Cocks were still having serviceability problems and they were green with envy when we turned up with ten aircraft. They said we would never get away with ten the following day – but we proved them wrong.

Like other fast jet bases, Coningsby was surrounded by open countryside, and the station had a love/hate relationship with the local village. Traders welcomed the wealth brought in by service families, although many of the inhabitants objected to the aircraft noise. The farmers were generally anti, and there was even one publican, close to the airfield, who actively discouraged RAF trade. Maintaining good public relations was a constant battle for the station commander, but some of the squadron's wives successfully integrated service and civilian interests. Jann Tucker, Mary Douglas-Boyd and Joan Hobby opened a boutique in the village. Jann, who was an energetic Welsh lass with an eye for business, later opened an extremely successful restaurant called Ratty's. For the officers, the social life at Coningsby centred around the mess, but each squadron adopted its own public house for off-base entertainment. The 6 Squadron officers used to meet at the Abbey Lodge, while 54 adopted the Bluebell. For combined 'stag' functions we tended to meet in the Fortescue Arms at Tattersall. I remember several hilarious evenings when the assembled company was entertained by a certain Brandy de Franc – a stripper from Nottingham, who had been discovered by the enterprising Flying Officer 'Scruph' Oliver. In fact Brandy became a popular star in the local pubs, specially after the vicar of Billinghay complained about her performance.

Apart from a lively competition in the mess, Nos 6 and 54 Squadrons worked well together. Our commitments seldom overlapped, and each squadron chose slightly different training aims. On 6 we were still involved with the CTTO trials, while 54 Squadron explored the possibilities for long-range deployment using flight refuelling. On 19-20 May 1970, Squadron Leader John Nevill, with Jim Straughan as his navigator, leading a pair of FGR 2s, established a world record by flying non-stop from the UK to Singapore, a distance of some 8680 statute miles, in 14 hrs 6 min and 55.6 sec. Another pair from 54 also attempted the record; the rest of the squadron deployed by staging. The record was soon broken by an airliner, as being civilian, that aircraft was permitted to fly a more direct route.

Following our Andoya detachment, we picked up additional crews who were holding at Coningsby awaiting the formation of No. 14 Squadron – the Phantom squadron destined for RAF Bruggen. This spread the flying fairly thinly but at least it kept the new crews current. We also started working up for annual renewal of our weapons qualification. The training would culminate in a four-week-long APC in Cyprus.

By now our experience with the Phantom was beginning to pay off. The majority of crews reached the required weapons standards, including the air-to-ground strafing qualification, before leaving the UK. Our subsequent deployment to Akrotiri on 5 May proved to be a most enjoyable sojourn in the sun. It was barely six months since our previous visit, and Cyprus was at its best before the heat burned everything to a crisp. The flying conditions were perfect. As before, the weapons programme was split between Larnaca and Episkopi, but we were faced with other unforeseen problems. One morning the range party arrived at Larnaca to find that the telephone wires had been stolen, which effectively closed Larnaca for the day. Later, our use of the bombing range at Episkopi Bay upset the commanding general's wife; apparently the aircraft noise unsettled her horse. We were obliged to enlarge the range pattern, giving the headquarters a wider berth. Instead of eight attacks per sortie, we could only get four – hardly worth the effort. This spoke volumes for the army's list of priorities!

We made full use of the opportunities for off-duty entertainment. As usual, the squadron party was a great success, although the senior matron at Cape Zevegari was a trifle miffed when we didn't provide her with a formal escort. She was lucky to get an invitation in the first place. But good relations were fully restored when Flight Lieutenants 'Frank' Mitchell and 'Gerry' Wells played the piano and guitar at a musical soirée in the Zevegari mess. The squadron officers also attended an evening of classical music at Curium, a restored Roman amphitheatre overlooking Episkopi Bay. Sadly it was not a live performance but the moonlit setting was magnificent. Our reverie was rudely disturbed when some idiot on the tier above broke a bottle of wine, making the seating arrangements uncomfortably sticky. I wondered if the ancient Romans had suffered similar indignities.

One weekend we borrowed a Land Rover and camped on a six-mile beach east of Kyrenia. For me, the northern coast was still the most attractive part of the island. Cyprus had gained its independence in 1960, and the light-blue berets of the United Nations peacekeeping forces were much in evidence. But not everything had changed for the best. In front of the entrance to the ruined monastery at Bellapais, there stood a majestic tree known as 'the Tree of Idleness', under whose shade sat old men and off-duty air force officers, sipping wine and coffee. The tree was still there, but time had taken its toll. The trunk was riven in two and the branches were heavily lopped. Now modern cafés crowded around, and the dusty square for dreamers had been replaced by a road.

Thankfully, though, little had changed in Kyrenia; it was still the same delightful old port, and on Sunday morning we had a few drinks at the Harbour Club before drifting back to Akrotiri.

Instead of returning to the UK, the squadron deployed from Cyprus to Cervia – a military airfield on the east coast of Italy, midway between Ravenna and Rimini – for exercise Dawn Patrol. Even in 38 Group it was unusual to get back-to-back assignments, but our morale was high, the aircraft were holding up well and the extra deployment was only for two weeks. Cervia was home to an Italian ground attack squadron in the process of converting to the new Fiat G91-Y, and they were doing little flying. The base commander freely admitted that he was looking to our detachment to bring the airfield facilities back up to speed. Cervia was a sub-standard NATO airfield: the taxi tracks were too narrow to take the RAF's VC 10 transport aircraft, which complicated the movement of our groundcrew.

Domestic accommodation and messing facilities were provided by the Italian Air Force. On the first weekend, our Italian hosts laid on a coach and driver to take us to Rimini and the republic of San Marino. The tented flight-line accommodation, provided by 38 Group, was pitched right at the edge of the paved area, barely thirty yards from the ASP. It was very much a case of living with the aircraft. The senior medical officer from Coningsby, who had specifically requested to join the detachment, was obliged to work closer to the front line than he ever intended, and his clinic got its fair share of partially burnt Avtur. During Dawn Patrol we flew simulated attack profiles against targets in southern Italy. My final task was to lead a multinational flypast over Aviano Air Force Base.

It was the strawberry season in Italy, and on the return to Coningsby every cockpit was stuffed with punnets. But there wasn't much room in the front cockpit, and whoever packed the boss's aircraft inadvertently stacked strawberry punnets on the g-suit test valve. When the boss started his engines his g-suit inflated almost to destruction. Which was a source of mirth for Dougie and me, until one of our engines refused to start. Time was critical but the groundcrew were determined not to miss their flight home, and they changed the starter motor in less than two hours. I had intended to do a high-speed run over Cervia, by way of a thank you, but the airspeed indicator failed on take-off and we were obliged to depart more sedately.

In any other aircraft the lack of both airspeed and Mach indication would have been cause for concern, but in the Phantom it was possible to maintain the correct speed by reference to the angle of attack indicator. Indeed the AOA indexer lights beside the gunsight gave the best indication of optimum speed during the approach and landing. During the return flight I pondered on the most likely cause of the failure. I remembered checking that the pitot head cover was removed on my first walk round, but someone might have replaced it while the starter was being changed. On landing at Coningsby, Dougie unstrapped, after confirming that the pitot head was clear, we both became righteously indignant. The groundcrew blew the pitot system out and recovered one over-cooked Italian bee.

David Harcourt-Smith got his group captain promotion in June and went to Command RAF Bruggen. Back at Coningsby, John Nevill was transferred from 54 Squadron to take over 6. Despite the disappointment that the post had not fallen either to Bill Rowe or to myself, the new CO was a popular choice. I had known John since Hunter days and he had been on the guard of honour at our wedding. The change brought about a general rearrangement of crews, and I teamed up with Flight Lieutenant 'Chas' Morgan. Chas was a cool, unflappable character and, like Dougie, his background was air defence.

If anything the pace of training quickened. Before this we had been working hard to stand still, but now the aircraft serviceability improved and we were constantly breaking new ground. Selected crews were regularly flying aircraft fitted with the massive Thorn EMI reconnaissance pod. The EMI pod, with its combination of optical cameras, side-looking radar and infrared line scan, was far in advance of other reconnaissance equipment in service with the RAF. Initially it was thought that the mounting of the recce pod would be a simple extension of the Phantom's operational capabilities, but it soon became clear that to get the best out of the system, both the crews and aircraft would need to be specially designated. The first specialist Phantom reconnaissance squadron – No. 2 Squadron – formed in RAF Germany in April 1971.

On 6 Squadron we usually flew four-ship simulated attack (SAP) sorties, but now we could programme at least one aircraft, sometimes a pair, to provide opposition. This added to the realism of our training and encouraged positive leadership in the air. We also experimented with different tactical formations. There was much debate within the squadron on the relative merits of singleton aircraft versus massed tactical formations, but in fact there was no real choice: of course the single aircraft was more vulnerable, but it might slip through unnoticed, either on a reconnaissance sortie or a nuclear strike. Conventional attacks usually required larger formations. The standard low-level battle formations – either spread or arrow – achieved the necessary concentration of aircraft, but they were entirely predictable. If the defending fighters found one aircraft they usually found them all. Furthermore, these formations did not make use of the Phantom's superior counter air capability.

In practice, we found that an 'escort' formation, where the main attack element was shadowed by a defensive pair some 4000 yards to the rear, was the best compromise. It was very difficult for opposing fighters to attack such a formation without exposing themselves to the escorts – although escort formation was of limited use against fighters with a head-on, look down/shoot down capability.

During July, as part of the continuing CTTO trials, we launched salvoes of 36 SNEB rockets (one full pod from each wing) against an instrumented target at Tain Range in Scotland. Even with inert warheads the SNEB's mud-moving capabilities were impressive. We also introduced night low-level navigation exercises, culminating in simulated bomb release – scored by Strike Command's Radar Bomb Scoring Units. The AWG 12 radar had no specialist terrain-avoidance mode, and we were therefore limited to the minimum safe altitude – nominally the highest terrain on track plus 10%. The margins for error were small. It was obvious that, in future, the army would require close air support round the clock, and John Nevill was determined to develop a night-attack capability on 6 Squadron. As yet there were no vision-enhancing night aids, so the targets had to be illuminated.

Our daughter, Emma Joanne, arrived on 19 August 1970, which was cause for much rejoicing – except that I had to join an HQ 38 Group pre-deployment recce of Decimomannu – an Italian Air Force base in Sardinia. I tried to dodge the commitment – after all, Jules was still in hospital with Emma and I was taking care of Stuart – but apparently no one else was available. So I lodged Stuart with the Douglas-Boyds and departed for Lyneham.

Decimomannu – or Dechi, as it was universally known to airmen – was a weapons training base. Originally, the range facilities had been shared by the RCAF, the German Luftwaffe and the Italian Air Force. Legend had it that when the Canadians had first arrived, the menu for lunch included roast kid, considered to be a great delicacy in Italy, which inexplicably had been translated as 'roast child'. The Canadians, to a man, opted for the fish – there's just no accounting for taste. But the Canadians had pulled out of Dechi in 1970, and their share of range time had been purchased for use by the RAF and the USAFE. The purpose of our recce was find out what was available on the ground, prior to the first RAF detachment – by No. 6 Squadron. It was immediately apparent that the USAFE, who had taken over the Canadian accommodation in its entirety, had secured for themselves the best deal. The RAF was left with an ill-assorted collection of sub-standard buildings requiring considerable work.

Anyway, the recce team made the necessary recommendations, and we were promised the work would be done *domani* – meaning tomorrow. That seemed unlikely, but I hoped that at least the domestic accommodation would be ready for the squadron's forthcoming deployment.

In September, the squadron was tasked to provide a role demonstration mock attack at the Farnborough Air Show. We preferred a role demonstration because it required minimum rehearsal: we could operate from Coningsby, and co-ordinated, pull-up and tip-in dive attacks were our bread and butter. Suitable fireworks and other special effects were provided on the ground. After three rehearsals our demonstration, in which eight aircraft attacked the target in thirty seconds, was suitably impressive. The following week I took six aircraft to RAF Gutersloh for Exercise Cross Swords, where we were tasked for close air support, with forward air control (FAC), against German armour. It was a minor commitment – but the Phantom's jet efflux chewed up Gutersloh's tarmac runway. The squadron eventually deployed to Dechi on the thirtieth. Much to my disgust, none of the work promised six weeks before had been done. Obviously, *domani* was the Italian equivalent of *mañana*. The RAF's combined mess was just a bare room, with equipment and provisions still in packing cases. Nothing had been done in the so-called operations facility; it was still a dilapidated building with foul-smelling, blocked toilets. Fortunately, the base's flying and weapons training facilities were better organised.

The air-to-ground range at Capo Frasca was manned by Italian Air Force personnel, but many years of co-operation with the Canadians had left its mark. Capo Frasca was ideal for academic weapons training. The range time was divided into twenty-minute slots, which were sufficient for each aircraft to complete ten attacks. We normally combined two types of weapons delivery – either retard bombing and SNEB, or 20° dive bombing and strafe – on each sortie. The programming was tight; each formation had to clear the range on time to make way for the next. It was then essential to land back at Dechi for a rapid turnaround in time for the next RAF slot. Our sortie rate was high – far better than we had previously achieved either in Cyprus or in the UK.

After the essential weapons qualification we increased the delivery speeds and switched to more demanding operational profiles. The range had the potential for more advanced training, but the IAF considered Dechi to be a punishment posting and the executive officers were reluctant to accept change. We also had problems collecting spares sent via commercial airlines to Cagliari airport, because the customs staff expected a back-hander for their co-operation. Even in those days corruption was quite normal in Italy.

We were not the only ones fighting an uphill battle at Dechi. One Friday, after a particularly difficult week, I was having a cool beer in the Italian officers' club when my German opposite number joined me. 'You know,' he said, 'ze British and ze Germans have much in common.'

I was about to observe that that must be why we were on opposite sides during two worlds wars, but he went on: 'Ze Italians – zey are different. You haz zem during ze first war, we haz them during ze second.' And with a final note of desperation: 'Now we boz has zem!' How right he was.

Dechi lacked the usual off-duty amenities. The Italian officers' club was a poor substitute for a normal RAF mess, and Cagliari had little to offer. But Forte's Village, a holiday resort on the south coast, offered a welcome haven at the weekends. We could book in for two days at preferential rates. Of course, the navigators could afford to relax more than the pilots, and this may have been why Bill Rowe – normally a most abstemious officer – occasionally 'tied one on' at Forte's Village. At such times, the utterly reliable OC 'A' Flight, custodian of the key to the boss's Mini, became something of a liability. On one occasion the key in question was marooned on a raft in the middle of the swimming pool. No problem to Bill, who, although fully clothed, was by that time convinced he could walk on water. He didn't make it, of course, and his suit never recovered. On another Sunday, Bill again lost the key and we had to hot-wire the Mini. I found myself in the unlikely position of being fed through the Mini's passenger window to reach the bonnet release. We eventually got back to Dechi and were having a cool beer in the Italian officers' club when Bill reached into his top pocket and found the ignition key.

The management at Forte's Village encouraged the squadron to practise its wet dinghy drills in the pool – there was little else in the way of free entertainment. In fact by midnight, the official entertainments programme at the Village had usually run out of steam – there was just a disco for the younger holidaymakers. One Saturday, I needed to get my beauty sleep so I left the party early and walked back to my chalet. Even at that time of night, the camp was well lit, so I had no reason to suspect trouble, but two smart young men stopped me to ask the time. As I checked my watch, I was pushed violently back over a third youth crouching behind. They put the boot in and someone lifted my wallet. I eventually staggered to the reception area and got some help. It was no big deal – just a few cuts and bruises and my ribs were a bit sore – but I had lost my money and my RAF Identity Card.

Next day I was interviewed by the Carabinieri. In a country where abduction, extortion and murder were fairly common, the odd mugging was not particularly newsworthy. But the staff at Forte's Village were anxious to avoid adverse publicity and I was given every consideration. The Carabinieri apologised but admitted they were unlikely to find the perpetrators. The squadron rallied round to help and I couldn't thank them enough for that.

It was standard practice among the aircrews to run a sweepstake on the weapons scores, and Chas and myself won the strafe with an average of 57%. Towards the end of the detachment, the squadron also organised a draw among the groundcrews for familiarisation flights in the back seat. It was quite amusing seeing the bravado of some of the 'hairies' evaporate once they found they had won – of course, by then it was too late for them to back out. I took Corporal Greaves for a low-level cross-country around the island, which he thoroughly enjoyed.

November 1970 saw a significant improvement in weapons training facilities in the UK; up to now the ground-attack squadrons had had to make do with programmed range periods and the semi-annual APCs. There was little opportunity for regular weapons practice, but now 38 Group made a determined effort to introduce applied training on a daily basis. The first breakthrough was the building of a tactical weapons range at Otterburn in Northumberland, where a number of different target complexes were laid out. This range could accept live SNEB and strafe attacks, albeit with practice ordnance, under the direction of a ground-based FAC. One day I recognised the voice on the other end of the radio as 'Tinkle' Bell – my old mate from RAF Germany, who was now doing a ground tour with HQ No. 38 Group.

Another innovation was the introduction of first-run attacks (FRAs) at the weapons ranges around the UK. In broad terms, given two minutes' notice (i.e. fourteen nautical miles out) the ranges would clear aircraft in for an FRA. Initially, SNEB or retard bombing were the preferred options because they caused least disruption to other formations using the range but, with the introduction of instant acoustic scored targets, strafe also became available. With the Phantom's range and weapons load it was possible to make live attacks at several different ranges, all in the same sortie.

March 1971 was a record month for me, and I managed to chalk up nearly forty-one hours' flying in the Phantom. The flying was mainly at low level, but the squadron had also started 'ghost trail' deployments to Cyprus. Under these arrangements, a pair of aircraft with tanker support would deploy non-stop to Akrotiri. We were not cleared to overly Italian airspace, so the total flight time was just over four hours. With the FGR 2's HF single side-band radio, it was possible to communicate direct with the UK even from Cyprus. The return journey on the following Monday was flown in two stages: Akrotiri to Luqa, and Luqa to a night rendezvous with a Victor tanker in UK airspace. We would then let down for a low-level cross-country around the UK. The first time I completed a ghost trail, I got nearly twelve hours' flying in two days – not bad for a fighter aircraft.

The following month we started night ground attack. Before the development of 'smart weapons', attacks on tactical military targets required some sort of dive delivery and weapon release at short range. In operational conditions we would have to use flares to illuminate the target, but for training purposes it was more convenient to use static lighting at nearby coastal ranges. The night targets, at Theddlethorpe range, were picked out with Gooseneck paraffin markers – a kerosene lamp shaped like a watering can, with a lighted wick protruding from the spout. At first the lack of visual cues outside the cockpit was unnerving, but the procedures were similar to those used by day and most of the crews quickly achieved qualifying scores in retard bombing and SNEB. I found 20° dive bombing an even blacker art at night.

The squadron deployed to Dechi again on 19 May. By now we were well used to the string of excuses the Italians used to close the range. So we enlisted the aid of Squadron Leader 'Tony' Park (the quiet member of the Cazaux team in 1959) – a weapons specialist from Coningsby – to oversee the range and, if possible, organise target lighting. The Luftwaffe had been seeking clearance for night attacks for some months, but the Italians were firmly opposed on the grounds that night flying was not included in the original agreement and there were no standard procedures. The boss eventually got agreement to a limited night-attack trial – of course, that didn't guarantee the full support of the Italian range staff. Of the ten nights we attempted to fly, we were treated to 'Da range – she is acclose-ed' on no less than five occasions.

At Frasca, Tony Park had organised sodium lighting. The effect was similar to the illumination provided by flares – which was adequate for bombing and rocketing, but for strafing you had to see the fall of shot. I was lucky enough to register hits, shown by sparks on the metal target frame, with my first burst and thereafter knew where to aim, but many of the pilots missed altogether. I have to say, night ground attack, especially for short-range weapons like the gun, could be quite hairy at times. And after the thrills on the weapons range, the minimal airfield lighting at Dechi provided a different brand of excitement.

The boss also talked the OC of the USAFE detachment into providing two Dart sorties for our use. It was little more than an introduction to Dart firing, and our gunsights were not optimised for air-to-air, but several pilots scored hits. Once again it proved the value of the Dart – but still staffs at the MoD remained unconvinced.

Thank heavens we were still welcome at Forte's Village. After the irritations of Dechi, good food and relaxation were the order of the day. It's a small world, though: I was at the pool-side one weekend when I met Pete and Hilu Ginger. It was great to see two old friends from Wattisham days. Pete had retired from the RAF following his tour on Treble One and was now working for the BAC at Warton. He had been test flying the Lightning, but was due to move over to the Jaguar. We had a long discussion on the merits of the Phantom's two-man crew.

Much to the disgust of the Germans, our night weapons trial at Frasca was highly successful. There was little love lost between the Luftwaffe and the Italians. At the final Friday-night beer call, the Luftwaffe colonel hurled a half-empty Coke bottle at the Italian OC ops, but he was wide of his target and the bottle hit me in the shin. I went down like a sack of potatoes. The Luftwaffe colonel stalked out, but was persuaded by the boss to come back and apologise. I was still on the floor, convinced my leg was broken, when this German officer strode over clicked his eels and bowed. 'Please accept my deepest apologies,' he said. The Italian colonel insisted on driving me to the base hospital for treatment.

I don't know what it was about Dechi – every time I went there I got assaulted. It was a great relief to get back to Coningsby.

On 12 June I led six Phantoms to Bad Soellingen, a Canadian base in southern Germany, as part of the NATO squadron-exchange programme. I took Captain 'Lou' Raina – one of our Canadian exchange officers – along as my navigator. Canada had recently abandoned the traditional designations of navy, army and air force and had adopted the rather colourless all-embracing title of Canadian Armed Forces. All personnel wore the same dark-green uniform and used army ranks. Lou Raina and his pilot compatriot, Captain 'Bob' Marion, had previously been RCAF flight lieutenants and would have preferred to remain so.

Soellingen was on the border between France and Germany, just west of Baden-Baden. No. 439 Squadron was equipped with F-104 Starfighters, an aircraft that had suffered an unenviably bad safety record, particularly with the Luftwaffe. In fact the F-104's loss rate was comparable to many other single-engined fast jet aircraft; the difference was, a far greater proportion of F-104 accidents were fatal. Not so with the Canadians, who took the realistic view that, if the engine quits at low level, you pull up, converting speed to altitude, and you eject.

In fact, 439 Squadron lost an aircraft on the day we arrived. The F-104 was *en route* for the annual Tiger Meet, attended by all squadrons bearing a tiger on their squadron badge. No. 439 Squadron RCAF was a founder Tiger member. The engine failed shortly after take-off and the pilot ejected. Funny thing was, this year 439 had decorated their Tiger Meet aircraft all over with black and yellow stripes. The effect was most impressive – no doubt it would have stolen the Tiger Show – but of course the unique paint job might cause a few problems for the inevitable crash investigation: in aviation circles, black and yellow stripes are usually reserved for marking emergency controls.

But the accident was soon put aside and we were quickly absorbed into the Canadian system. Canadian airmen have much in common with the RAF – we speak the same language. More SAPs, recce and close air support – but southern Germany was all new territory to us and, as one young Canadian pilot commented, Germany was a target-rich environment. In just one sortie it was possible to pick out more military hardware than there was in the whole of the UK.

The social programme was no less demanding, although we had prior warning from Major 'Gin' Smith, who commanded 439 Squadron's detachment to Coningsby. Gin had introduced us to the curious Canadian bar-game of Dead Ants. At the call of 'Dead Ants', all present, including any ladies, had to hurl themselves on to the floor, waving their legs and arms in the air. The last one down bought a round of drinks – all good clean fun, albeit slightly embarrassing at a cocktail party. The Canucks just didn't give a damn. As the Canadians taxied out for their final departure from Coningsby, someone in the tower whispered, 'Dead Ants.' It was almost the perfect call – but somehow 'Gin' Smith managed to raise his feet out of the cockpit.

It was a great pleasure at Soellingen to meet up with Major Peter Caws, whom I had last seen graduating at Gimli in 1955. Peter's career in the RCAF had more or less matched my own in the RAF, although it surprised me to hear that he was contemplating early retirement at the end of his present tour.

At the weekend I took the opportunity to visit my brother Ian, who was working as a contract draughtsman for the BMW company in Munich. Ian was enjoying life with a small group of expatriates from the UK, all working for the same agency, but I got the impression he missed England. After a fairly drunken weekend, Ian poured me back on the train for Baden-Baden.

The following Monday was a German national holiday – which meant no low flying – so our Canadian hosts challenged us to a golf match. The 6 Squadron team was short of two players, so John Nevill flew out from Coningsby with 'Dinger' Dell. We lost the match.

The detachment was a great success. We flew a lot of hours, and I gave 'Gin' Smith, Peter Caws and Colonel Burgess, the CO of 439, rides in the twin-stick Phantom. In fact Colonel Burgess made a perfect circuit and landing from the back seat – no mean feat for a first flight in the Phantom FGR 2. I had a couple of flights in the F-104-F. It was interesting to compare the two aircraft: the F-104 was smooth as silk at low level and very fast, but its manoeuvrability was limited at speeds below 450 knots. Even on such a short acquaintance, it was obvious that the Phantom was a far more capable aircraft.

I flew the return flight to Coningsby with Bill Hobby. *En route* we made a co-ordinated attack on a Nike missile site in Holland, and rendezvoused with another formation from 6 Squadron over the North Sea. With the Phantom's TACAN it was possible to get an accurate air-to-air range between aircraft during join-up; this facility was invaluable during flight refuelling operations.

I took leave during August and drove down to Weymouth with Jules and the children. After a relaxing holiday with the grandparents it was back to the cut-and-thrust of squadron life. By this time I knew my next posting would be to staff college; actually I had been nominating 'Staff College – on Exchange' as one of my preferences for some while. I wasn't that keen – but faced with the inevitable I thought it best to show willing. I had visions of a comfortable year abroad; I had not bargained on an exchange with the Army Staff College at Camberley – which was a horse of a very different colour.

But there was still work for me to do at Coningsby. In September I flew thirty hours of the most varied flying possible in fighter-type aircraft – from offensive support, SAPs, night low-level and flight refuelling. Night tanking was particularly satisfying; the tanker's floodlit wings were the only horizon necessary, and the hose basket was picked out by a circle of tiny pea bulbs. In October I flew one last ghost trail to Cyprus, before the squadron started a six-week period of weapons training.

This time we were committed to night ground attack at West Freugh, which was one of the few ranges in the UK large enough to accept the Lepus flare. The squadron had already done release trials with the Lepus, which was a large magnesium flare designed for photographic reconnaissance. The target at West Freugh was a raft anchored in Luce Bay. The procedure was for the flare ship to approach at low level, identify the target on radar and toss a stick of three flares to bracket the target area. A time switch in the Lepus ensured safe separation between the aircraft and flare ignition. The illumination provided by each flare run lasted for approximately five minutes, allowing eight conventional dive bomb attacks below the flares. But first, there was the problem of getting the whole formation out to the range. Close formation at night, without the usual visual cues, was hard work, and it would not have allowed time to set up the weapons switches. So our usual procedure was to fly in an extended radar trail, with aircraft separated two miles line astern. With six aircraft (i.e. two flareships and four bombers) the formation was spread over ten nautical miles. The FGR 2 was well equipped for this tactical snake, but even minor changes of flight path at the front end could be much magnified at the rear.

On the first night, Chas and I flew as 'Black three', but something went wrong at the back end. 'Black six' somehow overtook 'Black five'. The two aircraft must have passed very close to each other, yet the crews were none the wiser. But that was a matter for the debrief. The first load of flares was delivered accurately on target; the illumination was brilliant, but from 3000 ft one patch of sea looked much like any other and it was difficult to see the target. The bombing accuracy was poor, but it was a first attempt and no doubt the scores would improve.

On the second night, one of the flares failed to ignite. There was no way of knowing which one of the stick of three had failed, but we had been assured that if this happened the Lepus would remain ballistic (i.e. the retardant parachute would not deploy) and the flare would therefore be well clear of the weapons pattern. Even with just two flares there was ample light to continue. As I pulled out of my dive I glimpsed what appeared to be a grey telegraph pole, suspended from a parachute, flash past the nose at very close range. Obviously we had been given duff gen. Unlit Lepus flares did *not* remain ballistic, and the possibility of colliding with an unlit 'grey ghost' was far more hazardous than we had been led to believe. We amended our range procedures.

I flew my last trip on 6 Squadron on 10 December 1971. In three years I had managed to clock up 641 hours in the Phantom, and for the most part it had been unremarkable. That is not to say there hadn't been the odd moment of excitement. I had had my share of aircraft emergencies – the occasional single-engined landing, a fire warning which caused me to jettison three overload fuel tanks, numerous BLC malfunctions and the like – but it seldom got to the stage where the aircraft was in serious jeopardy. And, of course, there were the hairy incidents that were part and parcel of low-level fast jet operations, like the free radar letdown over Exmoor, the Lepus flare incident and the occasional low pull-out. For me, one of the most hair-raising incidents occurred when a junior pilot led me in for a formation landing in bad weather – I was in echelon starboard and he landed on the right-hand half of the runway. It was the only time I'd had to deploy the braking parachute while still airborne, but it worked and no damage was done.

I had had a successful tour but it had been hard work, and now I needed a rest. The turnover of squadron personnel had started as early as September 1969: Bill Rowe had left in May 1971 and Dougie-Boyd had taken over 'A' Flight. Now, as I handed over 'B' Flight to Squadron Leader Ian Tite from 228 OCU, I regretted having to leave.

I had mixed feelings about my forthcoming Camberley course. Even the inevitable round of farewell dinners combined with the Christmas parties did little to cheer me up. My concern mainly was due to my lack of confidence with the pen; but on top of that I knew nothing about the Army. Major Humphrey Tyack, our tame GLO, was a friendly enough character, but in my experience some army officers were unpleasantly arrogant. But at least Camberley was a pleasant part of the country and I had been promised a married quarter.

11
Staff college Camberley; staff tour at Headquarters No. 38 Group

We moved into Overlord Close at Camberley just after Christmas, in good time for me to start the short introductory course for foreign students and exchange officers. There were two other RAF squadron leaders on the course: Keith Harding, a helicopter pilot, and Roger Sweatman, a transport pilot. Wing Commander Gordon Massie was the RAF member of the directing staff (DS). Apart from Gordon, I think we were all rather surprised to be at Camberley.

Jules and I were the only RAF people living in married quarters. Apparently the architect who designed Overlord Close had received an award for innovation. Certainly our house was unique, and like much 1960s architecture, it was difficult to live with. The lounge resembled a squash court, complete with first-floor viewing gallery. The under-floor central heating and ice-cold ceiling – basically the roof of the house – produced a constant downdraft of cold air. The previous occupant had also been an RAF exchange student, and I inherited his khaki puttees and beret, along with a note advising me that both of these items were essential for the field work during the course. Actually the beret was a size too large, but by judicious tightening of the lace it more or less fitted. I also drew from the quartermaster a set of plain green combat clothing – again too large. Don't they have any small-size army officers? Compared to the British Army students, all with their own latest design disruptive-pattern kit, I could easily have been mistaken for an untidy heap of green laundry.

From a personal point of view, there were compensations for moving south of the Thames. Camberley was a pleasant little town, and we were closer both to Gab and our old friends in north-west London. We were surprised when my parents accepted an invitation to come and spend the New Year with us; Dad was notoriously reluctant to abandon the comforts of his own home. To mark the occasion, Jules took the lead by organising an impromptu family reunion. We managed to rope in the rest of the Bendell clan, and Mother was quite overcome.

My first assigned duty at Camberley was to look after a fellow student, Major Musa Adwan of the Jordanian army. No problem with that – Mussa and his family were living next door, but it was a bit like one guest acting as host to another. I could have done with a bit of help myself – the British Army had a strange way of handling visitors. Fortunately, Musa could speak a little English, but his wife Saleema and their four children were the proverbial fish out of water. While Jules introduced Saleema to the dubious pleasures of shopping in Camberley, I did my best to help Musa find a car. Of course he wanted a new car: the snag was he didn't have enough money. After scouring through the newspapers and visiting every dealer in the area we learned that the NAAFI manager wanted to sell his Austin Mini for just a few pounds more than Musa said he could afford. I left Musa to haggle over the price, but he did eventually buy the car. I have to admit a Mini was not the ideal choice for the Adwans – with six aboard it was cosy to say the least – but that didn't put Musa off and, as far as I know, the Mini never let him down.

While all this was going on I was trying to get to grips with the introductory course. There was much to learn. Almost from the word go we were submerged in a bewildering lexicon of army jargon, complete with new abbreviations and acronyms. We were issued with a sackful of reference material and the list of required reading grew longer by the hour. Of course, at Camberley, the army students, whatever their colour or creed, had an advantage over the RAF and Navy exchange officers: the pongos had grown up with platoons, companies, battalions, divisions, corps, and the like. The best advice offered to the exchange officers was that we should not expect to match the average British Army student – which proved to be correct. Unlike the Royal Navy and RAF officers, who viewed staff college as a necessary evil, the British Army officer's performance at staff college more or less dictated his future career. As a result, the British Army students were totally committed, at least to start with, and the atmosphere at Camberley was deadly serious.

During the introductory lectures there was a lively debate among the foreign pongos on the British Army's regimental system. Personally I cared little about the pros and cons; if the British Army believed in the regimental system for reasons of morale, then so be it. But their later insistence on maintaining the correct order of regimental seniority, especially when drafting operation orders, would return to haunt us all. Did it really matter that the Scots Guards were senior to the Grenadiers, or vice versa?

The Camberley course consisted of 180 officers, which included fifty exchange students. I was in a syndicate of twelve students in 'C' Division. It was quite usual for the first term of any staff course to be devoted to minor staff duties (i.e. service writing), which offered a wealth of opportunity with which to browbeat the hapless students. Camberley was no exception. Our syndicate was further blighted by the appointment of a newly promoted, thoroughly unpleasant lieutenant colonel of the Irish Guards as our DS. I have never subscribed to the belief that it is necessary to destroy the confidence of students before they can be taught the right way, but that was the philosophy of our first DS. Not only did he demolish the British students, he also harassed the foreign officers quite unfairly when their tardiness to respond during syndicate discussions was solely due to their difficulty with the language. After one particularly bruising session, even a fellow Guards officer felt obliged to apologise for the colonel's boorish behaviour. We all agreed the colonel was a pompous ass. It amazed me that the British Army should appoint such a man to instruct at their prestigious senior staff college. But enough of that. Our syndicate survived the first two months, although it was an unpleasant experience which tainted the rest of the year.

It was during this first term that I started to have problems with my left arm. The pins and needles sensation returned, particularly in my hand, but now the whole arm felt stiff. I thought it was probably due to a strain, because I had been burning the midnight oil trying to keep up with the work, and that fitted in with the medical diagnosis of fibrositis. After five sessions of physiotherapy, including heat treatment, the arm improved, but strangely I never recovered the normal sensation of touch in my left hand. It was a minor inconvenience; I was right-handed anyway, and no one noticed that I had to visually check what I took out of my pocket.

It was claimed that the real value of staff college lay in the people you met rather than in the acquisition of knowledge, but I was not convinced this held true for the exchange students at Camberley. Because of the overriding importance attributed to staff college by the British Army students, the social life at Camberley was slow to get off the mark and the exchange students tended to be on the fringe. Being RAF, I was one of the 'crabs', and Jules was known as Mrs Crab. We were invited to a few army parties, but they seemed rather cliquey – unless, of course, you were part of the horsy, hunting, shooting and fishing set. Jules and I found ourselves drawn more towards the overseas students – who, by and large, were charming company. Of course, for reasons of religion, many of them didn't drink alcohol, which sometimes made entertaining difficult. In March we invited a group of fellow students and their wives, including Venki and Rada Patel, to dinner. Venki was a major in the Indian army. As far as we were concerned it was just a pleasant social occasion, but when we let slip that it was also our wedding anniversary, the Patels took it as a great honour. Fortunately, there was no great cultural difference with Mike and Marlena Jeffery. Mike was a major in the Australian army – in fact he had won the Military Cross (MC) in Vietnam and had received his award from the Queen at Buckingham Palace. Mike and I played a comparably scrappy standard of golf, but it was a valuable safety valve. The Jefferys became our good friends at Camberley, and they have remained so ever since.

The atmosphere at Camberley eased considerably during the second term. Our studies now centred on field tactics, which was more practical, and our syndicate was fortunate to have one of the best instructors – Lieutenant Colonel J. Watts OBE, MC, Royal Irish Rangers. But more impressive to those who knew about soldiering, Johnny Watts had made his reputation with the Special Air Service (SAS) in Malaya and Oman, and we were about to be given a unique insight into modern tactical thinking by an expert. The work consisted of TEWTs – territorial exercises without troops. In the mornings, the students would walk the ground with map-board and coloured Chinagraph grease pencils, making plans either to attack or defend various objectives in Berkshire and Hampshire against mythical armies. After a leisurely picnic lunch, Johnny Watts would take us round again and tell us the way he would do it. In the warm, peaceful sunshine, some of the colonel's suggestions appeared bizarre. No doubt the local inhabitants would have been horrified to learn that their picturesque thirteenth-century village church would have to be demolished to clear the field of fire, but it was for their own good. And even if the colonel's solutions did not always conform to the 'pink' it was noticeable that other, more senior, members of staff often would attend Johnny Watts's debriefings.

The phase culminated in a *coup-de-main* assault on a heavily defended Cookham Bridge. Our plan was good – we took few casualties – but according to Johnny Watts it was too slow. He would have abseiled down from helicopters directly on to the bridge, and in all probability he would have succeeded single-handed. But the colonel knew his stuff and could quote from personal experience. He also gave us colourful snippets of advice such as, 'Beware the mad machine-gunner hiding in the rubble,' and, 'You have to put your minds in the shoes of your enemy.' But we always knew what the colonel really meant. Working with Johnny Watts was a refreshing change from the idiot treatment we had received during the first term, and did much to restore our rather battered self-confidence.

In between the field exercises we studied modern battles and in the process learned about land warfare in mountain, desert and jungle terrain. We studied in detail the classic armoured campaign of the Israeli/Arab Six-Day War. Colonel Watts also corrected the balance of thinking among the army students on the value of close air support in the ground battle.

On 1 June, Jules and I attended a small gathering in the commandant's office at which Major General Howard-Dobson presented me with a Queen's Commendation (QCVSA) for my flying on No. 6 Squadron. A totally unexpected honour, but we enjoyed the occasion.

A few days later the student body was briefed in the Alanbrooke Hall on the college's battlefield tour of the D-Day landings in Normandy. The intention was to bring to life the atmosphere of war, but most of the students were simply grateful to escape from the classroom. The tour concentrated on three vital roles played by British forces in Operation Overlord, namely: 6 Airborne Division's task to secure the left flank of the invasion beachhead; the assault on Gold Beach by 50th (Northumbrian) Division, specifically the action fought by the 6th Battalion Green Howards on D-Day; and the breakout by 11 Armoured Division to the east and south-east of Caen as part of Operation Goodwood on 18 and 19 July 1944.

We deployed to France on 3 June. As with the TEWTs, we walked the ground in Normandy with guest artists – men who had fought in the battle – as they recounted their experiences. We were all impressed by the cool, raw courage shown by these men. As an airman, I could appreciate the skill required by the pilots of three Horsa gliders who had made night landings in a tiny field alongside the bridge over the Caen Canal (subsequently named Pegasus Bridge) in the early minutes of 6 June 1944. And everyone paused for thought when Lieutenant Colonel A.J. Parry (a lieutenant at the time) explained how he had led the assault on the Merville Battery across barbed wire and minefield. Lieutenant Colonel R. H. Hastings, the CO of 6 Green Howards, impressed us with his leadership – here was positive proof of the value of the British regimental system. Sadly one of the regular artists – CSM Stan Hollis VC, 'D' Company, 6th Battalion, Green Howards, who had won the Victoria Cross for acts of extraordinary gallantry on D-Day – had died the previous February, but we listened to his voice on tape as we looked across the scene of his particular action. Operation Goodwood was fought in the Bocage, an area of narrow fields, orchards and sunken lanes better suited to defence than attack. In the warm sunshine it was difficult to imagine the blood-and-guts carnage that had taken place in 1944. Tanks had been destroyed, or in the jargon of the day brewed up, all around, but General Davidore-Golsmith (who was a tank squadron commander at the time) remembered exactly where each engagement took place. With typical British understatement the battle was portrayed as a hard-fought advance, the outcome of which was never in doubt – but in reality it was a brutal war of attrition which cost 11 Armoured Division over a third of its effective fighting strength.

Nor were the enemy forgotten. One of the guest artists was Colonel H. U. Von Luck, CO 125 Panzer Grenadier Regiment, who in desperation had ordered a German anti-aircraft battery to engage the British tanks. The gallant colonel was later taken prisoner on the Russian Front.

On returning to Camberley we switched our attention to the continuing campaign against the IRA. Up to that time, the British Army had considered the risk element of serving in Ulster beneficial to recruitment. But in February the official branch of the IRA planted a bomb at the paratroop depot at Aldershot, as an obvious reprisal for 'Bloody Sunday' in Londonderry. Two more bombs were planted in London in March, marking the start of the Provisional IRA's bombing campaign on mainland UK. This led to an immediate tightening of security around the so-called 'soft' military targets. Few would then have believed it possible that the IRA terrorist campaign would continue for another twenty-three years. At the time I was interested, because urban terrorism was the subject of my major staff college thesis, an opus of 3000 words – a daunting prospect. Particularly so since all I knew then about urban terrorism would comfortably fit on the back of a postage stamp.

The Alanbrooke Hall was an ideal venue for guest lecturers who came to talk about a wide range of subjects. Of course the students were expected to show a lively interest and ask suitably penetrating questions, but, as Lord Birkett said, 'Better to keep your mouth shut and be thought a fool than to open it and remove all doubt.' On 11 July we listened to a superb lecture on combat survival by Major J. M. Rowe, US Army, who had served as a military advisor to the South Vietnamese army in the early sixties, and had been captured by the Vietcong. The Major described how he had survived many years of barbaric treatment, until he eventually escaped by hailing a US Army helicopter gunship engaged in ground attack. For me, the presentation brought home some of the horror that many of my friends from Nellis must have been experiencing as POWs in North Vietnam.

Later in July the students were invited to attend a fire-power demonstration by the 7th Armoured 'Old Ironsides' Division, US Army, at Graffenwohr in West Germany. The course travelled in two RAF VC10 aircraft from Brize Norton to Nuremberg. One of the most impressive set pieces was to see a car sawn in half by a short burst from a Vulcan cannon mounted on an armoured personnel carrier. The Vulcan was the same gun I had used on the F-105 and the Phantom, but I had never before seen the results from such close quarters.

After the display we gathered at Graffenwohr for an alcoholic dinner party and exchange of gifts. We returned to the UK the following day, somewhat the worse for wear.

August was taken up with the mid-course leave. Jules and I teamed up with the Harwoods and hired a cottage near Praa Sands in Cornwall for a typical beach holiday with the children. We all needed the break. John and I played the odd round of golf – odd being the most apt description.

After Praa Sands we spent a week with my parents at Weymouth, then it was back to Camberley to work on my paper. Fortunately Joyce, my sister-in-law, offered to type my thesis – but I was still grappling with the writing.

Our attention now turned to joint warfare, which included liaison with visiting teams from the RAF Staff College, Bracknell and the RN College at Greenwich. The need for close co-operation between the services was emphasised. To us, it seemed that this was readily appreciated by the officers at working level, although co-operation was sometimes lacking higher up the chain. I was detached to work with an RAF team at Bracknell during Exercise Red Rice, where Jules was invited to a coffee morning with the air force wives. She returned that evening and asked if I knew a girl called Christine. Well, of course I did – but the last time I had seen her was in 1965, as she'd boarded the ship for Australia.

Christine invited us to a party at Bracknell. It turned out that she had met her future husband, a British army officer, while he was serving in Australia. Subsequently he was selected to attend the RAF staff college as an exchange student. It's a small world. It was good to know that Christine was now happily married with a son of her own.

The Jefferys were Anglophiles in the widest meaning of the word, and they were determined to make the most of their opportunities at Camberley. Even when Mike contracted mumps – an uncomfortable affliction at the best of times, but more so as an adult male – he hardly slowed down. One morning, when Mike was well on the road to recovery and Marlena was taking their children to school, he struggled out of bed and caught sight of his rather enlarged private parts. At that moment he heard the front door opening and called down, 'Hey, Marl, come up and have a look at this!' Unfortunately it was not Marlena –

but the cleaning lady came up anyway and, the way Mike told it, she was suitably impressed. A few days later the Jefferys hosted a fancy dress party; Marlena – who was heavily pregnant at the time – appeared as a mother superior, while Mike, arrayed in blue body stocking and scarlet tights, made a convincing Superman. Eventually, on 6 October, Marlena produced a charming daughter, Sarah, and Jules was invited to be her godmother.

After the joint phase, the work turned to NATO and the army's role in north-west Europe. By now the pressure of course work was slackening off.

The vital date – the day when the postings were announced – was 4 October. Gordon Massie broke the news to the RAF exchange officers. All of our postings had some connection with the army: Roger Sweatman was to be the RAF liaison officer with the SAS in London; Keith Harding was to join the staff at the junior division of the Army Staff College at Shrivenham; and I was to be posted as Ops 3 (Phantom) at HQ 38 Group, the RAF formation tasked with providing tactical air support for the army. It was not exactly my preferred choice – there would be little chance of flying – but it was better than the MoD, and at least I would be back with the RAF.

The course was almost finished, but we had one more major exercise to complete, and that dealt with a fighting withdrawal in the face of the expected Warsaw Pact's massive armoured thrust across the North German Plain. This had always been accepted as the most likely scenario and, in those days, even the most conservative estimate would have the Soviet forces reaching the Channel ports within four days. Of course, the joker in the pack was the employment of nuclear weapons. Most of the officers at Camberley accepted that, if the attack did come, NATO would use tactical nuclear weapons.

Mike and I teamed up with an aristocratic West German army officer – Lieutenant Colonel Klaus von Bodenstein – to consider the problem. Our more immediate concern during this exercise was a series of power strikes, which tended to limit the night work. We discussed the options at length by candlelight, and wrote furiously by day. As an outsider it was interesting to compare the differing strategies.

The staff college solution was for a progressive withdrawal using natural features to force the Soviets to concentrate in well-defined killing zones, and then to destroy them with tactical nuclear weapons. Klaus, on the other hand, was not prepared to sacrifice any German territory, much less use nuclear weapons on West German soil. He believed strongly in counter-attack, hooking behind the Soviet's leading elements and cutting their lines of supply. It was an interesting alternative. Fortunately, neither option was ever put to the test.

Traditionally, the students produced a Christmas pantomime. In December 1972 our course produced *Aladdin.* The standard was almost professional. Whatever else, there was no shortage of talent at Camberley.

After our final interviews (I passed with an honourable B) we wound down during the final week. We had all had enough. On their last night in London, the Jefferys invited us to see *Cosi Fan Tutte* at Covent Garden. The next day they embarked for Australia, and we moved a few miles up the road to RAF Benson.

We settled in quickly, and it was a relief to get back to the real world. Benson supported three disparate organisations: the Queen's Flight, equipped with Andover and Wessex aircraft; the Tactical Communications Wing (TCW), tasked with providing air-transportable radio links with the army; and last but not least, Headquarters No. 38 Group.

In 1972, No. 38 Group transferred from Air Support Command to Strike Command. This change had little effect on the role of the Phantom squadrons at Coningsby: 6 and 54 were still committed to close-air support on the flanks of NATO. No. 41 Squadron – a designated Phantom reconnaissance squadron – had just been formed in 1972, but this squadron was tasked by the joint air intelligence centre.

The atmosphere at HQ No. 38 Group was fairly relaxed. I took over from Squadron Leader 'Chuck' Coulcher and shared an office with Flight Lieutenant Tony Gordon, who worked for me. No less than five other members of the staff had previously served at Coningsby.

In May, Jules and I were invited to Coningsby to attend the sixtieth anniversary of the formation of No. 6 Squadron. The squadron had now been taken over by Wing Commander Danny Lavender, but many of our friends were still there. The guest of honour was King Hussein of Jordan. As a result of an extraordinary security gaffe, and much to her embarrassment, Jules wound up meeting King Hussein in the gents' toilet. Apparently the King was greatly amused – not so the security guards.

The wrinkles had been ironed out of the Phantom's annual training syllabus, and that part of my job almost took care of itself. In any case, by that time it was common knowledge that the Phantoms would soon be replaced in the close-air-support role by the SEPECAT Jaguar. If anything, my tasks in the air-support operations centre (ASOC) at the Tactical Field Headquarters were more challenging.

The ASOC was an essential link in the tasking chain between the army and RAF close-air-support squadrons. Most of our exercises with the army were simulated (i.e. CPX or paper exercises), but even so we had to deploy with the army to field locations and work from tented accommodation.

The HQ 38 Group elements deployed in three or four Land Rovers. In war, a tactical headquarters deployed in the field would be prepared to move every six hours, thus our kit was lightweight, rugged and flexible. My first exercise was to the Thetford training area in Norfolk, where I met Mike Wilkes from Camberley – or rather, I tripped over him on the second night out. Mike was sleeping under a concertina roll of barbed wire. In theory he should have been fairly safe (for the same reason I slept beside a Land Rover), but he hadn't allowed for yours truly blundering around in the dark. I have to admit I was getting a bit old for the camping game. It was fine during the day, when you could see where you were going, but at night in blacked-out conditions the mixture of mud, barbed wire, trees and recumbent army officers was rather trying. Added to that, the directing staff had a nasty habit of regularly dispensing CS gas canisters to simulate chemical attacks. We were equipped with nuclear, biological and chemical (NBC) suits and respirators, but life was far from comfortable. I usually finished a four-day field exercise totally knackered.

But the work was interesting. By now the anti-aircraft threat in the forward areas – posed by radar-laid guns and guided missiles, some even hand-held – was significant. The possibility of losing aircraft due to friendly fire – so called 'blue on blue' engagements – was very real. A system of airspace management, from corps in the rear to the forward edge of the battle area (FEBA), was needed. In previous years, when the ground-to-air weapons were far less efficient, we had relied rather naively on the rule that aircraft heading east were friendly and those going west were hostile. The facts that in the heat of battle troops on the ground might not be aware of their bearings and, at some stage, friendly aircraft would have to return on a westerly heading, were conveniently ignored. But now, something more sophisticated was needed. IFF (the equipment used to identify aircraft on radar) and flight-level sanctuaries were part of the answer, but they had to be backed up by sensible routing. In liaison with the army staffs I plotted a system of routes avoiding high-risk areas, which could be issued both to the tasking agencies and the ground forces on a daily basis. Each evening I produced map overlays showing the agreed minimum risk routes (MRRs) for the following day. These were delivered to relevant command posts by helicopter. From small beginnings, the MRR system gradually gained acceptance, and something very similar was eventually adopted across the central region of West Germany.

Life at Benson was very pleasant. At the weekends I usually played golf with Tony Gordon and Dick Barraclough at Goring Streetly – although, sad to say, my handicap stubbornly remained in the high teens. I was also able to spend far more time with the family, and we went to Cornwall again for our summer holidays.

Benson also owned two small motor boats which were moored on the Thames at Wallingford. Actually I was quite keen on boating, but my attempt to get the family interested was a dismal failure. Of course, it was difficult to be totally relaxed when you were on the river with a temperamental motor and neither anchor nor oars for use in an emergency. The absence of an anchor meant that the crew – Jules – had to step lively whenever we wished to tie up. We had barely started our first cruise when Jules had to leap ashore while I changed over fuel tanks. It wasn't my fault she landed in stinging nettles.

After a fairly heated exchange of words she agreed to give boating one more chance, and the following day packed a picnic lunch before we set off downstream. After negotiating the lock at Wallingford, one of the deepest on the Thames, we settled down to a peaceful day on the river. The children, wrapped up safely in life-jackets, were enjoying themselves, and people on the river seemed very courteous. But after thirty minutes or so the engine began to cough and splutter. We made it to the Beetle & Wedge for a medicinal brandy – the kids had lemonade. Then, after much cursing and swearing, I managed to coax the engine back to life. We found a fairly easy mooring to have lunch, which we shared with assorted biting insects and a herd of curious cows, then it was all aboard for the return trip. If we could have continued as planned, Jules might have been won over to a life on the river – but as we approached Wallingford we were hailed by an enormous ocean-going gin palace. Apparently their engine had failed, and could we give them a tow to the bank? Well, only too pleased to oblige . . . I told Jules to grab the tow rope as I gunned the motor – which was not that impressive. On reflection I should also have told Jules to tie the tow rope on to our boat. There was a strangled squawk from the rear and I turned to see Jules grimly hanging on to the towrope and slowly being dragged over the back end of our boat. She didn't actually fall overboard, but it was damned close.

So ended our days on the river.

Some time in September I assisted Group Captain 'Ray' Bannard in planning a role demonstration at RAF Wattisham – showing all the elements of 38 Group for the Royal College of Defence Studies. The scenario was a surprise attack to overrun and hold an enemy airstrip in hostile territory – but of course the real purpose was to demonstrate the considerable tactical firepower available to 38 Group. As far as I can recall, the display, which was accompanied by spectacular pyrotechnic ground effects, started with a formation of Phantom FGR 2s making a low-level, high-speed, conventional dive bombing attack – to soften up the enemy. This was followed by the arrival of four Puma helicopters, discharging thirty RAF Regiment gunners in full combat kit to secure the airstrip. Moments later a Hercules C-130 landed and unloaded a selection of support equipment, including Land Rovers with trailers. And finally four Harriers, supposedly requested by the regiment gunners, appeared, again at high speed and low level, to mop up the remaining opposition. The whole item, which was allocated just seven minutes, called for precise timing. Naturally 38 Group's contribution required several rehearsals and had to be approved by the headquarters' staffs. It was a great excuse to get out of the office.

In November the tactical headquarters deployed to Cyprus for a major CPX exercise. We travelled passenger-cum-freight in a

Hercules C-130 from Benson. Now I accept that the Hercules was a great aircraft, but few passengers would describe it as comfortable. In the mixed passenger and freight configuration, where the passengers were crammed into the available space like socks in an overstuffed suitcase, the Hercules could be hell. The standard-issue ear-plugs offered scant protection against the constant barrage of noise. After a bum-numbing six hours we stumbled off the aircraft at Kingsfield, a small military airfield some eight miles north-east of Larnaca.

The headquarters was set up at Pergamos, and old prison camp which had previously been used to constrain terrorist prisoners during the EOKA campaign. The facilities here were spartan but adequate. Besides, no one in their right mind would complain about a deployment to Cyprus – when the alternative could be Thetford Forest.

For some reason the role of the ASOC was played low-key during the exercise. When it finished, four of us, with Ken Hayr in the lead, hired a car to drive to the coast. We headed north through Salamis, dating from the twelfth century BC, to Prastio and Lefkoniko, tiny villages that time had forgotten, making for the Kyrenia Range. It was a part of the island I had not seen before – at least, not from ground level – and again I was struck by its simple, unspoiled and natural beauty. The road along the top of the range threaded its way through open pine woodland, with stunning views on either side. Then, quite suddenly, we found ourselves in the midst of a Turkish military encampment. It was touch-and-go as to whether we would be challenged, but we passed through unhindered. It was none of our business, of course: since independence, British military interests in Cyprus had been confined to the Sovereign Base Areas (SBAs) further south.

We stopped at Buffavento – a castle seven miles east of Kyrenia where Richard Coeur de Lion had installed his mother-in-law. Buffavento could be reached only by a steep goat's track which zigzagged 600 ft up the side of the mountain. Even for us it was a strenuous climb of thirty minutes, and I could well imagine that, once the old lady was up there, she would stay put. We were met at the entrance by a fit young Turk who offered us a drink of water from the castle's cistern. Apparently the cistern was filled by water draining from the roofs and gutters. When it was first built it had taken three years to fill, and since then had never run dry. The water was crystal clear and ice cold. On the next floor up, another guide, equipped with high-powered binoculars, pointed out Nicosia to the south-west and the distant coast of Turkey, over a hundred miles to the north. Someone had for themselves a splendid forward observation post.

We sorted out our accommodation in Kyrenia, had a delightful meal in a local Greek restaurant, and finished the evening learning to dance to bouzouki music.

Next day we hired a boat for a little water-skiing. On leaving the harbour we passed a heavily armed motor gunboat, moored out of sight from the town. The skiing was a laugh, but I was reminded that two-stroke fuel tasted just as foul in the Med as it had in Lake Mead. On the drive back to Pergamos we were left pondering the question: why can't these delightful people learn to share this beautiful island and live peacefully together?

Our return flight to the UK was noisy but otherwise uneventful. The great advantage of flying with HQ No. 38 Group was that the aircraft delivered you almost to your doorstep.

Then, in December, I was given the news I had been waiting for since graduating from Camberley: in July I would be posted to take command of No. 17 Squadron – a Phantom ground attack/strike squadron – at RAF Bruggen. My refresher flying courses were due to start in February.

I suppose for any career-minded military aviator, to get command of a frontline flying squadron had to be the plum job. Of course there were other wing commander flying posts, such as OC Ops, but I much preferred to be a squadron commander. And there was the additional bonus of serving again in RAF Germany. So I was over the moon.

Squadron Leader Frank Mitchell – another of my pals from No. 6 Squadron – arrived to take over my Ops 3 post at HQ No. 38 Group. It was always a little difficult when faced with a series of short courses, but Jules and I agreed that she and the children would stay at Benson during my refresher. I would commute home at the weekends, and for much of the time I would share the commuting journey with Squadron Leader Stu Penny. It was typical of the Air Secretary's Department that there was insufficient time for me to do full Jet Provost/Hunter/Phantom refresher courses. But from my experience in 1968, I agreed to ditch the Jet Provost and go straight on to a short

Hunter course at Chivenor, hopefully followed by a longer course on the Phantom at Coningsby.

With brand new wing-commander's braid (but unpaid, of course – with acting rank you were only paid when you were in post), I reported to RAF Chivenor on 3 February 1974. Squadron Leader 'Jim' Edwards – my partner in crime from training days – greeted me in the bar. He was now in charge of the Hunter simulator. Chivenor hadn't changed; it was still the same ramshackle collection of wooden huts, and if I closed my eyes I could still see the cook sprinting around the mess hotly pursued by Mike Calvey's badger. Even the evil-smelling coke stoves in the sleeping quarters were the same.

No. 229 OCU wasted no time. On 6 February, after two dual sorties in the Hunter T7, I flew solo in a Hunter F6. It had been many years since I had flown the Hunter, but the old skills quickly returned. If anything, my rapid progress was a reflection on the quality of the aircraft. Initially, the need to talk on the radio and fly the aircraft at the same time was a problem – how could I be so tongue-tied? But I managed to bang in a couple of very satisfactory air-to-ground strafing scores of 68% and 74% at Pembrey Range.

In just four weeks at Chivenor I flew twenty-two hours, all good-quality training and most of it at low level. Excellent value – I could not have asked for better. Sadly there was one fatal accident during the month – a young foreign student lost control in cloud and crashed.

Between Chivenor and Coningsby I managed to complete the sea-survival course at Mountbatten and the aviation medicine course at North Luffenham. I figured I was doing well in the limited time available. I reported to No. 228, the Phantom OCU, early in March. There were one or two familiar faces at Coningsby, but Nos 6 and 54 Squadrons had moved to RAF Lossiemouth for conversion to the Jaguar. Their Phantom aircraft at Coningsby had been taken over by Nos 111 and 29, who were working up to operational status as UK air-defence squadrons.

Nothing much had changed at No. 228 OCU; I was to be profoundly mistaken if I thought I could keep up a high rate of flying.

After the ground school, I eventually got airborne on 4 April – and was shocked to be reminded what a handful the Phantom FGR 2 was. In my experience, provided you remained in current flying practice it was relatively easy to maintain a high level of proficiency in the air, but the older you were, the more difficult it was to return after a prolonged period on the ground. I was never really convinced of the logic of the RAF's so-called 'balanced' career, because more often than not it put squadron executives, particularly squadron commanders, at a disadvantage when they were expected to lead from the front. At thirty-eight, I was past my prime for relearning fighter-pilot skills. There was never any danger of my failing, but it was intensely frustrating to be placed in that position. And that, of course, made no allowance for the inevitable lack of flying on 228 OCU.

The continuity was reasonable during the first month. In sixteen flying hours I covered the conversion syllabus, regained an instrument rating and flew four sorties of simulated air combat. But in May and June, when I moved to low-level attack and weapons qualification, the flying rate dropped to less than ten hours a month. On any frontline squadron such a low rate of flying would be considered a flight safety risk – and rightly so. Overall, in my four months at Coningsby, I flew only thirty-nine hours in the Phantom. I could have done that in half the time. Nor was I much impressed by the bland statement that I didn't need any more flying. It was the typical attitude of 228 OCU.

Yet again, I was pleased to get away.

Fortunately, on 1 July my promotion to substantive wing commander was confirmed, and the extra money was most welcome. Inevitably, our move to RAF Germany promised to be a little more complicated than any we had so far tackled within the UK, but we were learning fast. As a designated squadron commander I was entitled to an ex-officio quarter at Bruggen, which avoided the usual period of waiting. Nevertheless it was more convenient to travel separately. I planned to drive out first; Jules would fly out later with the children. Buying a 'duty free' car (i.e. without having to pay the UK purchase tax) was just one of the many perks of serving abroad.

My final week at Benson was hectic; even though the service paid the moving expenses, there was still a lot to do. Then, one Sunday morning in mid-August, I set out for Dover with our new Austin Maxi packed to the gunwales with those possessions deemed too fragile to be packed with the rest of the furniture. I must say, it was a relief to be on my way. In theory Jules and the children would catch the shuttle from Luton Airport in five days' time.

I made good time to Dover and the crossing was smooth. The route from Calais to Roermond was fairly straightforward – much of it was motorway standard – then I settled down to a leisurely four-hour journey, which would put me at Bruggen in time for a cool beer when the bar opened. The weather was fine, apart from a few isolated thunderstorms. I had just gone through one such storm when, quite suddenly and dramatically, I started to see double. This was not just a simple blurring of vision, I could literally see two of everything – one road directly ahead, and another identical road, with identical traffic, angled 30° off to my left. No matter how much I blinked or shook my head, with both eyes open, I could not get rid of the double vision. The only way I could continue to drive was by closing one eye; only then did the world return to normal. I broke into a cold sweat. This was a new and rather alarming experience.

I pulled into a service area. Perhaps if I rested, I thought, my sight would return to normal. But it was impossible to sleep, and after an hour I was back on the road, still seeing double. The last sixty miles or so were a waking nightmare.

The officers' mess bar at Bruggen was packed with old friends from 6 Squadron days. All were pleased to see me and anxious to help. Of course I couldn't tell them about my double vision; I had not yet worked out how best to deal with that.

I planned to stay in the mess until Jules arrived, so after a couple of beers I asked Jerry Wells to give me a hand unloading the car. He briefed me on the following day's programme. My arrival interview with the station commander was booked for 1030 hours and there was a married quarter waiting for me to march in.

After a final nightcap I excused myself and hit the sack. I still hoped the double vision would clear itself overnight, but by this time I was desperately worried.

Next morning there was no improvement. It was difficult to make believe all was well when you couldn't see straight. My interview with the station commander – Group Captain Peter Harding – was short and to the point. Apparently I had four days to take over the squadron from Wing Commander George Ord.

The rest of that day was taken up with briefings and meetings. At a time when I should have been alert, knowledgeable and keen, I was preoccupied. Somehow I coped, but again went to bed hoping that a good night's sleep would solve my problems.

On Tuesday, the 13th, my sight was no better. I flew a dual Phantom sector recce with Jerry Wells. The weather was murky, and not helped by seeing two of everything. I landed with one eye closed, but it was now obvious that I would have to seek help.

On the Wednesday it so happened that I had an appointment to see one of the junior doctors about medical liaison visits with 17 Squadron. After chatting for a while, I asked him if there was anything he could do to cure double vision, and explained my problem. The poor chap was quite confused, but as a result I was rushed to RAF Wegberg to see other, more distinguished physicians. I was not popular. This was Wednesday – sports afternoon and all that. Why couldn't I be attended to by the duty staff? But someone at high level must have insisted.

I was seen by two doctors that afternoon, the first of many sessions of being poked and prodded. And the questions they asked did not seem terribly relevant to me. Did your mother love you when you were young? As a child, did you wet the bed? Are you worried about flying? Indeed, I spent most of my time trying to convince these worthy gentlemen that my double vision was not due to a fear of flying, or, as far as I was aware, of any other mental condition. It was difficult to explain that, apart from the double vision, I was a fairly normal pilot who enjoyed flying and who was looking forward to commanding a squadron. No, I was sure there was something wrong physically.

Eventually one of them said, 'Well, I am not surprised you are seeing double, your left eye has drifted left.' Now we were getting somewhere. But as the afternoon wore on my hopes of taking over 17 Squadron began to fade.

Arrangements were made for me to be admitted to hospital the following day for a lumbar puncture.

Back at Bruggen I called to warn Jules that our plans might well change. I was invited to supper that evening with the Ords. George had planned this to be an informal briefing, but I found it difficult to concentrate.

Next day I reported to Wegberg, where a different team of doctors was on duty. With a local anaesthetic, the lumbar puncture felt like a dull punch in the back. I was a bit weak at the knees afterwards. They warned me that some patients suffered from post lumbar puncture headaches, and therefore I had to lie down.

I had a string of visitors that day, mostly doctors, and all of them were waiting for the outcome of the tests. One chap kindly arranged for me to be given an eyepatch, which saved me the bother of closing an eye. Jerry Wells came and reported that I was now OC No. 17 Squadron – but that evening the doctors decided to repatriate me to the UK.

I put a call through to Jules to tell her to hold on to the quarter at Benson.

I returned from RAF Germany on 19 July – Emma's birthday, and the day Jules and the children were supposed to fly out. The nursing staff dosed me up with pain-killers and gave me a supply of pills to use on the aircraft. I wasn't too worried; up to then I had been horizontal and hadn't suffered a hint of a headache – but nothing prepared me of the discomfort that was to come. After about ten minutes of the journey to Wildenrath the headache hit me, and rapidly progressed until the pain got so bad I could hardly see. The pills were not strong enough. There was no room to lie down on the aircraft, and by the time we eventually landed at Luton I was more dead than alive. Fortunately Jules and Mary Mitchell had driven over to meet me, and I was able to flake out on the back seat of the car.

I was depressed, my body had let me down and my future in the RAF seemed uncertain.

12
Wg Cdr Air Defence at Headquarters RAF Germany

It was a relief to get home. The nurses at Wegberg had told me that the post lumbar puncture headache would abate when my level of spinal fluid returned to normal. In the meantime it was advisable to drink plenty of water and lie down. Wegberg had also arranged for me to see the RAF's senior consultant neurologist – Air Vice Marshal 'Paddy' O'Connor – at the Central Medical Establishment in London. I was anxious to keep that appointment and hopefully learn the cause of the double vision.

On the following Monday I was not really fit to travel, but Henry came to the rescue and drove me to town. I spent the journey prostrate on the back seat; I couldn't even help with the navigation.

The Central Medical Establishment (CME) was located at Kelvin House on Cleveland Street, across the road from the Middlesex Hospital. But unlike the hospital, CME did not treat patients – it was a centre for RAF consultants and its primary role was to assess the medical employment standard (MES) of RAF aircrews. The doctors at CME were all-powerful: they could ground you permanently and even recommend discharge from the service on medical grounds.

The MES assessment was divided into three parts: A for flying duties; G for ground duties; and Z for geographic zone. Each part was assessed from 1 to 5. Up to now my MES had always been A1 G1 Z1 – meaning fully fit for flying and ground duties worldwide. It was an unusual consultation, with me slumped across three armchairs, but 'Paddy' O'Connor knew all about lumbar puncture headaches. Compared to the amateur interrogation at Wegberg, this was a thorough neurological examination, with all the usual implements – a small rubber mallet, a pointed stick and a tuning fork. Things progressed smoothly until the 'blind' test, when I had to identify by touch various items I was given. After the episode of 'fibrositis' at Camberley I knew that my left hand lacked sensitivity, although I still retained some feeling. It so happened that the first object was one of those small magnifying glasses which folded into an integral protective cover. I guessed what it was and, as an afterthought, added, 'And it's black', simply because magnifying glasses of that type usually were black.

'Paddy' O'Connor was not amused.

I also found it difficult to stand on one leg. Come to think of it, I was having some difficulty standing on two – my sense of balance was shot – but I put that down to a residual side-effect of the lumbar puncture.

'Paddy' O'Connor was unwilling to commit himself. I could understand that he needed more information, but I would have appreciated a man-to-man discussion on the possible causes for my symptoms, and an indication as to what further tests were needed. He did none of these, and I was left with the impression that this charming, no doubt eminent neurologist was somewhat removed from the real world.

O'Connor arranged to see me again the following week. In the meantime, he said, 'Go home and relax with your family.' That was a tall order.

It was virtually impossible to relax, when every waking moment I was reminded by the double vision. Indeed the uncertainty of what the future might hold in store was an enormous strain on the whole family. And there was nothing I could do about it. Of course, it did not help that most of our personal possessions were now at Bruggen – although thankfully, our friends at Benson gave their unstinting support. The Kembals brought around spare blankets and toys for the children, and the Mitchells loaned us a car for the duration, which was an absolute godsend.

As a result of the Turkish invasion of Cyprus, Frank Mitchell had been detached there at short notice. I remembered all the military activity we had seen around Kyrenia the previous November – could this possibly have been a dress rehearsal for the invasion?

Benson provided a car and driver for my second appointment at CME. 'Paddy' O'Connor had nothing new to say, but he arranged to see me again the following week.

After about twelve days the headache receded, although I was still a bit shaky on my pins. Then one morning, while shaving, I noticed a slight, almost imperceptible improvement in vision. The feeling of relief was almost euphoric – this was the first sign of recovery.

After three weeks or so my sight was almost back to normal and, naively, as it turned out, I thought I would soon be allowed to return to work. In fact I was thoroughly brassed off with the weekly visits to CME and the diet of meaningless platitudes. I had kept in touch with 17 Squadron through Squadron Leader 'Geoff' Culpit, an extremely efficient flight commander. No one had been posted in to take my place so in theory I still commanded the squadron. But 'Paddy' O'Connor, who seemed genuinely surprised that I wished to return to Bruggen, refused to be drawn.

Eventually, after four weeks, I was admitted for further tests to the National Hospital for Neurology and Neurosurgery at Queen Square, London. Group Captain 'Terry' Gledhill, a charming fellow who occupied the next bed, was recovering from brain surgery. In the mid-fifties 'Terry' had flown a Canberra through the mushroom cloud of one of the UK's early nuclear bomb tests. He didn't exactly glow in the dark, but his encounter with the radioactive cloud had done him a power of no good.

I have always disliked hospitals; they are apt to be full of very sick people. Strange though it may seem, even during the double vision, I felt reasonably fit. But that soon changed.

I can't remember all the tests, but a few stand out. One was to have numerous electrodes attached to my scalp, while I sat in a darkened room and watched a screen on which was projected a chequerboard pattern. Every half-second the black squares turned to white and the white to black. I asked what it was all meant to prove, but apparently this was a new test and the answer was hidden in the electronic traces, which could only be read by the experts. Another test, which was called an air myelogram, had to be done under a general anaesthetic and was a great deal more invasive. Spinal fluid was drawn off by way of a lumbar puncture and replaced by air, or oxygen. I was then rotated around on a special table, and the bubble of gas between the brain and the skull was followed on X-ray. Any abnormal swelling or area of pressure would have been immediately apparent. It was a sort of unconscious aerobatic sequence and, since I was clad only in one of those revealing open-backed surgical gowns, I must have let it all hang out. In the final test I stood, surrounded by a cordon of doctors and nurses, while they injected yet another drug. Whatever they were waiting for didn't happen.

Next morning a tall, distinguished doctor by the name of Roger Bannister, of four-minute-mile fame, was doing the rounds. 'Well, congratulations,' he said. 'You do not have a brain tumour. No – we think you have had a viral infection.'

Apparently, the medical documents I had brought back from Germany in a sealed envelope had been annotated 'suspected brain tumour', which probably explained why 'Paddy' O'Connor had been waiting for other symptoms to appear. This was the first time a tumour had been mentioned to me, and I wasn't sure whether to be alarmed or elated.

John and Cherry Harwood visited me on the Sunday and kindly offered to drive me home. Of course, by now I was laid low by yet another post lumbar puncture headache.

Two weeks later I returned to CME, confident in the knowledge that the worst was over and I would be allowed to return to work. It was probably the shortest consultation I ever had with 'Paddy' O'Connor. Obviously he had given my case a great deal of thought, and the news was bad. Despite being cleared by the national hospital, my MES was to be temporarily downgraded to A3 G2 Z4, which meant that I could only fly, either as or with a copilot, and for duty purposes I was restricted to temperate climates. It was a bitter pill to swallow; effectively I was grounded for a minimum of twelve months, and I had irretrievably lost 17 Squadron. The only saving grace was that perhaps, now that the decision had been made, I would be allowed to get on with the rest of my life.

I returned to Benson to await a new posting. After the knocks of the previous months my morale was at rock bottom and I was prepared for the very worst – possibly another tour at the MoD – so it came as a pleasant surprise when the Air Secretary's Department phoned to ask if I would accept the post of Wing Commander Air Defence at HQ RAF Germany. This was fantastic. In one simple move – most of which had already been accomplished – our lives would return to normal.

In October the family caught the shuttle flight from Luton. Olive and Gerry Wells met us on arrival at Wildenrath. The Rheindahlen Garrison and RAF Rheindahlen combined to provide administrative support for the staffs housed in the Joint Headquarters building. These included two British national headquarters – HQ RAF Germany and HQ BAOR (British Army of the Rhine) – and two NATO headquarters – 2 ATAF (the Second Allied Tactical Air Force) and NORTHAG (the Northern Army Group). The complex was huge – in all, about 13,000 personnel were employed at Rheindahlen and to this number must be added their numerous dependants.

In many respects the facilities provided at Rheindahlen were superior to those found in a similar-sized civilian town. We booked into Cassels House, the officers' transit hostel, where we stayed for a few days before moving into a flat at Beeker Heide, a suburb of the town of Wegberg. Only then could we collect our sticks of furniture from Bruggen.

Several RAF families, newly arrived from the UK, were housed temporarily at Beeker Heide. Our immediate neighbours were the Allens – Derrick was the dental officer at Rheindahlen, and he would eventually straighten out my front teeth – and the Ridleys. Norman Ridley was in the Supply Branch. He was also a reputable mountaineer. We only learned of Norman's climbing skills when a large black Labrador dog by the name of Randy accidentally locked Eileen Ridley out of their flat. It was all rather embarrassing for Eileen; not only was it against the rules to keep pets in the flats, but within the hour she was expecting guests to arrive for a sherry morning. Randy actually belonged to Eileen's brother, and she was only looking after him as a favour. After a panic telephone call, Norman arrived post-haste from the office. He scaled the outside wall to the second floor balcony and climbed in through the window. Small wonder the local German population tended to keep their distance from the Brits.

Later that day Randy cut his ear on a barbed-wire fence and, overnight, by dint of much head shaking, he managed to redecorate the Ridleys' flat in a fetching blood-red polka dot scheme. Randy had definitely outstayed his welcome; Norman had to redecorate their flat.

Four months later we moved into a married quarter in Bangor Walk at RAF Rheindahlen and settled down to one of the most enjoyable ground tours in the RAF.

I took over from Wing Commander Bill Maish, with whom I had previously served at Jever in 1957. With my air defence background and Lightning experience, I was well qualified for the job. In broad terms, Wg Cdr Air Defence was responsible for staff matters arising from the RAF's air defence forces based in Germany. At that time RAF Germany's order of battle included two air defence fighter squadrons: Nos 19 and 92 based at RAF Gutersloh, equipped with Lightning F2A aircraft, and No. 25 Squadron, equipped with Ferranti Bloodhound SAM missiles, with flights at the three 'clutch airfields', Laarbruch, Bruggen and Wildenrath. To handle these commitments, and also to maintain a continuous operations room cover at HQ RAF Germany, I had a staff of eight squadron leaders and five other ranks.

The RAF's main peacetime air-defence role in Germany stemmed from a tripartite agreement at the end of World War II between the Allied powers and the Soviet Union. According to this agreement, British and American air forces would police West German airspace, while Soviet air forces would police the airspace over East Germany. Since that time, the three committed nations had maintained air defence fighters at five minutes' alert. This was the same commitment held by the RAF Germany Hunter squadrons in the fifties.

The risk of conflict with the Warsaw Pact forces was ever present – the degree varying only with the current political climate. It was believed that the West would be given little notice of an all-out attack, and that all major NATO airfields would be high-priority targets. Hence the need for the hardening programme. According to intelligence assessments, the Pact's military forces outnumbered us roughly three to one, and some of their equipment was equal to if not better than ours. The odds were formidable but, in the air, we always thought we had the edge in training, flying skills, tactics and technological development. The threat of war was always taken seriously by military personnel in Germany; after all, it was perceived that we were holding the front line.

In wartime, the RAF squadrons had been assigned to SACEUR (Supreme Allied Commander Europe) as part of NATO's air defence forces. Over the years the Gutersloh wing had established an enviable reputation.

The serviceability of Lightning aircraft had steadily improved since my Wattisham days, and the squadrons regularly met their monthly flying target. The station usually achieved the highest possible ratings in the no-notice tactical evaluations (Taceval). Rumour had it that the multinational Taceval team considered Gutersloh to be the benchmark for efficiency in all-weather fighter air defence.

Morale was high at Gutersloh, and the Lightning F2A – with its large ventral tank and inbuilt cannon – was well suited both to the policing role and to the war role in Germany (which was predominantly at low level). I saw first-hand how the station prepared for its war role when John Howe – the man who had made his name during the introduction of both the Lightning and the Phantom – invited me to witness a station Mineval exercise. (The Mineval was a Taceval exercise assessed by station personnel.) Their performance was remarkable, bearing in mind that Gutersloh had not been hardened, nor had it been given funds to modify existing ex-Luftwaffe buildings.

The combat operations centre (COC) was located in the cellars beneath the station headquarters. John Howe sat with his executives on a raised podium overseeing the response to a multitude of exercise injects covering every conceivable emergency. The personnel had seen it all before, and the station reacted like a well-oiled machine. What impressed me (and no doubt impressed the average Taceval team) was the unhurried calm of the COC. John Howe ran a tight ship. The occasional 'Battle Flight' scramble, just to make sure the Lightnings could still meet the five-minute alert commitment, was light relief. There was none better than the Lightning for rapid reaction.

The only area in which Gutersloh failed – and no one could criticise them for it – was their inability to survive the constantly evolving Soviet threat. Unlike the Western powers, the Soviets had long considered chemical warfare to be a simple extension of conventional war. To keep pace with the perceived threat, NATO was in the process of introducing a massively expensive airfield-hardening programme. But Gutersloh was planned to become the future main Harrier base in RAF Germany, and all of its combat aircraft would disperse to field locations early in the transition to war. Hence the decision to exclude Gutersloh from the hardening programme.

Throughout RAF Germany, the constant preparedness for no-notice tactical evaluation and the round-the-clock commitment to QRA dictated life on the flying stations. The pace of life at Rheindahlen was far less intense, although the social round was fairly demanding. At regular intervals we dusted off the books containing the National and NATO alert procedures and went through the final preparations for war. Invariably these paper exercises lasted less than a week. At such times my specialist squadron leaders deployed to 2 ATAF's war headquarters in subterranean caves at Maastricht. I personally ran the HQ RAF Germany response cell from my office. The hours were longer than usual and there was the occasional all-night duty. We donned NBC kit for the inevitable chemical phases, but otherwise life was fairly routine. Of course, Rheindahlen was essentially a peacetime headquarters and, like Gutersloh, it was not expected to survive long in a real war.

By any standards the quality of life for a staff officer serving at HQ RAF Germany in 1975 was excellent. The cost of living was similar to that of the UK, and with generous overseas allowances service people had a greater choice of how to spend their money. We gathered an ever-increasing circle of friends, many of them with children of a similar age to Stuart and Emma. In addition to the Allans and the Ridleys, we met up with the Harnets and the Bellamy-Knights, to name but a few. Many of the friendships we made at Rheindahlen have stood the test of time. We also ran into the Coulchers – ex 38 Group – and the Milner-Browns. Anthony Milner-Brown was a Scots Guards Officer, and had been one of my fellow students at Camberley.

Of course, the opportunities for travel on the continent were unrivalled. At the weekends, depending on the weather, we either went sight-seeing at local beauty spots or would venture further afield – either in Germany, or across the border to Holland. Monschau, a picturesque village in the Eifel, made an interesting day out and we took Gab there when she visited in April. Caravanning was the only practical choice for longer holidays with the children. It so happened that my brother Tim, who was serving as an instrument tradesman with a Harrier squadron at Wildenrath, kindly lent me his caravan for our summer holiday. One morning in July we set off for the Cavallino Strip, just to the east of Venice – a mere 600 miles away. If I remember rightly we got all of five miles down the road before one of the children asked, 'Are we nearly there?'

We made it to Stuttgart on the first day and stayed with Ian and his fiancée Karen. Next day we made an early start in order to clear Munich before the rush hour. Then it was down through Austria to Italy. Half-way through the Brenner Pass we stopped to consult *Europa Camping*, that invaluable guide for continental campers. I had been driving for eleven hours and badly needed a rest, so I was relieved to find that the nearest available camp-site was just three miles off the motorway at Bolzano. As the crow flies, that was probably true – but it was not clear from the sketch map that only a bird could have made it that way. The camp-site was actually a base camp for climbing in the Dolomites, about 4000 ft above the valley floor. It was a bit tricky hauling the caravan up the one-in-three gradient, with hairpin bends every 200 yards. Fortunately we didn't meet any traffic, but I noticed that, the higher we went, both the trees and the conversation became more sparse. Even the children went quiet.

When we finally made it to the top, the air was crystal clear and the views were superb, but Jules vowed she would not be able to sleep, knowing that we would have to descend the following day. So we turned around and drove back down. Actually it wasn't as bad as going up, but when we got to the bottom the engine was making expensive noises – the water pump had blown!

The car was repaired, and three days later we hit the road again for Trento and Verona. There were many camp-sites along the strip, but the Audi NSU site – which had originally been founded as a holiday camp for German car workers – was popular with the Brits. The camp was run on Teutonic lines, with key times announced by bugle call over the loudspeakers: reveille at 0700 hours; quiet hours between one and three in the afternoon (Ve haff vays of keeping your children quiet); and last post at 2100 hours. It sounded more like a prison camp – but with typical German efficiency the toilet blocks were spotless, the site was regularly sprayed to keep down the mosquitoes, and we had everything we needed for a splendid seaside holiday.

For a change from the beach we would take a boat trip and rubberneck our way around Venice: St Mark's Cathedral, the Doge's Palace, the Bridge of Sighs, the Rialto . . . On another day we visited the islands of Murano, Burano and Torcello. For Jules and me it was a fascinating experience, although the children would have preferred to stay on the beach.

After two weeks of complete relaxation we retraced our steps to Rheindahlen. I shall never forget dicing with demon drivers and their intimidating heavy truck/trailer rigs along the Munich autobahns.

Overall, the holiday was a great success, although I had developed a nervous tic in my right eye and a slight speech impediment – which, thankfully, was short-lived.

By 1975 British defence commitments east of Suez had been markedly reduced and, pursuing their usual policy of cutting the defence budget, the Labour government instructed the armed forces to reduce manpower. The reaction of the services was perhaps typical: the RN, in true Nelsonian tradition, ignored the instruction; the army reluctantly agreed, but claimed they would rely on natural wastage; only the dear old RAF rushed to obey by introducing a compulsory redundancy programme for commissioned officers. The selection, based on branch, rank, age and seniority, was made by the Air Secretary's staff at the MoD. Fortunately, I was just outside the 'at risk' bracket, but four of my watch officers were made redundant. I had great sympathy for these men; all were qualified aircrew in their mid-forties, and had devoted their working lives to the service. Up to then the average RAF officer was unquestioningly loyal and, rightly or wrongly, expected loyalty in return. But in 1975, long before redundancy became recognised as a legitimate means of shedding excess manpower, many RAF officers saw the compulsory redundancy issue as a betrayal of trust. A career in the armed forces no longer offered long-term security.

But I had my own problems. My reduced MES had to be reviewed every six months. This usually entailed a visit to the CME – but in September 1975 I was instructed to report to RAF Wroughton for yet another lumbar puncture. Needless to say, I was not exactly enthralled by the prospect. I was fairly healthy at the time, having successfully avoided all the usual office bugs, and I jokingly suggested that my immune system maintained a higher-than-average state of alert. But if a lumbar puncture was necessary to return to flying, then so be it. However, I did plead with the doctors to do everything in their power to ameliorate the inevitable headache, and they agreed to use a small needle.

After spending five days in hospital, I visited my parents in

Weymouth. In retrospect it was probably not a wise decision, but family business needed my urgent attention. The pills held off the pain until I reached Weymouth, where I threw up at the side of the road, but the relaxation at home did me some good. Then, on the Sunday, I set off to return the hire car to Swindon. By now I had run out of pain-killers, and halfway back I had to find somewhere to lie down. Fortunately the weather was warm and sunny and I stretched out in a deserted meadow – what bliss. I must have fallen asleep, because some time later I woke up surrounded by a herd of cows. They didn't seem to mind.

Later that afternoon, while waiting for the London train at Swindon station, I again needed to lie down. I stretched out on a platform bench. Two old biddies complained loudly that drunks shouldn't be allowed to use public transport. On reflection I preferred the cows.

I stayed the night with Henry and Joyce, and reported to the CME the following day. Fortunately my lumbar puncture had proved to be clear. On 15 September I was given a full medical board and regained an A1 G1 Z1 category. I was cleared to return to unrestricted flying, although I suspect that 'Paddy' O'Connor was still unsure of my state of health. Nevertheless he accepted the board's decision and I was grateful to him for giving me the benefit of the doubt.

Back in Germany I was tasked to keep a watching brief on the airfield-hardening programme at RAF Wildenrath. The Harrier squadrons presently stationed there had no use for hardened accommodation, but the long-term plan called for Nos 10 and 92 Squadrons to re-equip with Phantom FGR 2s based at Wildenrath. The existing Lightning squadrons at Gutersloh would disband to make room for the Harriers. This would be the first opportunity for RAF air-defence squadrons to operate from hardened accommodation, and for the plan to succeed we needed to consider the practical implications. I did not know it, but for me this was the happy coincidence of being in the right place at the right time.

I took 'Rolly' Jackson with me to visit Wildenrath and Bruggen, where the hardening programme was more advanced. At Bruggen the newly arrived Jaguar squadrons were tending to duplicate facilities, only adopting a war posture when necessary. I though this was an expensive, inefficient and unnecessary luxury. Far better to train in peace as you would expect to operate in war. At Wildenrath the building work at three dispersed sites south of the runway was still in progress, but I could visualise how the Phantom squadrons would operate. It would be an exciting challenge.

Ever since the Berlin blockade, when the Soviets had blocked all surface links between West Germany and the city, the problem of maintaining Berlin access had exercised the minds of both politicians and military alike. During the original blockade, between June '48 and May '49, the city had been sustained by a massive Allied airlift, but the threat of a complete blockade still existed and denial of access remained a possible flashpoint for more serious Soviet adventures in Western Europe. The Allied nations most concerned with Berlin access (i.e. the United States, the UK, France and West Germany) had established a special joint headquarters – called Live Oak – adjacent to the Supreme NATO Headquarters outside Brussels. To the uninitiated, Live Oak was a slightly wacky organisation, but those who had studied the subject of Berlin access appreciated the problems. Certainly, it was hoped that political pressure would suffice to dissuade the Soviets from a further blockade. The military options were very limited and, bearing in mind the imperative to avoid any escalation of hostilities, extremely risky. For example, it was unlikely that the Soviets would ever allow a tri-national armoured battle group to advance along the Helmstedt/Berlin autobahn unopposed. Such action would inevitably lead to instant and overwhelming reprisal. The options in the air were slightly less provocative – after all, the Berlin airlift had been successful – but a multinational formation of transport aircraft, even one escorted by fighter aircraft, would be extremely vulnerable. And what would be the next move if an aircraft, from either side, was shot down?

But just because the military plans could not be perfected was no reason to sit back and ignore the problem. As Wing Commander Air Defence, I was RAF Germany's designated liaison officer with Live Oak, and I quite enjoyed working with the multinational staffs. An annual live air exercise was mounted from RAF Gutersloh, and this was backed up each year by two or three paper exercises at the Live Oak ops centre at Ramstein air force base near Kaiserslautern. The exercise scenario was invariably one of increasing political tension, with each successive inject pushing the staffs further towards authorising hostile action. It was all brinkmanship. From my experience at Nellis I was well used to working with the Americans, although strangely enough their reactions to the access problems were by far the most hawkish. This could all have been due to personalities, of course, but I suspect the Americans were still smarting from the political intrigues of Vietnam. The French and the Germans were less intransigent, and the French officers confidentially admitted that France should never have withdrawn from NATO. On a lighter note, the non-American exercise players were pleased to take advantage of Ramstein's excellent PX facilities.

In December I learned that I was to take command of No. 19 Squadron when it re-equipped with Phantoms at RAF Wildenrath in October 1976. I could hardly believe my good fortune. I was being given a second chance as squadron commander, and could bring to fruition all the plans I had worked on at the headquarters. My flying refresher training was due to start in March. The only fly in the ointment was that the Senior Personnel Staff Officer (SPSO) at HQ RAF Germany wanted to move the family back to the UK while I refreshed. As far as I was concerned, that was a non-starter – the children were settled into schools at Rheindahlen and I was not prepared to have them uprooted just to fill a square on some desk officer's charts. I won in the end, but the SPSO was not best pleased. I managed to pick up a good second-hand Renault 5, to give Jules her own personal transport while I was away.

Late in January, Jules and I spent three days' leave in West Berlin. On the advice from those who had gone before, we chose to travel by the British military train. The itinerary for the journey was detailed down to the last minute by HQ BAOR movements staffs. The first leg was by the standard German civil rail network. At Braunschweig we boarded the military train – the 'Berliner'. It was a bitterly cold, grey day, with snow trapped between the frozen lines. I could think of no better mode of transport, nor a more appropriate time of the year, to visit the DDR – the Soviet-controlled zone of Germany.

This was the Berliner's daily return to the 'divided city'. The train stopped at Helmstedt to change engines and take on the East German train crew. Fifteen minutes later we passed through the inner German border, with its heavily mined and fenced corridor which extended from the Baltic coast in the north all the way south to the Adriatic. Obviously, this corridor was designed to constrain the East German people rather than deter any invasion from the West.

Five miles inside the DDR, at Marienborn, the train stopped for Soviet border checks. It was a strange ritual: the passengers were not allowed to leave the train. Only the British officer in charge of the train and a fellow who went by the obscure title of TCWO and a Russian interpreter alighted to present all the documents to a Soviet army officer for checking. Outside, on the platform, the Soviet army guard, armed with Kalashnikov AK47s and smartly turned out in greatcoats and fur hats, were essential bit-part actors on the frozen scene. Even the massive civilian East German wheel-tapper, with her long-handled hammer, who was probably keeping an eye on the blind side of the train, appeared threatening. In the past, the Berliner had been boarded illegally by people desperate to escape from East Germany. To prevent this happening, each carriage was guarded by British military police and the inside carriage door-handles were wedged shut by wooden struts.

After an interminable twenty minutes we were on the move again.

Most of the journey was done at night, so there was little to see outside the train. We were having dinner in the restaurant car as the train rumbled through Magdeburg, where even the city lights seemed dreary by comparison with the West. At Potsdam the train stopped again to change the engine and guard.

We finally arrived at the Charlottenburg station in the British sector of Berlin at 2025 hours, and caught the service transport to the transit hotel at Edinburgh House.

There was much to see in Berlin but, with only two days available, we had to be selective. Our first impression was of a city living on its nerves. Late into the night the streets were packed with speeding traffic. Where were they all going? And the population seemed to be unbalanced: there was a small and dwindling number of elderly pensioners – people who had spent their lives in the city and were not willing to move – and an entirely separate workforce of young West Germans who were taking advantage of generous financial inducements to spend two years working in West Berlin. There was no solid middle-aged group to give stability, but perhaps that was the true nature of West Berlin – a city under siege.

On our first day we took in the popular attractions: the glitter and opulence of the Kurfurstendamm; and the Kaiser Wilhelm memorial church – nicknamed the Lipstick and Powder Compact – built next to the bomb-damaged ruins of the original church which were preserved as a reminder to West Berliners of the futility of war. We walked to the Reichstag and the Russian War Memorial, with its goose-stepping Soviet army guard. We could only view the Brandenburg Gate from across the infamous Berlin Wall. It was only from close quarters that one could appreciate the formidable nature of the Wall, with its barbed wire, armed guards, dogs and constant surveillance on the Soviet side. To defeat any grappling hook, the top section of the Wall was free to revolve. People still tried to escape; some got away with it, but the pathetic wooden crosses on the western side bore silent witness to the many who died in the attempt.

Because of my job at the headquarters I was not permitted to visit East Berlin, but Jules was free to go, and I used my contacts to get her a personal guided tour. Early next morning an official car, manned by two large RAF policemen, picked us up. They dropped me off at the tiny museum, devoted to the ingenious and hazardous escape attempts, overlooking Checkpoint Charlie. Everything was documented here, from tunnels and sewers to modified bubble cars.

Meanwhile, Jules and the two policemen drove through Checkpoint Charlie. According to Jules, East Berlin was dull and drab compared to the West. Restoration work was confined to a few main streets, but the rest of East Berlin was fairly run down. On that grey January day, Jules was impressed by the cemetery for the Soviet war dead at Trepto Park.

In the afternoon, with Jules safely back in the West, we visited the memorial at Plotzensee to the German people who had resisted Hitler's National Socialist dictatorship. As early as 1933, Plotzensee was infamous as a place of execution for political prisoners. Here the SS eliminated Hitler's enemies, either by guillotine, by garrotting or by hanging. Between 1933 and 1945, tens of thousands of ordinary German civilians had been executed. With typical Teutonic thoroughness, the details of each death sentence was recorded. The Plotzensee Memorial contained the execution chamber, complete with the original six meat hooks used for the hangings, and the execution diary. In the entrance courtyard stood a massive earthenware urn, containing soil from every concentration camp, to commemorate the systematic murder of six million European Jews and other minority groups. A sobering experience – but we were left with the impression that no simple memorial could ever do justice to the enormity of the crimes committed in the name of the Third Reich.

At 0715 hours on 29 January we boarded the Berliner for the return to Braunschweig. Even in daylight the DDR appeared to be a blighted land.

Now I could look forward to the flying refresher courses. On this occasion there would be sufficient time to do the job properly, with short courses on both the Jet Provost and the Hunter, before attending the Phantom OCU at Coningsby. On 7 March I said goodbye to Jules and the children and drove north to Rotterdam to catch the overnight ferry to Hull. It should have been a pleasant passage, but the North Sea was in an ugly mood that night and there was nowhere to sleep. It was snowing when we docked at Hull – welcome to Yorkshire.

At RAF Leeming I met up with some old friends who were on the same course, including Dereck Bryant, who was now a group captain destined to take over Coningsby, and Simon Bostock, an ex-Lightning man. The UK's air-traffic procedures had changed a bit since 1976, but otherwise the course held few surprises. One weekend I borrowed an aircraft and flew to Leuchars to stay with the Gordons. Tony Gordon had been posted to Leuchars from HQ 38 Group.

In the four weeks I spent at Leeming, I racked up twenty-six hours in the JP 4 – an ideal basic refresher course.

In late March, Jane Sadler called to say that Gab had died in hospital. This was sad news. Gab had previously suffered from breast cancer; we thought it had been cured, but unbeknown to us she had had a relapse. I immediately phoned Jules, who arranged to return to the UK for the funeral. Sadly I couldn't get away.

The Hunter refresher squadron had been redeployed from Chivenor, and now shared RAF Brawdy on the southern coast of Pembrokeshire with the new Hawk training squadron. The airfield had previously been used by the Royal Navy, but if the location was new to me, many of the staff pilots were old friends: George Glasgow, ex-

Wattisham; 'Bo' Plummer, ex-66 Squadron; Tom Eeles and Al Mathie.

It was while flying with Al Mathie that I sustained a badly wrenched neck, which kept me grounded for several days. Dereck Bryant and I were invited to dinner with Ian and Kathy Tite – again, small world. After his tour on 6 Squadron, Ian had lost his medical category. He had since been discharged from the RAF and was now employed as an operations manager for a local road haulage company.

The Hunter was an old friend, and I thoroughly enjoyed the refresher course. In three weeks I flew seventeen hours, and also completed a wet dinghy drill in the sea at Pembroke Dock.

I reported to RAF North Luffenham for the aviation medicine course during the last week of May. More pressure-breathing sessions, an anoxia run, the inevitable explosive decompression, which was followed by an equally dramatic repressurisation, during which one of the students stopped breathing and the rest of us suffered serious sinus and ear problems. This created near panic for the doctors outside the chamber. Fortunately, the student in question started breathing again and quickly recovered – so no harm done.

With a week to spare before the course at Coningsby, I took the opportunity to drive back to Rheindahlen for the summer ball. On this occasion the commander in chief had directed that there would be no official guests, so the evening was a wholly enjoyable gathering of friends. The time passed all too quickly. I did not relish the thought of another eight weeks at Coningsby, but took some consolation from knowing that this would be the last lap.

The return trip to Coningsby via Zeebrugge and Felixstowe was straightforward. Since my last visit in 1974, Coningsby had been toned down; in other words all the buildings had been painted green and the station had sprouted barbed wire. I was prepared for the usual lack of flying, but 228 OCU had finally got its act together. In five weeks I flew thirty-seven hours in the Phantom. Not only did I finish the course early, but I was far better prepared for squadron flying than on previous occasions – proving yet again the value of continuity.

Most of the crews on the course were destined for No. 19 Squadron, and two of the navigators – 'Forbes' Pearson, who was designated as one of the flight commanders, and John Cosgrove, the designated Nav Rad Leader – had previously served with me on No. 6 Squadron. The pilot flight commander was 'Wally' Walton from RAF Bruggen, who I suspect harboured aspirations to command the squadron rather than me. I also made contact with 'Graeme' Smith, the designated QWI, and 'Al' Munro – both presently serving with No. 29 Squadron at Coningsby.

I didn't hang around, and as soon as I finished the course I embarked for Germany. There was much for me to do at Rheindahlen in preparation for 19 Squadron.

13
Officer Commanding No. 19 Squadron (Phantom FGR 2)

I got back to Rheindahlen in mid-August. Apart from the personal administrative details of having to march out of the quarter and clear from the station, I wanted a briefing from the headquarters on the latest developments affecting the formation of 19 Squadron.

RAF Germany's overall plan called for the Harrier squadrons at Wildenrath to move forward to Gutersloh, as and when space became available with the disbandment of the Lightning squadrons. That process could not start until No. 19 (Phantom) Squadron was declared operational at Wildenrath. So I had just three months to work the squadron up to a combat-ready status and take over the Battle Flight commitment by 1 January 1977. The programme was tight: Wildenrath was not an established air-defence base, and at that time of the year adverse weather could well disrupt flying. Our aircraft and the bulk of the engineering personnel would come direct from No. 2 (Recce) Squadron at Laarbruch during the first week of October; some experienced Phantom groundcrew would also be transferred from RAF Bruggen.

Jules and I moved into a large, rambling bungalow at Wildenrath during the first week of September. Our immediate neighbours were Stu and Jenny Penny (by this time Stu was a flight commander on No. 3 Squadron, one of the resident Harrier squadrons). The bungalow was comfortable enough, although like many of the quarters built in the late forties as part of German war reparations, it was sorely in need of refurbishment. The central-heating system was fired by a temperamental solid-fuel boiler. In days of yore, when civilian staff were more plentiful, the quarters had been serviced by boiler men and gardeners. But now the residents stoked their own boilers and, instead of gardeners, each quarter had a small motorised lawn mower on the inventory, more suited to bowling greens and tennis courts than our patch of rough meadow grass. If I really put my mind to it, I could mow the lawn in four hours. Fortunately, the onset of winter would soon provide temporary relief from the mowing chore.

It was a pleasant surprise to find that one of the navigators assigned to 19 Squadron – Flying Officer Stuart Black – had already arrived. With a few days to spare I took advantage of an invitation by Wing Commander 'Des' Melaniphy, the CO of 4 Squadron, to fly with them on exercise in the Sennelager Training Area. No. 4 Squadron had changed markedly since its days at Jever, and Harrier operations in the field were a world apart from air defence, but it was interesting to see how close to getting it right Peter Anson and I had been at the MoD in 1967.

Wildenrath had been a Harrier base since 1970, and the station personnel were set in their ways. The Harrier squadrons invariably deployed for their day-only operational role, while the station's personnel remained well insulated. That was about to change – and being the first of the new order, 19 Squadron was viewed with some suspicion. The air-defence role required high states of readiness and rapid reaction round the clock. The system relied on a sophisticated ground environment, including early-warning radars and an extensive communications network, all the way from the Sector Operations Centres (SOCs) down to the crews manning the aircraft. Air defence squadrons needed the active support of a well-developed main base. In future most of Wildenrath's personnel would be fully committed to the station's operational role. That meant regular exercises and a comprehensive involvement in Taceval.

Wildenrath was also the first RAF air defence base to operate from hardened accommodation. With a few notable exceptions (Rheindahlen, Gutersloh and Gatow), the main RAF bases in Germany were hardened to a standard known as the First Generation NATO Hard. Typically, squadron-sized dispersals contained nine reinforced concrete aircraft shelters (HASs) which, it was claimed, would survive anything but a direct hit from a 1000 lb bomb. In addition to the aircraft shelters, each dispersal was provided with a hardened and filtered operations and briefing complex – inaccurately referred to as the PBF (Pilot Briefing Facility) – and an assortment of hardened equipment shelters (HES). Attached to the PBF was a non-hardened squadron headquarters building containing offices, a crewroom and minimal toilet facilities. This NATO-funded accommodation was the bare minimum necessary to support a dispersed squadron, but additional, nationally funded soft accommodation was needed for permanent occupation.

At Wildenrath there were three hardened dispersals south of the runway, all similar in size. While working at Rheindahlen I had earmarked Wildenrath's south-east dispersal (Bravo dispersal) as the preferred location for 19 Squadron. It had the advantage of having two HASs within a short distance of the normal duty runway, which would permit an easy and rapid access route for Battle Flight. By September the construction of the hardened accommodation on Bravo dispersal was well advanced and the communication links – telephone lines, radio and telebriefing – were being installed. But the work of resurfacing the main taxiway and making good the paved access to the aircraft shelters would not be completed in time for the arrival of our first aircraft. The construction of nationally funded soft accommodation for the groundcrews and the flying clothing section had not yet started.

Wildenrath's station executives would have preferred 19 Squadron to operate initially from a hangar on the domestic side of the airfield; this would neatly fit in with the rest of the station and conform with the accepted norm. But I resisted. Unlike the resident Harrier squadrons, the hardened accommodation at Bravo dispersal would be our permanent home – anything we did on the domestic side of the airfield would have little relevance to our operational requirements. Besides, I judged that a healthy separation from the Harrier way of doing things would be essential for 19 Squadron's morale.

Most of the aircrews reported for duty mid-way through September. It was obvious that they had been carefully selected; only two of the pilots were first tourists, the rest were relatively experienced either in air defence or with the Phantom in Germany. In the case of the navigators there were five first tourists, but I was reasonably satisfied with the balance of the squadron.

Within a week, Flying Officer 'Dave' Allen, the Squadron's Junior Engineering Officer (J Eng O), and Warrant Officer Thomas arrived from Laarbruch with some sixty former 2 Squadron airmen to prepare the dispersal for the imminent arrival of the aircraft.

One of the tradesmen from Laarbruch – Corporal Pickerel – who in civilian life was a qualified carpenter, was immediately pressed into service to furnish the ops room and provide notice-boards. It was a repeat of my experience with 6 Squadron: brand new accommodation, limited furniture, and no preconceived ideas. Essentially, we were starting with a completely clean slate and the specialists were free to make best use of the unique accommodation. The dispersal was a hive of activity, everyone working flat out to prepare for squadron occupation. Even the German contractor relaying the taxiway was swept along with the urgency of the situation, and that was exactly what I had intended.

On 27 September I drove to Laarbruch with Stu Black to pick up our first aircraft. The aircraft had already been painted with 19 Squadron's blue and white check markings on the fuselage and a Chinese Dolphin badge on the fin. Both symbols dated from the First World War – the dolphin was in recognition of the squadron being equipped with the Sopwith Dolphin fighter, which in 1918 was the fastest and most heavily armed fighter in service. By prior arrangement with Gutersloh, *en route* to Wildenrath we rendezvoused with a 19 Squadron Lightning F2A for airborne photographs. The difference between the aircraft was immediately obvious: the Lightning had just two Firestreak missiles and internal guns; the much heavier Phantom, in full air-defence configuration, had a Vulcan gun on the centreline, wing tanks and eight air-to-air missiles.

On arrival at Bravo dispersal I was obliged to park the aircraft in front of the first HAS – the only shelter with a completed access, as the rest of the taxiway was blocked with heavy tarmac-laying machinery. We were met by the station commander, Group Captain David Leech, and Air Vice Marshal 'Tim' Lloyd, the Deputy Commander RAF Germany.

The remaining nine aircraft, the groundcrews and the squadron's engineering officer (S Eng O) – Squadron Leader 'Colin' Terry – arrived during the next two weeks. I made sure that every man was aware that our primary aim was to produce a minimum of eleven combat-ready crews by 31 December.

Despite the unusual mix of heavy tarmac-laying machinery and sophisticated, high-tech aviation equipment, we continued to operate from Bravo dispersal. When the contractor finally left the site, the squadron mounted a line-abreast FOD plod. FOD is the acronym for foreign object damage, but the term is also used to describe any loose material that can be sucked into an engine.

Wildenrath slowly came to accept that 19 Squadron was in residence, although for several weeks the odd misguided Harrier pilot attempted to use Bravo dispersal as a relief landing strip. The practice finally stopped when I let it be known that, in future, any uninvited visiting aircraft would be comprehensively zapped – that is, redecorated – by 19 Squadron.

Our workup training started on 1 October. I shared the initial pilot checks with Wally Walton and Jack Hamill, an experienced Phantom QFI from Leuchars. Apart from the two first tourists, all the other pilots held Green or Master Green instrument ratings, which allowed us to continue flying even in marginal weather conditions. Long-term crewing up could wait; we needed to get the best possible value from the available flying, and to this end the crews were often mixed. By the second week I introduced an extended day/night programme. Fortunately air defence training can be accomplished as easily at night as by day.

Visual identification – or to use air-defence jargon, 'visident' – is a basic air-defence skill essential for the air-policing role in Germany. The task can be extremely demanding. Obviously, in clear daylight, identification requires little more than a routine interception – the degree of difficulty only varying with the target's height and speed. These variables also apply in cloud, or at night, when the interceptor might have to get closer to the target, sometimes even into close formation.

Our training for night visident was phased: Phase I, being the simple closing on a target displaying standard navigation lights, up to Phase VI, which involved closure on a blacked-out target on a moonless night. At times the only clue to the target's identity was the vague outline of a blacker shape interrupting the background pattern of stars. The FGR 2 was well suited to the visident role: it was an advantage to have a two-man crew when flying in difficult conditions, and of course the AWG 12 radar was better than anything we had used before. The most difficult targets for the Phantom – and for that matter the same applied to the Lightning – were aircraft flying at high altitude and low speed, for example aircraft similar to the Canberra or the American U-2. If the intercepting aircraft could not match speeds with the target, the fighter might have to resort to shadowing, that is weaving behind at a discreet distance.

Of course, training for Battle Flight was only part of our task, but with appropriate supervision, crews invariably acquired the other, less demanding fighter skills.

I exercised the boss's prerogative and chose Flight Lieutenant Norman Browne as my navigator. Without doubt Norman was the most experienced Nav Rad on the squadron, and I enjoyed flying with him. With his broad Ulster brogue and wicked sense of humour, he was one of the squadron's characters. At that time there was a waiting list for married accommodation at Wildenrath, but Norman neatly sidestepped the issue by taking on a hiring. He preferred to live off base within the local German community. The fact that he spoke German helped, of course, and he regularly played football as a member of his village team. Norman seldom spoke about the problems in Northern Ireland. Although I didn't hear about it until much later, he had had a remarkable escape while serving on exchange with a Fleet Air Arm Sea Vixen squadron. Apparently the underwater escape system had operated as he was climbing out of the aircraft and his seat ejected. Fortunately, the system automatically released the straps and Norman was thrown clear. He was dumped in an untidy heap on the flight deck behind the aircraft. The first able seaman to get to him fainted when the apparent corpse opened its eyes. Norman only sustained a few bruises, and was soon back on the flying programme.

It was a distinct advantage to inherit the aircraft and the bulk of the groundcrew direct from Laarbruch. The men were familiar with each individual plane, and our serviceability held up well during the first three months – the only exception being that of the AI radars. At that time the AWG 12 was notoriously difficult to keep serviceable: when one component was changed to correct a simple fault, the next weak link in the system would fail. And on 2 Squadron there had been no requirement to optimise the radar's air-to-air modes. The mean time between failure on the AWG 12 was supposed to be twenty-five hours, but few sets ever achieved this – and on some of our aircraft the

MTBF was measured in minutes. It would take many months for the radars at Wildenrath to achieve an acceptable level of reliability.

On Friday afternoons I held executive meetings attended by the flight commanders and engineering officers, at which we discussed the outline programme for the following week. This was normally followed by a full aircrew meeting. Then, in time-honoured fashion, most of the aircrew repaired to the officers' mess bar for happy hour (two drinks for the price of one). At one of the first happy hours I made the mistake of inviting the assembled company back to our house for bacon and eggs. Jules coped well – until an American Marine Harrier exchange pilot, known as Richard III, teamed up with someone from 19 and presented a 'double moon' against the French windows. Soon after that, 'Banjo' Munro somehow ruptured one of our bean bags and filled the lounge with thousands of tiny, statically charged, polystyrene balls.

Next day, Jules got flowers and an apology for the 'double moon', and one of the young navs – Pete Smith – kindly volunteered to patch the bean bag.

Routine use highlighted a few problems with the HASs. Most could be overcome by modifying our procedures, but because headquarters staffs lacked experience of HAS operations it was difficult to get our ideas accepted. For example, on return from each sortie we had to keep one engine running, to ensure power for the INAS while being repositioned in the HAS. Each HAS was equipped with an electric winch and wire bridle to drag aircraft back, but we found this procedure too cumbersome. Aircraft repositioning was better accomplished by pushing back with a tractor. Problem was, we needed an extra tractor. The massive steel doors of the HASs were powered by electric motors for opening and closing, but we found the doors could be opened faster manually. The doors also had to be fitted with large, drop-down steel bolts to stop them being slammed shut by the jet blast as the aircraft exited the HAS.

By far the most significant and the most difficult requirement to get across was the need for additional manpower. We found that our engineering establishment of ninety-four men was insufficient for HAS operations. In some respects, aircraft maintenance in the HAS, where a team of two or three airmen looked after one aircraft, was more akin to the American style of crew chief maintenance. For the system to work efficiently junior NCOs had to take on a greater share of responsibility. For example, corporal tradesmen needed the over-signing rights normally associated with chief technician rank, but senior RAF engineering staffs were reluctant to accept change, and so Colin Terry had to spend many hours writing up the case for increased 'merit posts'. Eventually, one year later, our groundcrew strength was increased by 25% to 117.

On 3 November Group Captain 'Steve' King, my previous boss at Rheindahlen, visited the squadron. He wanted to fly and I needed his support to make a few structural alterations to the squadron Headquarters. Problem was the building was divided into small offices none of which was large enough for a decent-sized officers' crewroom. I wanted to remove an internal wall, knocking two offices into one, but no one at staff level was willing to give the necessary approval. I flew Steve King in the squadron's two-stick aircraft, which at that time was being operated from one of the HASs earmarked for Battle Flight. The weather was distinctly unpleasant with solid cloud from 1,000 ft to 25,000 ft, but we managed a few supersonic interceptions. It rained steadily at Wildenrath while we were airborne, and by the time we got back the HAS was flooded to a depth of eighteen inches. The whole dispersal was prone to flooding after heavy rain. The German civil engineers claimed it was because the heavy construction work had disrupted the land's natural drainage – in their opinion nothing could be done. I was genuinely concerned about the unhealthy mix of water and high voltage electric cables, and about the possible disruption of vital surface communications, including telebriefing.

The groundcrew rescued us in a Land Rover and I took Steve King to our 'hole in the wall' coffee bar. I could not have wished for a better demonstration of the sort of problems we were facing. That same afternoon a gang of German labourers dug a deep ditch alongside the dispersal, which solved the drainage problem. And the beefier members of the squadron, armed with a sledge hammer, made short work of the breakthrough at squadron headquarters. Thereafter, co-operation with the headquarters staffs significantly improved.

The procedures detailed in RAF Germany's SOPs for the air-policing role could easily be applied to the Phantom squadrons. But in the case of its war role the FGR 2's look-down/shoot-down capabilities were new, so it fell to 19 Squadron to draft procedures for consideration by the staff.

Because of the close proximity of the Warsaw Pact forces and the minimal warning times, the air defence of Western Europe relied heavily on surface-to-air guided missiles (SAM). Only missiles could be held permanently at instant alert states and react fast enough to counter the expected massive surprise attack by enemy aircraft. NATO's European missile defence system was layered in both altitude and depth. At that time, the intelligence assessment was that the enemy air attack would be mounted predominantly at low level. The Allied missile defences were arranged so that attacking aircraft would first have to penetrate a low-level Hawk SAM belt – the LOMEZ. Behind that, and covering medium to high levels, was the Nike-Hercules SAM belt – the HIMEZ. The Fighter Engagement Zone (FEZ), where the Phantoms would be employed, was essentially below and to the rear of the missile engagement zones. Further back still the individual bases were protected by gun and short-range missile defence systems. The 'clutch airfields' were protected by No. 25 Squadron's Bloodhound missiles and RAF Regiment squadrons equipped with short-range BAC Rapier missiles and 40 mm Bofors guns.

Up to this time the fighter defence against low-flying aircraft was based on combat air patrols and visual search. But at an altitude of 1500 ft the AWG 12 could provide effective radar surveillance over a cheese of sky measuring 50 nautical miles ahead and 50 nautical miles across, from ground level to maximum altitude. With two Phantoms properly co-ordinated in a six-minute racetrack pattern it was possible to maintain continuous surveillance. Unlike visual search techniques, our radar was not degraded by weather or poor light conditions. Forbes Pearson and the other QWIs produced an excellent draft proposal incorporating a system of low-level radar combat air patrols (RCAPs), which utilised to the best advantage the FGR 2's unique capabilities. The draft was subsequently approved by HQ RAF Germany and became the new air defence SOP.

We held two squadron parties in November. The first was for the officers and their wives in the squadron headquarters. Even though the station had been informed of our intentions, an RAF police dog handler attempted to prevent our entry. The second – basically a thank you to the groundcrews for a job well done – was held at a German workers' GSO club on the domestic side of the airfield. On this occasion the RAF police breathalysed those leaving the party and one of my pilots was found to be over the limit. Enough was enough. We were used to a certain lack of co-operation from the Old Guard at Wildenrath, but I was not prepared to accept active confrontation. I made that point to the station commander. Fortunately, the follow-up tests on my man proved negative.

John Mitchell, whom I had known as a flight lieutenant on AFDS, but now promoted to group captain, arrived on 1 December to take over from David Leech. Wildenrath had finally relinquished its Harrier commitment and was now an air-defence base. We were informed by HQ RAF Germany that the Phantom squadrons would be declared to NATO as operational with missile and gun armament. This was logical and, to the average staff officer, did not appear to be a problem – but at squadron level it had a profound effect. The Phantom's gun configuration caused high drag and reduced sortie times, but more important was the question of aircraft generation. We knew that the aircraft could easily be loaded with missiles within the time allowed for NATO's aircraft-generation rates, but fitting and harmonising the SU 23 (Vulcan gun pod) was manpower-intensive and time-consuming. Despite the disadvantages, I decided that as a general rule, we had to fly with the gun fitted.

'Bob' Barcilon – the CO of 19 (Lightning) Squadron kindly invited Jules and me to the final squadron dinner at Gutersloh. It was a sad occasion, many of the Lightning people being preoccupied with thoughts of their imminent return to the UK. But the new 19 Squadron at Wildenrath was almost ready and I made tentative arrangements for the hand-over of the squadron's standard and other memorabilia.

On 21 December I drafted a signal to HQ RAF Germany declaring 19 Squadron operational. By a quirk of fate, within seven days three of my experienced pilots were sick: two with fractured bones and one, Graeme Smith, with a virulent case of chickenpox. But there was no going back now; those that remained fit would just have to work harder.

I thought it essential for morale to receive the squadron standard at a formal parade. I suspect HQ RAF Germany would have preferred this to be low key, because my request for some sort of military music produced one lone volunteer trumpeter – but it was the thought that counted. Due to bad weather on 30 December, we held the colour parade in No. 60 Squadron's hangar – the spectators half froze to death, but at least they stayed dry. 'Tim' Lloyd took the salute and afterwards was the guest of honour at a formal lunch in the mess.

We planned to take over Battle Flight at 2359 hours on 31 December, and hold two aircraft and crews permanently at five minutes' readiness until 31 March. Hopefully by then, No. 92 (Phantom) Squadron would also be operational and the Battle Flight commitment could be shared between the two squadrons.

I arranged with the Sector Operations Centre at Uedem (SOC 2) that the formal hand-over from Lightning to Phantom would be done while airborne, and to make sure nothing went wrong I crewed up with Flight Lieutenant Tony Parker in XV 439 well before midnight. The order to scramble came at 2355 hours, and we got airborne well within five minutes. There was just one minor glitch; one of my afterburners failed on take-off, but by that time I was committed.

The German population traditionally mark the New Year with fireworks. On 1 January 1977 No. 19 Squadron added its unique brand of display. We made contact with the Lightning pilot, airborne from Gutersloh, relieving him of the Battle Flight commitment, and spent the next hour cruising around at high altitude exchanging New Year greetings with the operations centres and radar stations in 2 and 4 ATAFs.

That marked the start of a difficult period for the squadron. For technical reasons – mainly to do with engine starting and INAS alignment – the reaction time of the Phantom FGR 2 was much slower than that of the Lightning. For example, a full INAS alignment, basically telling the INAS its precise position and heading, took fourteen minutes, although a 'rapid' alignment, albeit with slightly reduced navigational accuracy, could be done in two minutes. It was just possible to hold a five-minute state with the Phantom from outside the cockpit, but the crews had to stay close to their aircraft. The long-term plan was for purpose-built accommodation adjacent to the HASs, but in the meantime the crews had to make do with a cramped service caravan. The conditions were primitive: meals were delivered in hot boxes from the airmen's mess, and the only toilet was an Elsan bucket in the HAS – where one sat in splendid, albeit bum-freezing isolation. It was difficult for those on night shift (between 2000 and 0800) to get any sleep, so they had to be released from duty the following day. For safety's sake we planned on rotating Battle Flight crews every twelve hours, so each twenty-four-hour period absorbed four crews – roughly half our effective strength. Fortunately, after the first two weeks, the walking wounded had recovered sufficiently to share the burden.

In February I learned that my successor as OC 19 Squadron, Wing Commander 'Tim' Gauvain, would take over in July 1978. Although it was all of eighteen months away, it was a sobering thought – I was being short-toured to barely two years. I suspected that the 'posters' were taking their revenge for me bucking the system by refusing to move my family back to the UK while I refreshed. I immediately applied for an extension but should have known better – once the Air Secretary's Department had made up its mind, the plot was cast in stone.

A few days later I was dragged away to head a board of inquiry into the loss of a Buccaneer from Laarbruch. Apparently the aircraft had caught fire in the air and crashed at Volkel, a military airfield in Holland. Fortunately the crew had safely ejected. I picked up the rest of the board, consisting of a Buccaneer pilot and an engineering officer, from Laarbruch and we drove to Volkel. The causes of aircraft crashes are seldom clear-cut, but in this case within half an hour of arriving at the scene of the crash we found positive evidence that the starboard engine had suffered an uncontained turbine failure. In layman's terms, the high-temperature section of the engine, the turbine, had disintegrated and burst out of its casing. Of course, that would have to be confirmed by a detailed engine strip at Rolls-Royce, but the jagged exit holes in the turbine casing were unmistakable. The hot turbine blades had caused significant airframe damage and fire too. We also found evidence that the navigator's ejection seat had been incorrectly rigged and he was extremely lucky to have survived. In the course of our investigation on the seat, the board had to visit RAF Honington, and I took the opportunity to drop off a couple of bottles of plonk for the station commander, one-time boss of Six Squadron – Group Captain John Nevill.

It took all of two weeks to write up the board and submit our findings to HQ RAF Germany. The Buccaneer's Spey engines were subsequently modified to cure a design weakness.

I found the squadron in good spirits when I got back – although occasionally I had to intervene to curb some wild ideas. If I remember rightly it was 'Banjo' who suggested that the squadron should adopt a live dolphin, presently captive at a Dutch zoo. With visions of a large, stinking aquarium in the crewroom, I ruled that out. But Banjo's approach to the Bols distillery in Holland, seeking their advice on a suitable cocktail for the squadron was an inspired move. The idea was to produce a blue and white drink to match the squadron's colours. Blue Bols liqueur was a natural choice for the blue, but the problem was to find a suitable white mix. Not that we intended to mix them anyway – that would have defeated the object of the exercise. Bols suggested three combinations: condensed milk – which was right for colour but sounded and tasted vile – or cointreau, or schnapps. We had a tasting. Understandably the ladies preferred the cointreau combination; the schnapps was definitely a 'hair on the chest' type of drink. The Blue Bols had to be injected with a syringe to sit below the white/clear mix, where it would stay perfectly separated. We christened the cocktail the 'Blue Dolphin' and it was always down the hatch in one – a sure guarantee of success at any party.

Aside from these light-hearted moments, I was acutely aware that the extended working hours were taking their toll. At that time the executive officers were working at least eighty-five hours a week, and few officers got away with less than seventy – a commendable commitment, but we were not in a war situation. I was determined to reduce the hours spent on duty. To make matters worse, since forming in October there had been few opportunities for the aircrew to take leave, and the leave policy could only be relaxed when 92 (Phantom) Squadron became operational.

On 7 March we deployed four aircraft and six crews to RAF Valley for a missile practice camp (MPC). The aim of the detachment was to fire four missiles, two Sparrows and two Sidewinders, against remotely controlled Jindivik targets launched from Aberporth. An MPC was not competitive at a personal level in the same way as an APC – there was no counting of scores, and as long as a missile was launched within the firing parameters it should home on to the target. But it was important for the squadron to do well, since every missile launch was a reflection on the squadron's efficiency with its primary air-defence armament. Achieving a successful kill was a different matter. The MPC firings were in many respects trials sorties and the target profiles were deliberately chosen to explore the extremities of the missile's flight envelope. All the target profiles for 19 Squadron's firings were at low level, testing the FGR 2's look-down/shoot-down capability. I delegated command of the detachment to Wally Walton; I had fired several air-to-air missiles from the F-105, and there was still much to do at Wildenrath. The squadron was still committed to two aircraft and crews on Battle Flight, so we were fully stretched.

The Valley detachment returned on 17 March, when I had hoped to start an air combat training phase. Apart from routine PIS, there was little call for upper air work in Germany, but there were many occasions when we became involved in simulated air combat at low altitude, and the only way to train safely for this eventuality was to practise at medium altitude. Training for air combat was hard on the aircraft. To minimise airframe fatigue we reduced the all-up weight by removing the wing tanks and guns.

After less than a week, at 0430 hours one morning, John Mitchell called for the first Station Mineval – Exercise Wild Dog. It was essentially a shake-down training session – the first of many. Indeed, the pattern of one three-day Taceval type of exercise per month was normal for flying stations in RAF Germany. Each exercise followed the standard format: assessment of readiness including aircraft generation – 50% fully armed and serviceable in six hours, 70% in twelve hours – followed by an operational assessment, which of course included flying. The other main areas to be assessed were engineering support and the ability to survive.

I thought, for a first crack, the squadron performed well. We just met the aircraft generation targets, but the necessity of having the aircraft already fitted with guns was proven beyond doubt.

The pressure of work eased markedly in April, when 92 Squadron took their share of the Battle Flight. Of course it was a little inconvenient having to give up one of our HASs for 92's Battle Flight aircraft, but there was no shortage of parking space in Bravo dispersal, and for overnight storage we could always double up in the remaining shelters. We did attempt to operate with two aircraft in one HAS, but the engine exhaust fumes proved to be unacceptable in the rearmost aircraft.

Most of the crews got away at some point for a well-earned leave. I planned on taking the family to Oberammergau in southern Germany for a week's break, and just before we set out Barney called from the States to say that he was bringing his new wife – Jann – to Germany on honeymoon. We arranged to meet them in Oberammergau. I made a few rapid telephone calls and got them a room in the guest house where we were staying. It was a magical week. Oberammergau is famous for its Passion plays, which originated in the Middle Ages during the final outbreak of the plague. The townspeople promised that, if the plague stopped, they would put on a Passion play every five years. Well, the plague did stop, and the rest is history. Fortunately in 1977 there was no Passion play, otherwise we would not have been able to book accommodation for a whole week.

The night after the Barnhills arrived there was a heavy fall of snow, which was a great hit with the children. We visited all the local tourist attractions – the open-air Passion play theatre, the Winter Olympics site at Garmisch Partenkirken and King Ludwig II of Bavaria's royal palaces at Neuschwanstein and Linderhof. Legend had it that the King was mad, although Jules thought he was merely eccentric. But mad or not, he was clearly profligate with the money he raised on taxes – and that may have been the reason why he ended his days in suspicious circumstances on the shores of Lake Starnberger in 1886.

After three days I drove Barney and Jann to Munich to catch their flight home. On the last day of leave the family took the cable car up to the summit of the Zugspitze and visited the highest border-control post between Germany and Austria, at 6000 ft above sea level.

When we got back to Wildenrath, Rolly Jackson called to tell me that I would be leading RAF Germany's combined formation flypast for the Queen's Silver Jubilee Review at RAF Finningley on 29 July. That was almost four months away, but preparations started immediately. I took Norman Browne with me, in a Phantom, to the first briefing at Finningley on 15 April, and returned to Wildenrath the same day. The ops order called for each major frontline squadron to be represented by at least one aircraft, so the RAF Germany formation consisted of two Phantoms in line astern formation, with two Buccaneers and two Harriers forming a vic on the second Phantom, and a vic of five Jaguars at the tail end. One aircraft of each type flew as airborne spares. The shape of the formation was actually chosen by HQ RAF Germany, although for symmetry alone there were few options.

The first period of rehearsals started on 20 April. For economy of engineering support the Phantoms and Harriers deployed to RAF Wittering and the Jaguars operated from RAF Coltishall. Overall the Silver Jubilee flying display was programmed to last for thirty-eight minutes, and comprised fifteen formations involving 137 aircraft. Because of the numbers and variety of aircraft converging on Finningley from different bases, the routes and timing were carefully preplanned. Thus the RAF Germany formation was to take off from Wittering precisely on time to arrive over the display datum at 1606½ local time. The timing limits were plus or minus five seconds. Our route was via Coltishall (where the Jaguar element joined the formation) to Flamborough Head (where the two Harriers joined up and the spare aircraft broke away), and from there to the IP, fifteen miles from Finningley.

The first rehearsal was for leaders only. That was followed by three full rehearsals, one of which was severely curtailed by weather – although being in a Phantom we made it on time. Within ten days we returned to Wildenrath to await the final rehearsals in July.

In May the squadron was committed to Exercise Black Prince, the annual Berlin Access exercise mounted from Gutersloh. I led the British element of the tripartite fighter force. We flew what could best be described as high cover, in a series of racetrack patterns, above the three transport aircraft. The different national air forces worked well together, and when everything went according to plan the fighters were ready to oppose any hostile threat by manned fighter aircraft. Unfortunately the same could not be said of the SAM threat, for which there was no effective defence, and for that reason the tripartite air-access plan lacked credibility.

On 2 June we started our workup for our first APC to qualify in air-to-air gunnery. Previously this would have been done either in

Cyprus or at Deci, to take advantage of the better weather, but 19 Squadron had drawn the short straw and was destined to do its firing from RAF St Mawgan in Cornwall. Of course, Cornwall didn't qualify for a local overseas allowance, which effectively meant a reduction in pay, so it was difficult to generate much enthusiasm among the troops.

The RAF was still committed to the outdated banner target, and now, with the demise of the Meteors, we had to wait on the availability of the target-towing Canberras of No. 100 Squadron. In the event, a single Canberra was deployed to Gutersloh for two weeks in June and we flew a limited number of ciné sorties. The FGR 2's gun-sight had an air-to-air guns mode with radar ranging, but the system was not optimised for the heights and speeds we were using. Nor was there a fixed reference in the gun-sight to show the alignment of the gun. As a result, in its air-to-air mode, the FGR 2's gun-sight was less capable than the original Hunter GGS.

We deployed to St Mawgan on 20 June and had to spend the first week taking ciné before attempting live firing. Academic air-to-air gunnery had changed dramatically since the late fifties. The banner was still limited to 180 knots and we were still in the game of counting coloured holes, but to compensate for the Phantom's limited manoeuvrability the target-towing aircraft maintained a slow turn throughout the firing pass. The fighters attacked from a high perch position inside the turn and opened fire at 320 yards, with the aiming pipper sliding forward along the length of the banner.

As usual it was difficult to assess whether or not you had hit the target until after landing. The scores were expressed as a percentage of hits against rounds fired. NATO's minimum qualification criterion was two consecutive scores of 17.5%. It was surprising that after an average of only six shoots all fifteen of the squadron's pilots qualified – although few pilots were consistent and there were no high scores.

I finished the APC with an uncomfortable feeling that it was all a contrived performance – trick shooting to compensate for inadequate training and outdated equipment. How much cheaper and more professional would it have been to provide each Phantom wing with two Dart tow-rigs and a supply of Dart targets?

Later that year Graeme Smith and QWIs from 92 Squadron flew a successful, albeit limited trial, firing on a Dart towed by a German

Air Force Phantom. But the RAF pundits still refused to accept the validity of the Dart target system.

Towards the end of the St Mawgan detachment, we laid on a party for the resident officers and their ladies in the officers' mess. With Blue Dolphins to break the ice it was a roaring success. On the morning of the last day, the Hercules aircraft that was programmed to return the ground personnel to Wildenrath was cancelled. Instead they were transported back to Germany by Britannia Airways, and much to their irritation the aircraft landed at Hannover. Then it was by bus to Wildenrath, making a journey which would normally have taken two hours stretch to eight. No wonder they were peeved.

Meanwhile, back at Wildenrath, I learned that the station commander was going to call a Mineval on the Monday. I tried to get the squadron excused but John Mitchell would have none of it.

By 18 July the aircraft and crews participating in the Silver Jubilee Review were back in the UK for the final rehearsals. Once again we took up residence at Wittering, and the support provided by the station was first class – no one questions the priority of a Royal Review. As far as we were concerned there were no changes to the ops order, but a TACAN beacon had been installed at Finningley to assist with navigation. In the event this was a valuable aid; the final run-in heading was 210° – directly into the sun – and (typically in that part of the UK) the in-flight visibility was poor. Compared to the Coronation Review in 1953, when more than 600 aircraft had taken part, the Silver Jubilee Review of 1977 was a minor commitment.

We flew just three rehearsals before the Review on 29 July. We repeated the flypast for Finningley's Open Day on 30 July, and I simply extended the flight plan to lead the Phantoms, Buccaneers and Jaguars back to their respective home bases in Germany. The Harriers did not have enough fuel for the round trip and had to land at Wittering. I think everyone enjoyed that detachment; it made a pleasant change from the total and all-consuming commitment in RAF Germany.

Some weeks later a medal to commorate the Queen's Silver Jubilee was struck. In the manner of such awards an allocation was made to each station, and at Wildenrath medals were awarded to all the senior executives. I got one and suggested that Norman Browne, who had been the lead navigator of the RAF Germany formation, should also get one – but nothing came of it.

The concept of radar combat air patrols was highly successful. By now we had established three training RCAPs over Germany: one covering the North German Plain; one to the east of the Ruhr; and one centred on the Moehne Dam. Another RCAP was planned in Belgium airspace over the Ardennes. Few offensive attack aircraft could get through without being detected. In theory we could have taken them out with head-on attacks, but without an airborne IFF we had no means of positively identifying targets at fourteen miles – the maximum effective range of the Sparrow missile. Initially we solved the problem by detaching one fighter to investigate, and report 'Hostile' or 'Friendly', while the fighters remaining on the CAP readied themselves for immediate weapon launch. But this procedure wasted fighter resources and reduced the overall effectiveness of the CAP.

During August, as a result of a liaison visit with No. 349 Squadron of the Belgian Air Force – equipped with F-104s – we agreed to co-operate on RCAP missions. The F-104 had no radar capability at low level, but Phantom crews could act as airborne directors to launch the F-104s at the targets. In theory, the Belgian pilots identified the targets, and the Phantoms on CAP went through the drill of launching the Sparrow missiles. The effectiveness of these sorties depended on the F-104 pilot's reactions. Some interceptions were brilliantly successful, others were disastrous, but liaison at this level was always useful. Meanwhile, the Belgian squadron gained valuable experience at low level prior to being re-equipped with the General Dynamics F-16s.

I made it squadron policy to encourage personnel to take at least one long leave break each year, to give them a chance to get away from Wildenrath. In mid-August, Jules and I packed the caravan and set off with the children to the south of France. The feeling of freedom as we drove away from Wildenrath and beyond immediate recall was almost palpable. We had allowed three days' motoring to get to the south of France.

We spent the first night at Mullheim, the second at a delightful little camp-site beside the river in Montelimar, and eventually booked into a camp-site about two miles east of Port Grimaud.

We spent the first four days on the beach, and when we tired of sea, sun and sand, we toured the local area – to Saint Tropez, the ancient town of Grimaud, Nice and all the other beauty spots in between. We met some army friends from Rheindahlen – they were camping at an adjacent site – and we visited the Pearsons, who had rented a mobile home along the coast. I envied the Pearsons for not having to tow a caravan.

After twelve days' blissful relaxation we set off for home. I chose to go via Italy and drive north to Switzerland. My brother Henry was working and living in Zurich at that time and we planned to visit them before calling on Ian and Karin at Neuhausen on our way north. Henry and Joyce were delighted to see us, and they introduced their brand new addition to the family – Andrew. After two nights in Zurich we headed for Neuhausen. Then, after a night with Ian and Karin, we made the long but familiar haul back to Wildenrath.

I was finding that holidays on the continent were becoming a strain. I had had a nasty fall the day before we left for the south of France – in an awkward moment my feet had suddenly gone from under me – and three weeks later I still carried the bruises. I was also exhausted – although that was to be expected after our adventures. More worrying was the realisation that my reserves of energy were so low – no longer could I mow the lawn in one go. I was aware of getting old, and resolved to pace myself better in the future.

During August the Battle Flight pair was relocated in a hangar on the north side of the airfield while work proceeded on the purpose-built alert accommodation at Bravo dispersal. Everyone was relieved to say goodbye to the revolting caravans. As I've mentioned, it wasn't practical to hold the five-minute state from the hangar accommodation, but Wildenrath was granted temporary dispensation to revert to a ten-minute state.

The Wildenrath wing also lost out on the NATO Squadron Exchange Scheme, but as an alternative we arranged to run a 'fighter meet', a sort of fly-in for all the NATO fighter squadrons. Traditionally, fighter meets are wild parties. The host station has to have a lot of space, plenty of beer and fairly indestructible facilities. Wildenrath's was held in an empty hangar. In those days the Royal Netherlands Air Force – the 'Cloggies' – had the worst reputation of all. Certainly things started to get out of hand when one Dutch pilot, much the worse for booze, challenged other squadron pilots to walk across the hangar rafters while being shot at with air-sea-rescue emergency flares. The station medical officer – 'Doc' Russel – took one look at that lot and decided to go home. Fortunately no one was shot down. I don't know how a brand new builder's skip came to be left outside the hangar – but at some time during the evening a private car was loaded into it and set alight.

Fortunately, the normal run of entertainment at Wildenrath was more sophisticated. We had the usual dining-in nights, October Fest binges, the occasional soirée where we'd listen to Monty Sunshine's Jazz Band, balls and the inevitable Burns suppers. On 19 Squadron the keener sportsmen asked if they could enter a team for the annual football trophy, the Aircrew Cup. I had reservations; the competition for the Aircrew Cup was notoriously cut-throat and we could ill afford any sports injuries. But the 'Jockstrappers' were determined to compete, and thought they had a fair chance of winning. So I relented – on condition they won the trophy. Of course, every member of the team had to be serving on the squadron, but the rules on including engineering officers were fairly relaxed. Colin Terry actually played in goal for a couple of games, but Dave Allen was our real ace in the hole. Before he'd joined the RAF, Dave had played professional football for Dundee United. Norman Browne played, of course, and the rest of the team were fairly capable.

By September we had made it through to the final against No. 3 Squadron, ably led by their CO, Wing Commander Dick Johns. I didn't participate; not only was I not good enough, but I was finding it difficult to run. For some reason, even when I walked fast my right toe dropped and I tended to trip.

They played the match on the headquarters pitch at Rheindahlen, and the non-playing members of the squadron turned out in force to support the home team. No. 19 Squadron eventually won 3–1, with 'Noddy' Halsall and John Cosgrove both scoring. That evening we dined out with the Terrys, the Cosgroves and the Sabins at the Berg Wegberg. The pace of life at Wildenrath was such that it seemed only yesterday that we'd first formed the squadron. These officers were the first of the original members to be posted. Each had done a splendid job, and I recommended Colin Terry for a formal award. Two replacements had already arrived: the new nav rad leader was Ian Dorman-Jackson, and Squadron Leader John Gilbert took over the engineering responsibilities from Colin Terry.

By this time the noise complaints had reached worrying proportions. The Phantom was of course a noisy aircraft, especially in the circuit, and while this was accepted by the local population during daylight hours it was totally unacceptable at night, particularly during the summer months when our night-flying programme extended into the small hours of the morning. John Mitchell imposed a number of training restrictions: first by limiting circuits and overshoots after 2300 hours and banning all take-offs after midnight. But we really needed a concerted 'hearts and minds' programme to win the support of the locals. Each flying squadron was allocated a town. I was instructed to make contact with Erkelenz, a small town some five miles south-east of the airfield. From initial telephone calls it was apparent that no one on the town council spoke English. So one morning I collected Norman and Banjo, who spoke some German, and drove to Erkelenz, where we had an appointment at the town hall to see the Burgermeister, Willy Stein, and Barthel Jansen, the Stadtdirektor.

Our first meeting was a little stilted – we had nothing in common – but to get the ball rolling, I suggested that the members of the town council and their wives might like to visit the squadron during a normal working day. I was pleasantly surprised at the enthusiastic response – about fifty dignitaries turned up by civilian coach, and we packed them into the PBF.

With the help of the station's interpreter I had transcribed my introductory briefing spiel into phonetic German: 'Mine dammen und mine hair . . .' etc. One particular phrase I remember was 'shtackle-dats-roum' – barbed-wire fence. My parrot-fashion speech was well received, but unfortunately it gave the false impression that I was fluent in German. The crunch came when the visitors unleashed a barrage of questions.

Even so, the good burghers of Erkelenz were impressed by a Phantom scrambling from inside a HAS. Finally we took them to the officers' mess for a stiff round of Blue Dolphins.

A few weeks later we received an invitation for the squadron's officers and their wives to visit Erkelenz. The town was steeped in history and had once been a key staging post on the trade route between eastern Europe and England. We found that Erkelenz's colours were blue and white – similar to 19 Squadron – and by happy coincidence the town distilled both a blue liquor and a fiery clear schnapps. In typical German tradition, before we departed, Willy Stein presented me with a pint of 'Erkelenze Blau' to finish in one – but I delegated that particular duty to Banjo.

And it wasn't over yet. We were invited to attend a dinner dance in the town hall that evening. So it was a mad scramble back to Wildenrath to get changed into our finery. I suppose I was a bit under the weather and Jules insisted that I had something solid before we left home. I had the bright idea of eating a poached egg from a plate while balanced on a stool in the bath. Unfortunately the plate slid off the stool and dumped the egg and toast in the bath. After much ferreting around I rescued the egg intact. It tasted quite good – the toast was a bit soggy, though. Jules just had to let that story slip out during the return trip to Erkelenz, but I was past caring.

The 'hearts and minds' campaign had a suitably beneficial effect on public relations: the noise complaints diminished, and it was noticeable that the squadron regularly received invitations to attend functions in Erkelenz. For our part, we occasionally arranged for a flight of Phantoms to fly over the town on formal occasions.

Wildenrath had many official visitors, and these were farmed out to the various squadrons on a pro-rata basis. On 19 Squadron we averaged one visitor per week; our first was the Member of Parliament Mr Winston Churchill – grandson of the great wartime statesman. But everyone on the station was involved in the visit of HRH the Duke of Gloucester on 12 October. Sadly the Duchess, who was due to accompany her husband, was indisposed. In the nature of such royal visits everything, down to the minutest detail, was rehearsed. I gave my standard squadron briefing – fortunately not in German – and the squadron laid on a set-piece scramble. We were told that the Duke was interested in architecture, but I doubt that he was much impressed by our hardened accommodation. Jules and I were among the many guests who attended the official lunch in the officers' mess.

The grand finale was a wing scramble of twenty aircraft.

Apparently the Duke enjoyed his visit; I personally thought he was a charming chap and, as expected, the visit was a welcome boost to the station's morale.

The work on the purpose-built Battle Flight accommodation was completed in late September, and Battle Flight returned to Bravo dispersal. The crews could now live in relative comfort less than twenty yards from their aircraft. Provided there was no call-out, it was possible to get a decent night's sleep and I had no qualms about committing the crews to twenty-four hours on duty. The completion of the Battle Flight accommodation was the final building block on Bravo dispersal while I was with 19 Squadron.

We had come a long way since first occupying the site, and much of the work had been done on a self-help basis. We had reinforced the vulnerable sections of the perimeter with barbed wire and sandbagged strong points. The station wouldn't supply the wire, but Forbes Pearson found a stockpile in a remote bunker on the airfield and the aircrews immediately put it to good use. We had used the 'rapid runway repair' engineers on detachment from the UK to construct a hidden track and car park in the woods. Every HAS was now equipped with an enclosed cabin to accommodate the groundcrew and protect the documentation. I would have liked to instal racks to hold a complete weapons reload in every HAS, but that was too advanced for conventional thought at the time. The squadron's engineering personnel had improvised a redundant Bowser shelter to act as hardened quarters for the off-duty groundcrews. Phase 2 of the NATO hardening programme would provide proper accommodation for groundcrews, but in the meantime our makeshift arrangements were better than nothing.

I was well satisfied with the standard of communications, both within the dispersal and between the PBF and the station's Combined Operations Centre. We had six hand-held Storno radio sets, which were essential for the control of our engineering resources – I would have liked more Stornos for ground defence but these could not be provided. At one stage the engineers attempted to improvise an intercom system using baby alarms, but their range was insufficient and we had to fall back on the old-fashioned field telephones.

After a long fight with the catering staffs we had managed to establish a feeder in the airmen's soft accommodation. The choice of food was limited and the standard did not match that routinely provided at Canadian or American flight line feeders, but the meals were hot and served in a fraction of the time it took to use the messes on the north side of the airfield.

I was rather pleased with the squadron's progress. In one year, Bravo dispersal had been transformed from muddy, disorganised chaos into a pristine, rather impressive military organisation. We were now thoroughly familiar with all aspects of operation from a hardened site. The changes necessary to convert from a peacetime to a war footing could be completed in minutes rather than hours. In most cases it was simply a question of changing clothing, ripping off the Velcro-backed squadron badges from flying suits and drawing personal weapons. When an alert was called the S Eng O automatically took over the role of ground defence commander for the dispersal, leaving the duty aircrew executive officer free to allocate crews to aircraft and run the flying programme.

A Maxeval was called in October – similar to a Mineval, but called and assessed by the staff of HQ RAF Germany. It was a tough three-day exercise, but then it had to be – the next call-out was likely to be a full-blown evaluation. Although Taceval was essentially a no-notice exercise it would have been poor military practice not to have assessed the likely time-scale and risk. It was now eight months since the Wildenrath wing had been declared operational, and by any standards our Taceval was overdue. We guessed it would be in November, although we didn't know the precise date.

The format of the NATO Taceval was standard, although the exercise inputs were infinitely variable. A multinational team arrived without notice to witness Phase 1 – readiness – which included the recall of personnel and the generation of armed aircraft. There might then be a short break before Phase 2 – the assessment of operational effectiveness – which normally involved seventy-two hours' continuous operations. During Phase 2 the base's support functions and ability to survive attack were also assessed. It was a practical war-game played in real time, with specialist umpires on hand to report on the unit's response. I was fairly confident that 19 Squadron was up to scratch. We had trained hard for the past year and our procedures worked smoothly.

I remember excusing myself during one air raid, just to see how the troops were reacting. The dispersal was sealed up tight as a drum – not a soul to be seen – but moments later, after the all-clear, when four aircraft were scrambled, the dispersal became a hive of activity. There was something about RAF Germany that engendered in everyone a determination to give it their best shot.

The Taceval team actually arrived at Bravo dispersal shortly after 1400 hours on 7 November. I happened to be looking out of my office window as the cars drew into the car park and a group of visitors purposefully headed for Battle Flight. Phase 1 of our long-awaited Taceval, which we subsequently learned was code-named Exercise Capital Clown, was under way. I keyed the 'squawk box' to the ops room, and within seconds Bravo dispersal was alerted. This was during normal working hours, so the station's recall plan was hardly needed.

The first exercise injection was to scramble Battle Flight, which thankfully went off without a hitch. Since October we had planned our routine servicing programme to conserve aircraft hours, and on 19 Squadron we easily produced six aircraft in half the allotted time. Meeting the 70% target in twelve hours was more difficult, as inevitably we had to recover aircraft from deeper servicing. Even up to the eleventh hour it was looking doubtful, but with fifteen minutes to go two aircraft came up and the crews checked in on telebrief to the COC. We actually produced 80% of our aircraft, fully armed and serviceable, within the allotted twelve hours. Having convincingly met the aircraft generation target, the armourers set about downloading the live weapons.

Phase 2 started next morning at 0600 hours. I chose to do the first shift on the ops desk, since this was the best position to command and monitor the squadron's response. The Battle Flight remained intact, but I split the rest of the squadron into two shifts, ensuring round-the-clock manning. Aircrews were allotted to each aircraft, and held the alert states dictated by the COC. Crews at thirty minutes or longer were free to return to the PBF, but experience had shown that most crews preferred to remain in the HAS. Once manned up, the aircraft tended to remain serviceable and each crew could fly up to three consecutive sorties before they had to be replaced. Any spare personnel in the PBF were used to relay briefing information to the crews manning the aircraft, although this could also be done using the telebriefing links. The Taceval team called the shots, but typically two or three exercise injects were in force concurrently. Some were minor, lasting but a few minutes, while others might remain in force for the duration of the exercise. Although the British NBC equipment was considered to be the best in the world, any nuclear, chemical or biological inject severely disrupted the squadron's working practices. Even in winter, wearing a gas mask while engaged in hard physical labour caused heat stress. And this was a potential killer.

At that time NBC protection for crews while airborne was less well developed. Although we had flown a few strictly controlled sorties with experimental masks and filters, our main protection was to use 100% oxygen, but the aircraft's cockpit pressurisation was not filtered. We also knew that our decontamination measures on the ground were rudimentary. But in all probability we were as good as any other nation – bar those of the Warsaw Pact.

I flew just two sorties during Capital Clown – one day and one night. And by the morning of 10 November I was fairly sure that the squadron had performed well. The weather had been abysmal since the start of the exercise, with low cloud and continuous rain. But we had not missed a scramble, and we appeared to have reacted properly to every inject.

There was just one major hiccup during the entire exercise and that occurred during a rapid re-arm turn-round: when all the AIM-9 pylons at Wildenrath failed the 'no volts' checks. I should explain: to guard against an inadvertent weapon release it is essential to check there is no stray electrical current in the armament circuits. On this occasion all the AIM-9 (Sidewinder) pylons registered a small, irregular voltage. This had not occurred before on such a wide scale. Wing Commander Keith Fenner – OC Eng Wing – eventually solved the mystery when in desperation he poured warm water on one of the pylons as it lay on the hangar floor – and the pylon produced a small electrical charge. Clearly the pylon had picked up a deposit of chemicals, probably from the corrosive cocktail of fumes that hung over the Ruhr like a yellow deathcap, that had reacted with the rain. In effect the pylons had become batteries.

Unfortunately Keith solved the problem just two minutes outside the allotted time.

The final Taceval event was a wing scramble to launch all the remaining serviceable aircraft, but due to weather this was downgraded to a mass taxi down the runway. Remarkably the wing finished the exercise with a final serviceability of 90%. I led ten aircraft from 19 Squadron on to the runway.

Exercise Capital Clown finished at midday. We were acutely aware that the reputation established by the Lightning wing at Gutersloh would have been hard to match. After a nail-biting delay the leader of the Taceval team gave us the final ratings. Incredibly, Wildenrath had achieved the coveted Rate 1 (excellent) for: readiness, operational effectiveness and the ability to survive. But because of the AIM-9 pylon 'no volts' problems it had dropped to a Rate 2 for support functions. These results were outstanding. We had aced it! A great cheer went up from the assembled company.

With Taceval over we could afford a concentrated programme of Air Combat Training. We also liaised with the Buccaneer and Jaguar squadrons at Laarbruch and Bruggen, who were seeking active fighter opposition during their routine attack profiles. The guaranteed supply of targets was useful, but we also hoped to persuade the strike/attack crews that their cavalier attitude to safe routing and sanctuary flight levels was fraught with danger. Up to now the mud-movers had believed that on their return they could afford to ignore the standard procedures and could evade Allied air defences by flying fast and low. This may have been a reasonable assumption during the fifties and sixties, but it was no longer valid. The SAM systems were much improved, and now the Phantom FGR 2, with its look-down radar and forward hemisphere weapons, was the first of a new breed of fighter that largely negated the advantages of high speed. Now, returning aircraft were better advised to conform with the air-defence safety procedures. In the event of them not being able to comply they were supposed to reduce their cruising speed to less than 200 knots.

I am not sure that we ever managed to convince the strike/attack crews, but the mutual training produced some hairy mock engagements and spirited debriefing sessions. On one such occasion I was giving Keith Fenner a back-seat ride in our twin-stick aircraft. My policy on giving air-experience flights to visitors was quite straightforward: first we had to have an aircraft to spare and, second, any such flight had to be part of the normal training programme. Keith had been muttering for some while that in his capacity of OC Eng Wing he had been providing all the support for the squadrons but no one had yet offered him a flight in a Phantom. He had a point – one fine day we kitted him out to fly on a Jaguar affiliation exercise. The sortie was all at low level and there was plenty to keep a nervous passenger occupied – but Keith was already a qualified private pilot and I didn't expect him to have any problems. Keith was surprised by the effectiveness of the Phantom's controls, but for the first twenty minutes he coped well. Then, shortly before we joined the CAP, a flight of four Jaguars in standard low-level combat formation appeared head-on over the top of a ridge. The combined closing speed must have been well in excess of 800 knots. I immediately took control and ordered an inwards turn-about – meaning the separate elements of my formation would turn hard towards each other through 180° – to follow the Jaguars. It was a recognised tactic which invariably gained the initiative. Whichever way the Jaguars turned, they would face both a head-on threat and a separate attack from their six-o'clock.

The Jaguar leader fell into the trap of turning about also – or maybe he just wanted to play. For the next thirty seconds we were committed to a wild, high-positive-g engagement. The professional aircrew would have been well used to the gyrating kaleidoscope of earth, sky and aircraft (our missiles were of limited use in this type of engagement, though we managed to track two of the Jaguars in the gunsight), but Keith Fenner may well have been disoriented. I tried to give him a running commentary of the fight, but he didn't say very much. When we got back to Wildenrath he immediately reported to the station medical centre.

Some weeks later Keith took me for a trip in a single-engined Cessna at the private flying club at Laarbruch. We swanned around for a bit and flew down to Wildenrath. It was good fun, but Keith's idea of a steep turn was 45° of bank with the nose steady on the horizon – no wonder the poor chap had gone quiet in the Phantom.

Keith seemed to attract misfortune like a moth to a candle. When the station commander's residence suffered a main drains blockage, the civilian plumber decided to blow out the obstruction with an air hose – presumably compressed air had done the trick before. But on this occasion the blockage held and the contents of the sewer came up through the Fenners' toilet. Unfortunately Keith was sitting on it at the time. The shit went everywhere. Rita was sworn to secrecy, of course, but it is difficult to keep that sort of thing under your hat.

December was the first month since February when Wildenrath did not have a Taceval-type exercise, and we got to do a lot of flying. On 20 December we held a Squadron Open Day, featuring Santa's HAS Party for the children. It was all highly successful. The adults also enjoyed their share of the traditional festivities, including a squadron party in the PBF.

By the start of the new year we had launched into a new round of training, and the less experienced crews had to be brought up to speed. A station Mineval was called on the 17th of the month.

The pressure of work had stabilised since the frantic pace of early 1977. The average working week was now fifty-five hours, although some of that was between midnight and five in the morning, and could therefore be deemed unsocial. Each squadron now had fifteen crews, although a small proportion were still upgrading to combat-ready status. Fully qualified aircrew from a UK squadron typically took two months to upgrade, while a first tourist straight from the OCU would take six.

We also introduced visident training against Shackleton early-warning aircraft. With careful use of airbrakes and flap, it was just possible to match the Shackleton's normal cruising speed, but at low level there was little room for error. The intercepting fighter had to stay above the target – making a 'lights out' visident rather difficult, proving yet again the value of the two-man crew.

With our imminent return to the UK I had to turn my attention to family matters. Lack of continuity was a perennial problem for service children's education. Before his eleventh birthday Stuart had already attended five different schools. Only the very brightest pupils could cope with this degree of disruption, and most children were disadvantaged – so Jules and I decided that the time had come for Stuart to attend boarding school. Fortunately, at that time the Service Education Allowance covered three-quarters of the boarding fees.

Neither Jules nor I had any previous experience of this sort of thing. We elected to go for the south of England, because I was destined to attend the Air Warfare course, and after that I would probably do a staff tour. We spent hours poring over the list of schools, eventually narrowing it down to a short-list of two – Douai and The Oratory, both near Reading. The next step was to see what they were like and the family returned to the UK to make the final decision during the last week of February.

Douai was a fine school but a trifle too heavy on religion for Stuart. The Oratory, between Henley and Wallingford, was modern by comparison and seemed to our uneducated eyes better suited. Stuart also preferred The Oratory. With the benefit of hindsight, I am not sure now that we made the right choice.

With the main purpose of the leave fulfilled, we stopped off with Jerry and Olive Wells at RAF Coltishall. Jerry was now instructing on the Jaguar OCU. Next day, Saturday, Jules and Olive went shopping in Norwich while I took the children to see *Star Wars*, the newly released blockbuster film.

On Sunday a message came for me to call Wildenrath. When I got through, they passed on the sad news that Julie's mother had died. Jules took it well. Of course she was fond of her mother, but like me, I suppose, she had followed a different path.

We lodged the children with Jerry and Olive and drove to Shrewsbury for the funeral.

I was determined to enjoy the last eight weeks of my tour. Soon after I got back to Wildenrath the squadron received an invitation for three officers to attend Erkelenz's Karnival breakfast in the town hall. I took Norman and Banjo as my interpreters. Karnival is a typical German quasi-religious festival, a last fling before the restrictions of Lent. The breakfast was followed by a procession through the town, for which the squadron had entered a decorated float. We found ourselves standing on the float throwing sweets to the children. It was great fun and did much for the squadron's burgeoning liaison with the town.

I also let it be known on the squadron that, from now on, I expected to fly at least once a day. Unfortunately, the staffs at HQ RAF Germany had other ideas. On 16 March I was appointed president of a court martial to be held at RAF Laarbruch on 29 March. I could have done without that: this was serious stuff, and since three airmen were jointly charged with serious offences the case was far from straightforward. Fortunately, a judge advocate – a professional lawyer – would be in attendance, but I still had to bone up on my *Manual of Air Force Law*.

It was an interesting experience: on the second day we found the three guilty and awarded substantial prison sentences, although subsequently our findings were overturned because the German civil police identification procedures were ruled inadmissible in English law.

My tourex date had been brought forward to June so that I could return to the UK in time to start the Air Warfare course in July. The timing was unfortunate, in that it clashed with other commitments at Wildenrath. No. 19 Squadron was due to deploy to St Mawgan on 1 June for its annual APC and, because of a 2 ATAF Tactical Air Meet, the officers' hostel at Wildenrath would not be available for regular use. This meant Tim Gauvain would not be able to move his family to RAF Germany, and we would have nowhere to stay while Jules cleaned the quarter. It was annoying, but rather than complicate the hand-over I elected to stand down before the squadron deployed. We would have to make do with the restricted accommodation.

I took full advantage of my last chance to get in a full month's flying in April, and on the 10th of the month, with 'Noddy' Halsall as my navigator, I clocked up my thousand hours on the Phantom. The lads organised a celebratory glass of champagne on landing.

As expected, our social calendar was filed with farewell suppers and formal dinners, and the squadron dining-out night was a typically noisy affair. For reasons which I have never understood, the presenting of commemorative gifts had been banned, but on 19 Squadron we bypassed the ruling by paying a monthly contribution to the Silver Fund. In practice each officer thus paid for his own parting gift. I already had more than enough pewter tankards, so I chose a plain, silver-plated cigarette box. And I presented the squadron with a 'close painting' of the official squadron badge – the original had been lost long before the squadron had moved to Wildenrath.

We got home late on 28 April after our formal dining out from the mess. Paddy called from Weymouth almost straight away, with the news that Mum had been rushed into hospital with severe stomach pains. The prognosis was uncertain, and I felt slightly guilty at not being able to help. But at least Mum would get proper treatment. Henry and Therese had driven down to Weymouth to be on hand.

I didn't sleep much that night, and eventually sat in the lounge to watch the dawn come up. Mum had been very frail the last time we visited Weymouth, and she would often fall asleep in her armchair. I was never much concerned about her health before, but perhaps it was true that she had grown old before her time. Then again she had every right to be tired; she had lived through two world wars and had given birth to nine children, seven of whom had survived.

Both of Mum's parents had died of cancer, and she had a morbid fear of the disease. But even though she was physically worn out, her iron determination was undiminished.

Like many of her generation she did not approve of cohabiting before marriage, so in her eyes, Ian's and Karin's planned marriage – at Neuhausen, on 2 May – was vitally important. Mum was determined that nothing should stand in the way of the wedding, and she instructed Paddy not to tell Ian and Karin about her illness.

Henry called at eight o'clock in the morning to tell us that Mum had passed away, and I broke the sad news to Ian and Karin. Their immediate reaction was to delay the wedding, but we talked for a while and when they learned of Mum's dying wish they decided to go ahead. I am sure it was the right decision; whatever else the Bendells' religious upbringing had taught us, life was for the living.

Henry and Therese, with Jaquie and Therese's daughters Helen and Belinda, caught the night ferry and arrived at Wildenrath on 30 April. Later that day we drove in convoy to Stuttgart. I counted it a singular honour to be chosen as Ian's best man, and I was determined to make my speech in German. With Ian's help I cobbled together a few phonetic words for my parrot-fashion German. It was a quiet, registry office wedding; my only concern was that I might have difficulty signing the register – but more of that later.

The reception was held in one of the excellent local inns, and my speech went down well – until it came to my final joke about a farmer shooting a donkey between the eyes, and his new wife protesting. I should have said *shootzen*, but in my haste to get to the punch-line I said *shitzen* – which has an entirely different meaning. The assembled company erupted with laughter – well, at least I didn't have to explain that 'Ich niche spreken ze Deutsche'.

Altogether it was a truly memorable day, and I like to think that somehow Mum was watching over the proceedings.

Then it was a mad dash back to Wildenrath and on to Weymouth for the funeral. I managed to hitch a lift to Lyneham and back in an RAF Hercules – leaving Jules to make final preparations for a joint farewell party at our quarter with Stu and Andie Robertson.

I rolled up minutes before the party was due to start. This event was for the benefit of the squadron officers and their ladies, and it was a great success.

During the final month, much of my time was occupied with writing up the necessary officer's confidential reports. Generally I considered myself lucky to have had such a strong supporting team on 19 Squadron: all had worked extremely hard and they deserved credit – but to do them justice was a time-consuming business. It was also important to let each officer know where he could improve.

As it turned out there were few opportunities in May for me to fly. The squadron's main task was to practise air-to-air ciné against the banner in preparation for their forthcoming APC and, since I would be handing over to Tim Gauvain before they deployed to St Mawgan, it was inappropriate for me to use up valuable training hours.

On 18 May, after a standard low-level CAP sortie, I led four aircraft in close formation over a new stretch of autobahn, to coincide with its official opening by the Bergermeister of Erkelenz. A photograph of Willy Stein standing in the back of a vintage Mercedes, with the Phantom formation overhead, subsequently appeared in the local press.

On 26 May Norman Browne and myself flew our last sortie together on 19 Squadron.

On the same day I went to see Doc Russel to ask if he would refer me to a civilian specialist who might tell me what was wrong. Bill was quite surprised, until I explained that I was presenting an increasing number of worrying symptoms: the lack of feeling in my left hand; the inability to run; an occasional difficulty holding a pen – hence my concern at Ian's wedding; and an unaccustomed urgency to pee during happy hour. I was also deadly tired – although this could in part be attributed to the frenetic pace of life in the recent weeks.

But this felt like a different order of tiredness. I was utterly exhausted – and I was only sleeping fitfully. Individually, none of these symptoms was particularly disabling, but taken together they were cause for concern. I was losing confidence in my state of health. Something was wrong, and I suspected it might be serious.

Now, having completed a successful command tour, I was about to hand over all responsibility for 19 Squadron. The stress of command – which I doubted was ever the root cause of my problems – no longer existed and, since I didn't want to repeat the experiences of 1974, I thought the best course was to consult a civilian practitioner in the UK.

Of course there was no way Bill would refer me outside the service, but after listening he arranged for me to see the neurologist at RAF Wegberg, Squadron Leader D. G. Fowlie, that same afternoon.

Russel and Fowlie were the first two doctors who actually listened to what I had to say. After a lengthy consultation, Fowlie agreed that my symptoms were potentially serious. He could not do the necessary tests at Wegberg to make a firm diagnosis, but he made an appointment for me to see Wing Commander R. J. Davies at RAF Wroughton when I returned to the UK.

I was a bit choked when I handed over to Tim Gauvain on the morning of 27 May. In fact I had every reason to be pleased. Tim was taking over a highly proficient Phantom air-defence squadron. Graeme Smith was due to take over from Wally Walton, so the level of experience would be preserved. The squadron could not have been in better shape.

I bade a final farewell to the aircrews as they taxied out for their deployment to St Mawgan, then there was nothing left to do on Bravo dispersal, so I went home to help Jules with the packing. Everyone took back more from Germany than they arrived with, and with thirteen large Tri-wall packing cases we were no exception. Wildenrath was now wholly committed to the Tactical Air Meet, but after the interview with Doctor Fowlie I had neither the energy nor the inclination to become involved. We spent our final night at Wildenrath with our neighbours, Jean and Derrick Lewis – and departed the station in convoy, with Jules driving her Renault and me in the Maxi, on 7 June 1978.

14

Staff tours at Headquarters Strike Command; invalided from RAF

We moved into a married quarter at RAF Cranwell early in June. For me there was the dubious satisfaction of finally being selected to attend a senior staff course at the very same station to which I had been denied entry some twenty-five years before. Several former acquaintances of mine were stationed at Cranwell: Air Vice-Marshal David Harcourt-Smith was the commandant of the RAF college, and David Leech was now group captain operations on the staff of the College of Air Warfare. I also learned that Wing Commanders Frank Mitchell (ex HQ 38 Group) and Jack Pugh – who had just completed a tour as OC Ops Wing at Gutersloh – were due to join the same course.

I had two weeks' grace – which should have been a relaxing interlude after leaving my responsibilities as squadron commander at Wildenrath. The house at Cranwell was comfortable and, courtesy of Pickfords, our possessions had arrived from Germany with minimum damage. Last but not least, the children were safely installed in schools on the station – Stuart was not due to start at The Oratory until September. But after the total commitment of Germany I found it difficult to unwind, and the impending medical appointment at Wroughton hung like the proverbial Sword of Damocles.

On 18 June I took the train to Swindon, Wroughton's joining instructions having discouraged the use of private transport. I didn't know what to expect.

Ward 12 was reserved for neurological patients. Was I some kind of nutcase? I was even more alarmed to hear that all patients arriving on Ward 12 were automatically given a lumbar puncture – a macabre sort of initiation ceremony. To those in the medical profession a lumbar puncture is a minor procedure – but I had done it all before, several times over, and I certainly didn't relish the thought of that wretched headache. Fortunately, the following morning when I saw the consultant neurologist, Wing Commander Roy Davies, he suggested that the results of my previous lumbar puncture at Wroughton, in September 1975, might be sufficient.

No doubt I had physically deteriorated since I was last in the clutches of the doctors, and the tests at Wroughton, which were similar to those done at the National Hospital in London, proved it. Now, with my eyes closed, I had lost all sense of balance. By feel alone, with either hand, I could no longer tell the difference between a golf ball and a matchbox. And how was it possible to mistake a fifty pence piece for a ball of cotton wool?

They repeated the chequer-board test, and the technician explained that one of its purposes was to measure the reaction of the optic nerves. There was a significant difference between my right and left eye, which might explain why I still occasionally suffered from double vision.

On the Wednesday I was driven to RAF Halton for a brain scan. That at least was new.

Roy Davies called me into his office on Thursday and quietly broke the news that I had multiple sclerosis – usually abbreviated to MS.

My initial reaction was one of great relief. At last someone had put a name to the illness that was causing all my alarming symptoms: the pins and needles at Andoya; the fibrositis at Camberley; and of course the double vision at Bruggen. At last I knew I was not going mad. It was only later, after Roy Davies discussed the disease in more detail, that the true significance struck home. There is no cure and no effective treatment for MS, so it was welcome to the grey world of the incurably ill. But as Davies pointed out, MS is seldom life-threatening. At that time I still had aspirations of promotion to group captain and, now that my career was likely to be cut short, promotion seemed even more important, if only to ensure the best possible pension. Roy Davies hastened to assure me that I should have no immediate worries on that score – his report would only state that my central nervous system (CNS) was damaged.

With these thoughts (and many more besides) whirling around in my brain, I called Jules and asked her to pick me up from Grantham on Friday evening. I had intended to delay telling her about the MS until

I got back, but she insisted. I hadn't even sorted out my own thoughts on the subject, let alone figured out a way to soften the blow. Of one thing I was certain: my having MS must remain confidential – at least for the time being. Looking back, this self-imposed burden was unnecessary.

Fortunately, the Air Warfare course was informative rather than testing, so I had plenty of time to come to terms with my predicament. My main concern was that I wouldn't be able to cope with all the travelling. In those days the Air Warfare course travelled extensively by bus, and I had to plan carefully so that I could hold on between rest breaks. There was only one occasion at which I came close to being seriously embarrassed. After a five-day tour, we were on our way home, on the A34 near Abingdon, when the coach broke down. The coach driver set off to find a telephone, and the choice for the passengers was either to stay aboard or hike the short distance to RAF Abingdon. Aware of the need to be close to a toilet, I joined Jack Pugh and the others as they struck out for Abingdon. It should have been an easy two-mile stroll along country lanes, but after a mile my bag weighed a ton and my right leg was visibly seizing up. I muttered something about a badly ricked ankle, to explain why I was limping – the first of many excuses I would use in the coming months to maintain the charade of good health.

With Jack's help I eventually made it to Abingdon, but it was a salutary reminder for me to be more careful in future.

The major writing task on the course was to produce a five-thousand-word paper on a given military subject. There was a wealth of experience within the student body, and the papers often presented innovative ideas which were subsequently submitted to the appropriate MoD staffs for consideration. Had it been left to individual choice, I would have written a paper on airspace management in the Central Region. But three of us – Frank Mitchell, Graham Pitchfork and myself – were tasked to produce a joint paper on AST 03, the air staff target to select a replacement aircraft for the Harrier and Jaguar for use in the close air support role in the 1980s and beyond. It was a challenging project, and we spent many hours discussing the various options during the interminable bus journeys.

As far as I can remember the Harrier offered far better potential for development than the Jaguar. The Harrier could react faster and, due to dispersed operations, it was relatively invulnerable to counter-attack from the air. Against this had to be balanced the Jaguar's greater weapons load and better reliability. The Jaguar was the first British military aircraft to have reliability and ease of maintenance included in its design specification. But at the time, for precision close air support, both the Harrier and the Jaguar were limited to daylight attack, delivering their weapons from close range. And both aircraft were committed to overflying the target, making them vulnerable to hand-held guided missiles. So, while we recommended that the Harrier should be developed further, we concluded that in future the best option for close air support would be an armed helicopter equipped with stand-off, all-weather, guided weapons.

After much badgering by successive commanding officers, my brother Tim was finally persuaded to apply for a commission, and he arrived at Cranwell for his initial officer training in July. It was good to meet up again, although neither of us had much time to socialise. I watched his passing-out parade, where the salute was taken by my previous boss, Air Vice-Marshal Peter Bairsto.

Tim invited Jules and me to the graduation dinner. We also managed to get over to Coningsby for a meal with Tony and Jann Tucker at Ratty's. Tony had recently retired from the RAF.

I had an interesting conversation with Mary Mitchell when she attended the autumn ball at Cranwell. Apparently, following my double vision episode at Bruggen and the desperate day when she and Jules had picked me up from Luton, her brother-in-law, who was a doctor, had suggested that I was possibly suffering from MS. How right he was. But I couldn't admit it, even to Mary.

Towards the end of the course Bill Wratten – now serving on the Air Secretary's staff at Barnwood – came to announce the course postings. Frank Mitchell and Graham Pitchfork both got operational front-line flying squadrons. Having had six months rest I envied them, but there was no going back for me. Instead I was posted to Headquarters Strike Command as the command flight safety officer (CFSO).

I had always preferred to keep a healthy distance from flight safety. Not that I had anything against flight safety per se; it was just that at squadron level safety reporting procedures generated mountains of paperwork. On the few occasions I had become directly involved, I had been an unwilling member of a board of inquiry, anxious to get it over with and get back to flying. So this was a new area for me.

When the other members of the course heard about my posting they chuckled and muttered darkly about poacher turned gamekeeper.

Despite my concern, Strike Command at RAF High Wycombe probably was the best location for me to cope with long-term disability. The family would be close to our friends, and Stuart, now safely installed at The Oratory, would be less than an hour away.

To my surprise, the 'dream team' of Mitchell, Pitchfork and Bendell won the Plenderleith Commemorative prize for the best paper written during the course, and our names were duly inscribed in the memorial book. Of course, we knew our ideas on AST 403 would never be politically acceptable to the RAF staffs – armed helicopters and their ilk were traditionally procured and controlled by the army and navy – and as far as I know nothing more was done about our paper. But honour was satisfied some years later, during the Gulf War, when American helicopters armed with guided weapons were used with devastating effect against the Iraqi forces.

On 14 December 1978 we moved into a married quarter at RAF High Wycombe and I took over from Wing Commander Pat King, whom I had first met at Jever in 1957. By now the famous wartime RAF commands – bomber, fighter, coastal and transport – had reverted to Group status within Strike Command. The AOC in 'C' Strike Command – Air Chief Marshal Sir David Evans – commanded all operational RAF forces in the UK.

Headquarters Strike Command was so large it was humourously referred to as MoD West. Headquarters Air Support Command, at RAF Brampton, commanded the necessary training and technical support facilities for the front line.

On reflection my attitude to flight safety was probably the same as any other professional aircrew. In a peacetime air force it is all a question of striking the right balance between flight safety and realistic training. While there is always an element of risk in military flying, there is no point in killing people just for the sake of realism. The system of checks and balances in use in the RAF reduces those risks to a minimum. I had always worked on the premise that accidents caused through lack of foresight were entirely avoidable.

Traditionally, in the RAF, the boss of the squadron sets the standards, and the flight commanders ensure that his policy is applied. On 19 Squadron I was prepared to listen to advice from any quarter, but I made the final decision and no one was left in any doubt. The *modus operandi* of the Flight Safety Branch at the headquarters had evolved over the years to suit the senior air staffs. As the CFSO, I answered directly to the senior air staff officer (SASO) – Air Vice-Marshal Mike Knight. My staff consisted to two pilot specialist aircrew squadron leaders, Glyn Chapman and Dave Bourne, an engineer squadron leader, Dave Johncock, and a retired squadron leader, Jack Wheeler, who edited the *Strike Command Flight Safety Review*. We were supported by an all-civilian registry staff of two clerical assistants and a typist. Rumour had it that I personally vetted the Flight Safety Registry's staff. Of course it wasn't true, but the story was too good to deny, and I have to admit the two clerical assistants, Lynda and Jo, added a refreshing touch of glamour to the corridor. Our typist, Carol Linehan, was worth her weight in gold. Small wonder the Flight Safety Registry was the centre of attention for all the young bloods, and occasionally an older roué. Ours was a close-knit, happy, working staff.

During my time as CFSO there was an average of between twelve to seventeen major accidents per year in Strike Command, about one third of these being fatal. There was nothing particularly new about these figures. Obviously, each type of aircraft was technically unique, and approximately half of our accidents were due to some sort of technical failure; from a staffing point of view, these occurrences were usually straightforward. Of the remaining fifty per cent, half were due to some sort of natural hazard – bird strikes, weather, etc. – and the rest might at some point have involved human error. These were more difficult to resolve. The age-old pilot errors were still being made, but these accidents were often due to a culmination of factors. In some air forces the question of blame for a flying accident is deferred to a separate court hearing, but consideration of negligence falls within the remit of a properly convened RAF board of inquiry. For this reason negligence is precisely defined in Queen's Regulations. Even so, considerations of blameworthiness remain a difficult area. Clearly it is inappropriate to assume negligence if the precise cause of the accident cannot be established, but this can be complicated by other factors. For example, if the aircraft was deliberately being flown contrary to regulations – then there must be an element of negligence.

Every accident had to be investigated, and it was the responsibility of the relevant group commander to convene the boards of inquiry. At this stage we simply maintained a watching brief. On completion, the boards were passed to Headquarters Strike Command for further staffing and the drafting of comments for the AOC in C. In fact the staffing of boards of enquiry formed the bulk of our work. First we passed the board to the relevant desk officer for comment. In the meantime one of my staff would summarise the board, reducing it to some twenty pages, the concise summary leading logically to a considered, balanced comment. Occasionally we found inconsistencies, and the board would have to be sent back for reconsideration. Contrary to the popular belief that senior staff officers are far goo busy to plough through many pages of turgid detail, most would read the boards from cover to cover before releasing their draft comments. The work was interesting, although it could be frustrating when some staff officers agonised over the precise wording of a piece of work. On one occasion our summary had to be redrafted fourteen times before it was accepted – and the final draft was remarkably similar to the first. I think it was Bill Maish who coined the title of 'wordsmith' for the CFSO's task.

The CFSO post was considered to be high profile. There were certain advantages in working directly for the senior executive staff (the SASO, the DC in C, and the AOC in C), but it was a double-edged sword. Regardless of the hour, it was my job to inform the senior staffs whenever an accident occurred. Thus I was constantly on call and, on most occasions, I was the bearer of ill tidings. It was difficult to avoid the flak, but Mike Knight had a light touch.

I usually got into the office by 0820 hours in time to read the overnight flight safety signals and be ready to field questions at the SASO's morning briefing. This was attended by the principal air staff officers. I remember after one freezing night when, to keep warm, the RAF police guard on an aircraft dispersal had rerouted a ground equipment heating duct and had inadvertently started a fire. The group captain security was extremely selective reporting this incident, and simply suggested to SASO that the guard deserved a 'good show' for extinguishing the fire. He might just have got away with it, had I not pointed out that his men had started the fire in the first place.

Ever the optimist, I had hoped that once we were settled in at High Wycombe the MS would remain in remission, but slowly over the next six months I stiffened up. I had to abandon my bicycle as a means of getting to work, and even the short walk from the car to the office was becoming difficult. I was running out of excuses for my shambling gait; but it was probably the rumour – behind my back, as it were – that I had a drink problem that finally forced me to come clean.

First I cleared it with Roy Davies. He agreed it was sensible to let my boss know that I had MS, and in the meantime he arranged for me to start a course of adrenocorticotrophic hormone (ACTH). Normally administered by injection in hospital, at room temperature ACTH has the consistency of thick syrup, but I preferred to be treated as an out-patient at the station's medical centre.

In fact Mike Knight was away at the time, so I spoke to his deputy, Air Commodore Ray Davenport. I also called Bill Wratten at Barnwood; as the desk officer responsible for my postings plot, he had an immediate interest. Fortunately the CFSO post was not much sought after, and Bill kindly arranged for me to remain at Strike Command for the foreseeable future.

ACTH was not a cure – no doctor could actually explain how it worked other than to suggest that it reduced inflammation – but it offered temporary relief from the symptoms of MS. The course of treatment lasted for twelve days – eighty units for the first three days, slowly reducing to twenty. For me the effect was quite dramatic: on the first evening I vividly remember standing unaided and walking normally for the first time in many months (an exaggerated burst of energy was a known side-effect of ACTH). Other side-effects, such as the disturbance of sleep patterns, the retention of body fluids and the complete loss of taste, were less welcome – but I would willingly have accepted these if the drug had provided lasting relief. Unfortunately the beneficial effects of the drug wore off as the dosage rates reduced.

Over the next eighteen months I had four more courses of ACTH, and the effectiveness of the drug reduced each time I took it. By 1980 I was getting little benefit at all, and in December of that year I stopped taking it.

One of the great frustrations of having MS is that you can no longer plan ahead – your future is uncertain – and that saps your confidence. I have to say though that the dropping of the charade of fitness was a great relief – not only for myself, but also for Jules.

In due course we had to tell the children; it would have been grossly unfair and probably unsuccessful to attempt to do otherwise. As children often do, they took it in their stride. Not having to move every two years also brought its advantages – Emma could settle down at the local school and Jules took a job as a tracer in a civil engineering company.

Some people are embarrassed by illness. Even some of my associates at work avoided contact – they just didn't know what to say – but they soon came round when they realised I hadn't changed and that I didn't mind talking about MS. As a professional officer I was still prepared to give of my best, but no one was going to push me around. In theory, a medical downgrading should not debar promotion, but in a highly competitive RAF career, having MS was a grave disadvantage. For all practical purposes my fate was sealed.

The admission that I had MS also marked a turning point in my attitude to the disease. Prior to this I had simply coped with each episode of impairment as it arose. It was not exactly a case of passive submission, but neither had I taken any positive steps to fight back. In an effort to find out more I sought advice from the MS Society. They were very pleasant, but appeared to concentrate on outings and social events rather than therapy. I suppose I was a bit wound up by then, but what really put me off was a bland statement in one of their magazines that the best way of dealing with MS was to ignore it. Clearly these people were living on a different planet. But they did suggest some useful reference material, and many years later I made use of an excellent respite care home subsidised by the society.

What is MS? The first point to make is that every patient with MS is different: their symptoms are unique, and the progression of the disease may well be different. By the same token there is little to gain from comparing MS patients. It might help to visualise the CNS – that is, the brain and the spinal cord – as the body's main electrical circuit. Every nerve fibre in the CNS is encased in a fatty tissue called myelin which provides nourishment and insulation. Messages are transmitted from the brain or the spinal cord to the muscles, which either contract or relax to make the desired movement. Sclerosis is Latin for scar. For reasons not yet fully understood, when MS strikes, the body's immune system attacks the myelin sheath; this causes a plaque and eventually a scar which reduces the efficiency of the nerves. In simple terms, the messages to the muscles are no longer properly co-ordinated. A signal to tell a muscle to contract may not arrive at the same time as the signal to tell the opposing muscle group to relax – a condition known as ataxia. With MS the physical damage is limited to the central nervous system, but its effects can manifest themselves in any part of the body. Often, with cruel perversity, MS strikes at the limbs and skills vital to normal work – professional cameramen have been known to lose their sight, teachers slur their speech, and musicians lose their hearing and manual dexterity. In 1979 there were at least 50,000 confirmed cases of MS in the United Kingdom.

Less than 3% of the cases of MS are malignant – meaning the onset is serious and rapid, leading to death within three years. This form of MS is more commonly seen in younger age-groups. In the vast majority of cases the pattern of the disease either presents itself as a series of well-defined relapses and remissions or as a chronic deterioration. The prognosis seems to depend on the person's age. Typically, if MS strikes in the mid-twenties it is likely to go into remission, sometimes for years, before striking again; but if it first strikes in the mid- to late-forties the difference between each relapse and remission is much less marked. With advancing age even the relapsing/remitting form of MS tends to become chronic – but there are no hard and fast rules. Everyone is different.

Bearing in mind that I had already suffered from MS for at least nine years, I was in reasonable shape. My reserves of energy were low, but the only other symptoms were a slight loss of co-ordination and occasional double vision. I could only walk for about fifteen minutes before I had to stop and rest. When muscles are not regularly exercised they tend to shorten, which further reduces the range of movement.

So, after completing the course of ACTH, I started regular physiotherapy at RAF Halton. By limiting my physiotherapy to lunchtime sessions, I was able to continue working normally. Similar to other people with MS, I was badly affected by heat and stress. I also suffered from fatigue; sometimes after physiotherapy I could scarcely walk.

Life throws up some odd coincidences. Within weeks of admitting to MS we learned of a dozen or so other victims. Stuart's housemaster at The Oratory, Michael Connolly, who had recently been diagnosed, invited Jules and me to the first meeting of what was to become the Reading branch of ARMS. This is a charitable organisation concentrating on research into the disease. To my way of thinking, ARMS was far more positive than the MS Society, although Reading was too far away for me to become actively involved. The Reading branch was about to start an extended trial on diet. I was never convinced that diet was the principal factor in MS, but there was good evidence to suggest that it played some part. MS is more prevalent in the temperate latitudes, both north and south of the equator, but within this distribution there are known to be focal points. For example, in Norway the disease is concentrated in the inland areas, where the diet is rich in dairy produce, yet in the coastal regions, where the diet is predominantly fish, the incidence of MS is rare. On the strength of this, Jules decided that a change of diet might help, so we switched to a low-fat regime avoiding saturated animal fats. We tried to eat fish at least once a week.

My father died on Christmas Eve 1979. Since losing Mum he had become a sad, lonely old man. He didn't want to move away from his friends in Weymouth, yet he was unable to look after himself. His health had deteriorated. After a bout of food poisoning during the summer and worsening emphysema, he was admitted to hospital. The rest of the family did their best to help. Jules and I drove down on the Friday to sit with him but I had to get back to High Wycombe to complete my final course of ACTH.

Dad died two days later.

My father didn't have much to show for seventy years' hard living. He didn't leave a will, and it took me a week to sort out his personal affairs. The whole family came to the funeral. In one hectic afternoon we shared out the few personal possessions and shut up the house. I had been paying Dad's mortgage since 1965, and if I had been in better health we might have held on to the house, but I was unsure of the future and Weymouth was the wrong area. Eventually I sold the house and raised enough money for a deposit on a property in the High Wycombe area.

I could still do a full day's work, but by now I needed a walking stick to get around. Fortunately the CFSO's job did not require much travelling: just one annual flight safety symposium at one of the main flying stations for the group and station flight-safety staffs – which I chaired – and an occasional visit to the Inspectorate of Flight Safety at Adastral House. For the latter I was always given service transport.

Of course I was well supported, both by my staff and my superiors. During my time as CFSO, in addition to Mike Knight I served John Fitzpatrick and Laurie Jones. At the MoD, the successive inspectors of flight safety – Ken Hayr, David Leech and Tom Stonor – were all friends of mine. For the most part I could also count on co-operation from other senior staff officers at HQ Strike Command. One or two thought I was inclined to be flippant, but they didn't appreciate that humour was all that was left of my much-depleted self-confidence.

The headquarters participated in the usual preparation for war exercises, and in these, the flight safety staffs were responsible for an airspace deconfliction programme. It was a poor substitute for positive close control, but this would only come with the introduction of sophisticated airborne command and control systems. My problem with no-notice call-outs was that I could not respond rapidly.

It is a mistake to think that flight-safety staffs had a direct influence on the aircraft accident rates. The best that we could do was to draw attention to the likely hazards by way of the flight safety publicity and by publishing the findings of selective incident and accident reports. But with two aircraft types – the Jaguar and the Hunter – perhaps I can claim to have improved the RAF's accident record.

By 1980, Strike Command had had fourteen major Jaguar accidents for which no satisfactory explanation could be found. These accidents invariably culminated in high-speed impact with the ground, and they were all fatal. SASO asked me to investigate. Obviously something was wrong – and why were there no successful bail-outs? After studying the boards of inquiry it struck me that in all cases the interval between the time the aircraft was known to be under normal control and the subsequent crash was extremely short – typically less than ten seconds. At first glance there was nothing strange about that – the Jaguar usually operated at low level, where the safety margins were reduced – but in one accident the aircraft was known to be above 10,000 ft when it appeared to have gone out of control. This was a dual-instrument training sortie, and the instructor had just asked for clearance to practise unusual positions. In this routine the instructor puts the aircraft into an extreme attitude and the student has to recover, purely on instruments – it is part of a standard RAF instrument-rating test. But in this case the aircraft crashed within nine seconds. The other common factors were: all the aircraft were fitted with underwing fuel tanks, and all the accidents occurred within thirty minutes of take-off, when the underwing tanks would have been only partially empty. There was no evidence of any aircraft breaking up in the air but, since no emergency calls were made, presumably whatever was happening was both sudden and violent.

According to the records at the MoD there was one other similar Jaguar accident, which occurred during the release-to-service trials at Boscombe Down. It involved a dual aircraft, fitted with external stores. The test crew, Colin Cruickshanks and Clive Rustin, were investigating the aircraft's flight limitations, including how far and how rapidly bank could be applied. Fortunately they started the test at high level, because shortly after applying moderate aileron the aircraft suddenly departed from normal flight. The manoeuvre was so violent that the pilot lost his grip on the controls. They could not regain control, and both crew members successfully ejected at about 4000 ft (just 4 seconds before ground impact). Ideally a fighter/bomber aircraft should have full freedom of roll but, as a result of the Boscombe Down trials, among other restrictions with fuel in the underwing tanks, the Jaguar was restricted to low rates of roll at a minimum of plus 1g. From my experience of ground attack, I knew how difficult it would be to comply with this essential limitation.

Putting two and two together I surmised through familiarity in squadron service that insufficient attention was being paid to the Jaguar's release to service and, in all probability, the aircraft was being flown beyond its limits.

My paper was sent to HQ 38 Group and the Jaguar OCU for comment. They made a great song and dance about it and denied that there had been any malpractice, but they were ordered to modify the training syllabus and to comply strictly with the release to service. The unexplained Jaguar accidents ceased.

The case of the Hunter was relatively straightforward. In 1983, after thirty years in service, the aircraft was beginning to show its age. We were still using the Hunter as a lead-in for advanced training and for providing flying experience for crews holding between OCU courses. Many senior staff officers had fond memories of the Hunter, so it was unpopular to suggest that the time had come to say goodbye. On the face of it the aircraft was still reliable, except for a few worrying, inadvertent releases. When things start to drop off aircraft you have to ask questions. Quite simply, the Hunter's wiring was wearing out and, when I looked at the servicing man-hours required for each flying hour, I found that the servicing load had tripled in three years. I drew this to the attention of the deputy commander, Air Marshal Sir Peter Bairsto, and a short while later the single-seat Hunters were withdrawn from service. Statistically, that probably saved Strike Command five or six accidents a year.

In November 1980 my MES was permanently downgraded to A4 G3 Z4, meaning that I was only fit to fly as a passenger and I was restricted to temperate climates. I could hardly complain – the RAF doctors had delayed the formal decision for as long as possible – but the immediate effect was that I lost my flying pay and took a salary cut of some £200 per month.

I must have been doing something right, because in the New Year I was appointed as an officer of the Order of the British Empire (OBE). This honour came as a complete surprise and, in due course, the family accompanied me to Buckingham Palace for the investiture. Afterwards we had lunch with the Harwoods and Peter Saddler at the RAF Club.

In the following years several wacky treatments and extreme diets were hailed as miracle cures for MS. For example, the snake-bite treatment, where for a price one could check into a clinic in Florida for the doubtful privilege of being injected with rattlesnake venom. I also tried acupuncture from an amateur practitioner at the CME, but like many MS patients I soon developed a healthy scepticism for such claims. With an incurable illness, whenever you try something new you are apt to get a psychological lift – and then you are reluctant to give up the treatment, just in case it is actually doing some good. If you adopted them all you could finish up with a very strange way of life. So I tended to ask the question – could I live with this regime? I was neither brave enough nor desperate enough to take on extreme new treatments for MS, unless of course there were a definite cure. But none appeared, and I slowly deteriorated.

Up to now it had been convenient to live in service married quarters, moving the family around in gipsy fashion from posting to posting. But ill-health had changed all that – I was no longer mobile. In theory I could be asked to leave the service at any time. Although, having said that, the RAF had a well-deserved reputation for their considerate treatment of those suffering medical problems.

Every six months I was examined by Roy Davies. Usually he could not detect a significant change, but I knew the disease was slowly taking its course.

In all this uncertainty it was important for the family to put down roots, and in April 1981, after scouring the local area for private accommodation, we bought a house in Walters Ash. It wasn't our ideal home, but it was adequate for our needs, and it was barely a mile from the headquarters. We fully expected to move elsewhere when the children finished their education and I retired but, even as I write some fifteen years later, we are still living comfortably in the same house.

In July of that year we spent an enjoyable family holiday with Ian and Karin, Henry and Joyce and their children, Jackie and Andrew, and my sister Paddy. Karin had borrowed a rambling mountain chalet just outside Unken, a small Austrian village eighteen miles south-west of Salzburg. For those of us travelling from the UK, Austria was a tedious three-day drive, both there and back – but it was worth it. I had just bought a new Honda Accord, which was a joy to drive. We took the scenic route, night-stopping at Longuyon and Stuttgart. The chalet was comfortable and there was plenty to keep us all occupied in Austria. The holiday clashed with the wedding of Prince Charles and Lady Diana Spencer and, because of that, Jules had threatened to cancel, but Henry jury-rigged a TV aerial and we saw it all on an ancient black-and-white set. The children probably remember the swimming pool and the salt mines, and the adults will remember the ice caves. I wasn't fit enough to sample either of these but, with Henry and Paddy, I viewed the Grossglockner glacier a twelve-mile river of ice slowly gouging a broad valley through the mountains – one of the most powerful forces in nature that, since the last ice age, had sculpted much of western Europe into its present form. We also visited Hitler's 'eagles' nest', now converted to a grand tea-room overlooking Berchtesgaden. I think we all enjoyed eating out.

On the return journey we again stopped at Stuttgart, but took a different route back to the UK through Luxemburg and Belgium, night-stopping at Bastogne, of Battle of the Bulge fame.

In an unexpected coup on 2 April 1982 Argentine forces seized the Falkland Islands. After the well-publicised withdrawal from our commitments in both the Far and Middle East, there is little doubt that Argentina's military junta was convinced that Britain was neither willing nor able to retaliate. It was a reasonable assumption – had not Margaret Thatcher been Prime Minister. But as history records, within three days a British South Atlantic task force sailed from Portsmouth. The Royal Navy took the leading role in Operation Corporate but, right from the outset, Strike Command's forces played a significant part. The RAF was closely involved with resupply through Wideawake airfield on Ascension Island, and later with offensive action by Harrier aircraft from No. 1 Squadron and Victor and Nimrod aircraft.

In a reversal of national policy, expenditure on defence was sharply increased. Trials that in peacetime would take months to complete were completed in days. Ships were refurbished, modified and pressed into service. Great strides were made in long-distance communications. Air power was enhanced by the development of the ski-ramp modification to the Navy's carriers and by the widespread adoption of air-to-air refuelling. All committed Harriers were fitted with AIM 9L (Sidewinder) missiles. Laser-guided bombs and Shrike anti-radiation missiles were procured from the United States. Many of the desk officers based at High Wycombe were actively employed in the ops room deep in the bowels of the old Bomber Command bunker. But all I could do was watch from the sidelines.

Operation Corporate was a stunning success. The Argentine forces surrendered on 14 June, and within a week my old friend Bill Wratten was on his way to take over as the first station commander at RAF Stanley. Life at High Wycombe returned to normal.

In due course Roy Davies retired and was replaced by Wing Commander 'Bob' Merry. I was somewhat concerned – after all, the RAF's neurological consultant was the master of my fate – but Bob

Merry was, and still is, a charming chap. In February 1983 he arranged for me to be admitted to the RAF's medical rehabilitation unit at Headley Court for two weeks' intensive physiotherapy.

When I first went there, Headley Court was used for the treatment of RAF officers and senior NCOs, with occasional patients of similar rank from the army, and civilian employees from the MoD. The big house at Headley Court, which is used as the officers' mess, was originally owned by Lord Cunliffe and was completed at the turn of the century. He made a hobby of collecting panelling from old houses, and many of these are still preserved. There is no wallpaper in the house; from cellar to attic, every room is lined with wainscot – and most of it is very old. The Jacobean panelling (dating from 1619) in one bedroom is believed to have come from Hinchingbroke Castle, and legend has it this panelling brought with it the ghost of one of Cromwell's sisters. I never saw the lady myself, but allegedly she was dressed in green and regularly appeared descending the main staircase – presumably heading for the bar. Apparently the ghost has now been exorcised. Which is sad – I can well believe in the spirit world – after all, who of us can be certain we have never seen a ghost? But to return to temporal matters – in 1949 Headley Court was gifted to the RAF as a charitable trust on condition that it be used as a medical rehabilitation unit for flying personnel. The aim was to return those who had been either injured or seriously ill to full physical fitness in the shortest possible time.

I was still able to get around using my walking stick, but I hadn't bargained on the chill, blustery wind. At the entrance to the station headquarters I was literally blown off my feet. It was not the first time I had fallen, and it certainly would not be the last. At the time I could just about get up on my own, but people appeared from every corner of Headley Court. I was given an immediate dressing down – apparently it is a rule at Headley that if you have to use a stick, you must always use two.

The treatment at Headley was tailored to meet the needs of the individual. Each day started with ten minutes of warm-up exercises followed by intense physiotherapy and occupational therapy. Lunch was taken in the mess, and treatment was continued in the afternoon. The programme was specifically designed for those recovering from physical injury. Indeed, most of the patients either had sports injuries or had been involved in road traffic accidents – although on later occasions there were a few casualties from the Falklands. Typically the sporting injured would arrive at Headley Court, disabled and underconfident, and six to eight weeks later they would emerge fully mended in mind and body. It was different for the neurological cases. The effectiveness of treatment following brain injury or stroke, or even MS, was far less predictable. The fact that neurological damage did not always respond to repetitive exercise and hard work flew in the face of the Headley Court ethos. The fitness freaks' cliché of 'no pain, no gain' no longer applied. If my calf muscles were stretched a fraction too far my leg would go into a ramrod spasm that even the beefiest physical training instructor could not break. But the physiotherapists trained to deal with neurological cases were outstanding. I remember Sergeant Dave Flint was particularly successful with me. Mind you, he had his own brand of torture, like immersing a foot or a hand in a bucket of crushed ice and water for ten minutes or so to reduce spasticity. If you don't think that's painful, try it some time.

I attended Headley Court on three further occasions, two in 1984 and the final session in March 1986. By 1985 the centre had been expanded, with additional treatment facilities and a forty-bed hospital, to cater for the needs of all ranks in all of the UK's armed services. By now my right side was becoming progressively more disabled. My right toe dropped, causing the foot to drag. Even more disabling was a frozen right shoulder that severely restricted arm movement, and my right hand was beginning to curl like a bird's claw. I could still write with it, but I had to use an elastic band to wrap my fingers around the pen.

It is difficult to define precisely the benefits I got from Headley Court. No doubt the physiotherapy slowed the debilitating progress of MS, but exercise is not a cure. In March 1986 I was fitted with a splint to counter the toe drop, but my right shoulder failed to respond to painful cortisone injections into the joint. Aside from the treatment I met some remarkably brave people at Headley Court – it was a humbling experience.

But get back to 1983. In August I was warned that I would be posted to take over as the deputy senior personnel staff officer (DSPSO) at

High Wycombe in December. It was not a punishment posting: after five years as the CFSO and five more on continuous call-out, my practical experience was becoming dated and it was time for a change. But I was worried; this was a completely new area for me. Whilst I was well used to the CFSO's job I knew nothing about personnel staff work, and I was not sure I could handle the change. I remember discussing it with the Allens when they invited the family down for a short sailing break on the Solent. Of course there was no point in whinging about it – besides, I needed a break.

I took over as the DSPSO from Wing Commander 'George' Etches on 13 December. The P2 branch, for which I was responsible, dealt with routine personnel matters arising from commissioned officers serving in Strike Command. My immediate boss was Group Captain Derrick Spackman (later succeeded by Group Captain D. E. 'Min' Larkin), and he reported directly to AOA – Air Vice-Marshal Keith Sanderson. I had two squadron leaders working for me – Mike Webb and Janie Henderson – plus a retired officer, Tony Sargeant, and a civilian clerical officer – as well as a small clerical staff to run the registry. I was also the first reporting officer for Squadron Leader 'Roger' Langdon, who was filling the South Atlantic Admin Co-ordination post. As a recent war zone, far removed from traditional RAF transport links, the Falklands had many varied and immediate needs. Much of the staff work was done through teleprinter/satellite communication links, although telephonic voice communication was also available. South Atlantic business was crisis management on a grand scale.

At that time the RAF was just introducing computers to streamline and improve the conventional paper-driven systems. But during the transition period access to computers was limited, and we found ourselves having to maintain both paper and computer records. Officers' postings were handled entirely by Barnwood, and we simply maintained a watching brief; we also had ready access to officers' records. But annual confidential reporting was never computerised, and this provided a steady flow of work.

Unlike criminal offences, which were subject to the due process of law (i.e. police investigation, summary of evidence and court martial) and dealt with the P1 staffs, the P2 branch staffed adverse reports raised on officers who had infringed Queen's Regulations. These covered a wide range of misdemeanours contrary to the good order and discipline of the service. I have to say it was an area which, in itself, was often misunderstood. For example, when an officer was convicted of a drink-drive offence by a civilian court, an adverse report was also raised by the RAF. Some would claim this was unfair and amounted to double punishment for the same crime, but that would exaggerate the severity of the service's action – usually the offending officer would be interviewed and admonished by his AOC. When viewed in the context that the RAF had a right to expect exceptionally high standards of behaviour from its officers, the system of special reporting was eminently fair. With the possible exception of drink-drive offences, the raising of a formal adverse report usually was the last resort following the officer's failure to heed informal warnings. There was seldom any doubt about the validity of such reports, and our staffing procedures were similar to those used in the flight safety branch. We staffed the reports and drafted comments for AOA. When a report was approved, AOA would direct that appropriate action be taken. Contrary to popular belief, special adverse reports were not considered during promotion boards.

However, if the nature of the offence was serious enough to recommend discharge from the Service, the case would be remanded for consideration by the Air Force Board. In my experience their lordships were inclined to be lenient, even when the defendant was a total loser. On the other hand, cases of deviant sexual behaviour invariably resulted in dismissal from the service.

Some of the situations we dealt with were highly amusing, but overall the staffing of special adverse reports was a tacky business. I once confided to a fellow officer, who was more widely experienced than me in such matters, that much of my time was taken up with individuals who deserved least. He said that was always the way – and, of course, he was right.

On 1 March 1984 Ken Hayr – now the air officer commanding No. 11 Group – organised a 66 Squadron reunion dinner at Bentley Priory. Sir Peter Bairsto was due to retire later that year, so this was also a farewell dinner for the boss and Lady Bairsto. It was a memorable evening, which no less than twenty officers attended with their ladies. Needless to say, after a quarter of a century many of us were showing our age, but memories were still bright and the hangar doors stayed open far into the night. Then, on 11 May, I drove with John Nevill and Bill Hobby to RAF Coltishall for No. 6 Squadron's 70th anniversary dinner night. King Hussein of Jordan was the guest of honour. I spoke to him later that evening and he remembered meeting Jules in the toilet at Coningsby.

The problem with squadron reunions is that you seldom meet the mates you served with when the squadron was the best in the air force. In fact we three were the only representatives of the heady Phantom era. No doubt these Jaguar pilots were worthy successors, and they were certainly polite, but I came away with a slightly uncomfortable feeling that I had somehow intruded on someone else's private party.

It is known from post-mortem evidence that with MS, the damage caused to the CNS is very similar to that found in deep sea divers afflicted with the bends. The only recognised treatment for the bends was immediate repressurisation. In 1982, ARMS sponsored a study of hyperbaric oxygen – that is, the breathing of oxygen in a pressure chamber. The results suggested there might be some benefit. It is standard practice to breathe oxygen in high-performance aircraft, and at Wildenrath, when unbeknown to me I was already affected by MS, I had noticed that my walking was easier after a sortie. I was determined to try this treatment – but my immediate problem was to find a suitable pressure chamber. Neither the navy nor the RAF were willing to help. Of course the chambers at North Luffenham designed for high-altitude work were not suitable for hyperbaric oxygen therapy. Only chambers designed to operate a higher than ambient (rather than low) pressure, such as those used for the treatment of bends, worked in the right physical sense – but these were jealously guarded by the doctors. In any case, such chambers were not suitable for regular, long-term therapy.

I had almost given up the idea when I heard that the Chiltern branch of ARMS was about to start hyperbaric oxygen treatment at Prince's Risborough. At that time the founder member and leading light in the Chiltern project was Mr Leslie Gardner, who with a gallant band of supporters had raised the money to buy a pressure chamber.

I started hyperbaric oxygen therapy in September 1985. The chamber at Prince's Risborough held up to six patients at a time. We were taken down to a set depth below sea level – most patients preferred sixteen feet, or half of an atmosphere, but it was a matter of choice. Once down we breathed oxygen for one hour. I seemed to get some benefit; after treatment I could walk further and my bladder control improved, but these benefits were temporary.

Even twelve years later, I am not sure if there is any long-term benefit from hyperbaric oxygen therapy, but if I miss out for three weeks I feel the need to dive. Maybe it's all psychological.

I returned home from my final session of treatment at Headley Court on 29 March 1986, just in time for my fiftieth birthday. I don't take much notice of birthdays, but I suppose fifty is something special. I thought Jules had arranged a quiet lunch at the house with six of our friends, but I was totally conned. Jules disappeared at about ten in the morning to see the chiropodist – or so I thought – while I put the finishing touches to a display of squadron badges. The next thing I knew was that Gary Barnhill walked in. In the next hour more than thirty of my friends and family pitched up. I was totally overcome, and almost cried in my beer. Jules is good at organising surprise parties.

And that was not all. A few weeks later Jules and I went on an aerial tour of London in a Gazelle helicopter from 32 Squadron. It was listed as a training flight from the headquarters to the Thames Barrier and back, for Squadron Leader Bill Ritchie and our erstwhile neighbour, Derrick Lewis.

MS is a long, hard haul, and despite my best efforts to keep mobile I continued to deteriorate throughout 1986. I was having to start progressively earlier in the morning to get ready for work. I could no longer cope with no-notice call-outs, and I was aware that my usefulness during exercises was ever more limited.

It was probably the deep-seated fatigue that finally beat me. It was more than just lack of sleep; with MS the ataxia constantly drains energy. On some days I could only walk 50 yards before I had to sit down. I used to be a competent handyman, either around the house or with anything mechanical, but now I couldn't even change a standard three-pin plug. It was intensely frustrating, but there was no point in getting angry about it. With MS, anger is a complete waste of energy.

I always said that I would quit the RAF before I was asked to leave. In September, as Jules and I drove to Wroughton for my six-monthly check with Bob Merry, we agreed that the time had come. Bob was genuinely relieved to hear the news – I suspect he was steeling himself to inform me of the same decision. But, mainly for pension benefits, I asked that my final day of duty be delayed until after 30 March 1987.

I was admitted to Wroughton Hospital for two weeks' medical assessment in November. By this time Wroughton was a joint RAF/Army facility. I was still reasonably independent, although I needed assistance with the bath and I had difficulty with the high hospital beds. The muscle spasms which stopped me bending my right leg occurred more frequently now, and I was prescribed Baclofen, a muscle relaxant. I can't say I enjoyed the stay but, as usual, there were many patients not with MS who were far worse off.

I handed over the DSPSO duties to Wing Commander Geoff Brindle on 9 January 1987 and, after farewell interview with AOA and the DC in C, I was posted supernumerary to RAF High Wycombe. That meant I no longer had to report for duty. It snowed on the following Monday, and I remember my great relief at being able to relax at home.

My career in the RAF wasn't over yet; I still had a few loose ends to tie up. On 11 February I attended a full medical board at the CME, and was downgraded to A4 G5. The G5 assessment meant that I was unfit for further service. The next day Jules and I were invited to attend a formal guest night for the Honourable George Younger – Secretary of State for Defence – at the officers' mess. This was also to be my final dining-out night. The AOC in C apologised that there would be no speeches, which was fine by me – at least I wouldn't have to sing for my supper. Next day I was elected an honorary member of the mess.

The average service officer, retiring at the age of fifty-five, had to find a job, both to boost his income and to keep himself occupied. For me, work was no longer an option. I had enquired about employment and several old friends had written offering advice, but the prospects of finding a job were bleak. Besides, I felt totally drained and it took me best part of six months to recover.

On 2 June, Jules drove me to Eltham Palace for a day's resettlement course, run by the army, on the financial aspects of retirement. I was a little concerned about our financial situation; the service's gratuity and pension were straightforward, but if this was our only income then clearly we would have to economise. At that time there was no information available to me on possible disability benefits. My concern about money was ill-founded, although it took the best part of a year finally to award me a war pension.

My last day of paid service was 18 June 1987. I have no complaints about the way I was treated; in my case the RAF was eminently fair and compassionate. My career was a wholly enjoyable challenge in which I experienced more success than failure. I received the standard letter of thanks for long and valuable service on behalf of Her Majesty the Queen. I also received a personal letter of thanks from the air secretary – Air Vice-Marshal Tony Mason – which was most kind.

After thirty-four years of service I was a civilian again.

My story is not one of blood and guts. As a young man I had regretted never having to fire my guns in anger; and as far as I am aware no one ever shot at me. That was just the luck of the draw, and now seems unimportant. My only claim to fame is that, along with many thousands of others, I played my part in winning the Cold War. And I had my moments of excitement – four thousand hours of fighter flying saw to that.

To the many friends I made along the way, thank you for the company. I just wish I could start all over again – so here's to the next time.

Glossary

A/B	Afterburner (USAF)
ACTH	adrenocorticotrophic hormone
ADI	Attitude Director Indicator (flight instrument)
AFB	Air Force Base (American)
AFC	Air Force Cross
AFDS	Air Fighting Development Squadron
AI	Airborne Intercept (Radar)
AIM 7	Sparrow – Air intercept missile
AIM 9	Sidewinder – Air intercept missile
Angels	Air Defence term for thousands of feet – altitude
AOA	Angle of attack or Air Officer Administration
AOC in C	Air Officer Commanding-in-Chief
AOC	Air Officer Commanding
APC	Armament Practice Camp
ARMS	Action for Research into Multiple Sclerosis
ASOC	Air Support Operations Centre
ASP	Aircraft Servicing Platform
AST	Air Staff Target
ATAF	Allied Tactical Air Force
AVTAG	Jet aviation fuel
BAC	British Aircraft Corporation
BAFV	British Armed Forces Voucher (equivalent to £1)
BAOR	British Army of the Rhine
BLC	Boundary Layer Control
Bogey	Airborne reporting code for hostile contact
BOQ	Bachelor Officers' Quarters (American)
CAP	Combat Air Patrol
CCTS	Combat Crew Training Squadron (USAF)

CFE	Central Fighter Establishment
CFSO	Command Flight Safety Officer
CME	Central Medical Establishment
CNS	Central nervous system
CO	Commanding Officer
COC	Combat Operations Centre
CPX	Paper exercise
CTTO	Central Trials and Tactics Organisation
D/F	Direction Finding
DC in C	Deputy Commander-in-Chief
DDR	Deutsche Demokratische Republik (East Germany 1949–90)
DFCS	Day Fighter Combat School
DH	Direct Hit
DS	Directing Staff
DSPSO	Deputy Senior Personnel Staff Officer
EOKA	Greek Cypriot terrorist organisation
FAC	Forward Air Controller
FEBA	Forward Edge of the Battle Area
FEZ	Fighter Engagement Zone
Flag or Banner	Towed airborne gunnery target
FOD	Foreign Object Damage, or any loose matter that could damage engines or aircraft
g	the force of gravity
GCA	Ground Controlled Approach
GCI	Ground Controlled Interception
GGS	Gyroscopic Gun-sight
GLO	Ground Liaison Officer (Army)
HAS	Hardened Aircraft Shelter
HES	Hardened Equipment Shelter
HF	High Frequency radio band
HIMEZ	High Missile Engagement Zone
HSI	Horizontal Situation Indicator (flight instrument)
IFF	Identification Friend or Foe
ILS	Instrument Landing System
INAS	Inertial Navigation and Attack System
IOT	Initial Officer Training

IRA	Irish Republican Army
IRE	Instrument Rating Examiner
IRT	Instrument Rating Test
ISS	Individual Staff Studies
J Eng O	Junior Engineering Officer
JC & SS	Junior Command & Staff School
kts	Knots – nautical miles per hour
LOMEZ	Low Missile Engagement Zone
Maxeval	Evaluation assessed by Group Staff
Mayday	International distress call
MC	Military Cross
MCS	Management Control System (USAF)
Minival	Evaluation assessed by the Station Staff
MoD	Ministry of Defence
MPC	Missile Practice Camp
MRR	Minimum Risk Route
MS	Multiple Sclerosis
MTBF	Mean Time Between Failure
NAAFI	Navy Army and Air Forces Institute
NATO	The North Atlantic Treaty Organisation
NBC	Nuclear, Biological and Chemical
NCO	Non-Commissioned Officer
NOFORN	US eyes only
NORTHAG	Northern Army Group (Western Europe)
OBE	Officer of the Order of the British Empire
OC	Officer Commanding
OCU	Operational Conversion Unit
ORP	Operational Readiness Platform
PBF	Pilot Briefing Facility
PC	Permanent Commission
PI	Practice interception
POW	Prisoner of War
PX	Post Exchange (American)
QFI	Qualified Flying Instructor
QNH	Altimeter pressure setting that gives altitude above mean sea level
QRA	Quick Reaction Alert

R/T	Radio/Telephony
RADA	Royal Academy of Dramatic Art
RAE	Royal Aircraft Establishment
RAF	Royal Air Force
RCAF	Royal Canadian Air Force
RCAP	Combat Air Patrol employing AI radar
RHAG	Rotary Hydraulic Arrester Gear
RN	Royal Navy
S Eng O	Squadron Engineering Officer
SACEUR	Supreme Allied Commander Europe
SAM	Surface-to-Air Missile
SAP	Simulated Attack Profile
SAS	Special Air Service
SBA	Sovereign Base Area
SNEB	68 mm unguided air-to-ground rocket
SOC	Sector Operations Centre
SOP	Standard Operating Procedure
Splash	Reporting code for destruction of target
SPSO	Senior Personnel Staff Officer
TAC	Tactical Air Command (USAF)
TACAN	Tactical air-navigation system
Taceval	Tactical evaluation
TCW	Tactical Communications Wing (RAF)
TEWT	Tactical Exercise Without Troops
UHF	Ultra High Frequency radio band
USAF	United States Air Force
USAFE	United States Air Forces in Europe
V/STOL	Vertical/Short Take-off and Landing
VHF	Very High Frequency radio band
Visident	Visual Identification
Wg Cdr	Wing commander
Wg Cdr Ops	Wing Commander Operations Wing

Index

Headings have been listed in full, for explanation of acronyms please see glossary pp.324-7.

Index

Index

Index

Index